SEASON OF FEAR

SEASON OF FEAR

BRIAN FREEMAN

Quercus
New York • London

Quercus

New York • London

ISBN 978-1-62365-407-8

Library of Congress Control Number: 2015930241

Distributed in the United States and Canada by
Hachette Book Group
1290 Avenue of the Americas
New York, NY 10104

Manufactured in the United States

10 9 8 7 6 5 4 3 2 1

www.quercus.com

For Marcia
and in memory of Ali Gunn

Sin crouches at your door.
It desires you, but you must overcome it.

—G<small>ENESIS</small> 4:7

PROLOGUE
TEN YEARS AGO

He marched through the orange grove in quick, angry steps, crushing the litter of fruit that sweetened the night with a citrus perfume.

The sandy soil, still damp from the afternoon rain, modeled the design of the hard rubber treads on his boots. He made no effort to hide his trail. In the days ahead, they would follow his footprints back to where he had parked the stolen pickup truck. They would take photographs and make casts and review dozens of brands of footwear. They would tell the world that he bought Herman Survivors at Walmart, like thousands of other hunters. They would find the GMC Sierra abandoned in the parking lot of a Sonny's Real Pit Bar-B-Q in Haines City, and the truck would lead them to the garage of a 1950s-era rambler half a mile from the Gulf Coast in Indian Rocks Beach. The owner, a snowbird from Wisconsin, would be unaware that the truck was missing.

None of it would make any difference at all.

They would never find him.

A film of sweat from the sticky heat covered his body and festered under his black clothes. Trickles of moisture invited the mosquitoes and midges to feast on his face. He ignored the whine in his ears and the flutter of moth wings. He walked past the arrow-straight rows of trees like a soldier, focused on where he had to go and what he had to do.

Time was passing. He needed to hurry.

He saw the sanctuary high above him, cresting the hillside. The stone tower shimmered in the glow of spotlights. People could see it for miles from the swampy lowlands. The tower looked out of place, like something stripped from a European cathedral, too perfect and ornate for the scrub lizards and dripping Spanish moss of central Florida. Its pink marble shined like candy. Ceramic grilles adorned the stone, depicting flamingos and baboons cavorting in Eden. Adam and Eve were pictured on the tower. So was the snake, whispering sweet nothings in Eve's ear.

Now he would crash the party in paradise. An invisible wraith. A bearer of death.

Kill the fortunate son.

"*What are you doing?*"

He stopped dead. The hot wind brought the orange trees to life. Clusters of ripe fruit swung from drooping branches. He looked back, but he was alone with the voice in his head.

"*What's happening? I'm scared.*"

He beat his forehead with a gloved fist to drive the memories away, but he found himself reliving the sensations anyway. The panic. The fear. Blackness and light whipping through his brain, faster than he could see. A shudder rippling through his body, a blow to the chest. And blood. So much blood, pooling and flooding like a crimson lake in the moonlight.

"*Why is there so much blood?*"

He remained motionless, waiting until the tiny voice went away. There was too much at stake to obsess over things he couldn't change. He couldn't afford to give in to emotions now. The only emotion he could allow into his heart was hatred. If he could channel his hatred, if he could taste its bitterness, he could do what he needed to do.

The orange grove ended at a slope that led to the hillside sanctuary. It was the highest mountain in a flat state. He climbed, with the tall grass crowding him. He beat away the insects now, because they had become insatiable, flocking around him like a biting cloud. Their whistling chatter was deafening. He used a penlight on the ground and saw lizards skittering back and forth across the trail ahead of him. He felt as if he were trudging through a primitive rain forest, thick with humid air that weighed on his chest.

Five minutes later, at the crest of the hill, he broke free onto a beautifully manicured lawn, where a garden party was under way. He saw the flicker of torches making silhouettes of the crowd assembled on the grass. Human noises burbled from the glitterati: laughter, rumbling voices, the clink of wine glasses. A hundred people, maybe more. Carillon bells played inside the tower, clanging out across the hilltop. The tune was familiar.

He slipped a hood over his head and steeled himself for the things to come. Awful, necessary things. He was a man with a mission. It was just that no one would know what that mission was.

"Birch wanted a magical night," Diane Fairmont murmured as she studied the crowd from the dais that had been constructed on the lawn. "I guess he got one."

"I guess he did," Tarla Bolton replied.

Tarla swept her long blond hair from her face. Her friend was right. The night really did sparkle. Below them, beautiful people wandered in and out of the dancing shadows like fairies. She saw tall men in suits and tuxedos. They were all men with money, which was what every politician wanted at his event. Women wore summer dresses fluttering in the hilltop breeze. The young women spilled cleavage from silk. Older wives eyed the interlopers with sideways, cynical stares.

They drank Chardonnay. They laughed. They inhaled the moist wind of the Florida night and smelled yellow jasmine. The bells of the tower played, reminding Tarla of children banging spoons on old metal buckets.

"Do you know what the bells are playing?" Diane asked.

Tarla cocked an ear, letting her diamonds dangle, and then she laughed. "It's probably something old and classical, but it sounds like Supertramp. Remember that song?"

"Which one?"

"Goodbye Stranger."

Diane's face soured at the irony. "It's about one-night stands, isn't it? Birch probably asked them to play it."

She turned away from Tarla and sat down in the chair behind the microphone. The loyal wife's chair. When Birch spoke, the cameras would all catch her there. Smiling. Applauding. The woman behind the man, dressed in a conservative ensemble, attractive but unthreatening. That was the image Birch wanted for her now. Voters didn't like trophy wives living in the governor's mansion.

Tarla watched her friend wither in the heat. Diane's skin was pale, not its typical gold from the summer sun. She'd spent most of the evening ducking the crowd. When Diane twisted her neck to stare at the pink tower, Tarla noticed a sharp stab of pain on her face. "Are you all right?"

"It's nothing."

"You don't look good," Tarla said.

"I'm fine," Diane insisted. "Drop it, darling, please. The campaign is exhausting. I'm tired."

Tarla weighed whether to push her friend, but she decided that now wasn't the time. She had several more days before she needed to be back on set in Mallorca, and she was staying with Diane in Birch's mansion, the way she did every summer. They could talk more later. Tonight was for politics. Tonight they had to wear masks.

Tarla and Diane had grown up together in the sleepy central Florida town of Lake Wales. They'd spent their earliest summers here in the Bok sanctuary, swatting no-see-ums as they lay in the grass near the tower, talking about boys and dreams. Tarla knew that her best friend had always looked at her with naked envy since those days. Tarla was slim, blond, tall. She'd escaped Lake Wales for Hollywood as a teenager and did what no real person should be able to do. She made it. She became an actress. She made movies and money. When the two girls both had out-of-wedlock sons at age twenty-one, Tarla could afford to shuttle her son, Cab, to movie sets around the world, while Diane relied on food stamps to feed Drew.

Birch Fairmont hired Diane as his secretary at Welsh Capital when Drew was ten. He chose her for her body and breasts as much as her Microsoft Excel skills. Age thirty, single mother, unapologetic about stealing a married man, which was what she did when Birch divorced his first wife. She had never pretended that her affair with him was anything but mercenary. She'd gotten exactly what she wanted: the mansion in the Mountain Lake Estates, the island vacations, the permanent security for her son. Though it had come with a steep price tag, which Tarla could see written on Diane's face

Tarla took the chair on the dais next to her friend. The other chairs were empty, but Birch and his entourage would soon fill them for the speech to the wealthy guests. *Vote for me, but more than that, give me money.* Not that Birch needed it. He'd funded most of his campaign from his own venture capital millions.

"You heard they found that poor girl?" Diane asked.

"What girl?"

"The one who went missing. Alison, I think. Fourteen years old. It was in the news over the weekend. They found her body hidden in a ditch. Terrible."

"Did you know her?"

"No, but I should write to her parents. Imagine what they're going through."

Tarla didn't know what to say. She didn't understand the criminal mind; she couldn't comprehend how one person could inflict suffering on another. It mystified her that her only son had chosen to immerse himself in solving crimes. With his looks, Cab Bolton could have been an actor or model, but he investigated murders instead. Tarla hated it. She thought he had chosen his career as a kind of rebellion against her Hollywood world.

"I saw Drew this weekend," Tarla went on, thinking of mothers and children.

"Yes, he just got back home."

"How is he?" she asked, knowing the answer, which was: *Not good.* Diane's son had battled drugs most of his life and had largely surrendered in his fight with addiction. It had been a source of heartache for Diane—and arguments with Birch—throughout their marriage.

"The doctors say he's better, but he's been better before," Diane replied. "Sooner or later, he starts again."

"I know. I'm sorry."

"You're lucky with Cab."

"I am, but Cab's a loner like me. He shuts me out."

"I don't know if that's true," Diane said.

Tarla smiled. "No? He spent more time with you than with me when he was here this summer. Avoiding his mother is his avocation."

"He loves you, and he's a gem," Diane lectured her, in a terse voice that said: *You've got everything.*

Tarla didn't protest. Diane was right.

Her friend's gaze landed on her husband in the crowd. Birch Fairmont was easy to spot. His voice was loud, his laugh exaggerated so that everyone could hear him. He had a lion's mane of gray hair that shined like wax under the torches, and a bronzed Florida tan. Normal people wilted under the humidity, but Birch glowed. He was big, with a prominent nose, plump cheekbones, jutting chin, and a stomach pushing over his belt. He wasn't tall, but he had charisma and confidence, the kind of magnetism that drew people to him. He was tailor-made to sell to the voters.

"Lyle and Caprice think he's really going to win," Diane said.

Tarla was unimpressed. "So I hear."

"He got into the race as a protest. No one expected him to make any noise. Now Lyle says he's in the lead."

"The incumbent died, and the new Dem is left of Nancy Pelosi," Tarla scoffed. "Chuck Warren, the Republican, cozies up to right-wing nutjobs. Birch looks like a statesman by comparison to those clowns."

"It's a big thing," Diane insisted. "Caprice says this election could be the start of a national third party movement."

Tarla laughed, which was the wrong thing to do, because she knew it annoyed her friend. "That's what they said about that wrestler in Minnesota, too. Does Birch plan to shave his head and wear a feather boa?"

"It's not funny, Tarla," Diane snapped. "I believe in this."

"I'm not questioning the message," Tarla replied, "just the messenger."

Tarla refused to hold her tongue about Birch. She'd spent too many years seeing Diane locked up like a bird in a cage, singing when he told her to sing. She also knew that Diane was right. Birch might actually win. A scary thought. All the polls put him ahead, but polls didn't mean much two months before the election. The other parties wouldn't roll over. Chuck Warren was already hitting Birch on gun rights. The Democratic campaign manager, Ogden Bush, was promising an onslaught of negative ads. Tarla wasn't sure that Birch and his team knew how to play dirty enough to come out on top.

It was nine o'clock. The bells in the tower fell silent. Whispers swept through the crowd; the elegant guests looked around expectantly. Tarla saw Birch mounting the steps of the dais, with the yes-men of his campaign behind him. Birch's smile was wide and false. He was already in love with politics, the smell of power, the fawning operatives trailing in his wake. He wasn't the kind of man who would change Washington for the better. He'd be seduced by it like all the others.

Tarla had never liked Birch, and he knew it.

She stood up as he approached her. He was resplendent in his black suit, his teeth bleached as white as ivory. His eyes traveled over Tarla's silver beaded dress, diving into her cleavage like a spelunker into a cave. He put his arms around her in a bear hug, squeezing her full breasts. His hand fell to the small of her back, and she thought he would have cupped her ass if the media hadn't been there to watch him.

"Thank God there's a podium," he whispered. "You always give me such a hard-on, Tarla."

"You're a pig," she whispered back.

Birch laughed, as if they'd shared an intimate joke. *My dear friend, the Hollywood star.* He leaned down to kiss his wife's cheek, and his face was full of faux devotion. Tarla was an actress, and she knew acting when she saw it. He murmured in Diane's ear, and Tarla was close enough to hear what he said.

"For God's sake, Diane, you're not at a fucking funeral. Look like you're *happy*."

Diane forced a half smile onto her face for the cameras. Birch faced the podium and waved at the crowd with both arms. The assembly erupted with applause. Around him, two dozen donors and campaign staffers filled the empty chairs on the dais, clapping as they sat down. It was a warm night; their faces shined with sweat and were red from free booze. Tarla recognized most of them. Corporate orange growers. Disney executives. People with fat checkbooks.

Lyle Piper, Birch's chief of staff, hovered behind the candidate, barking instructions into a cell phone. His fiancée, Caprice, did the same. The applause continued; people repeatedly shouted Birch's name like a religious chant. Lyle was small next to Birch, with a slight frame and birdlike skinny fingers. He had thinning blond hair cut like a conservative CEO's, and he acted the same way. In the times Tarla had met him, she didn't recall Lyle ever smiling. He was intense and preachy about everything from tax policy to cholesterol. Even so, he was less of a hypocrite than other politicians she'd met. He walked the walk about personal responsibility. Lyle had lost his parents four years earlier, at age twenty-four, and since then, he'd been a surrogate father to two younger siblings. Not an easy job.

Lyle slipped an arm around Caprice's elbow. Lyle Piper and Caprice Dean were a political power couple in Florida, but they were idealistic in a way that only young people could be. They still thought they could change the world. They thought a new, centrist political party would be different from the other two. They thought Birch Fairmont would be the face of something that could tear down the extremes on both sides.

Tarla could have told them right then that they were naive.

Caprice leaned down to Diane. If Lyle looked older than his years, she looked younger. She was pretty and full-figured, with long dark hair, fresh-scrubbed skin without a hint of a Florida tan, and bookish black glasses propped high on her rounded nose. She wore a burgundy waistcoat, black slacks, and high heels smudged with mud. Her voice cracked with excitement. "Isn't this great?"

"Wonderful," Diane said, her own voice hollow.

The two political aides sat next to Diane on the dais. Birch raised his arms to quiet the crowd, but they may as well have been celebrating the balloon drop at a convention. It was Labor Day, and they had all seen the polls. They smelled momentum, which was like adrenaline in the veins of political junkies. This was their man. Birch Fairmont, candidate for the United States Congress in the Twelfth District from the newly formed Common Way Party.

Tarla kept an eye on Lyle Piper and was surprised by what she saw. The cameras had left him, and something black flitted across his face. He clasped his hands in his lap and stared at his leather shoes with a stony expression. Caprice grabbed his hand, and the mask of enthusiasm slipped momentarily from her face, too. Whatever they told the world, they both knew the truth about the candidate at the podium. They were dancing with a devil. That was politics.

"My good friends," Birch said to a new round of cheers. The microphone broadcast his voice around the park. The tower shimmered a hundred yards away. The floodlights illuminated the stage, but the crowd was lost in shadows, and beyond them, on the fringe of the lawn, the world was black. The park disappeared into the surrounding jungle.

Tarla eyed Diane, who had a peculiar expression on her face. Her friend watched Birch with pride, fear, and hatred.

"My good friends," Birch repeated.

More cheers.

"In less than two months, we will show America that we can choose something other than divisive rhetoric and empty slogans," he continued, diving into his stump speech. "That we can find consensus among our differences. That we can rely on good sense, not nonsense. That there really is a common way for all of us."

Tarla saw Birch's photo on signs thrust into the air and waved by volunteers. The caption above his face read: *The Common Man*. She shook her head at the hubris of it all. Birch was many things, but he was not common. He was a businessman worth a hundred million dollars. Definitely not common.

"I need you with me!" Birch shouted.

He waited for an elevated energy in the voices of the crowd. That was how you built people into a frenzy of full-throated excitement, with each applause line louder than the one before. Instead, he got no reaction, except a low burst of uncomfortable clapping that died as quickly as it started.

Unsettled, Birch tried again.

"I need every one of you to be part of the common way!"

Heads turned, but no one cheered. Low voices murmured in an uneasy ripple. Birch was visibly annoyed. He looked over his shoulder at Lyle and mouthed: *What the hell?*

Like the rest of the crowd, Lyle's attention was focused elsewhere. He and everyone else had become aware of a man on the corner of the dais. He'd come from nowhere out of the shroud of the night. He was dressed completely in black: black long-sleeved nylon shirt, black tight jeans, black gloves over his hands, and—like a Dickens ghost—a black hood over his head. His presence froze them all into motionless silence. Tarla sucked in her breath as she saw him. She knew. Everyone knew.

Something bad was about to happen.

One person took action. She recognized him; he was the director of one of the largest corporate citrus farms in the area. Married. Father of three. He was on the dais in the second row, and he stood up and pushed to the front and marched toward the man in black. He got within ten feet before the man reached behind his belt with a gloved hand, which reemerged holding a semiautomatic pistol. He lifted his right hand and calmly fired one shot into the head of the citrus farmer, who crumpled and slipped off the dais to the thick lawn.

The explosion, like unexpected thunder, woke up the crowd. Chaos descended. Screaming began; the audience turned en masse, like a wave, and stampeded toward the tower, where overgrown trails led out of the park.

The man in black was unaffected by the tumult. He was on a mission, marching along the front of the platform toward Birch Fairmont. The VIPs in the rows of chairs sat paralyzed, watching the violence unfold. A woman in the back row stood up to escape, but the man in black fired, hitting her in the shoulder, her torso blooming with red as she wailed and sunk to the wooden floor. No one moved again.

Smoke burned in Tarla's nose from the smell of the bullets. She found herself dizzy, seeing the man come closer. Birch had the look of a man on a falling plane, a man staring at his mortality seconds away. This instant, you are alive; the next instant, you will be dead. He faced the gunman with his fists clenched; he didn't run, because there was nowhere to go. His face went dark with frustration.

"You son of a—"

Birch didn't finish his curse. The man in black fired four times, one two three four, *boom boom boom boom*, each bullet streaking into Birch's chest, carving out ribs, organs, and blood. Birch staggered but didn't fall, and the man fired again, another round flush in the heart, and Birch's knees sagged. He grabbed for the podium, missed it like a blind man, and fell sideways, gasping out cherry-colored blood. His white shirt was crimson. His tanned face was ashen.

"*Birch!*" Diane screamed.

The man in black swung around and thrust the gun in Diane's face, but Tarla stood up and put herself between them. She had only one thought in her head, to protect her best friend. The barrel, inches away, fed smoke into her nose and mouth and made her choke. The metal almost touched her forehead. She couldn't see his eyes behind the black mesh, but she was close enough that she could smell his sweat and see the tiniest tremble in his hand. In her heels, she was taller than him. It was strange, what you noticed at a moment like that. He was a killer, but he was just a man.

She thought of her son, because she wanted him to be her last thought on this earth. Cab, six-foot-six, blond, funny, cynical, wicked smart, gorgeous. Cab, the one thing she had ever created in her life that gave her nothing but pure pride.

Then the gun was gone from her head. Gone, leaving her alive. Tarla could barely stand with nausea and relief. Birch's blood pooled around her feet. *It's over*, she thought, but she was wrong. The man in black pointed his gun at Lyle Piper. Lyle had a look of dazed confusion on his face, as if he had stumbled into a bad dream. Next to Lyle, Caprice's young voice warbled like a soprano, screaming out words that climbed into disbelief, almost unrecognizable.

What are you doing what are you doing what are you doing what are you doing?

Tarla watched in mute horror as the man fired again, one kill shot, no mercy. Just like that, Lyle keeled backward, and Caprice was spray-painted with blood and brain. He was dead, and she was alone.

One word, one scream, long and endless and riven with loss, wailed from the dais. *No no no no no no no!*

Vertigo descended on Tarla, overwhelming her senses. The world made circles, breaking up the way a kaleidoscope whirls and spins. She blinked once, and the gunman was gone, and she heard sirens and saw the multicolored flash of lights. She blinked again, and she was in a hospital bed miles away.

PART ONE

THE EXTREMES

1

"Chayla," the union official said, stabbing the elevator button in the lobby of the Tampa Hyatt Regency. "What the hell kind of name is that for a storm?"

His younger companion chuckled as he sipped a Starbucks cappuccino, which left foam on his upper lip. "Hey, it's better than Debby. Chayla sounds like some kind of evil witch, you know? Like she could seduce you and wipe out your home and you'd thank her for it. Debby, that's like being mugged by a Girl Scout."

"Yeah, well, I don't care what name they give the things. This baby hits, we're talking hundreds of millions in damage. That's a lot of Do-si-dos, Brent. You guys are watching the weather maps?"

"Sure we are. Some models have landfall on the Gulf Coast by Wednesday of next week, but it could still turn north to New Orleans, and all we'll get is rain."

The union official, whose name was Walter Fleming, poked a half-eaten chocolate donut at his well-dressed companion. As a rule, Walter didn't like hotshot political aides. They were too smart for their own good. Nobody could be as dumb as really smart people, particularly when they worked for the government. "Just don't blow this, okay? Nothing loses votes faster than a messed-up disaster. Especially if it hits next Wednesday, huh? The Fourth of July?"

The political aide smirked behind his coffee cup. "Relax, Walter. We're on it. Besides, if it comes our way, it's more work for your boys, right?"

Walter scratched his wiry gray crew cut, which hadn't changed since his marine days. "It's not about that, and don't let anyone hear you talking that way."

The two men wore lanyards and badges from the industrial union meeting at the convention center. Walter had been the number-two man in the union's leadership hierarchy for more than fifteen years. He had no interest in the top job. The union leader had to wear expensive suits and put up with reporters and send out Twitter updates, whereas Walter could wear jeans and do the real political work behind the scenes. If anyone in Tallahassee wanted something important done without publicity, they knew who to call. Not the top dog. They called Walter.

The political aide—Brent Reed, thirty years old, curly black hair, goatee—had made the call to Walter when their poll numbers started going south. Reed was just the messenger boy. The call went much higher up the campaign food chain, but nobody at the top wanted to get their hands dirty. That was Walter's job. After fifty years in Democratic politics, ever since he was an eighteen-year-old kid, Walter knew everybody who mattered in Florida, and he knew how to get things done.

"Jeez, these elevators are slow," Walter complained as they waited in the lobby.

"Yeah, there's never an electrical worker around when you need one," Reed joked.

"Funny. That's real funny."

Brent slid an iPhone out of his pocket and scrolled up the screen with his thumb. Walter figured he was probably checking his Facebook page, "liking" some post about a Vegas vacation or a cat in a sweater. Dumb kids.

"Anyway, you can say you told me so," Brent went on, fixated on his smartphone screen as he sipped his coffee. "Looks like Diane

Fairmont's numbers are for real. She's up three over Ramona Cortes in a three-way race. Eight over you-know-who."

"I told you so. People haven't forgotten what happened to her husband ten years ago. Her favorability is, what, sixty-five percent? That's a lot better than our boy. He's down around thirty-seven right now."

"Maybe we should shoot his wife," Reed joked again. "He can compete with Diane for the sympathy vote."

Walter eyed the hotel lobby, then bunched the silk lapel of Reed's suit coat in his beefy fist and hissed at the tall, slim aide. "You want to read a remark like that in the papers? Keep your goddamn voice down."

"Chill, Walter. There's no press around."

"You better learn, there are spies *everywhere*. You have to talk like everything coming out of your mouth is going into an open mike. Haven't you figured out that this is a war? The Republicans cottoned on to that a long time ago, and the Common Way folks have done a hell of a good job of catching up."

Brent shrugged. "That's why we called you, isn't it?"

"It took you long enough."

"Maybe so, but my people are getting nervous. They want to see some progress. What should I tell them?"

Walter shook his head. If he'd learned one thing in fifty years, it was that each new generation had to learn the old mistakes all over again. Give a kid a master's degree in public policy from FSU, and he was still a moron. Walter, who was six inches shorter than Brent Reed and a hundred pounds heavier, exhaled a cigar-tinged breath. "We'll talk about this in my room. Not here."

"Whatever."

The elevator doors finally opened. A handful of hotel guests exited into the lobby. Most were delegates from the convention who greeted Walter like a celebrity. He pumped their arms and chatted them up, paying no attention to the impatient political aide with him. Brent held the doors open until the elevator's alarm buzzed, and then Walter shouldered inside and hit the button for the Hyatt's sixth floor with his fat thumb.

Just as the doors began to close, a bare arm slid between the narrowing gap, as if waving a magic wand. The doors reversed course, and a girl joined the two of them in the elevator compartment. Walter stuck out a sleeve of his tweed sport coat to keep the doors open until she was safely inside. She was young. Everybody looked young to Walter, but he figured she couldn't be more than twenty years old. She wasn't short, but she was anorexic-skinny: all bones, no curves, flat breasts. Her jaw worked; she was chewing gum. The girl wore a pink tank top that didn't even reach to her belly button, and her cut-off corduroy shorts were cut off so high that Walter could see the slope of both butt cheeks when she turned and faced the door. She pushed the button for the tenth floor.

"Wow," Brent said.

Walter's idea of "wow" was Kim Novak, but the girl in the elevator was cute, the way his youngest daughter was cute. She had pink-painted toenails poking out of flip-flops. Her hair was long, lush, and black; her face was pale and freckled, with a tiny oval mouth. A silver cross dangled from her right earlobe. He couldn't see her eyes, which were hidden behind sunglasses with leopard frames. She tugged on the strap of an oversized satchel purse, which was slung over one arm. She wore earbuds, and the music from the iPod squeezed into her skintight back pocket thumped so loudly that Walter could hear the screaming lyrics of the song. The girl hummed, and her hips swung rhythmically, and her head bobbed.

"What the hell is that noise?" Walter asked Brent. "Is that supposed to be music?"

"Sounds like Rihanna. 'Roc Me Out.' Rihanna, that's a good name for a storm."

"This girl is going to be deaf by the time she's thirty," Walter said.

Brent's eyes were locked on the sway of the girl's shapely backside. "What?"

"Forget it."

"Anyway, I need to take something back to my people," Brent went on. "Do we have any dirt on Common Way yet?"

"Upstairs," Walter repeated through gritted teeth.

"Oh, hell, you think this girl can hear a thing we say?" Brent raised his voice and called to her. "Hey, sweetheart, rock me on the floor, okay? Man, that ass of yours could stop traffic."

"Jesus, Brent!"

"Forget her, she's in her own world," Brent told him, and he was right. The girl couldn't hear anything except Rihanna. She danced as the elevator ground upward. "So?"

"Fine, we got nothing so far," Walter said. "I told you this was going to take time. We'll turn up something we can use, but we need to keep a low profile. If Common Way catches us spying, it's game over."

"Were you able to get someone inside the campaign?"

"That's my business, not yours. And it's better for you if we keep it that way." He added after a pause: "Remember, Ogden Bush works for them now, not us. You don't want him connecting the dots. He knows me."

"Bush. Fucking turncoat."

"It's politics. We screwed him, he screws us. Sooner or later, we'll want him back on our side. In the meantime, sit tight, and let me do my job."

"When do you plan to deliver? After the election? That won't do us much good."

"We can't make shit up out of thin air. It's got to be legit."

"Well, we're paying a lot of money, and we expect results. Something needs to happen soon."

"What's the rush?" Walter asked.

"Our boy is watching the needle sink. He's not happy. He's about to make some decisions that none of us want."

Walter took a moment to grasp Brent's meaning. "Are you saying he's thinking of dropping out of the race?"

"Better to bow out than to get beaten. Live to fight another day, you know? He'd rather see Diane win than Ramona Cortes."

"When?"

"Depends on Chayla. He doesn't want to announce until we see what happens to the storm. Plus, we've been thinking that you'd be able to dig up something that would be worth sticking around for. That's why we called you, Walter. So what do you want me to tell him?"

Walter rubbed his grizzled beard. "Tell him to hang tight. Don't do anything stupid."

"What if there's nothing to find?" Brent asked.

"There's dirt," Walter insisted. "These guys made a mistake somewhere, and we're going to throw it in their faces. But it won't make any difference if he's already out of the game."

The elevator doors opened on the sixth floor. Walter stamped outside. He had Stoli in his room, and he needed a drink. He was angry with Brent; he was angry with the idiots in Tallahassee. Politics. The years passed, and nothing changed. Every election was a race to the bottom.

Brent tapped the young girl on the shoulder and held the elevator open with one hand. She didn't take off her sunglasses, but she popped an earphone out of her ear. "Huh?"

"I like your music," Brent said.

"Whatever," the girl replied. She replaced the earphone before Brent could say anything more. Walter smiled, and Brent looked deflated. The girl was good with a brush-off.

The odd thing was, as the doors closed, Walter studied the girl and thought: *I've seen you before.*

Peach Piper tugged the black wig off her head and shoved it inside her satchel purse along with her iPod.

Her real hair was blond, cut super-short in a pageboy style that barely swished across her freckled forehead. She whipped off her sunglasses. Her eyes were Atlantic blue. She yanked her tank top over her head—no bra—unzipped her short-shorts and shivered in the elevator in nothing but purple bikini panties. Eyeing the elevator buttons, she dug a Magic Kingdom T-shirt and loose white cargo pants out of her purse and practically jumped into them. She replaced her flip-flops with Crocs and her cross earring with a big gold hoop.

When she was done, she grabbed a crushable nylon backpack from inside the purse, squeezed the purse and her clothes inside, and shrugged the backpack onto both shoulders just as the elevator doors opened on the tenth floor. A black woman and her young son boarded the elevator, and the boy looked at Peach and giggled and whispered to his mother. Peach realized that her cargo pants were unzipped, and she discreetly tugged the zipper up as she pushed the button to return to the lobby.

The doors opened on the sixth floor again to let on two more convention delegates. She noticed with fleeting concern that Walter Fleming and Brent Reed remained in the hotel hallway. Fleming's back was to her. That was good, because the old union boss was the one Peach was worried about. He was smart and observant. Brent Reed was just a moron. He looked right at her in the elevator, and Peach gave him a big toothy smile, and he was completely oblivious.

He hadn't recognized her from the bar the previous night, either, when she was a redhead in a little black dress. Or from the food truck near the riverfront, when she was a Marlins fan with a baseball cap and gold tracksuit.

Peach rode the elevator down and wandered through the lobby. She exited into the hot June afternoon, jogged across the street through traffic, and made her way two blocks to a small park by the river. It was a perfect day, or as perfect as Tampa got during the sweaty summer, with a blue sky and Gulf breeze. She sat down on a bench between the palm trees, steps from the green water, and retrieved the Sony voice recorder from the side pocket of her satchel purse and plugged in her headphones. Rewinding, she listened to the elevator conversation between Fleming and Reed.

Hey, sweetheart, rock me on the floor, okay? Man, that ass of yours could stop traffic.

Moron.

Peach ran through the recording three times and then dialed the office number for the Common Way Foundation. The foundation was headquartered in a high-rise bank building only a few blocks away, but Peach actually worked in the foundation's opposition research department, which was squeezed into unmarked offices on the seedy end of downtown. The phone rang, and her brother Deacon answered on the second ring.

"Hey, Fruity," he said.

"Hey."

"Where are you?"

"Near the river. I'm coming back."

"How'd you do?"

"Stalking Reed finally paid off."

"He didn't make you, did he?"

Peach didn't answer.

"Sorry, I know that's an insult," Deacon said, and she could hear his smile. "So what did you find out?"

"You better call Caprice and have her talk to Ms. Fairmont."

"They're already at the media schmooze-fest at Diane's house. Is it important?"

"Yeah, I think so. Walter Fleming is coming after us. I think he's got some kind of spy inside Common Way."

"Well, we figured. Is that it?"

"No, there's more," Peach said. "Tell her the governor is thinking about dropping out of the race."

2

Cab Bolton watched from the second-floor balcony as Diane Fairmont put on her political face for the television interviewer. She looked at ease in the spotlight. Natural. Warm. Comfortable in her own skin. She sat in an ornate chair near the fringe of a pond in her Tampa mansion's hilly gardens. Huge lily pads floated on the green water. A white swan lazily floated behind her and stirred ripples on the surface. Makeup people hovered around Diane like flies, making sure her skin didn't sweat, making sure she had the right flush for the camera.

The interviewer, an Asian man in his twenties, gestured at the swan and said something that made Diane laugh. Her smile looked sincere, and her dark eyes glittered with intelligence. She was in her midfifties now, like Cab's mother. She wore her golden brown hair in a sensible bob, shiny but not showy. Simple pearl earrings, but no other jewelry. Her suit was dark—serious, reliable—but her blouse was light blue—friendly, inviting. She kept her hands neatly folded in her lap and her legs pressed together. The entire look had probably been poll-tested.

Cab was surprised at how easily Diane had adopted a public image, because the woman he knew from his past had been a lonely introvert, hiding her emotional wounds. He wondered if her new persona was an act, but he was willing to believe that people didn't always stay the same as they aged. It had been a long time since he'd seen her. Their paths hadn't crossed since he spent a week at Birch Fairmont's house in June ten years earlier, during the summer that changed everything.

The summer that ended on Labor Day in death and blood.

He leaned on the white stone balcony, which was framed by columns that graced the front of the estate. The gardens below were lush with palm trees, weeping willows, gnarled oaks, and overgrown saw palmettos. Bronze sculptures of herons and fish dotted the lawns, and fountains sprayed out of the ponds like canopies. Through the web of greenery, he could just see the asphalt of Bayshore Boulevard beyond the estate walls and the calm water of Hillsborough Bay. They were inside the urban boundary of the Tampa peninsula, but this was a private world, carefully secluded from outside view by a stone wall and thick, carefully pruned hedges.

Even so, politics demanded that Diane invite the media to a meet and greet. Voters needed to size up their future governor. Hence the dark suit and sensible heels and understated appearance. Hence the softball questions from sympathetic talk show hosts about her years as a single mother with a checkbook to balance. Yes, she was rich now, but she hadn't always been rich, and her life had been marred by more than its share of tragedy.

"Champagne, darling?" a sparkling voice asked.

His mother appeared on the balcony, surprising him. Tarla never gave any warning before she dropped into his life. She just appeared and disappeared. They'd arrived separately that evening at Diane's gated estate. Cab had driven more than 150 miles along Florida's west coast from his home in the beach town of Naples. Tarla lived much closer to Diane, on the top floor of a Gulf Coast condominium in Clearwater, half an hour away. He'd been looking for her since he got to the party, but Tarla was good at not being found until she wanted to be found.

"Sure, why not?" Cab said.

He took a sip from the crystal flute that Tarla handed him. The champagne was superb: dry and effervescent. Diane could afford the best, and it didn't hurt to make the media people a little drunk while they asked their questions.

"Do you know why they call Florida the Sunshine State?" Tarla asked, with a wicked little arch of her blond eyebrows.

"Why?"

"Because 'Waiting to Die' looked like crap on the license plates."

Cab rolled his cornflower-blue eyes. "Do you really want to be making jokes like that when your best friend is running for governor? The eighty-five million senior citizens around here might not appreciate your sense of humor the way I do."

"I'm practically a senior citizen myself, darling."

"Please," Cab told her. "You're fifty-five, and you look like Naomi Watts."

"Well, aren't you sweet."

He wasn't lying. Tarla had retired from the movie business several years earlier, but she still looked like a Hollywood star. In truth, so did he. Anyone could see they were mother and son: matching eyes, matching sun-bleached blond hair, both with sharp, angular faces. Cab was six-foot-six with a long neck that emphasized his height. He had a gangly walk, not always graceful but easy to remember. He kept his short hair gelled, making spikes that sometimes resembled a sea urchin's shell. His nose was shaped like a ski jump, and he had a baby-smooth complexion that always looked as if he'd just shaved. He wore a one-carat diamond in his left earlobe, and he was particular about his tailored suits even on the most humid Florida day.

He could blend in on Rodeo Drive or South Beach, but he didn't really fit in at most crime scenes. That didn't bother him. If people wanted to underestimate him because of his looks, it made his job easier. The trouble was, he knew that he really didn't belong in the police world, as many of his colleagues regularly reminded him. He wasn't sure if he belonged anywhere. At thirty-five, he was still figuring out what he wanted to be when he grew up.

"I appreciate your being my date tonight," Tarla said.

Cab grinned. "I wouldn't miss it. Politicians and reporters are my two favorite kinds of people after serial killers."

"Sarcasm doesn't suit you, Cab."

"And yet I stick with it," he replied.

"It's only two and a half hours from Naples to Tampa. Not such a long drive."

"More like two in the Corvette," he admitted.

"Well, see? I don't feel guilty. Unless I'm stealing you away from a romantic weekend with Wawa."

"It's Lala," Cab said, "and you're not."

"Ah." Tarla sipped her champagne and fixed her son with knowing eyes. Her blond hair, which had never sported a gray root in her entire life, tumbled around her shoulders in curls that were casually messy. "Everything still rosy there?" she asked.

"We're fine. Sorry to disappoint you."

"Did I say I didn't like her?"

"You didn't have to. She's Catholic, Cuban, and Republican."

"I have no problem with Cubans, darling," Tarla replied, smiling.

"We're fine," he repeated. "Lala got pulled into a special assignment. I haven't seen much of her lately. We talk on the phone now and then."

"Oh well, phone sex has its place in the world."

Cab rubbed his forehead in exasperation. "Seriously, mother?"

"I'm teasing, darling. My, you really are crabby tonight."

He drank his champagne without replying. He wouldn't have admitted it to Tarla, but his relationship with Lala had been strained for weeks. Lala Mosqueda was his sometimes partner on the Naples police and his sometimes lover. They'd begun a relationship several months earlier. Lala was not a casual fling and not into casual sex, and that was a terrifying prospect for someone like Cab, who had spent a dozen years not trusting any woman who came close to him. They were opposites in almost every way: Lala small, dark, and intense, fiercely religious and conservative; Cab absurdly tall and birdlike, blond, and generally unserious about everything except his work. Particularly religion and politics.

Even so, the two felt an attraction like magnets and steel. In the spring, Cab had traveled to Door County, Wisconsin, for an ugly, difficult murder investigation, and he'd spent much of the time driving the remote dirt roads, talking to Lala on his cell phone and realizing how much he missed her. When he came back to Naples, they'd tried being a couple again, but their relationship had been one step forward, one step back. It didn't help that she'd been away from Naples and mostly out of touch for several weeks. It also didn't help that his liberal Los Angeles mother couldn't understand the attraction between her Hollywood son and a right-wing Cuban cop.

"Do you really think I look like Naomi Watts?" Tarla asked.

"I do."

"My breasts are bigger than hers," his mother said. "Of course, mine have had a little help along the way."

"I try not to think about it," Cab said.

"Give me your honest opinion. Which one's perkier tonight?"

"Pass," he replied.

Tarla laughed, a throaty chuckle that had made moviegoers and costars go weak in the knees for thirty years. Her body was still pencil thin; she worked out with the same frenzy she had when she was on-screen. She leaned in and whispered, "You realize I'm kidding, right?"

"Yes, I do."

"Fine, give me your glass. I will find us more alcohol."

His mother disappeared with a swish of apricot satin. Cab shook his head, because Tarla was Tarla, and there was nothing he could do to change her. He was still getting used to the idea of having his mother back in his life. For years, she'd lived in Hollywood and then London, while he bounced from the FBI to the police to private investigative work and back to the police in locales from Barcelona to Rhode Island. His inability to stay put had earned him the nickname Catch-a-Cab Bolton. However, he'd endured the sweaty Gulf Coast for more than two years now: partly because he was tired of running, partly because of Lala.

Three months ago, Tarla had concluded that Cab was finally putting down roots. She'd moved from London to Florida without so much as a phone call to warn him of her arrival. He'd still been on his investigation in Door County when she showed up at his condo to find Lala, nude, stepping out of his shower. Things had gone downhill from there between the two women in his life.

He liked having his mother close to him, but he was also glad that he had convinced her to buy a Gulf-shore condo not far from Diane, rather than her original plan, which was to locate herself in Cab's building in Naples. Two hours along I-75 between them was just about right. He also couldn't blame his mother for all the trouble between him and Lala. He'd done a good job of pushing her out of his life.

Cab watched Diane's television interviews going on in the garden below him. He couldn't hear any of the back-and-forth, but he knew it was all about politics, which to Cab was nothing more than the art of helping voters decide which candidate was the better liar. The young Asian host had finished, and another reporter—a woman with coal hair who made him think of Lala—was settling in to take her turn. In the pause, Diane's gaze wandered, and her eyes met his in the dusky space between the lawn and the balcony. Her composure broke for only a moment. Ten years—it had been ten years. She nodded at him and gave him the smallest smile. He returned the acknowledgment.

That was all; that was the moment he'd dreaded for so long.

"She's born for this, isn't she?"

He turned toward the voice, actually grateful for the interruption. A man joined him on the balcony. "I'm sorry?" Cab said.

"Diane. She's so smooth with the press. I told her she should have jumped into the race ten years ago. She would have won in a landslide. Who knows where she'd be now? Hell, maybe the White House."

"Her husband had just been murdered," Cab pointed out.

"Well, sure, that's my point. She was a shoo-in."

The man craned his neck to stare up at Cab. Most people did. The man on the balcony was smaller by a foot, and he was forty but trying hard not to look more than thirty. His jet-black hair was tied in a long ponytail. He bulged with muscles, and he had a saddle-brown Florida tan. He was dressed in a black T-shirt, pastel green sport coat, white pants, and Top-Siders with no socks. The big red button on his coat read, "Governor Diane."

"I know you, right?" the man said. "You're Tarla's son, the detective."

"That's me."

"Garth Oakes," the man told him, jutting out a hand. He had a rock-hard grip. "I'm an entrepreneur. Fitness videos. You've probably seen my ads on TV. *Beat the Girth . . . With Garth!*"

Sometimes, living in Florida, Cab found himself wandering into a Carl Hiaasen novel. "Sorry, I don't watch a lot of television."

"Hey, well, never mind. If everybody looked like you, I wouldn't have a business, right?" Garth cradled a mug of herbal tea in his hand, with the string of the tea bag dribbling down the side. Cab smelled cinnamon and clove. "I remember you from the bad old days in Lake Wales. You visited Birch's place that summer, right? You're like a giraffe, who can forget that?"

"Most people say I'm more like a heron," Cab replied.

"A heron. Yeah, funny. I see it. Anyway, I was around there a lot back then. I did massages and workouts for Diane a few times a week. Part exercise, part therapy. Me and her, we're close. She really needed someone to talk to, you know? First there was Birch, and then she lost Drew a year later. One-two punch. That was rough, huh?"

"No doubt."

"Me, I think it was worse losing her son than it was when Birch died. She spent hours crying on my shoulder. When she wasn't crying, she was talking about taking down the fucking drug dealers. Make 'em pay. You don't want to see that lady angry, I'm telling you. Not like I'm saying she wasn't upset about Birch. I mean, your husband gets murdered, that's a terrible thing, but Diane and Birch—well . . ." His voice trailed off.

"I don't think Diane would be too happy to hear you talking like this, Garth," Cab pointed out.

"Oh, hey, just between us boys, right? Diane and Tarla are besties. I figure you're in on all of this crap."

Cab put a hand on the man's shoulder. The fabric of the green sport coat felt cheap, like a thirty-dollar knockoff from a big-box store. If Garth was selling fitness videos, he wasn't selling many of them. "Excuse me, I have to go find my mother."

"Yeah, sure, good talking to you."

Cab left Garth on the balcony, sipping his tea and standing with his legs spread apart, like he owned the mansion. Inside, he found himself in a marble-floored hallway that stretched the length of the house. Double-wide doors led to a master bedroom. Diane's room. She had purchased the bayside mansion a few years earlier, when she moved from the small inland town of Lake Wales to the large coastal city of Tampa. There were too many memories in Lake Wales, she'd told Tarla. She associated the town with her childhood, with Birch's murder, with Drew's suicide. In Tampa, she could start fresh, in an estate a short drive from the Common Way Foundation headquarters. The foundation, launched with millions donated in the wake of Birch's assassination, had been the center of her life for a decade.

He stood in the doorway, spying on her suite. The artwork, the bedding, the heavy red wallpaper all showed tropical birds. An overhead skylight cast a circle of light on the bed. There was no clutter in the room and nothing personal except for a photograph on the baroque nightstand of Diane's son, Drew, and another photo from childhood of Diane with Cab's mother. He saw no photograph of Birch Fairmont.

Cab headed for the end of the hallway, where white carpeted stairs led to the first floor. As he descended the steps, he found himself face to face with an attractive woman heading in the opposite direction. She had alabaster skin and long, highlighted chestnut hair. Her face brightened as she saw him.

"Mr. Bolton, there you are," she said.

"Here I am."

"Your mother said you were upstairs. I've been looking for you."

Cab smiled warily. "Oh?"

"My name is Caprice Dean. I'm the executive director of the Common Way Foundation. Tarla probably mentioned that I wanted to speak to you tonight."

"Actually, she didn't," Cab said, "but I'm usually the last to know when it comes to my mother."

Caprice laughed. "I understand how that goes."

"What can I do for you, Ms. Dean?"

"As it happens," Caprice said, "I want to hire you."

They sat in a gazebo in the gardens, where the foliage made a quiet grove. Cab had counted at least fifty people in and around the estate, but the trail that led here was hidden from prying eyes. They both had champagne, fizzing with bubbles. The octagonal shelter was open to the air and situated in the flow of a damp bay breeze. Fountain grass bowed between the pillars.

"It's beautiful, isn't it?" Caprice said. "It's so secluded here. That's what Diane likes about it. You could believe the city doesn't exist at all. Mind you, the barbarians are inside the gate tonight."

"You mean the media?" Cab asked.

"Obviously," she replied with a smirk.

"Well, if Diane values her isolation so much, why did she run for governor?" he asked. "Politicians don't have a zone of privacy anymore. She knows that."

Caprice nodded. "You're right. It's open season on candidates these days. Honestly, we argued about it for a long time. I thought we should recruit someone else to be in the spotlight."

"So why did she?" He smiled. "I assume it wasn't solely the counsel of Garth Oakes."

Caprice laughed. "You've met Garth, have you? I'm not a fan, but Diane likes him. No, the campaign was Diane's call all the way. She felt it was her responsibility to lead the ticket."

"Why were you opposed?" Cab asked.

"Oh, don't get me wrong. I thought we should be in the race, too. We've spent ten years at the foundation advancing our agenda from the outside. Influencing the debate. Supporting and opposing specific candidates. Now we're ready to get into the game."

"In other words, the governor is politically weak this year, and you hate the idea of a staunch conservative like Attorney General Cortes landing in Tallahassee."

"That's true, too," she acknowledged.

"Diane is ahead in the polls," Cab pointed out. "Isn't that a good thing?"

"It is, but there are also crazies who want to paint a target on her chest. Just like Birch."

"You think she's at risk?"

"I do. That's why we'd like your help."

"Oh? What kind of help?"

Caprice didn't answer right away. She pushed her champagne glass in a small circle on the marble table between them. A ringlet of lush brown hair fell across her forehead, and she brushed it back. Her eyes examined him curiously. "You know, Tarla warned me about you."

"Did she?"

"Yes, she said you were the least ideological person on the face of the earth."

"Guilty," Cab said.

"So you don't understand."

"Understand what?"

"Why all of this matters."

She said it intensely, with a serious face. She was passionate, just like Lala. He wondered why he found himself drawn to women who were so different from himself. Women who wore their hearts on a sleeve. Women who followed a cause with flags held high. Cab was nothing like that, but Caprice was obviously a true believer, and the truth was, he found her very attractive.

It was partly her looks. Younger, she would have been pretty; mature, nearing forty, she was beautiful. She had a smooth, soft face and dark, inquisitive eyes. He liked the whiteness of her skin, which was so un-Floridian. She was obviously comfortable with her body, which was fleshy in an erotic way, not stick skinny. She wore a midnight-blue dress that afforded a view of her strong legs well above her knees and of the swelling curves of her full breasts. She had an open, unflinching stare, not at all shy, not girly or cute. Her directness was as appealing to him as her physical features.

"It's not that I don't care," Cab said.

"You just think all politicians are the same."

"Exactly."

"Well, we're not." Caprice stood up and moved to the opposite side of the gazebo. Her movements had grace. She turned around, leaning back on the stone ledge. "I was a political science major at

UCF. I hated both parties, and I still do. They're all about ideology, not common sense. My boyfriend, Lyle, he felt the same way. We were both ambitious. We committed ourselves to the idea of an independent, centrist party that would truly compete against the Republicans and Democrats, not simply be a spoiler movement. With Birch's campaign, we thought we had taken the first step."

"I'm sorry. I know what you lost that day."

"With all due respect, Mr. Bolton, you don't. I'm sure your mother told you what we went through on that dais, but you can't understand what it's really like to lose someone you love, to stand there covered in his blood and brains."

Cab didn't reply. This wasn't a game of tit for tat, but in reality, he had lost someone he loved in a violent way, too. On a beach outside Barcelona, he had come face to face with a woman named Vivian Frost. He had never fallen so naively head-over-heels in love with anyone like he had with Vivian, and he knew he never would again. He'd given up everything for her, including his job with the FBI, only to discover that she was partnered with a terrorist—that she'd been part of a conspiracy that led to the deaths of twenty-seven people in a bombing at a Spanish train station. She'd lied to him. Manipulated him.

There, on the beach, he'd shot her in the heart.

He knew what loss was like.

"Something like that changes you," he said, joining her on the other side of the gazebo.

"Yes, it does," Caprice agreed. "Diane and I started the Common Way Foundation that same year. The violence outraged people around the country, and they supported us financially. The assassination was an attempt to silence what Lyle and Birch tried to do, and the foundation honored them and their principles. We stayed outside the process, but we took sides. We put a thumb on the scale. We pushed candidates and policy, and we didn't hesitate to rip both parties for their unwillingness to tell the truth. We learned our lesson."

"Which was?"

"Play hardball," Caprice said.

"Hardball. Is that why you hired a dirty tricks specialist like Ogden Bush for Diane's campaign?" Cab smiled and added: "I may not be political, but I do read the papers, you know."

Caprice winced at the man's name. "Ogden was Diane's choice, not mine."

"Still, he's a Democrat with a reputation for running fiercely negative campaigns, isn't he? Doesn't that fly in the face of your 'we're not all the same' speech?"

"I suppose you could say that," she agreed. "Ogden fell out with the Dems a couple years ago, so he sells himself to the highest bidder. He was helpful to us on voting rights legislation last year. I didn't think we wanted him on the campaign, but Diane thought he could help her make inroads with liberal voters. In politics, we can't always be particular about who we sleep with."

She leaned closer to him. Their shoulders brushed together.

"So what do you need me for?" he asked.

"I told you, Mr. Bolton, I want to hire you."

"Call me Cab," he said.

Caprice's face softened. "Okay. That's an unusual name. Why Cab?"

"Tarla was in a deli eating stuffed cabbage when her water broke."

"How cute. Is that true?"

Cab smiled but didn't reply. He had no idea what was true. Tarla had never told him. Just like she had never told him who his father was. He'd made up stories over the years to fill in the gaps.

"You don't look much like any detective I've ever met," Caprice went on. "Do most Naples detectives have spiky hair like that?"

"It's a pomade from London."

"I like it. The diamond earring?"

"A gift from a wealthy older woman."

"And how tall are you? Eight feet?"

"About that."

"Your suit looks like it costs what I make in a month at the foundation."

"About that."

"You don't apologize for having money, do you?"

"No. It is what it is. Tarla's wealthy, and she made me wealthy, which means I can do whatever I want. In my case, that usually means dealing with people doing ugly things."

"Which is why I want to hire you."

"I already have a job," Cab said.

"Actually, I talked to your lieutenant in Naples. He didn't seem too upset to let me borrow you for a while."

"I don't imagine he would be. He doesn't think I look much like a detective, either. Unfortunately, talking to my lieutenant behind my back makes me inclined to say no to whatever you have in mind. I don't like being manipulated, Ms. Dean. That may be how things work at the Common Way Foundation, but it doesn't work with me."

"Hear me out," Caprice said, with a soft grip on his arm as he turned to leave. Her fingers were warm.

Cab shrugged. "What do you want?"

"Diane's in jeopardy. I'm worried someone's planning another assassination attempt."

"Hire a bodyguard."

"I have."

"So why do you need me?"

"I want you to find out what really happened ten years ago," Caprice said, "and whether it could happen again."

"The FBI concluded that a right-wing militia group was behind the assassination. Its leader, Hamilton Brock, is in prison."

"For tax fraud," Caprice said, "not for murder. No one talked, and they never determined exactly who pulled the trigger. The militia is alive and well even with Brock behind bars. You think he can't direct things from inside his cell?"

"Talk to the police. The FBI."

"I've done that, and they're looking into it. However, one thing I've learned at the foundation is that we get better results when we do things ourselves. I don't want third parties I can't control. I want my own man."

"You think you can control me?" Cab asked.

"I'd like to try," Caprice replied, with a double entendre that neither of them missed.

Cab felt heat on the back of his dress shirt. "I don't do security."

"Security's not what I want. I want to know who wore that hood and pulled the trigger. Who killed Birch and Lyle? That's the only way we can stop them."

"You're talking about digging into a ten-year-old crime after a massive investigation turned up nothing," Cab said. "There were no witnesses. There was no gun, no DNA. The militia stonewalled. This man was a ghost. I'm not sure why you think I'd be able to make inroads where the FBI failed. Besides, you're making a big leap. If there really is a credible threat against Diane today, chances are it has nothing to do with the past."

"Sometimes it takes fresh eyes to see clearly, Cab. And I'm not wrong about the threat." Caprice carried a satin clutch that matched her dress. She undid the clasp and reached inside. She withdrew a folded piece of paper and handed it to Cab. "This arrived at the foundation last week."

Cab unfolded the paper. It was a copy of a newspaper article from ten years earlier, featuring a photograph taken at the Bok sanctuary in the wake of the murders. He saw bodies prone on the dais. Police. Shell-shocked survivors, including his mother, Diane, and Caprice, all of them ten years younger and ten years more innocent.

Someone had written across the photograph in a blood-red marker.

I'M BACK. MISS ME?

3

"City of Tampa."

The mural, like an oversized picture postcard, was painted on the brick wall of an ad agency building across the alley between Franklin and Florida Avenues in the northwest corner of downtown. Peach saw it every day when she squeezed her two-tone 1980s-era Thunderbird into spot 52. Each block letter spelling out the city's name featured a cartoon rendering of a different local tourist attraction. The Sulphur Springs Water Tower. The Plant Museum.

Places she'd never found time to visit.

The window was open, letting in the heavy evening air, making her clothes damp. Peach didn't mind; she hated the cold and loved the heat, even during the ferocious summer days. She stared at the mural, wondering why she'd never visited the Plant Museum in the years she'd lived here. Justin had told her once that the bronze sculpture of the Spinning Girl inside the museum looked like her, with her hair cut way up her forehead, her far-away eyes, and her breasts as shallow as Florida hills. She figured she should go see the sculpture sometime and see if it spoke to her. Maybe, in another life, she'd been the artist's model. Peach was a firm believer in reincarnation.

She left the engine running and turned on her radio. She hadn't felt like listening to music these past two weeks, but she could go for some Train or Bruno Mars or even Adele, although she was pretty much over Adele now. She punched the channel for the satellite pop blend, but instead of her sad songs, she heard some awful, screechy opera in a language that was probably German or Russian, where the words needed a lot of spit.

Justin.

Justin with his Beethoven T-shirts. He'd switched the channels on her radio again, and she was only finding out now. *I'm telling you, Peach, there's not a note of music worth listening to that was written after 1849.*

She shut off the radio and got out of the car. Next to her T-Bird, in spot 51, was a ten-year-old silver Mercedes SL convertible. For its age, it was in perfect condition, washed every week, sporty engine purring at eighty miles an hour on the back roads. Her brother Deacon babied it, just the way their older brother, Lyle, had. She ran the pad of her little finger along the chassis. Smooth. Lyle would have been pleased that the two of them still owned the car.

He'd only owned it for a month before—

Before.

Peach had been thinking about the past again. She'd been reminded two weeks ago how many people had been stripped out of her life. At age eight, she'd been orphaned when her parents died on a missionary trip in Colombia. At age twelve, she felt as if she'd been orphaned again when a soldier of the Liberty Empire Alliance gunned down her oldest brother, Lyle, along with Birch Fairmont.

Now she was twenty-two, although people usually mistook her for a teenager. Now it had happened again. Another death. Another loss.

Peach felt numb.

She peered down the city streets. It was early evening, but it was June 29, a Friday, and it would still be light for hours. The streets weren't busy. There wasn't anything to bring out the after-work crowd in this sleepy section of the city. By habit, she checked the windows and balconies in the nearby apartment buildings to see if anyone was watching her. Deacon said she was paranoid, but she couldn't stop. When she decided she was alone, she veered across the parking lot to the office door.

The location of Common Way's research department was a drab, mostly windowless building with a brown metal roof. Half the building was vacant. The rest of the space was taken up by a cubicle farm owned by the foundation. She let herself in through double-wide doors on the side of the building facing Florida Avenue, only a block from the 275 freeway. The number was 1100, but the last zero had slipped sideways, making it look like an eye examining the traffic.

Peach hated being in the office. The space was claustrophobic, with dirty white paint on the walls. She didn't like being inside, sitting at a desk, making phone calls, clicking keys on a laptop. She liked the old ways of doing things. Paper. Film. At home, she didn't even use a computer or a tablet.

Once anything about you is digitized, you don't own it anymore. Soon you don't even own yourself. Justin.

She wanted to be where the people were. There was safety in numbers. She was desperately shy and had no real friends, but she liked watching people, studying them, analyzing them, listening to them. That was what she did best. Humint, Deacon called it. Human intelligence. Peach was their oppo girl. She was the one they sent when they needed someone who could blend into a crowd and come back with evidence of what their enemies were saying.

Peach didn't like thinking of other people as enemies, but that was what they were. They had proven that over and over again.

Inside the office, she stared over the beige fabric walls of the cubicles. She heard the cacophony of voices and the rattle of keys. It was campaign season, and everyone worked late. She followed the building wall toward her brother's office. The wall was taped over with news about politicians and policies. It was a low-tech bulletin board where researchers shared information that didn't necessarily make it online. Gaffes. Issues. Photographs. Things they could use against people.

She flopped down in Deacon's guest chair and rocked nervously back and forth. Her brother sat in front of his computer, and his fingers flew.

"Hey," she said.

"Hey, good job today. You got the recorder?"

Peach reached into her pocket and handed him the Sony voice recorder that she'd used with Walter Fleming and Brent Reed.

"I'll run it through Dragon and get it back to you," Deacon said.

"Uh-huh."

"I talked to Caprice. She said to keep the lid on the news. She thinks if the story about the governor breaks too early, it'll force him to deny it and stay in the race."

"Duh."

"You going back to the convention tomorrow?"

"Yeah, probably. I don't have anything else to do."

Deacon stopped working and stared at his sister. "Look, why don't you knock off for the day. Go home. Forget about the weekend. Someone else can cover it."

"I don't know. Maybe."

"Did you eat?"

"I had half a salad."

"You need to eat."

"Whatever," Peach said. "I'm not hungry."

"I know you're upset."

"I'm not upset. I'm nothing. That's what bugs me, you know? I don't feel a thing, and I don't know what to do about it."

"I told you, go home," Deacon said. "Get some sleep. Or go work out. Go for a run."

"Maybe," she said again. "You going home soon?"

"Later. I want to hit the gym."

Deacon worked out every day. It was the only way to get past the stress of politics. He was skinny and strong, but he had a soft-edged face with unruly red hair and bedroom blue eyes. He was a dead ringer for their father. Same long nose with a little hook. Same dreamy smile. He rarely shaved, giving him a stubbly strawberry beard. Women really went for Deacon. At the gym, girls homed in on him as if there were some kind of pheromone in his sweat. He never got serious about anyone, though. The two of them were all about work.

They'd lived together since Lyle was killed. Back then, Lyle had been their surrogate father. She and Deacon hadn't really been close during those years, because Deacon was an angry kid after their parents died. Angry at them. Angry at Lyle. Angry at the world. To Deacon, who was six years older, Peach was an annoying little girl, and he was a teenager with better things to do. That changed after Labor Day. At age eighteen, with money they inherited from Lyle, he bought a little house in Tampa, and Peach moved in with him. Caprice hired him to work at the new foundation. When Peach turned eighteen four years ago, she joined the foundation, too.

"Go on," Deacon repeated. "I'll see you at home. Make some tater tots or something."

"Yeah, okay. See you later."

Peach pushed herself out of the chair and navigated the maze to her own cubicle. The desk was uncluttered, and the monitor was dusty. There wasn't even a calendar on the cubicle wall. She had three photographs pinned up with thumbtacks. One was of Lyle next to his new Mercedes, in August of that last summer, looking fussy and proud. The other was of Deacon, two years back, on a Sunday outing to Honeymoon Island on the Gulf. Sunglasses, no shirt, tanned and fit. The last picture showed a man not much older than herself, with a porkpie hat, a handlebar mustache like a cartoon train robber, and a mock scowl for the camera. He was tall and beanpole skinny, with arms folded across his scrawny chest. He wore baggy jeans and a T-shirt showing "The Scream."

Justin.

She got up and went to the next cubicle and sat down in his chair. There was nothing in the small space to remind her of him anymore. They'd taken everything away. The computer was new. The drawers were empty. They'd even removed the poster of Mozart on the wall and the kitten calendar she'd given him for Christmas. All that was left was his voice in her head.

Justin on Florida. *It's the cockroach capital of America. And there are lots of bugs, too.*

Justin on money. *My parents have money, and they're the unhappiest people you'll ever meet. They keep sending me money, because they want me to be unhappy, too.*

Justin on poetry. *The greatest poem ever is Blake's "The Tyger."*

Justin on sex. *Nothing screws up love faster than sex. So if we never have sex, we'll always be in love.*

They never had sex.

"Hello?"

Peach looked up when a voice interrupted her memories. A Hispanic woman in her midthirties stood in the opening of the cubicle. She held a cup of coffee in her hand and wore black glasses that looked straight out of Clark Kent and the 1950s.

"Who are you?" Peach asked.

The woman didn't have time to answer, because someone else appeared behind her and nudged her into the background the way an actor occupies center stage. The frown on Peach's face deepened.

"Oh, Peach, there are you," Ogden Bush announced. "Congratulations, I heard about your coup with Walter and Brent today."

"You did?"

Bush smiled. He had the arrogant smile of a wolf living among chickens. "I hear about everything. That's my job."

His job was to direct opposition research for Diane's campaign. Target the Republicans. Target the Democrats. Plant media stories. Craft negative ads. He'd spent two months inside the building since Diane formally announced her candidacy. The activities of the political foundation had been unofficially swallowed up by the activities of the campaign, and they were squeezed together in the same space. Bush had hired his own staff, who worked side by side with Peach, Deacon, and the other foundation employees. The political operative had his hand in everything now.

Peach didn't like him, but she didn't like many people. *We are alone, Peach. Alone and on our own.* Justin.

Ogden Bush had no allegiance to Diane or the foundation. He was a hired hand who followed the money. Ten years before, he'd been on the opposite side of the fence, working for the liberal Democrat against Birch Fairmont. Now he was on Diane's side, because she was the one paying the bills. Bush was clever and tough, but Peach didn't trust people who went where the wind blew.

He wasn't tall for a man, barely five-foot-nine, and he'd just turned forty. He had ebony skin. A generous-sized ruby ring adorned one finger. His coal eyes had the sharpness of a hawk that missed nothing, but he also had a way of looking through her, not at her, as if she were no more than prey. He kept a thin, neat mustache on his upper lip and a trimmed chin curtain along the pointed line of his face. His black hair was shaved short, with smudges of gray above both ears. He wore suits a size too small to emphasize his sleek, toned body. The suits were expensive and fashionable, because he wanted everyone to know how successful he was.

"People only pay attention to you if they know you can do something to them," he'd told Peach when they first met. "Good or bad, it doesn't matter."

Bush squeezed the shoulder of the woman in the cubicle doorway. "This is my newest researcher, Annalie Martine. Take her with you to the convention tomorrow. I'd like her in on the humint side of things."

"I work alone," Peach said.

"Take her with you," Bush repeated, ignoring her protest. "She'll be a quick study. She's got great references."

Peach said nothing. She hated being paired with strangers. Bush knew it, but he didn't care.

"I figured Brent Reed's mouth would trip him up sooner or later," Bush went on, his voice honey-smooth. "What about Walter Fleming? Did he say anything of interest?"

"He talked about you," Peach said.

"Oh?"

"He was concerned about you figuring out what he was doing. I think he's got a spy somewhere inside the campaign."

"Well, that would be Walter's style," Bush said. "Don't worry, he's a crafty goat, but I know how he operates. Anyway, show Annalie the ropes, okay? I'm counting on you, Peach."

Bush disappeared as his phone began to ring, and the musky cloud of his cologne went with him. Annalie gave Peach an apologetic smile. She looked uncomfortable. "Sorry to drop in on you like this."

Peach shrugged. "Whatever."

"Um."

"What?" Peach asked, but then she realized she was sitting in Justin's chair and that Justin's chair now belonged to this new woman. This stranger. "Sorry," she said, getting up.

"No problem."

Annalie didn't sit down. They stood in the cramped space together, barely two feet apart, eye to eye. They were the same height. Peach was skinny, but Annalie had curves under her black T-shirt and jeans. She would have looked younger and hotter if she'd lost the glasses and untied her black hair from the severe bun that was pulled back behind her head. She was pretty, with mellow golden skin and smoky eyes, but she wasn't trying to be attractive.

"I know it's hard when new people get dropped on you," Annalie said. "I'm lucky to be here. I need the job."

"Ogden said you had hotshot references," Peach said.

"Well, my father works for a big foundation donor."

"You ever done oppo work before?" Peach asked.

"Sort of. I worked for a woman who did private detective work in Jacksonville. You know, cheating hubbies and stuff."

"On the street or in the office?"

"A little of both."

"You must have guts to take this job," Peach said. "You're not afraid that it's cursed or something?"

Annalie cocked her head. "Cursed? I don't get it."

"Ogden didn't tell you about the guy you're replacing?"

"No, he just said a position opened up on the research team. I figured the last guy quit or was fired or something."

"He didn't quit," Peach said. "He didn't get fired. Justin was murdered two weeks ago."

4

The sun sank into the Gulf waters, and Cab expected it to sizzle like an egg hitting a hot frying pan. The Florida sunsets never got old. The strips of clouds turned as pink as cut roses, and the sandbars took on rainbow colors. He cast his eyes down from the twentieth floor toward the white sand of Clearwater Beach. Swimmers and shell hunters stood up to their ankles in the hot water, silhouetted by the sun. Around them, umbrellas dotted the beach like drips of bright paint.

He pulled out his phone and dialed Lala Mosqueda's number. The call went to voice mail, the way it always did lately. He'd left several messages. She hadn't returned them.

"Wawa?" said his mother. Tarla stood in the doorway between the sliding glass doors, still in the dress she'd worn to Diane's party.

"That stopped being funny a long time ago," Cab said.

"I'm sorry, you're right." His mother joined him on the balcony, leaning her bare elbows on the railing. The warm breeze off the water rustled her hair. "So what does she call me? The Hollywood witch?"

"It rhymes with that," Cab said.

"Well, good for her," Tarla said, smiling. She added, as if she were checking on whether he wanted his coffee black: "Are you in love with her, or is it just the sex?"

"Next subject."

"Oh come on, darling."

"I wasn't born with the love gene," Cab told her, which was a lie. He'd been wildly in love with Vivian Frost in Barcelona. "However, I'm also not into meaningless cheap flings."

"I detect a little bit of an accusation in that statement."

"Maybe you do."

In his lifetime, he couldn't remember his mother seriously involved with anyone. She'd drifted from affair to affair, and she'd broken up more than one marriage. He loved his mother, but there were days when he didn't always like her. She was beautiful, and she was a loner, and he blamed her sometimes for making him the way he was.

In other words, he was a lot like her.

"I'm not trying to split the two of you up," Tarla said. "If you want to make it work with Lala, make it work. However, let's be honest, darling. I saw you with Caprice Dean this evening. There were sparks flying."

"She's attractive. That's all it is."

"Is that a sin? I've known Caprice for years. She's pretty, smart, serious, and she's going places. If Diane wasn't running this year, Caprice probably would, and as young as she is, I think she'd win. That's the kind of woman you belong with, Cab."

"I really don't need romantic advice from you, mother," he said. "Did you know Caprice wanted me to do investigative work for her when you asked me to come up this weekend?"

"She may have mentioned it," Tarla said.

"So you lured me here under false pretenses."

"Would you have come otherwise? Besides, this way I get to see you. I didn't leave London for the cultural life of Clearwater. The seafood is wonderful, and the boys on the beach are cute, but otherwise, it's a bit of a wasteland. I'm here because of you, Cab. Unless you'd prefer I go away."

"I didn't say that," Cab replied. "I'm glad you're here."

He wondered if that was completely true. They'd always had a close but codependent relationship, and sometimes he rebelled against it.

Growing up, he had traveled with Tarla to movie sets all over the world, and although he had met famous people and stayed in amazing places, he felt homeless, as if he had no roots. Tarla was also intensely private, shutting him out from parts of her life, including the truth about his father. He'd learned to do the same. When he had a chance to leave, he did. At eighteen, he went to UCLA, graduated in three years, and to his mother's shock, he chose law enforcement when he could have chosen acting. She'd been prepared to find roles and open doors for him, but he didn't want the Hollywood life.

Now she was retired. Now they were together again, after nearly twenty years in different corners of the world. It was like starting over.

He turned and went inside. The condominium was ice-cold compared to the summer heat. He hadn't been to Tarla's place in several weeks, and she'd been decorating in the interim. The sprawling apartment looked like her. Cool. Modern. Expensive. It wasn't a place where you would sit down and put your feet up.

Tarla joined him from the balcony. She went to the bar and poured herself a glass of wine, and she held up the bottle with an inquiring glance. He shook his head. She drank more than he remembered.

"So why is Diane running for governor?" Cab asked. "You always told me she didn't want to get her hands dirty. She wanted to work behind the scenes."

Tarla shrugged. "I'm not sure her heart is in it, but she saw an opportunity and couldn't say no. The governor has been wounded by the kickback scandal involving his chief of staff. Ramona Cortes, the Republican, is another scary right-winger."

"Ramona's not really so scary," Cab said mildly.

Tarla's eyebrows arched toward heaven. "You've met her?"

"She's one of Lala's cousins," he said. "One of about two hundred or so."

"Charming. Well, Diane was getting pressure from foundation donors to get in the race to block her. They're afraid if Ramona becomes governor, she might decide to nuke Oklahoma."

Cab smiled. "Extremes are in the eye of the beholder. Do you really believe in the virginal purity of the Common Way Party?"

"Me? I'm a wild-eyed, woolly tree hugger, you know that. A Democrat's Democrat. But Diane is my best friend, and she'd make a good governor. I believe that."

Cab said nothing.

"I know you don't like her," Tarla added, "although I don't know why."

"That's not true."

His mother sat down next to him on a sofa that was black and umber, with striped hexagonal pillows. "You've ducked every occasion where she and I were together. You didn't even come to Drew's funeral, though I basically ordered you to be there."

"That was nine years ago, and I was busy with a murder investigation in Newport. I sent flowers."

"Yes, how thoughtful," Tarla snapped. "Drew shot himself, for God's sake. Diane was hysterical. She tracked down that awful drug dealer in a bar and had to be physically restrained from attacking him."

"I remember," Cab said.

"I'm just saying, Diane has lived a life that's far more difficult than you or I have ever had to deal with. You don't have a clue of what she's gone through, Cab. She's a good person, and I want to support her in any way I can. If you can help, I wish you would."

"I told Caprice I would look into it," Cab said.

"You did?"

"I did."

Tarla drank her wine and flushed a little with embarrassment. "Oh. Well, good. Thank you."

"I already have an appointment with Chuck Warren in the morning."

"The fascist?"

Cab smiled. "Not all Republicans are fascists."

"Warren is."

"Well, he was the GOP candidate for the congressional seat ten years ago. After Birch was killed, he got tarred for being too cozy with right-wing extremists. I'd like to see what he says about what happened back then."

"You really think he'll tell you the truth?" Tarla asked.

"No, but lies are more interesting. I usually learn more from lies than I do from the truth."

"You live in a strange world, Cab."

"No stranger than yours," he said.

"True." His mother smiled, but then her face darkened. "Do you think Diane is in any danger?"

"I don't know. Threats to political candidates are dime a dozen, but this one is pretty specific."

"Caprice thinks whoever killed Birch may be focused on Diane," Tarla said.

"What do you think?"

"Me? I have no idea. How would I know?"

"You were there," Cab said.

Tarla stood up and refilled her wine at the bar. "I don't think you should waste your time on the past. Ten years is a long time ago. I doubt there's any connection."

Cab joined her at the bar. "You've never told me much about what happened to you that night."

"I don't remember it," she said. She pulled away from him, and the casualness in her voice was unconvincing. She was a bad actress when she played herself. "I fainted, Cab. I woke up in the hospital. The night was erased from my brain."

"You were inches away from the killer. Closer than anyone else who survived."

"I don't remember him," Tarla insisted. "People tell me I protected Diane, but I don't even remember doing that."

He kissed the top of his mother's head. "I'm sorry. I know it must have been awful for you."

Cab didn't push her for answers, because Tarla wasn't a person who could be pushed. If you poked her, she shrank like a turtle deeper into her shell. He also knew that his old axiom was right again. You could learn more from lies than you ever could from the truth.

Tarla was lying.

There was something about that night that she didn't want him to know.

5

The deer sprang out of nowhere, like a monster from the closet. It wasn't there, and then it was.

Peach gasped in surprise, and her foot dove for the brake. The Thunderbird jerked to a stop, throwing her against the safety belt. The young doe, momentarily frozen, stared curiously into the car's headlights, and when Peach switched the lights off, she saw its spindly legs clip-clop casually between the trees toward the lake.

"*See the little white cross?*" she'd told Justin on their weekend getaway to Lake Wales last month. "*You have to be careful when you drive here.*"

Peach closed her eyes.

When she touched her hands to her face, she realized she was crying. She pushed open the car door and climbed out into the darkness, her knees buckling. She grabbed the door to steady herself, then took uneasy steps into the grass. Insects descended on her, buzzing and biting. She looked around for the deer, but it had already disappeared toward the water. Her feet were wet. She imagined for a moment that she was standing in blood, but when she looked down at the dirt and pine needles, she saw that it was just rain pooled on the ground from an afternoon squall.

Peach was alone on the sprawling trails of Lake Seminole Park. She and Deacon lived in a pink bungalow on Ninety-Eighth Street in

Seminole, which was a straight shot across the Gandy Bridge as she headed west out of Tampa. Their house, where they'd lived for ten years, was on the other side of the fence that marked the park's eastern border. She wasn't supposed to be in the park at night, but the security guards all knew who she was. To them, she was Peach Paranoid, but she was also the girl who had lost her parents in Colombia and her oldest brother in the Labor Day shooting. Let her be paranoid. Let her park wherever she wanted.

She didn't like to have her car seen at her house. She didn't want anyone knowing who she was or where she lived. Instead, she drove the T-Bird to the very end of the park's paved roads, near deserted picnic grounds. Twenty yards away, a sidewalk led to an open gate in the fence. She got out and slipped between the squat palm trees. She heard rustling and cackling from a brood of chickens that wandered in and out of the park from a nearby hobby farm. A peacock screamed not far away. She ducked through the gate and hugged the fence for another block until she was across the street from their house.

Overgrown oaks crowded the roof. The house dated to the 1960s and was surrounded by a warped wooden fence that Deacon was always promising to fix. The roof needed help, too; it was missing shingles from the last big storm, and it leaked over the toilet in her bathroom, dripping on her head. A sign warned trespassers of dogs, but they had never owned a dog. She didn't see the Mercedes in the driveway, and she didn't expect Deacon for hours.

She let herself inside. The house smelled of the fish she'd microwaved for dinner the previous night. The two of them weren't the best housekeepers, especially during campaign season. Junk mail and newspapers filled the counters and tabletops. The open wooden surfaces were gray with dust. Rather than turn on a light, she made her way in the dark toward her bedroom on the south side of the house, looking toward the park. There, she pulled the heavy curtains shut and switched on an overhead light.

Half a dozen white department store mannequins stared at her with empty eyes. She could see them in the full-length mirror, too, as if the bedroom were populated with ghosts frozen in odd poses.

Deacon thought it was weird. She'd named them when she was a teenager: Sexpot, Ditty, Petunia, Rickles, Harley, and Bon Bon. They wore different wigs and outfits, suitable for disguises. A long-haired hippy. A blond bombshell. A punk-tattooed biker chick with fire-red hair. She'd been all of those women in the past year.

She hadn't spent much time being herself.

Peach kicked off her Crocs and flopped backward onto her twin bed. She spread her arms and legs in an X and stared at the ceiling, which was webbed with hairline cracks in the plaster. She knew she should eat, but she wasn't hungry. All she wanted to do was sleep, but she hadn't slept for days.

Her phone rang. Sighing, she squeezed it out of her pocket. The number was blocked.

"Hello?"

"Is this Peach Piper?"

"Who is this?" she asked.

The Georgia-accented voice on the phone drawled at her. "Ms. Piper, my name is Detective Curtis Clay of the St. Petersburg police. I'd like to talk to you about a colleague of yours named Justin Kiel."

They sat on the beach on the shore of Lake Wales, surrounded by children splashing in the water. Across the lake, they could see the expensive shoreside homes climbing the shallow hill, with manicured lawns that reminded her of antebellum plantations. The air was filled with the motor whine and gasoline smell of powerboats pulling inner tubes across the lake.

Peach wore a one-piece yellow swimsuit, and she had her arms wrapped around her knobby knees. Justin wore trunks that lay like a tarpaulin across his long, skinny legs. They were both damp from bobbing in the lake. He took off his porkpie hat and plopped it on top of her wet hair like a crown.

"There, that looks good," he said.

Peach giggled. "You're silly."

As they sat with sand on their bodies, Justin took her hand, and in the silence, she realized: He's my boyfriend. They'd worked side by side at the foundation for a year, and she'd grown as close to him as she ever had to another person, but she'd never thought of it as being anything more. Except now it was.

Peach had never met anyone like him. He was quirky, with his little round hats and his old-fashioned mustache. He had a pimply face that most girls probably wouldn't like. Paper-straight bangs tickled his eyebrows. He was only two years older than she was, but he talked older, like someone who had lived a long time. He had an opinion about everything, delivered with the pompousness of a professor giving a lecture. He was hacker-smart about computers, but he kept almost his entire life off the grid. No cell phone. No credit cards, not even a checkbook. Cash only. He loved visiting antique stores and estate sales and buying hundred-year-old bric-a-brac—anything without a power cord, anything with dents and bruises and water stains, anything with a history of people who had owned it and had a story to tell.

All these years alone, and Peach had finally found a kindred spirit.

"So do you think I'm wrong?" she asked him. She realized she was nervous about what he would say.

"You are never wrong. About what?"

"Well, I mean, the celibacy thing."

"You decided that a long time ago, right?" Justin said. "It's what you believe in. I respect that."

"Don't you want sex? Men always do."

Justin scratched his head. His wet hair stood up like matchsticks. "People can be really close without having sex. I think it's cool that you want something different."

It wasn't the first time he'd told her that, but if they were really going to do this—boyfriend, girlfriend—she wondered if he'd feel that they needed to be physical. If she was going to do that with anyone, it was him, but the very idea of sex made her feel unclean. It was okay being naked, if he wanted that. It was okay kissing and holding. She'd just told herself as far back as she could remember that she would always be a virgin.

"Does it bother you being here?" Justin asked.

"What do you mean?"

"Lake Wales. Where your brother was killed."

Peach hesitated. "Yes."

"I'm sorry. I shouldn't have suggested it."

"No, that's okay, I told you I would come."

"Have you been back since it happened?"

"I haven't, but it's a beautiful place. It should mean something other than death."

"Do you remember that time?" he asked.

"Bits and pieces." She thought about it, and then she said: "My parents have mostly faded from my memory. Now Lyle is fading, too. I can't really hear him in my head anymore. He's going away. That's why I work at the foundation. It keeps a little bit of him alive."

They were silent for a while. The intense sun dried their skin, and she could feel her face and shoulders pinking up and freckling. A jogger with a golden retriever ran along the shore in front of them, spattering water and damp sand.

"Do you like what we do?" Justin asked.

"Like it?"

"The work. Do you enjoy it?"

"I don't really think about that. I'm good at it. It's important."

"Is it?"

She turned her head and shadowed her eyes with her hand to stare at him. "What are you saying?"

Justin took a slow breath. "It's just that some days I wonder who the good guys are and who the bad guys are, and whether there's any difference."

"We're the good guys," Peach said.

He smiled. "You are, that's for sure."

The sky was blue, but there was a cloud crossing his face. "What's going on, Justin? Is something wrong?"

"No, nothing."

He leaned closer and kissed her cheek without saying anything more. She was surprised. Usually, Justin beat a subject to death before he would let it go. He would talk and talk until she raised a white flag. Not this time. It made her a little unhappy. She didn't like the idea that he might be keeping something from her.

"I only got us one motel room," he said. "Are you okay with that?"

"Sure."

"One bed?" he said.

"Yeah."

"But no sex," he told her. "Don't worry."

"I'm not worried."

"You trust me that much?" he asked.

"You're about the only person in the world I trust," Peach said. She stared at him with all the intensity she could find, because she wanted him to realize she was serious. "You can tell me anything. You know that, don't you?"

"Did you know Mr. Kiel well?" Detective Clay asked.

Peach lay motionless in bed, with the phone at her ear. The vacant eyes of the mannequins stared at her, wondering what she would say. She was silent for so long that the detective repeated the question.

"No," she said finally. "I didn't know Justin well at all. We were basically strangers."

Her answer prompted an awkward pause. "That wasn't what I heard."

"Well, that's how it was."

"You worked regularly with Mr. Kiel, didn't you?"

"Sometimes."

"But you were strangers?"

"We were colleagues," Peach said. "That's all."

His drawl got a little cooler and less Georgia-friendly. "Ms. Piper, you do want to see us catch whoever did this to Mr. Kiel, don't you?"

"Sure."

"So if you can help us with information, you'll do that, won't you?"

"There's not much to tell."

The detective breathed into the phone, like a sigh. "Did you know that Mr. Kiel sold drugs? He was a dealer?"

Peach wanted to scream. Her breath felt ragged in her chest. *He wasn't! That's a lie!* "No."

"Did you ever see him selling drugs? Or using drugs?"

"No."

"Did he sell you drugs, Ms. Piper?"

"No."

"I'm not in narcotics. You can be honest with me."

"I said no."

"You're aware that Mr. Kiel was shot in a drug sale gone bad, aren't you? Drugs were hidden in the motel room where his body was found."

Peach felt the bed going round and round in circles. She got to her feet, made it to the wall, and slid down to the floor. Her free hand clenched into a fist. Her eyes squeezed shut.

"I only know what I read in the newspaper."

"Do you know if Mr. Kiel had any enemies?"

"I don't."

"What were you and he working on when he was killed?"

Peach wiped her nose. "What?"

"I said, what were you and he working on when he was killed?"

"Nothing."

"You weren't working together?"

"No, I hadn't seen him in days. We hadn't talked." That much was true. He'd dropped off the radar for a week. She'd been in a panic. *Where are you? What's going on?*

"Was Mr. Kiel working on his own? Did he tell you anything about that?"

"No, nothing."

He never said a word. Whatever was going on in his life, he'd left her out of it.

"Is there anything else you can tell me, Ms. Piper?"

"No. I don't know anything."

"Well, I appreciate your help."

She thought he was being sarcastic with her. There was nastiness at the back of his throat. The silence told her that he'd hung up, and she pressed the phone to her lips and wondered why she'd lied to him. She did want Justin's murderer caught. She did know things that no one else knew. Without her, the police would write it off as another drug killing. A cocaine statistic. Everyone would believe that he was something that he wasn't.

Justin would say: *It doesn't matter, Peach. We all die, we're all dust. Legacy is a fiction.*

But it did matter.

She could tell them something important to help them find the truth. They were searching his apartment, but that wasn't where the answers were. He had another place, but she didn't know where it was. A safe house. A hideaway.

Peach looked up the number for the St. Petersburg Police Department, and she called, still sitting on the floor. When the receptionist answered, she asked for Detective Curtis Clay. She would talk to him; she would give him what he wanted this time. Everything she knew.

"One moment, ma'am," the woman on the phone told her. And then: "What was that name again?"

"Detective Curtis Clay."

"I'm sorry, ma'am, there's no detective working here by that name. Maybe you have the wrong location. You may want to try Tampa or one of the other Gulf cities."

"He said it was St. Pete," Peach insisted.

"I'm very sorry, ma'am, we don't employ a Detective Clay. Would you like me to ask another—"

"It's my mistake," Peach interrupted sharply. She hung up the phone.

6

Like thousands of other foreclosure homes around the Tampa peninsula, the house on Asbury Place was slowly becoming an eyesore. The
previous owners had abandoned the property in April, leaving Florida
to move in with family in Salisbury, North Carolina. Grass in the yard
had grown six inches high, mixed with weeds that had gone to seed.
The fifty-year-old elm tree bending over the roof had dropped thick,
crooked branches that littered the driveway. Rust stains dripped down
the stucco from sagging gutters. The windows were boarded over and
spray-painted with graffiti.

For the bank, the house was one more property on a long spread-
sheet. It was the fifth house in the same neighborhood to suffer the
same fate. No one had time to look after all of them.

The house was two blocks from the placid bay waters.

Two blocks from Diane Fairmont's walled estate.

That was the crazy democracy of Florida, where million-dollar
mansions were next-door neighbors to garbage homes with pickups
rusting on the lawn.

He'd parked half a mile away, near a condominium complex just
off Bayshore Boulevard. No one would notice or remember his car. It
was after midnight on a hot evening alive with the song of katydids.

He followed the street beside the bay with a Dolphins baseball cap tugged low on his forehead. Sunglasses, even at night, covered his eyes. The headlights of a few cars lit him up from behind like a silhouette, but otherwise, he was alone. At West Alline, he followed the sidewalk in the darkness to the abandoned home on the corner.

Most of the other houses around him were unlit, but he heard the blare of party music from open windows half a block away. There were voices from people in the garden, but he couldn't see them, and they couldn't see him. The smell of cigarette smoke drifted down the street.

He dodged the fallen branches on the driveway. The front door was sheltered by overgrown hedges, and the lamppost near the steps had been shattered by rocks. NO TRESPASSING signs were posted on the door and the front windows. He'd first broken in three weeks ago, and since then, he'd replaced the lock, so he had his own key. It would be weeks before the bank discovered the invasion. Or maybe the police would arrive first. Either way, by then it would be over, and he would be gone.

He let himself inside and closed the door behind him. The shut-up house was musty and hot. The power and water had long since been turned off, leaving the house to cook in the humid summer. He followed a hallway on his left through the mudroom to an attached garage, where he slid a backpack off his shoulder and turned on an emergency lantern. Cockroaches scattered, disappearing under the metal shelves and into the rafters. Spiderwebs made silky nests in the corners. The concrete floor was smeared with oil where cars had been parked for years.

He'd hung a cork bulletin board on the nearest wall, covered with a collage of thumbtacked articles copied from Florida newspapers. Some were only weeks old. Some went back for years.

He studied the headlines.

**FRANK MACY GETS EIGHT YEARS
ON MANSLAUGHTER PLEA**

**ONE YEAR LATER, MORE TRAGEDY:
FAIRMONT STUNNED BY SON'S SUICIDE**

**COMMON WAY FOUNDATION INFLUENCE
GROWS—AND SO DOES CONTROVERSY
FAIRMONT TO ENTER GOVERNOR'S RACE**

He removed a piece of paper from his backpack and pinned it up with the others. This article was new—only hours old—taken from the website of a local television station. It included a grainy photograph of Diane Fairmont from the video feed of an interview conducted in the garden of her estate.

Two blocks away.

He took a red marker from his backpack and drew a circle around Diane's head. With two quick slashes, he made crosshatches, turning the circle into a target. He could smell the intoxicating aroma of the fresh ink. Like an artist, he scrawled a single word across her body.

REVENGE.

He didn't have time to admire his handiwork. The frame of the house thumped with the weight of footsteps. Somewhere else in the house, muffled but unmistakable, he heard breaking glass.

Someone was inside. He wasn't alone.

He doused the lantern and stole inside, where his eyes adjusted to the shadows. The carpet was hard and worn under his boots. He listened and heard nothing, but something was different. The air pressure had changed; a window was open. He also smelled a noxious sweetness. Feces. Someone had used one of the waterless toilets.

He unsheathed a knife from a back pocket. The camouflage blade had saw teeth and curled to a fierce point. His hands were securely covered in hospital gloves, leaving no prints.

Music filled the house, a teen-pop song by One Direction. The volume was loud enough that a neighbor might hear it and come to explore—or call the police. He traced the warbling boy-band music to a back bedroom, where the door was closed. He hid the knife behind his palm and silently twisted the doorknob. He eased the door open.

A candle wavered on the floor, throwing off dancing light and a strawberry scent. The room was vacant of furniture, but he could see dents in the carpet where a bed had been placed. Flowered wallpaper had begun to bubble and curl as moisture got underneath it. A broken, boarded window was pushed open, and he could see waving tree branches in the backyard. Sticky air blew through the bedroom. The music came from a battery-operated iPod dock at his feet, and he squatted and shut it off. He saw a wine bottle tipped on the floor, spilling Cabernet like blood. A wine glass lay broken beside it.

As the music stopped, a young girl appeared in the doorway of the walk-in closet next to him. Her feet were bare. She wore panties and a light blue mesh camisole. Her shoulder-length brown hair was dirty and curly. Her eyes flicked to the speakers, and then she saw him there, waiting for her.

"Oh, shit!"

She made a break for the window, but he was ready for her. He grabbed one wrist, twisted it, and yanked it behind her back. She howled in pain, but he clapped a gloved hand over her mouth.

"*Quiet.*"

"I'm sorry, I'm sorry!" she begged when he removed his hand. "Jesus, I didn't know anybody was here!"

He shoved her toward the bedroom wall. "Who are you?"

She folded her arms and danced on the balls of her feet. "I'm Tina. Look, can I just go? With all these abandoned houses, I figured no one would care if I crashed here."

"Why are you here? Where do you live?"

"I lived with my boyfriend until two days ago. Bastard threw me out because I ran up a two-hundred-dollar cell phone bill. I mean, hello, who doesn't have unlimited texting these days?"

"How old are you?"

She shrugged. "Nineteen."

"How did you find this place?"

"I drove around looking for somewhere I could crash. The house looked empty. I said I was sorry, okay? You beat me to it. Fine. Take it, I'll go someplace else."

"Did you tell anyone where you were?"

"Nobody, I swear, nobody else is going to crash your crib, man. I'm not looking to party. Besides, no phone, remember?"

He looked at her. She was young, foolish, and sweet. Half-teenager, half-woman. A tattoo of a sunflower peeked from her shoulder. Her skin had bikini tan lines. She misread his eyes, and her head cocked, and her mouth bent into a flirty grin. She took a strand of hair and twisted it around her finger.

"Hey, maybe we could figure something out," she said. "Like, maybe we could share the place."

She bunched the lacy trim of her camisole with both hands and pulled it over her head, baring her chest. Her breasts were small, with chocolate-brown, erect nipples and a teardrop birthmark under her left cup. She tugged back and forth on the elastic of her panties, as if she were working the handlebars on a bicycle. When she peeled them halfway down her hips, he saw the curly fuzz of her pubic hair.

Tina bit her lip and came closer. "Like what you see?"

He let the jagged knife slide down his hand, until the handle was in his grasp. The blade was an ugly, deadly thing. She didn't notice it.

"This could be like me paying rent, huh?" she said. "What do you think?"

She really was cute, trying so hard to get what she wanted, which was a place to stay the night. He ran the gloved fingers of his other hand along her cheek, then into the hollow of her neck, then down to her right breast, which he cradled in his palm. His thumb flicked her nipple, and she purred.

"That would be great," he said, "except for one thing."

She nestled against him, reaching for his zipper. "What's that, lover?"

"DNA," he said.

7

"It makes you wonder how they do it, right?" Chuck Warren asked. He gestured across the busy street, where a billboard featured an attractive thirtysomething couple playing with three children in a Florida back-yard. The tagline advertised a local doctor who performed vasectomies using no knife and no needle. "I mean, what's the deal? Do they use garden clippers or what?"

"I'm not eager to find out," Cab replied.

"You and me both. No snipping for me. Not that I'm looking to have more kids, but who knows? If I'm eighty and I still have two marbles rolling around in my head, I might want to put my other marbles to good use." He chuckled.

"Are you married, Mr. Warren?"

"Divorced. Twice. It cost me the gross national product of Brazil both times. That's two and out for me. From now on, I drive, but I don't park. What about you, detective? Are you married?"

"No."

"And you've got money. Smart man. That's the way to keep it."

Warren sipped coffee from a ceramic mug with his own face on it. It was Saturday morning, and Cab felt the Gulf heat tightening his eyes and shrinking his face like a mummy. The sharp creases in his charcoal suit were flattening like a wrinkled shirt in the shower. They stood on open green lawn in front of a radio station headquarters building, in the shadow of half a dozen enormous white satellite dishes. To their left, cars shot westward off the Tampa bridge to the crowded Gulf cities. The smell of dead fish wafted from the nearby beach.

One of the drivers on the highway spotted Chuck Warren and honked loudly. Warren waved back and gave a thumbs-up sign like a manic leprechaun. Two more drivers leaned on their horns in support, but another driver jerked an arm out his window at Warren with the middle finger extended.

Warren offered a cheery return salute. "Socialist," he said, laughing.

He sat down on a bench near one of the satellite dishes. Balancing his coffee mug on the bench, he slid a cigar from the pocket of his navy sport coat and offered it to Cab, who shook his head. Warren lit the cigar, puffed, and picked up his coffee again. "So do you listen to my show, detective?"

"Sorry, no."

"You a Socialist?"

"I'm a nothingalist."

"I just figured, Hollywood mama and all, you had to be a crazy Dem."

"No, just crazy."

"Well, sooner or later, we all have to take sides," Warren said.

The former congressional candidate—and current radio talk show host—was in his early fifties but looked younger. He was about five-foot-eight. He had shock-white hair, as wiry as a brush, and a smooth face that had probably seen its share of Botox and plastic surgery. His cherubic expression—easy smile, twinkling brown eyes—belied his reputation for extreme rhetoric. He was, according to his website, a happy patriot, relentlessly cheery as he tore into left-wing politics. He had charisma. All once-and-future politicians did. As much as you could dislike a politician on television, Cab decided, it was hard to dislike one in person.

Warren crossed his legs. He wore dress slacks and tan loafers. He looked to be in good shape for his age, but he had enough of a pooch to suggest that he liked steak dinners.

"So what can I do for you, detective?" Warren asked. "I love helping our boys in blue. Even ones with earrings."

Cab smiled. Everyone mentioned the earring. "I'm not here in an official capacity. Not as far as the Naples police goes."

"Well, in what capacity are you here?"

"There are concerns that Diane Fairmont may be at risk like Birch was ten years ago. Possibly from the same source. I'm trying to find out if that's true."

Warren chuckled and shook his head. He didn't get angry; he got amused. "What, is this part of her campaign strategy? Have you been conscripted by the folks at Common Way? I'm not really looking to be a political punching bag for that crowd. Been there, done that."

"Are you still bitter about what happened ten years ago?" Cab asked.

Warren sucked on his cigar and blew out a sweet cloud of smoke. He had puffy Santa Claus cheeks. "Not really."

"It ruined your political career."

"True, but it made me a millionaire." Warren poked a thumb at the radio station behind him. "Look, detective, ten years ago I was the Republican candidate for Congress in the Twelfth District. It was my fourth run at it. I never cleared forty-five percent. I was a nobody, an electrician with barely a dime to my name. Look at me now. Millions of people hang on my every word. Bill O'Reilly has me on speed dial. I've got a mansion on the inland waterway. I'm blessed to live in this country."

"Except back then, you finally had a chance at winning the race, and Birch Fairmont took that away."

Warren squinted into the beating sun. He slid out sunglasses from his pocket and put them on his face. "Okay. Sure. Ten years ago, the Democratic incumbent dropped dead of a stroke. The Dems replaced him with a newbie liberal who suffered from foot-in-mouth disease. Talked about Fidel like he was some kind of George Washington. So yeah, I was running neck and neck in the polls."

"Then Birch got in the race," Cab said.

"That's right, he did. Or rather, Lyle Piper pushed him in. Lyle was the political brain behind Common Way. Him and Caprice Dean. Suddenly we had a three-way race, and Birch's numbers were pretty strong for a while. He got a lot of buzz, and buzz gets you free face time on TV. Even so, I was going to win in the end. People have a way of coming home to their spouse after they have drinks with that pretty stranger in the bar."

"You don't think Birch would have pulled it off? Everybody said he had the momentum."

"No, I don't. The race was always going to be between me and the Dems. Ogden Bush was running their campaign, and the word on the street was that Ogden was going to bury Birch with negative ads. Pop his balloon. It would have worked, too. Birch's numbers were paper-thin."

"What did you think when Birch was killed?"

Warren gulped coffee. His face on the mug had the same big smile. The Happy Patriot. "I thought that was the end of my political career, and I was right. And no, I'm not minimizing what happened. It was terrible. However, I knew what it meant for my campaign."

"Namely?" Cab asked.

"The mainstream media would blame me. They'd been trying to crucify me from the beginning. That Orlando reporter, Rufus Twill, kept hyping bullshit stories about me and the Alliance. Chuck's a radical! Chuck's a right-wing extremist! Chuck's in bed with the Nazis! I knew the rest of the media would start talking about 'hate speech' and calling this a political assassination and pointing fingers at me. Which is exactly what they did. Hell, some people thought I had Birch killed to get him out of the race."

"Did you?" Cab asked with a small smile.

Warren grinned. "I told you, I love cops. They can't resist asking gotcha questions. No, not true. See, if I wanted to get Birch out of the race, I would have set him up with a hooker a week or two before the election. I wouldn't have killed him. Dead people get sympathy. The last thing my campaign needed was Birch Fairmont made into a martyr."

"The FBI think Hamilton Brock and the Liberty Empire Alliance were behind the assassination."

"So they say."

"You don't think so?"

"I think the feds conducted the most exhaustive investigation since Lincoln or Kennedy, and they didn't find a shred of real evidence linking Ham to the murders. That's a little funny, don't you think?"

"Hamilton Brock was a donor to your campaign. So were several of his lieutenants."

Warren took the cigar and jabbed it at Cab, but without any malice in the gesture. The man relished the give-and-take of political debate. "Well, first, I don't control who gives me money. Anybody wants to open a checkbook, I think that's their God-given American right, and I don't care what they believe. Second, Ham says those contributions were phony. He knew it would hurt me more than help me to have his group associated with my campaign."

"And yet you obviously know him," Cab said.

"Sure, I do. I've interviewed him on my show from the Coleman penitentiary. You ask me, Ham's a political prisoner. They needed to put someone away for the murders at Bok, so they trumped up tax charges against Ham, in order to pretend they'd done their job."

"You think he's innocent."

"I do."

"So who killed Birch?"

"I have no idea," Warren said.

"Do you think Ham Brock knows?"

"You'll have to ask him. I'm not saying it couldn't have been some deranged sympathizer acting on his own. Maybe it was. I just don't think it was Ham or any of his boys. They're too smart. On the other hand, there were also nasty rumors about Birch during the campaign."

"Rumors?" Cab said.

"Oh, yeah, some ugly stories buzzed around the grapevine. Ogden was behind most of them, so who knows whether any of it was true. I didn't peddle the dirt myself, because it would have made things worse. After Labor Day, you couldn't say a bad thing about Birch.

Getting killed makes you a saint. From what I hear, though, Birch was no saint."

"How so?"

"Oh, let's just say that Birch and Diane weren't exactly one big happy family. That was all for the cameras."

Cab stood up. He smoothed his suit and tugged the knot on his tie a little tighter. Warren remained sitting comfortably on the bench, with an arm slung around the back. Pungent smoke surrounded him like a halo.

"What about this year?" Cab asked. "Feels like déjà vu all over again, doesn't it?"

"Politically? Sure it does. The governor is cruising toward reelection, and then miraculously he gets bogged down in a corruption scandal involving his inner circle. The mainstream media pegs Attorney General Cortes as another crazy Tea Party Republican, just like me. Hell, Ramona was on Ham Brock's legal defense team, so she must be a radical extremist, right? And in marches Diane Fairmont of the Common Way Party to save the day. Like the Church Lady would say, how *conveeeeenient.*"

Cab cocked his head. "Are you suggesting Diane had something to do with the scandal involving the governor?"

Warren leaned forward with his elbows on his knees. "I'm saying Common Way has built a reputation as a centrist organization that's above the fray, and that's a bunch of crap. They're as ruthless as either of the other parties. Come on, who did they bring in to handle oppo work when Diane got in the race? Ogden Bush riding a new horse with the same dirty ass. So don't tell me Diane Fairmont is anything other than politics as usual."

"You do sound a little bitter."

"I just believe in knowing my enemy."

"Diane's your enemy?" Cab asked.

"This country has many enemies," Warren replied, "inside and out."

"How well do you know her?"

"Well enough to hope she loses. Do *you* know her, detective?"

"We've met," Cab said.

The radio host opened his mouth, closed it, and chomped his lips over his cigar. Finally, he said, "Word of advice from me to you. Don't trust her."

"I'm not big on trusting anyone in politics," Cab said. "That doesn't mean she's not in danger."

Warren leaned back against the bench. "Maybe, maybe not. I'll leave that in your hands. If you ask me, the whole thing is probably a political ploy."

"But?" he asked, hearing the man's hesitation.

"But let's face it. Common Way has bought itself a lot of friends over the years. They've bought a lot of enemies, too."

Do you know her, detective?

We've met.

Ten years ago.

The campaign had been in its infancy when Cab visited his mother while she was staying with Diane at Birch Fairmont's estate in Lake Wales. All of the political activity was happening elsewhere around the state. Cab never met Lyle Piper or Caprice Dean while he was there. He never saw Birch Fairmont that week in June. He was twenty-five years old, and his life was over.

He'd come from Barcelona, after the killing of Vivian Frost, after the internal security investigation that was kept tightly under wraps. No one wanted Cab or his story in the spotlight. His world had come to an end that summer, but he'd said nothing to Tarla, nothing to anyone, about what had happened. It was the beginning of his game of hopscotch, moving from place to place, jumping from job to job.

His mother had known that something was wrong, but she'd been unable to pry the truth out of him. In reality, she hadn't tried hard. She'd been busy filming television commercials, bolstering her millions with advertising sponsorships in anticipation of her retirement. Selling out, as she cheerfully put it. She'd been away most days, tramping around the orange groves with film crews.

Cab stayed at Diane's house, tunneling inside himself. He'd spent the days reliving his time abroad, his relationship with Vivian, the things they'd said to each other, the lies she'd told. He'd been looking for an escape.

That was when Diane found him.

Diane, who was living in her own kind of hell with Birch.

There were nasty rumors.

Cab sat in his candy-red Corvette outside the radio station, and he remembered that week with more clarity than he wanted. It was a vivid week in a vivid, terrible year. They'd spent hours together. He'd listened to Diane talk about her life, the struggles with her son, Drew, Birch's affairs. She was depressed. She was lonely. He was riven with guilt. They were primed for a mistake.

He remembered the afternoon that last day when she reached for him, and he reached back. They were both voracious with need, stripping off their clothes in the heat of her bedroom, with the summer air blowing inside. The two of them, naked, hungry. Her mound, moist as he kissed it. Her gasping scream as he entered her. She hadn't had sex with Birch in four years, she said. He hadn't had sex since Vivian, and he thought he could erase her memory in a single afternoon in Diane's bed. He remembered the lust of being inside her, this woman who was his mother's best friend, and he remembered the burning shame afterward.

He left Florida that night. He never saw her again.

He began to run.

Cab heard the vibrations of his phone over the purr of the Corvette's motor. He wondered if it was Lala, finally calling him back, but it wasn't. Her absence made him angry. He needed her.

"Cab, it's Caprice," she said, her voice as fruity and intoxicating as a tropical drink.

"Yes, it is," he said.

"What are you doing?"

"Actually, I'm about to drive to a federal penitentiary."

"Hamilton Brock?"

"That's right."

"Well, good luck. And thank you for helping Diane."

Cab wondered if he'd ever really helped Diane, now or in the past. He remembered their eyes meeting the previous night, just for a moment. It brought back the guilt and shame. "I guess I can't say no to my mother," he said.

"Really? Here I thought you couldn't say no to me."

Caprice was flirting with him, and he liked it.

"Are you checking on your new employee?" he asked.

"No, I wanted to see if you would go to dinner with me tonight."

"Tonight?"

"It's Saturday, Cab. That's when people go out to dinner."

"Is this work or a date?"

"Does it matter?"

"I guess not."

He thought about Diane, and the recollection of the afternoon he'd spent with her was still arousing. He thought about Lala and the intensity of their relationship. Fire in bed. Arguments out of it. And for days now—silence.

"So?" Caprice asked. "Shall we dance?"

"Yes, we shall."

"Excellent. The Columbia in Ybor City at eight o'clock. Don't be late."

8

Peach watched Annalie Martine from her Thunderbird. The newest foundation employee—the woman who'd replaced Justin—sat at a table outside an ice cream shop in Indian Shores. The Saturday noon-time traffic on Gulf Boulevard was a parade of weekenders making a beeline for the sand. The strip mall where Annalie waited was tucked among pastel hotels and condos, and bikini-clad teenagers pushed and giggled past her toward the white beaches. Annalie lazily licked a single scoop of maple nut ice cream from a sugar cone.

She had let her hair down since the previous day. Literally. Her lush black hair cascaded to her shoulders. She wore stylish sunglasses that slid down her nose as her skin sweated in the heat. No more Clark Kent frames. She wore shorts and heels, and her legs were crossed. Her black tank top sported the letters *D.C.* in a block white font across her chest. The tank top dipped low, offering an ample view of cocoa-skinned cleavage.

Peach wandered across the parking lot. When she passed Annalie as she went inside the shop, the thirtysomething woman glanced idly at her but made no sign of recognition. Peach wore a mousy brown wig today, taken from the head of Bon Bon Mannequin, and the hair was bushy around her face. She wore big red sunglasses, jeans, and an untucked striped button-down blouse.

Inside, she ordered mocha chip ice cream, took the cup outside, and sat in the chair next to Annalie.

"I'm sorry, I'm waiting—" the woman began, but then she stopped and said: "Oh. Peach?"

"Hi."

"It took me a second to recognize you."

"That's the plan," Peach said.

Annalie stripped off her sunglasses and pointed at herself with an inquiring glance. "So, do I pass inspection? You said dress to get noticed."

"Looking good."

"Thanks." Annalie licked her cone. "You live near here?"

"Not too far."

"Where's not too far?"

"A few miles."

Annalie's eyebrows flickered. She didn't miss the fact that Peach wasn't offering specifics. "Why did you want to meet so far west? We're heading back into the city, aren't we?"

Peach shrugged. "Sorry, force of habit. I used to meet Justin here. He had a place on the Gulf a couple miles south."

"Nice."

"Parental money."

"Well, I wouldn't know what that's like," Annalie said with a sigh. "Anyway, I came early and walked on the beach." She tilted her chin toward the blue sky. "Beautiful day, huh? It's like the calm before the storm. Everyone says Chayla will be bad."

"Storms don't scare me," Peach said.

"No? Me, I worry about waking up in Oz. Sounds like the weather people think Chayla will make landfall around the Fourth of July."

"Unless it veers away. They never know." Peach checked the time again. "We should probably go. The convention takes an afternoon break in a couple hours. People will be outside smoking. We'll want to be listening."

"Listening for what?"

"Whatever we hear," Peach said. "It's amazing what people will say. Do you smoke? You'll fit in better if you smoke."

"Occasionally. What about you?"

"I don't smoke. I don't drink. But I can fake it."

Annalie grinned. "You don't drink, and you don't smoke. So what do you do?"

"What?"

"You know, that Adam Ant song? 'Goody Two Shoes'?"

"I don't know it."

"Wow, I'm way too old," Annalie sighed.

"Can you drive?" Peach asked.

Annalie pushed the last bite of her cone into her mouth with one finger and stood up. "I'm the banged-up Corolla," she said, pointing at a black car on the far side of the parking lot.

Peach finished her cup of mocha chip and deposited it in the wastebasket outside the store. She grabbed her backpack and followed Annalie to the old Corolla. When they got inside, Annalie looked sideways at her as she started the engine.

"I get the feeling you don't like me," she said.

"I don't know you," Peach replied.

"Is it because of me taking over from Justin? Was he like your gihow or something?"

"Gihow?"

"Guy I hang out with. Sounds better than partner or boyfriend or live-in or whatever."

"Oh." Peach felt herself shutting down at the mention of Justin's name. "No, nothing like that."

Annalie stared at her, as if she knew that Peach wasn't telling the truth. "Okay."

"Do you have a gihow?" Peach asked.

"Me? No way. No time."

She said it breezily, but Peach didn't believe her. This woman was gorgeous. She had to be fending off passes from guys day and night.

They drove south on Gulf Boulevard, trailing a shuttle bus headed for Pass-a-Grille. She'd traveled this stretch of asphalt thousands of times: sometimes alone, sometimes with Deacon, sometimes with Justin. To Peach, this was Florida, with every building squeezed so tightly together that they looked as if they were holding their breath. The sidewalks were crowded with bare flesh. She saw turtle-like men with little heads jutting out of enormous torsos. Sagging old women in floppy hats. Boys with big bulges and girls with wiggling cheeks. Behind the buildings and parking lots, only steps away, the Gulf teased her, as motionless as glass, glinting with a million sun drops. There was hardly a wave cracking the surface now, but in a few days, the Gulf would awaken like a monster and hurl itself against the land. Chayla.

Justin on storms. *Hurricanes make you feel small. It's good to feel small every now and then.*

"I looked up Justin's murder," Annalie said. "So it was a drug thing, huh?"

"That's what they say."

"You don't think so?"

"I'm not a cop," Peach said. "I have no idea."

"I just thought, you worked with him, you'd know something."

"I don't know anything."

They stopped at a stoplight. Peach cracked the window, and a briny sea smell wafted inside. A crowd of teenage boys hooted at them as they ran through the crosswalk toward the beach.

"If Justin was your friend," Annalie said, "you must be sad. Or angry."

"What do you mean?"

"I mean, you look like you're working pretty hard not to feel anything, which tells me you feel something big way down deep. I think you were close to Justin, and you won't say so."

"You just met me," Peach said. "You don't know anything about me."

Annalie accelerated again. The engine rattled.

"Your parents were killed when you were eight," she said. "Your oldest brother was murdered when you were twelve. The guy you worked with for a whole year just got shot selling cocaine. I guess I know some things, or at least how to find them. I'm a researcher, and

I know how to read people's faces, too. You're not the mannequin you like to think you are."

Mannequin.

It was probably nothing, but Peach didn't like that Annalie used that word. As if it were a message: *I know you, I know what you keep in your bedroom. You can't hide from me.* She didn't like being grilled for her secrets. Everyone wanted something from her these days, and it all involved Justin.

"Stop the car," Peach said.

"Hey, sorry. I was out of line. I get in people's faces too much. It's a character flaw."

"I said stop. Pull over."

"Why?"

"I can't do this. Not now. Not today."

"Look, Peach, I didn't mean anything—"

Peach pushed opened the door of the Corolla while it was still moving. Annalie jerked on the brakes, and horns wailed behind them. Peach undid the seat belt with clumsy fingers and spilled into the street, ignoring Annalie, who shouted at her. She left the car door hanging ajar and ran between the pink condos for the Gulf beach.

The water was hot. It didn't cool her down at all. Peach's bare toes squished in the wet sand. The cuffs of her jeans were soaked. She'd tied the laces of her Chuck Taylors together, and she spun the shoes from her hand like clunky tetherballs. She walked, staring at the shells in the surf. She'd run for a half mile, ducking under fishing lines and dodging Frisbees that landed in the water. People looked at her because she was crying, but no one said anything. It was Florida. People broke up, and they went to the beach to cry.

Annalie was right. Peach had been lying to Deacon, and to herself, about feeling nothing. She'd been in love with Justin, and now he was gone, taken from her. Like her parents. Like Lyle. The emptiness was so great it made her want to swim into the deep water and drown herself. Justin had been someone she'd never anticipated, the one man she had ever invited to share her solitary existence. She had gotten up every morning anxious to hear his voice and see his face. He made her smile.

They had sworn to be loyal to each other forever. No one else knew. Not Deacon or Caprice or Ms. Fairmont or Ogden Bush. It was like being married, but better. They had something more sacred than love or sex.

That was what hurt the most, because Justin had betrayed her. He'd shut her out of what was happening to him and what he was doing. He'd gotten killed. She couldn't bear the loss of him, but even more than that, she couldn't bear not knowing *why*. It was not drugs. It was something else. Something he couldn't share with her.

Why?

Peach stood on the sand and stared at a four-story apartment building on the other side of the strip of beach, fifty yards away. The building was stucco, painted a fading shade of red that got worn each season by the salt and wind. Balconies and picture windows, one above another, jutted over the dune. Wooden steps led down from the rear door. It wasn't a new building, but the condos were expensive. Everything was expensive here.

Justin's place.

This was why she'd come here. This was why she'd escaped from Annalie's car. She needed to see his apartment again. She needed to find out what he'd been hiding from her.

Peach trudged up the sand. She passed an old woman sprawled in a white plastic lounger under the shade of an umbrella. She had brown wrinkled flesh. Spanish music played from an old battery radio beside her. Peach knew her, because she was Justin's neighbor, a widow who lived one floor above him. Mrs. Jabohnne. The old woman's eyes slitted open at the noise of Peach's footsteps, but she made no sign of recognition.

At the top of the beach, among flowers and long grass, Peach wandered under the shade of the first-floor apartment deck. Sand leached into the building's covered parking lot. She saw a faucet, and she turned on the water to wash her feet. When they were clean, she shoved her damp feet back into her sneakers. She still had Justin's key to let herself inside.

The building smelled musty. Bugs clung to the walls. She waited for the elevator, listening to it hum, and then took it to the second floor. Outside, in the open-air hallway, she turned right and opened the metal screen door. She let herself into Justin's apartment, which was stifling. More than eighty degrees. Only the ceramic tile under her bare feet was cool. The apartment was dark, with the lights off and the vertical blinds in the living room mostly shut, letting in narrow cracks of sun. It still smelled like him. Justin loved scented oils, and the aroma of cherry blossoms permeated the space. She expected him to wander from the bedroom, towel knotted around his scrawny waist, toothbrush hanging out of his mouth like a cigarette.

He didn't.

The apartment was sparsely furnished. It had always been that way. He kept almost nothing personal here. None of his antiques. None of his papers or photographs or books. When they came here, he left his work in the car, but at some point when he was alone, the work disappeared. He put it somewhere. Not here. He'd been open about the fact that he had another place, but when she asked him about it, he'd said: *It's not safe for you to know. Not yet.*

Drugs, the police would say. That was where he kept his drugs. But they were wrong.

She needed to find out where he lived his other life. His safe house.

Peach passed the kitchen and went into the living room. He had leather sofas and a big television, and rocking chairs by the window that looked out on the beach. They'd sit there night after night, sipping tea, watching the sunsets. He'd read poetry to her and play classical musical, no matter how much she said she hated it. It was all too dark, loud, and strong.

She stood by the windows, watching the water. Looking down, she saw a dead, desiccated salamander on the tile floor. She had no idea what she was looking for here. If the police hadn't found it, she wouldn't either. Maybe there was nothing to find, no clue to his secret, and yet she knew Justin. He would've left a message for her. Something.

Justin on life after death. *I want to come back and haunt you. Keep an eye open for me.*

She looked around the dusty apartment and willed him to make contact with her. She was here. She needed him. *What was it that you didn't want me to know? How do I find it?* She could tell from the clutter that the police had already pawed through the cabinets and drawers. Justin was typically very organized, and most of the apartment was in a state of chaos.

Or maybe it wasn't the police. Maybe it was someone else.

Peach wandered into the bedroom, which also faced the Gulf. Sheets had been ripped off the king bed and lay in a crumpled pile on the floor. The mattress had been knifed, exposing padding and springs. Looking for drugs. Looking for anything. On her left, double doors led to the deck. The apartment bathroom was there, too, where she would shower before bed and in the mornings. She'd practically lived here. That last week, when Justin disappeared, she'd spent every night waiting for him, and he never returned. He'd been somewhere else.

Where?

She picked her way around the debris. Justin kept a dresser on the wall opposite the bed, and the drawers had been removed and overturned. Clothes lay heaped on the floor. She recognized his T-shirts, his cutoffs, his boxer briefs, and his athletic socks. There were personal things, too, scattered on the tile. Tins of breath mints. Batteries. A wind-up Snoopy toy. Local restaurant menus. Even a box of condoms—unopened—which made her wonder if he'd been rethinking his willingness to remain celibate with her. Or maybe she hadn't been the only girl in his life. She didn't want to believe that.

Peach spotted a small book on the floor, and she bent and picked it up. It was old, bound in fraying green cloth, with embossed gold letters on the cover. She'd found it at an antiquarian bookshop months ago and purchased it for Justin as a gift. It was a book of poems by

William Blake, his favorite poet. Every time she'd visited his apartment, it had been on his nightstand, next to his bed. The pages were delicate and yellowed.

She didn't have time to open the book to "The Tyger."

Instead, someone bellowed at her from the bedroom doorway. "Put your hands in the air right now!"

Peach wheeled around in surprise. A big man filled the doorway, with a gun pointed at her chest. She gasped and thrust her hands upward with her elbows bent. The book was still in her hand.

"What the hell are you doing here?" the man demanded.

Peach struggled for something to say, but she said nothing. Behind her sunglasses, she studied the man. He was in his forties, with wavy blond-and-gray hair. He hadn't shaved. He wore a tan sport coat over a collarless black T-shirt, with navy slacks and black sneakers. His clothes fit snugly; his frame was heavy. A film of sweat made a mustache on his upper lip.

"Who are you?" he said, dragging aside a flap of his coat so she could see a gold badge dangling from his belt.

A cop?

No. She recognized the Southern drawl in his voice. This was the man who had phoned her, claiming to be Detective Curtis Clay of the St. Petersburg police. He was a liar and a stranger, and looking at him, she knew that he was no cop. He was here for the same reason she was here. To find Justin's secrets.

"Whoa, chill, buddy, my name's Rebekah," Peach said, modulating her own voice so it sounded like a New Yorker's. "I'm crashing with my mom in the condo upstairs. Could you put that gun away?"

The man who called himself Clay kept the gun pointed at her. "I asked what you're doing here."

"Jeez, I thought I smelled smoke. I figured I better check it out, you know? Mom's like the manager here. We've got snowbirds who are gone a lot, and she watches over things, so she's got a master key."

"Bullshit," he said. "Tell me who you really are and what you're looking for."

"Hey, I already said—"

"I know what you said. You're lying. How did you know Justin Kiel?"

"I didn't know him at all. I don't know who owns this place."

He stared at her in the dim, dusty space. "Show me your ID," he said.

Peach shrugged, but she wasn't going to do that. "Yeah, well, show me yours," she said.

"Excuse me?"

"I'll show you mine if you show me yours."

The man took a menacing step toward her. She could smell him as he came closer; he smelled of menthol, like the goopy pain patches she wore when she pulled a muscle. He holstered his gun. He dug in his coat pocket and came out with handcuffs, which dangled from his fingers.

"Maybe you'll feel like talking after a few hours in jail," he said.

She didn't know where he planned to take her, but it wasn't jail.

Peach bolted. She dove into the bathroom and locked the door. The man chased after her, but he stumbled on the debris and fell with a loud curse. She yanked open the glass shower door. Inside the shower, a small window near the ceiling faced the beach. She reached as high as she could and was barely able to undo the lock and slide the window open. Noise and wet sea air rushed through the space.

The man's shoulder crashed into the locked bathroom door. It splintered and came off its frame, tumbling inward.

Peach grabbed the window ledge and pulled herself up the wall, but her shoes slipped on the tile. Her feet pedaled helplessly. She jumped, propping both hands against the frame and squeezing her elbows into the tight open space of the window, which was barely wide enough for her body. Her head jutted outside, then her shoulders and torso, and she could see the green water and the people on the beach and the sand and grass two stories below her.

She also saw Annalie Martine on the beach, running from the shoreline, arms waving, black hair flying.

Curtis Clay grabbed her ankles inside the shower stall and dragged her backward. Like a mustang at a rodeo, she bucked wildly, trying to dislodge him as she clung to the window frame. His grip was as tight as a bear trap, but when he yanked on her foot, her shoe came off. He stumbled, hitting the shower wall hard. The water turned on, blasting the stall, and when he lurched for her again, his feet slipped under him on the wet tile. He crashed down.

Peach squirmed through the window and threw herself outside.

She was free, she was falling. Her body twisted in midair. The Gulf dune roared up to meet her face.

9

I'M BACK. MISS ME?

Cab unfolded a copy of the newspaper photograph that Caprice had given him, with the warning scrawled in the thick ink of a red Sharpie. He held the paper so that Hamilton Brock, the leader of the Liberty Empire Alliance, could see it. The two men sat in uncomfortable plastic chairs six feet apart. A video camera watched them from a corner of the ceiling.

"Who sent this?" Cab asked.

Brock's dark eyes flicked to the page and studied the ten-year-old photograph, but he said nothing. His face was devoid of expression.

"Bring back memories, does it?" Cab went on. "Kind of like Springsteen, right? Glory days?"

Brock's eyes refocused on Cab with barely veiled contempt, but he remained silent. So far, he hadn't said a word since Cab introduced himself. The hour-long drive north on I-75 to the Coleman Federal Correctional Complex, which was located in Middle-of-Nowhere, Florida, in flatlands across from grazing cattle, felt like a waste of time. Brock had no interest in talking.

Cab had expected a hardened skinhead, but Hamilton Brock looked more like a suburban soccer dad. He was a high school football quarterback, ex-army, auto mechanic, father of four. At thirty-nine years old, he had neat black hair, no tattoos, and a physique that looked prison-lean, but not ripped. His face was carefully shaved. He sat with his hands folded in his lap and his long legs pressed together. His posture was perfect.

Ten years ago, Brock had been an all-American Wally World shopper with a 2,200-square-foot house in Bartow. His wife homeschooled their kids. They had annual passes to Disney World. At night, he'd recruited converts in the basement of a Lakeland church to a volunteer militia whose website advocated mass deportation of illegal aliens, an electrified fence on the Mexican border, a ban on Muslim immigration, defiance of the Internal Revenue Service, and—among blog posts Cab had reviewed—forced sterilization of welfare mothers who gave birth to a third child. The Liberty Empire Alliance had also stockpiled dozens of assault weapons, handguns, ammunition, plastic explosives, barbed wire, copper, canned goods, bottled water, and doses of the anthrax antibiotic Cipro in a U-Stor facility raided by the FBI in Fort Meade.

You never could tell.

Cab tapped a long finger on the newspaper article again. "The Orlando reporter who wrote this? Rufus Twill. He wrote a lot about you and your group back then. Somebody repaid him by beating him within an inch of his life. Is that how you deal with people who don't see the world the way you do?"

The room was silent except for the rustle of the paper and the ticking of a decades-old clock high on the wall. Brock's mouth twitched. His head tilted a fraction, and he looked toward the floor and shook his head with disdain.

"Right, I don't get you, you're misunderstood," Cab said. He waited until Brock met his eyes again, and he added: "I know about your father, Mr. Brock. Thirty-one years with the same company, and then his job was outsourced to India. He spent three years looking for another job and didn't find one. He shot himself when you were seventeen. You found the body."

There was no emotion in Brock's face. The man had channeled his emotions into hatred long ago. He also had smart eyes, as penetrating as a snake's stare. Hatred and intelligence were a dangerous combination.

"Chuck Warren says you're innocent," Cab went on. "He called you a political prisoner."

Brock showed the barest flicker of interest at the mention of the Republican's name. "Mr. Warren is correct. That's exactly what I am."

"Oh, so you can talk," Cab said. "Good. Actually, I knew you could talk, because you've been on Warren's show. I was able to dig up the archives online. Here's one of my favorite quotes: 'People accuse us of hoarding weapons because we want to overthrow the government. Not true. We need to be armed for when the government comes to overthrow us.'"

The man's eyebrows arched with irony, and he cast his gaze around the prison visiting room.

Cab smiled. "I get it. They really did come for you."

"Yes, they did."

"The jackbooted thugs of the FBI?"

Brock exhaled with a loud sigh. He leaned forward and spoke in an unusually quiet voice. "You make jokes, Detective Bolton, but did you know that government officials with automatic weapons raided my home and the homes of half a dozen other patriots and kidnapped our children at gunpoint? Nineteen children hauled away and stripped from their parents. The oldest was eleven years old."

"They wanted to make sure you didn't use the children as hostages. Human shields. It's been done before by extremist groups."

Brock shook his head. He was talking now. He wanted to talk.

"The government was the one using children as hostages. Not us. This is the same government that waged a legal battle to have our children permanently taken from our custody and relocated under different identities so we could never find them again. Is that the America you serve, detective?"

"The feds lost that fight," Cab said, "thanks to another branch of government called the American judiciary."

"True enough. If you have children, I'm sure you will welcome a two-year battle against the behemoth of the federal government to enjoy the freedom to keep them. Not that we have many freedoms left in this country. Those of us who defend American values wind up here."

"You're here because you didn't pay your taxes, aren't you?" Cab asked.

"I'm here as a scapegoat, because the government needed someone to blame for a murder they couldn't solve."

That was what Cab expected Brock to say. It was the standard excuse of a guilty man. The trouble was, based on everything he'd read about this man, he expected him to be proud of what he'd done. To tell everyone, to take credit. Not to deny it and hide behind a lie.

"Most people think the government solved the murders," Cab said, "but they couldn't make the case because you and your allies stonewalled the investigation and destroyed records. Dozens of militia members disappeared. Including, most likely, the shooter."

"We were standing up against a witch hunt," Brock said. "This was a vendetta."

"Even Chuck Warren thinks the murders could have been committed by one of your Alliance members acting on his own."

"That isn't true."

"Actually, I believe you," Cab said, "because I don't think anyone in your group would go forward with a plan like that without your say-so."

Brock nodded. "That's why I know it wasn't one of us."

"Are you really saying you didn't want Birch Fairmont dead?" Cab asked. "Birch and the Common Way Party were ferocious enemies of your movement. Their policies on gun control and immigration were anathema to your group. Birch was a supporter of aggressive legal authority to combat domestic terrorists. That's what he called you, Mr. Brock. Birch Fairmont said you and the Liberty Empire Alliance were the poster children for domestic terrorism. And he was on his way to joining the United States Congress, where he would have had considerable power to target groups like yours."

"If you're asking me to say I'm sorry that Birch Fairmont was killed," Brock said, "I won't do that. He was an enemy of free people."

"But you didn't kill him."

"I'm not in the business of making martyrs of my enemies. That just gives them more power."

"Do you know who did?"

"I assume it was someone who wanted *me* in *here*. They got their wish. They took down a patriot like Chuck Warren at the same time. Obviously, we had a mole inside the Alliance. Someone who was able to point the authorities at us. As it is, they had to settle for trumped-up tax charges when they couldn't link us to the murders."

"So you think you and the Alliance were deliberately targeted. Set up as fall guys."

Brock shrugged. "Here I am."

"Are you still the leader of the Liberty Empire Alliance?" Cab asked.

"I still have a voice," Brock said in the same quiet, determined tone he had used from the beginning. "They can lock me up, but they can't silence me until they put a gun to my head and pull the trigger. They can't change the truth of what I say. Did you know that in less than thirty years the founding race of this country will be in the *minority*? The takers are outbreeding us. This will no longer be America. It will be *Hispanica*."

"I guess I better be nice to my girlfriend," Cab replied. "She's Cuban."

Brock tensed. For the first time, Cab saw a flash of anger, as if rage bubbled under the man's skin.

"More jokes," Brock said. "Do you think this is funny? Millions of people feel the way we do. We have allies and converts everywhere. More and more people are hearing our message. Workers. Mothers. Fathers. Even police officers, detective. And prison guards."

Cab ignored the diatribe. Instead, he held up the newspaper photograph again. "Let me ask you again. Who sent this?"

"I have no idea."

"Is Diane Fairmont in danger?"

"If she is in danger, she has no one to blame but herself. People who try to stage a coup always run the risk of the guillotine."

"A coup?"

"That's what the Common Way Party is planning," Brock said. "That's what this campaign is about. She has been systematically erasing the obstacles on her way to power. If you don't think it's a conspiracy, you're naive."

"Ramona Cortes is the GOP candidate this year. She led your defense team nine years ago, didn't she?"

"Yes, she did. Real Americans all over this country contributed money for our defense. Ms. Cortes was the best. However, it doesn't matter who represents you when the system is rigged to assure your guilt."

"Are you still in touch with Ramona?"

"No."

"But you share her politics," Cab said. "If it were a two-person race, if Diane were out of it, Ramona would be winning. You'd like that."

Brock stood up. "You're wasting your time. This election isn't about me or the Alliance. We're simply pawns. Just like last time. If we didn't exist, the Common Way Party would have had to invent us."

"One more question," Cab said. "If you wanted Diane killed, could you arrange it? Could you make it happen from here?"

Brock smiled. "Do you believe that if I wanted *you* dead, I could make sure you never walked out of this prison?"

The threat was so calm, so casual, and so real that Cab felt a chill. He didn't reply. He reached for a joke and didn't find one.

"Actually, I do believe that," Cab admitted.

"See, that should tell you something," Brock said, enjoying Cab's discomfort.

"What's that?"

"If I wanted to kill Diane Fairmont, she'd already be dead."

10

The day washed away.

Peach and Annalie sat in cheap folding chairs on the beach at Honeymoon Island, which was connected to the Gulf Coast by a causeway from the town of Dunedin. Peach propped her leg on a third chair. She'd twisted her ankle as she landed, and it was tightly taped with an athletic bandage she'd bought at Walgreens. Her other foot dipped in the hot surf. Her body ached, and she had scratches on her face and arms. Whenever she moved, she felt the grit of sand inside her clothes.

Annalie's phone rang, playing a song by Gloria Estefan. "Rhythm Is Gonna Get You." Peach watched Annalie check the caller ID and ignore it. It wasn't the first call she'd ducked.

"Do you need to be somewhere? You don't have to hang out with me."

"No, I don't need to be anywhere," Annalie replied, shoving the phone back into her pocket. She wore a wide-brimmed yellow hat, and her face was shadowed from the sun. "Saturday afternoon at the beach is pretty great, particularly since I thought I'd be working all day."

She toasted Peach with a tilt of a warm beer bottle. Offshore, speedboats sliced the waves. The beach around them was crowded and noisy. Dozens of seagulls dodged the children and picked at the foam. Pelicans skimmed the surface with lazy wings. Peach and Annalie sat in the midst of the calm water, near an uprooted palm tree half-buried in the sand. A cooling breeze took the edge off the heat, but when Peach closed her eyes, she felt the burn on her face.

"You change your mind about calling the police?" Annalie asked. "If some guy's out there pretending to be a cop, they should know."

"They'd say it was all about Justin and drugs," Peach said. "They'd figure that's why I was there, too. Besides, I can't get the police involved in anything without talking to Deacon and Ms. Fairmont."

"Justin was murdered. This isn't political."

"Everything's political."

Annalie shook her head. "Well, it's your call. Just watch your back, okay? You can identify this guy, and he knows it. Maybe he's the one who killed Justin, did you think about that?"

"Yeah, I thought about it," Peach said.

She'd thought about it, but she didn't believe it was true. She didn't think the killer would risk coming back, not after the police had already torn Justin's life apart. Whoever the man was in Justin's apartment, he was looking for answers, like her.

"You don't believe his death was about drugs, do you?" Annalie asked.

"I have no idea."

"I'm stepping into his shoes, Peach. I have a right to know if I'm putting myself at risk." Annalie reached out and put a hand on Peach's wrist. "Do you know what Justin was working on before he was killed?"

"I don't."

Annalie shivered, even in the heat. "I have to tell you, all this dirt-digging we do gives me the creeps."

"So why'd you take the job?"

"Why else? I need the money."

"I thought your father worked for a big foundation donor."

"He does, but he's not rich. Besides, I pay my own bills. I never had any interest in political crap, but after nine months without a job, I was running pretty low on cash. So my dad made a couple calls."

"I assumed you had Washington ties," Peach said.

"Why'd you think that?"

Peach pointed at Annalie's D.C. tank top, which was ringed with sweat on the hot afternoon. The woman looked down, as if she'd forgotten what she was wearing. She shook her head and smiled.

"Never been there. Somebody gave it to me." She added: "Listen, I know this isn't just a job for you. It's a cause. I get it."

"You're right," Peach said.

"That must have been awful for you and Deacon ten years ago."

Peach watched the translucent green water. The waves swelled and broke in white ribbons. She saw a sailboat jutting like a shark's fin out of the distant horizon line. "Yeah. It was even harder on him than me. I mean, just like that, Lyle was gone and Deacon had to take care of me. I didn't make it easy."

"Seems like you guys get along now."

"Oh, yeah. We couldn't be more different, but we're a team. It helps that we're working on Lyle's legacy. The Common Way Party was everything to Lyle. So much that he didn't always have a lot of time for us. Especially not that last summer."

"I'm sorry."

"Hey, campaigns are crazy. I get it now."

"Do you know Diane Fairmont well?" Annalie asked.

Peach dipped a hand in the surf and let warm water spill through her fingers. "I've met her. I don't know her well. She doesn't come over to the research wing very often. We're the dirty little secret that nobody wants to talk about."

"Dirty?"

"Some people think so," Peach said.

Annalie was quiet. A small Cessna flew over the beach, its motor whining. "Can I ask you something?"

"What?"

"A few months ago, the governor was looking unbeatable. He was way ahead of Ramona. Then his chief of staff got caught taking kick-backs from construction contractors, and his numbers tanked. Diane got in the race and vaulted ahead of both of them in the polls."

"What's your point?" Peach asked.

"Is it possible that Common Way was involved?"

"What do you mean? The governor is a sleaze. He surrounds him-self with sleazy people."

"You can be a sleaze and still be set up," Annalie said.

"What are you saying? Do you think *I* had something to do with that? Because I didn't."

"I never said you did, but sometimes special projects go on behind the scenes. People get recruited to do things they don't want to do."

Peach's eyes widened. "*Justin?* That's who you mean, isn't it? You think Justin was involved in setting up the governor's aide."

"I don't know. Is it possible?"

"No!"

"And yet you don't think his death was about drugs."

Peach stood up so fast that the chair spilled into the water behind her. Her leg buckled under her weight, and Annalie leaped to her feet and kept her from falling. Peach shrugged off the woman's help. She realized that she'd said far more to Annalie than she ever intended. Annalie was good. And smart. She knew a lot more about humint work than she was letting on.

"Let's go," Peach said.

"I'm sorry. I had to ask. I need to know what I'm getting into."

Peach splashed toward the wet, sandy fringe of the beach. Seagulls scattered into the air. "You're wrong about Justin."

Annalie grabbed her shoulder and stopped her. "Maybe I am, but that doesn't explain why you went to Justin's apartment. What were you looking for?"

"Nothing."

"Don't insult me, Peach. I know that's not true." Annalie dug in a pocket. "Were you looking for this?"

She held up a small book bound in fraying green cloth. Much of the gold lettering on the cover had flecked away. It was the book of old English poetry by William Blake that Peach had given to Justin. She'd thought she lost it when she fell from the apartment window. "Give me that," she said.

"There's an inscription," Annalie told her. "I looked through the book when you were in the drugstore. *Then they followed / Where the vision led / And saw their sleeping child / Among tygers wild.* That's from a poem called 'The Little Girl Found.' It's not a man's handwriting. Is it yours? Did you give Justin this book?"

"Give me that!" Peach repeated, ripping it out of her hand.

"The Little Girl Found. Is that you?"

"That's none of your business."

"You loved Justin, didn't you?"

"I said, that's none of your business."

"Did he love you?"

"Why do you care?" Peach asked. "What difference does it make?"

"Because if he loved you, maybe he told you his secrets."

"He didn't."

"Are you sure?"

"I didn't find a thing in his apartment," Peach said, and the bitterness was obvious in her voice.

"Justin wrote something in this book," Annalie told her. "It's on the page for the poem 'The Tyger.' Does that mean something to you?"

Peach's fingers tightened on the ragged cloth of the book. "What did he write?"

"Look."

Peach turned the brittle pages. She knew exactly where the poem was. She found it—*What immortal hand or eye / Could frame thy fearful symmetry*—and Annalie was right. Someone had written a single word on the page. Not someone. Justin. It was his handwriting. There was no mistaking it.

The message had to be for her, didn't it? This was their poem. They'd read it over and over in bed, so many times, with such emotion that it was like the words of the poem had taken the place of sex between them. Every stanza was burned into her memory, and she could hear it in Justin's voice.

He wouldn't write on that poem to anyone but her. He'd written one word, but not a word. A name.

What made no sense was that it wasn't her own name on the paper. Instead, Justin had written: **ALISON**.

11

Cab couldn't take his eyes off Caprice.

The sconce lights, shaped like torches, played shadows across her white skin. She wore a sleeveless black dress, and her strong arms ended in manicured hands and scarlet nails. Her full brown hair covered the straps of her dress and swished in little curls across the slopes of her breasts. A double gold chain hugged her neck, and gold hoop earrings peeked out between the locks of her hair. Her deep-red lips folded into a smile as he watched her.

"Like what you see?" she asked.

"I do."

"I do, too," Caprice said. "You may have noticed I'm pretty direct."

"So I gather."

"You're tall, and you look like a movie star. People see you and think, he must be somebody. It turns me on to be seen with you."

"Here I was thinking the same thing about you."

Caprice didn't duck the compliment. She didn't bat her eyes at him and protest: *Me? At my age?* Instead, she took a sip of expensive Albariño and said: "Oh, I know I turn you on."

"Am I that transparent?" Cab asked.

"Yes, you are, but your mother called and told me." Caprice laughed. "How's that for a pickup line?"

"Actually, it's not the first time I've heard it."

She laughed again. He liked her laugh, which was confident and smart. "Knowing Tarla, I bet not. She's a force of nature. Do you ignore her advice? Or are you one of those sons who protests and protests and then does what she wants anyway?"

"I'll let you know when I figure it out," Cab said.

He glanced over the iron railing at the dining area below them, which looked like the patio of a Spanish villa in the romantic light. They were on the mezzanine, which was a narrow alcove at the top of a tiled staircase, with a dozen tables discreetly overlooking what was called the Don Quixote room. Cut flowers adorned the tables. The mosaic designs reminded him of Andalucía. The Columbia in Ybor City was a mammoth destination, but its subdivided dining rooms managed to feel intimate.

"Do you like the piquillos?" Caprice asked, dipping her little finger in Manchego cheese and licking it with her tongue.

"Superb."

"I can't believe you've never been here. It's a Florida institution."

"The waiters know you," Cab said. "Is this where you take all your men?"

Caprice tilted her head, as if debating whether to be honest. "I do come here a lot. This is my favorite table."

They were at the end of the mezzanine, largely invisible to others around them. "Just like a cat," he said. "Keeping your back to the wall."

"Actually, it's a spy's table," Caprice said. "I can look down and watch people, and they don't know I'm doing it."

"You didn't answer my question," Cab pointed out. "Do you take all your men here?"

Caprice brushed one of her hands back through her hair. "I mostly come here with lobbyists and donors to talk about policy. I don't have much time for romance. Frankly, I need to be careful about who I'm seen with. Politics is a public business."

"And yet you're here with me," Cab said.

"I wouldn't mind being photographed with you. I wouldn't mind doing a lot of things with you." She took a crab croquette from one of the tapas plates in front of them. "Don't misinterpret. I'm not in the market for a relationship, but I do like having someone who looks good in a tux when I have to go to events. And afterward, well—"

"Friends with benefits?"

"We don't even have to be friends. I have plenty of friends. Some men would call that the perfect arrangement."

"Yes, they would."

Caprice put a hand over his and rubbed his index finger in a provocative way. "Am I embarrassing you? Like I told you, I'm direct. Usually, you get what you want by taking it, rather than asking."

"Did I say I was complaining?" Cab asked.

"No, you didn't. Good." She bit into the croquette and brushed Cuban cracker crumbs from her lips. "Tarla said you run like hell from real relationships."

"She'd say I run like hell from her, too," Cab said. "And she's probably right. Having a rich, famous, beautiful mother who wants to control your life isn't the unqualified blessing you might think."

"I'm sure."

"My girlfriend probably says I run from her, too," Cab added.

Caprice left her hand where it was. "Ah."

"She's Cuban. She's a cop. Tarla doesn't approve."

"I suppose she's beautiful."

"She is."

"Well, then why are you here flirting with me?" Caprice asked.

"Because Lala and I can't seem to make it work between us. I'll take most of the blame for that, but she and Tarla aren't entirely guilt-free. And to be candid, I find you very attractive, which makes it hard to say no."

"Then say yes."

"I'm having a good time," Cab told her. "Let's leave it at that for now."

"Fair enough."

Cab leaned back in his chair. He heard the throb of flamenco music and the click of castanets from somewhere in the restaurant. The aromas of mussels and chorizo rose from the table. "It surprises me that there's no man in your life."

"My career is my life," she told him.

"Is that lonely?"

"Not for a driven woman like me. There hasn't been anyone serious since Lyle."

"I'm sorry."

Caprice traced a nail around the rim of her wine glass. Her eyes were reflective. "Can I be honest with you? Lyle and I were never really romantic soul mates. We shared political values and ambition. It was a relationship of common interests. Which isn't to say that I didn't love him. I suppose that must sound awful, given what happened."

"No. You were both young."

"Yes, we were. Lyle was so rigid, too. Inflexible. That made it difficult. It's funny, because our whole mission as a third party is not to let ideology be the enemy of the greater good. I don't really blame him, of course. He felt so responsible in his personal life. He was trying to be a father to his younger siblings, and that was tough. Anyway, I swore to myself I wouldn't have that kind of relationship again, and when we got the foundation up and running, I never sought out opportunities. Too busy saving the world, I guess."

"Married to the cause?" Cab asked.

"Something like that." She read his face and added: "I know. You don't believe in causes."

"One man's cause is another's obsession. The Liberty Empire Alliance is a cause, too."

"For evil, not good."

"Who gets to say which is which?" Cab asked.

Caprice winked. "Me."

"You think we'd be better off with a benevolent dictatorship? Give the people what they need, regardless of what they want?"

"Maybe we would. I could think of worse people than us to overthrow the government, but let's try a third party first. A party where compromise and common sense aren't dirty words. A party that doesn't look for all-or-nothing solutions."

Rather than argue, Cab took another garlic-and-chili shrimp. Caprice was right; he didn't believe in causes. Once you really believed in something, you could make excuses for anything. The ends always justified the means. It wasn't a long journey from Diane Fairmont to Hamilton Brock.

"Speaking of the Liberty Empire Alliance," Cab said.

"Ah yes, you went to prison today. And you talked to Chuck Warren, too. How did those conversations go?"

"Pretty much as you'd expect."

"Do you think Hamilton Brock is behind the threats against Diane?"

"He says if he wanted Diane dead, she'd already be dead. That may be true, but it doesn't mean Brock doesn't know or suspect who's doing this. As for Chuck Warren, he thinks the threats are just a political ploy."

Caprice cocked her head. "You mean, we made it all up to get sympathy for Diane?"

"Yes."

"What do you think?"

"I'm assuming the threat is real until I prove otherwise. That doesn't mean I don't have doubts. If I find out you and your people are playing me, I won't hesitate to expose it."

"I'd expect nothing less." She added: "So what's your next step?"

Cab reached inside the pocket of his suit coat. He still had a copy of the article there, with the threat scrawled across it. He unfolded the page and tapped the newspaper byline. "Rufus Twill. He was an Orlando reporter. Some boys from the Liberty Empire Alliance nearly put him in a wheelchair a few years ago. I suspect he still keeps pretty close tabs on them."

Caprice frowned. "I don't like the idea of getting the media involved."

Cab couldn't help where his mind went. He thought: *Or is that exactly what you want?* Press. News. Headlines. He wondered if he was a marionette, and if Caprice was a sexy puppeteer who was guiding him exactly where she wanted him to go. He shoved the article back into his pocket without replying.

"There's something else," he told her. "I need to talk to Diane."

"Is that really necessary? Diane is busy with the campaign, and I don't control her schedule. I'm not sure how she can help you."

"Neither am I, until I talk to her."

She pursed her lips. "The thing is, I didn't tell Diane that I was asking you to look into this. She's not convinced the threat is real. She doesn't want to be seen as exploiting what happened back then."

"Well, real or not, I need you to set up a meeting," Cab said. "It doesn't have to be long. Fifteen minutes."

"What do you hope to learn?"

"She was there when Birch was killed. She may remember something that would point me in the right direction."

"Diane won't talk about the murders," Caprice said. "She doesn't give interviews about it."

Cab pictured Diane's face in his head. He saw her eyes across the courtyard and the look that had passed between them the previous night. A look of remembrance, guilt, and desire. He remembered her ten years ago, too, when her eyes were closed and her mouth was contorted in pleasure, and her body was underneath his own.

"She'll talk to me," he said.

Outside the Columbia, a black luxury sedan pulled to the curb to collect Caprice. The street was crowded. The driver, who had the heft of a bodyguard, got out and opened the rear door for her. Caprice balanced gracefully on the tips of her shoes to kiss Cab on the cheek. She whispered in his ear.

"Would you like to come home with me?"

"That's tempting," he said, "but I can't."

She eyed the street around them. He thought she was looking for photographers. People watching them. Smartphones spying on them. She put her warm fingers around the back of his neck, and he bent down this time, and they kissed. Her tongue slipped between his lips. Her nails were sharp enough to leave scratches.

"Just so you know what you're missing," she said.

Caprice got into the town car, and the driver shut the door. The car drove off, and Cab, still a little breathless and with the taste of lipstick on his mouth, dodged the traffic as he crossed the street. His red Corvette was parked at a meter in front of a brick building that sold hand-painted tile. The top was up. He unlocked the door and folded his stilt-like legs inside.

That was when he realized the car wasn't empty.

Lala Mosqueda sat in the passenger seat.

She said: "Are you sleeping with her?"

Cab dangled his keys from his finger. "Nice to see you, too."

"I've been wondering whether you were serious about our relationship," Lala said. "I guess I got my answer." She pushed open the passenger door.

"Wait." Cab reached across the car to take her hand.

She turned back to him and sat silently. Her dark eyes were on fire. The breeze outside had rustled her coffee-black hair, and it was a web across her golden face. She was dressed in black, making her almost invisible.

"I'm not sleeping with her," he said.

"Why not? I could see the flush on her face. She wants you. She'd probably give you a hell of a ride."

"You want to play games? Fine, I'll call her now. Funny thing is, she calls me back. There's not a lot of that going around."

Lala's lips turned downward. "I'm on a work assignment, you know that. I'm busy."

"So why are you here? How did you find me?"

"You checked in on Facebook," Lala said.

He smiled. "Right. Damn that Zuckerberg."

"I figured it was an invitation. Or a taunt."

"Could be," Cab said.

"So what, did you want to throw it in my face that you're seeing someone else?"

"I'm not seeing anyone. Including you, apparently."

They sat in angry silence. They did that a lot. When they were together, there was always heat, which was good when they were in bed and bad when they took out their resentment on each other. In some ways, it was easier when they were apart. When he'd pursued a murder investigation in Door County in the spring, he couldn't stop thinking about her. Their longing for each other was palpable every time they talked. Then, when he came back to Naples, they'd fallen into their usual pattern. Reaching for each other and then pushing the other away.

Tarla didn't help. Tarla, with her cutting remarks, trying to drive a wedge between them. His mother feigned innocence, but she didn't like Lala, and Lala didn't like her.

He could feel the heat. As angry as they were, they wanted each other. He could almost feel her breasts cupped in his long fingers and hear her telling him what she wanted. If he reached for her, they would kiss, and then they would drive somewhere and make love, and minutes later, they would have their daggers out again. He wondered what it was between them, because it wasn't just physical. He knew her body as intimately as he'd known any woman's; he'd long since memorized every tiny imperfection that made her perfect. The birthmark on the inside of her thigh. The ticklish, knobby bones of her knees. The crescents under her eyes when she'd slept badly, which she covered with makeup. She was beautiful, but not in a Hollywood way like Tarla. She was real. She had a real job. She had family she loved and family she hated. She worried about real things: money, kids, storms, death. Being around her made him feel real, too.

"How's Tarla?" Lala asked, getting to the heart of the problem.

"Tarla is Tarla. She's never going to change."

"Is she still making snarky comments about me?"

"Yes."

"Do you want to tell me what she said?"

"No. I told her to knock it off, but she won't. We both know that."

"We sure do," Lala said.

"Is that why you didn't call back? Because I'm with her?"

"Partly. Of course, I didn't realize that a weekend with your mother also included tongue time with a leggy brunette." She added: "Let me guess. Tarla set you up with her."

"Yes," Cab admitted.

"Big surprise. Who is she?"

"Her name's Caprice Dean."

Lala's head turned sharply. "Are you kidding me? From the Common Way Foundation?"

"You know her?"

"She works with Diane Fairmont, right?"

Cab nodded. "Tarla and Diane are best friends. I've told you that."

"Well, you're playing in powerful circles, Cab. I guess that's where you belong."

"Caprice asked me to do a job. It's not personal. I won't deny that she's attractive, and I won't deny that it's pretty clear there could be something there with her if I wanted it. I also won't deny that I'm pissed as hell that you've been ignoring me for weeks."

"What's the job?" Lala asked.

"Someone may be targeting Diane Fairmont. There may be links to what happened to her husband ten years ago. The FBI and police are looking into it, but Caprice wanted someone working for her."

"Or under her," Lala said.

"Funny."

"The feebs have the resources for this kind of case. You don't."

Cab shrugged. "True enough, but it's not that simple."

"Because of your mother."

"Right. Like I said, she and Diane are friends."

"Diane is a candidate for governor. You have no idea what you're getting yourself into. This is a hornet's nest, Cab."

"You may be right," he admitted.

Lala opened the car door again. "It was a mistake to come here. I'm sorry to ambush you."

"Why did you?"

He felt her dark eyes on him. He saw the fullness of her lips, and he urgently wanted to kiss those lips. He missed her, and he felt like a fool.

"Because I believe there is something in you and me that is worth salvaging," she told him.

"I do, too."

"Then—and I can't stress this strongly enough—I suggest you *not* have sex with Caprice Dean."

He chose not to take the bait. "When can I see you again?" he asked.

"I don't know."

"Nice."

"I'm not trying to avoid you. I've got an assignment that's keeping me away from Naples. You know that."

"Well, you've got my number," Cab said, "so call me maybe."

Lala couldn't help herself. She laughed. She got out of the Corvette, and her movements were like a cat's. Her black clothes fit like a second skin. When she leaned back inside, her face had turned serious again. "Does Tarla know about you and Diane? Your history together?"

"Only if Diane told her," Cab said.

"Is it a problem for you?"

"Not so far, but I haven't seen Diane yet."

"I meant what I said, Cab. Be careful. You may find yourself in over your head with these people. Even you."

"I appreciate the advice."

"No, you don't." Lala shut the door, and she was gone.

12

Peach sat in the dark. It was past midnight. She didn't like air-conditioning, and the house was damp and hot. She wore a spaghetti strap T-shirt and a roomy pair of Deacon's boxers she'd grabbed from the laundry. Her small feet were propped on the dusty living room coffee table, and her taped ankle throbbed. Sexpot Mannequin kept her company. Sexpot had hard nipples on crazy-big breasts, one arm cocked behind her head, and oddly muscular abs. She usually hung out in Peach's bedroom wearing a baby-doll and a long blond wig.

The mannequin thing was strange. She knew that, but she didn't care. Some people collected stuffed animals. Some people dressed up Barbies. She liked having these faux women around, who were blank slates on which she could fashion new identities. They were her alter egos.

Justin on her mannequins. *I'm not sure they like me. I think they're worried I'll steal you away.*

Outside, headlights beamed through the picture window, and she heard the purr of the Mercedes engine. Deacon was home. She listened to his footsteps and then the rattle of the key as he let himself inside. He brought a smell of sweat with him; he'd been at the twenty-four-hour gym. She said nothing, and he didn't see her in the living room shadows. He headed through the foyer to his bedroom at the back of the house, and a couple minutes later, she heard the loud bang of the pipes as he took a shower. Their bathrooms were old, and the water was rusty.

It was just the two of them. Peach and Deacon. They had the typical relationship of siblings who were close and not close, totally different and totally alike. They lived together; they worked together; they spent time together. Even so, he was six years older, and she still felt like a little kid around him. He had never tried to be a father to her, just an older brother with his own life. Unlike Lyle. When their parents died, Lyle had jumped into the role of fill-in dad, as if it were his calling. It changed him. It was weird how quickly Lyle aged in those years. Losing his hair. His voice deepening. Becoming so serious and strict.

She idolized Lyle, but that was the fuzzy glow of memory. He wasn't perfect. He'd often been harsh and judgmental with both of them. He could be neglectful, especially that last year, when politics constantly took him away. The Common Way Party was his priority then, not her. She remembered a long weekend in Tampa that last August. Deacon and Peach had gone on the road with Lyle, but instead of having fun in the city, Lyle had packed fundraising meetings into his schedule night and day, leaving them alone. Then, to make things worse, Peach contracted a case of pneumonia that left her hacking and feverish. Lyle acted as if it were her fault—like she was being sick just to inconvenience him. He'd insisted that Deacon drive her back to Lake Wales, and that had prompted a big argument, because Deacon wanted to stay. Then Deacon hit a deer on the road, damaging Lyle's precious new Mercedes. Another big argument. Peach had been practically delirious, but she had never forgotten the curses flying for days.

Those were among her last memories of Lyle, and she didn't like it that way.

The shower stopped. Not long after, Deacon turned on the light, making her squint. He stood in the living room doorway, with his muscular body wrapped in a worn bath towel.

"Fruity," he said in surprise. "I didn't know you were still up."

"Couldn't sleep."

He sat down on the old sofa next to her. She could feel warmth radiating from his skin, and his wavy red hair was damp. "What's Sexpot doing in here?" he asked.

"Oh, you know her. She gets around."

Deacon laughed. "You get anything at the convention today?"

"Actually, I didn't go. The new girl, Annalie, hung out with me at the beach."

"Good for you." He pointed at her taped ankle. "How'd you do that?"

"I stepped wrong in the sand. It's nothing. I'm fine."

She thought about telling him about her visit to Justin's apartment—and her confrontation with the stranger pretending to be a St. Petersburg detective—but she knew Deacon would be stern. He was overprotective, like Lyle, and he wouldn't like the idea of her sticking her nose into Justin's murder.

Was that what she was doing? She hadn't really admitted it to herself, but it was true. She didn't believe his death had anything to do with drugs. He'd been hiding something from her, and whatever it was had gotten him killed. She thought about Annalie. *Sometimes special projects go on behind the scenes. People get recruited to do things they don't want to do.*

"Can I ask you something?" she said.

"Sure."

"Do you know what Justin was working on before he was killed?"

Deacon shook his head. "No, Ogden pretty much had him under his thumb those last few weeks."

"Ogden did?"

"Well, it looked that way. I saw Justin in his office a lot. You know how Ogden works. He keeps us walled off, so he can dodge the blame if things go wrong. Why? What's going on?"

Peach shrugged. "It's nothing," she lied. "Annalie was wondering if she needed to follow up on any of Justin's projects."

Deacon hesitated, as if deciding whether to believe her. Then he slapped her on the leg. "Okay, I'm going to bed." He got up, tightening the knot of his towel. "You mind if I take Sexpot to my room? I like it when she watches me."

"Ewww," Peach said.

Her brother laughed. "I'm kidding. Get some sleep."

"I will. Hey, Deacon?"

"What?"

"Do you know anyone named Alison?"

He scrunched his mouth and thought about it. "Alison? I don't think so. Who is she?"

"It's a name Justin mentioned."

"Well, there's an Alison Kuipers at the law firm that Ms. Fairmont uses. She signs off on legal questions for some of the jobs we do."

"So if Justin had concerns about something, he would have called her?"

"Yeah, could be."

"Thanks," Peach said. "It's not a big deal. I was just curious."

Deacon mussed her hair, which he knew she hated. "Go to bed, Fruity. It's late."

"I will."

Peach waited as Deacon returned to his bedroom. He turned off the light behind him, leaving her in darkness. The pale glow of a streetlight down the block made Sexpot's white limbs shimmer. Peach wondered what it would be like to be empty at the core, dressed up so that people saw whatever they wanted to see.

Maybe that was her.

She waited half an hour without moving. It was past one in the morning. When she stood up, her twisted ankle protested, but she limped toward the front door. Not making a sound, Peach slipped out of the house, past the warped gates and the NO TRESPASSING and BEWARE OF DOG signs. She crossed the street in the humid haze and crept beside the fence guarding Lake Seminole Park. The ground under her feet was damp. At the gate, she slipped into the bug-infested woods and slapped away insects that tried to fly up her nose. They swarmed her, as if they were trying to warn her away.

She ran to her Thunderbird.

She knew there was no going back now. She was all in.

The monitor on Peach's desk glowed in a rectangle of white light. Around her, the foundation research office was dark. She'd left the overhead fluorescent lights off. Her T-Bird wasn't parked in its usual spot, number 52, across from the Tampa mural. Instead, she'd parked outside an apartment building two blocks away, which wasn't visible from the office's double doors.

She didn't want anyone knowing about her late-night visit, but she knew she was leaving electronic footprints. That was the risk she had to take. If someone looked, they would see that her pass card had been used to enter the building at 1:52 a.m. If someone looked, they would also see that the dormant foundation computer account for Justin Kiel had been accessed at 1:57 a.m.

She knew his password. She hoped that no one had thought to completely deactivate his account, but when she keyed in *Tyger1827*, it was as if Justin had never died. His files were still there. His office e-mail was still there. She assumed the police had been through everything following the murder, but they were looking for evidence of drugs, suppliers, and customers. Peach knew there was nothing like that to find.

She ran a search of his files. *Alison.*

She ran a search of his e-mail. *Alison.*

Both searches elicited no results. She tried again with the last name that Deacon had given her—Kuipers—and got no hits again. If Justin had been in touch with the attorney at the foundation law firm, he'd done it offline. Peach knew him. He wouldn't have left digital records.

His e-mails made her sad. Many of them were to her. As she scrolled through his file of sent messages, she found herself smiling. Then crying. He wrote to her about work. He wrote to her about music and poetry. He wrote to her with his little philosophies about the world. He wrote to her every day, and then he didn't write to her at all. That last week, he dropped off the radar completely. As she studied his account, she saw that his last sent message was dated a week before he was killed. He hadn't been in the office those last several days.

However, Peach studied his mail folders and saw two draft messages. Unsent. When she opened the folder, she saw that both messages had been composed the evening before his death, and for some reason, he'd left them undelivered. She wondered where he had written them, because he hadn't been in the office that night. She'd been here herself, alone.

The first message was to her, and it included an attachment. Peach held her breath as she clicked on the draft e-mail, wondering what she would find. She expected something deep, something secret, that only she would be able to interpret.

Instead, the mail message said simply: *Cool place!*

She opened the attachment, which was a JPEG photograph taken with her own phone. She saw herself. Justin had taken a picture of her in front of a restaurant called The Crab Shack on Gandy Boulevard. They'd eaten there several months earlier and spent hours over beer and Chesapeake-style blue crabs, hammering and picking meat from the tiny bodies. It was a happy memory. She looked carefree in the photo, with a big smile on her face, mugging and pointing her thumb over her shoulder. The restaurant, which was a tin-roof dive, was behind her, its exterior packed with kitschy decorations. A Land-Shark surfboard. A neon lobster in the window. Beer buckets and scrap metal crabs.

Peach studied the photo, and when the glow of her memory faded, she looked at it again and thought: *That's not right.*

Something was wrong, something odd, but the more she looked at it, the less she trusted her instincts. It was just an old photo. She'd seen it before. No big deal. And then she thought: *Why would Justin send me this again?* Why that photo. Why that night of all nights.

She sat in the darkness, but she had no answers. She clicked the Send button, and almost immediately, her phone beeped as the e-mail arrived at her account.

Peach opened the second unsent message. This one was to Ogden Bush. It read simply: *I need to see you.*

Justin was trying to meet with Bush the night before he was killed, but he never sent the e-mail. Something secret was going on between Justin and Bush. That was what Deacon had suspected: *Ogden had him under his thumb.*

Peach logged off the account and switched off her monitor. The office was black, so she took a flashlight from her desk drawer. Following the light, she left her cubicle and made her way along the rear wall to Bush's office. The door was closed and locked, but that didn't matter. This had been Deacon's office until Bush bumped him out to a smaller desk during the campaign. Peach had a key, and she let herself inside.

The office smelled like Ogden Bush, which meant it smelled like heavy, expensive cologne. She cast her light around the room. Even in the short time he'd worked here, he'd filled the office with personal memorabilia. Photos of himself with Democratic politicians and Miami hip-hop celebs. Headlines from winning campaigns and from scandals that had engulfed his opponents. Plaques from Florida charities. College trophies for tennis. He carried his huge ego and his high-powered connections with him wherever he went.

Peach spotted the file cabinet behind his desk. Using her flashlight, she quickly opened and shuffled through his desk drawers. She figured he kept a backup key in the office, and she was right. When she yanked open the bottommost cubbyhole drawer, she found a silver key taped underneath it.

She opened the file cabinet. The top drawer was stuffed with folders, seemingly in no order. She shuffled through them, but they were mostly historical, dealing with political maneuverings dating back for years. One of the folders was labeled with the name Chuck Warren. Another, immediately behind it, bore the name of Birch Fairmont. She was tempted to look, but for the time being, she ignored them and moved to the second drawer.

The folder she wanted was at the front, as if it had been recently reviewed. The name on the tab said "Justin Kiel." Peach pushed the tight folders apart and tried to squeeze the file on Justin out of the drawer, but before she could get it, she heard a muffled noise breaking the dead silence of the office. It was the street door opening and closing on the other side of the building.

Someone was coming inside.

Peach slammed the drawer shut. She switched off the flashlight and stumbled to Bush's office door. She pulled it closed behind her and crab-walked to the first open cubicle, where she threw herself inside, hugging the wall. Overhead, the fluorescent lights flickered to life, bathing the entire room in a bright, noontime glow. She heard footsteps and whistling. Someone walked down the corridor, passing immediately next to the cubicle where she was hiding, and she recognized an aroma that she'd smelled only moments earlier.

Cologne.

Ogden Bush. He was here in the middle of the night.

She heard the man continue to his office door. His keys jangled in his hand. He pushed the key into the lock, but then she heard something that made her hold her breath. The door shoved open under his hand. It wasn't locked. She hadn't closed it completely when she made her escape.

The jangling stopped. The whistling stopped.

Bush retraced his steps. She could sense his closeness. He was so near her that she could hear the measured in-and-out noise of his breathing.

"Hello?" he called, his voice smooth and suspicious.

Peach waited. She kept as still as one of her mannequins.

"Is anyone there?" Bush demanded.

He waited, listening, as a full minute passed. Then another. Peach squirmed, uncomfortable in the tight space beside the cubicle wall. An overwhelming desire to pee made her squeeze her knees together. Finally, Bush turned back, and she heard him go into the office and close the door behind him. She decided to press her luck and get away, but as she unfolded her legs and crawled to the cubicle doorway, she heard his door open again. She didn't have time to hide. If he stopped, if he glanced inside the cubicle, he would see her.

Bush walked right by her. Short, suave, confident. He swung his briefcase in his hand, and he marched down the corridor without a sideways glance. He was whistling again. She saw his head bobbing in time to the tune on his lips. His suit looked as lush as silk, and his shoes had a mirror shine. Moments later, the office lights went off again, and she was alone, hugging her knees and staring into nothingness.

She gave him ten minutes to make sure he was gone. She knew she should leave quickly, but before she did, she checked Bush's office one last time. She unlocked the door. Unlocked the file cabinet. Opened the drawer.

The file on Justin was gone.

Bush had taken it.

13

Cab parked his Corvette in a gravel driveway outside a white bungalow on the shore of Lake Hamilton, which was a long, slow drive from
the Gulf in the center of the state. He climbed from the cold sports car
into the afternoon heat. The temperature was in the nineties, and the
sky over the lake was cloudless and baby blue. It was Sunday, July 1,
and if the weather forecasters were right, Chayla would reach central
Florida by Independence Day and surge ashore with sixty-mile-an-
hour winds. Right now, the rotating storm, which looked like the
Milky Way inching through the Caribbean, felt a long way off.

He wore a dark navy suit and burgundy-framed Gucci sunglasses.
He'd polished his leather shoes that morning, and though the shine
never lasted more than a day, Cab liked to keep them that way. Standing in the hot sun, with his hands in his pockets, he felt sweat gather-
ing on his skin like a glaze brushed on St. Louis ribs.

The house where Rufus Twill lived was old and unkempt. Spanish moss dripped from the trees and made decaying brown piles on
the roof. The aluminum siding was crusted with dirt. Dead flowers
drooped from clay pots dangling from the gutters. Twill, who'd spent
twenty years as a reporter for an Orlando newspaper, was living on
Social Security disability income now. He lived alone. Never married.

Cab rang the doorbell, and when no one answered, he removed his sunglasses and peered through the oval window in the house's red front door. He could see through the small living room to the patio windows looking out on the lake, but he didn't see anyone inside. He wandered to the rear of the house, where a wide lawn, with overgrown grass and weeds, sloped toward the water. He saw a rickety dock with a new, brightly painted airboat tied to one of the posts. Twill lived on the southeast shore of the kidney-shaped lake, and Cab could see trees and thick marshes lining the far banks. He walked out to the dock and picked his way to the platform over the dirty, shallow water. Overhead, a bald eagle floated on the air in graceful circles.

His phone whistled in his pocket. Two voice mail messages had arrived during the drive inland. The first message was a familiar voice.

"Cab, it's Caprice. I enjoyed last night. We should do it again. I set up a private meeting for you with Diane tonight at 9:00 p.m. Call me after if you want a late drink."

He thought about Lala's very specific suggestion not to have sex with Caprice. A late drink at her place would likely lead to bed. As appealing as that idea sounded, he decided he wouldn't call her. He hoped his willpower lasted through the evening.

The second voice mail message was a complete surprise.

"Cab, this is Ramona Cortes. I believe we met briefly at a family wedding over the winter. I'd like to talk to you at lunch tomorrow. Let's say the Pilot House at the Tampa Yacht Club at 1:00 p.m. Call my aide if there's a problem."

Ramona had a slight hint of a Hispanic accent in her prosecutorial voice. Cab knew her enough to know that there was steel at the heart of her personality. Lunch with the attorney general wasn't a request. It was an expectation. Drop everything, and be there.

Things were getting interesting.

Cab slid his phone into his pocket, but he didn't have time to think about what Ramona might want with him. Instead, a voice called to him from the end of the dock: "Get those long arms in the air, friend."

Cab turned around slowly. A small black man in his fifties stood in the overgrown grass. In one hand, he cradled a foot-long baby alligator. In the other, he held a grimy revolver with a wooden grip and eight-inch barrel that looked as if it hadn't been fired since the 1970s. Cab spread his fingers wide and cocked his forearms.

"I'm Detective Bolton, Mr. Twill. We spoke on the phone."

"Yeah, I talked to somebody. Let me see a badge and a photo ID, so I can see who you really are."

Cab kept his hands up as he walked back along the dock, which shifted under his feet, almost throwing him into the lake. "I hope I don't look like a member of the Liberty Empire Alliance," he said.

"You'd be surprised."

At the end of the dock, Cab peeled back the lapel of his coat and reached inside with two fingers to extract his wallet and badge. Twill leaned forward to study his credentials, and when he was satisfied, he shoved the big gun into his paint-streaked cargo pants.

"Can't be too careful," Twill added.

"I understand. You should probably clean that gun. It's just as likely to blow up in your face as it is to shoot somebody else."

Twill shrugged. "It's not loaded. I hate guns."

"I'm not a big fan either," Cab admitted. "Who's your friend?"

"This is Boots." He used one finger to stroke the head of the alligator, which watched Cab with beady eyes and snapped its jaws.

"Alligator Boots," Cab said. "That's funny."

"Boots could take your finger off if he were so inclined."

"Well, one of my guiding principles in life is never to stick my fingers in an alligator's mouth," Cab said.

Twill allowed a smile to crease his face. His skin was a light oak color, with mottled darker spots on his forehead. He wasn't tall, and he was skinny, with bony arms left bare by a loose gray tank top. He wore a Chicago Cubs baseball cap. One of his chocolate-brown eyes stared at Cab, and the other was fixed, like glass. A milky scar ran along the line of his misshapen chin.

"So what is it you want, detective?"

"Are we off the record?" Cab asked.

"You don't have to worry about that. Since the beating, I don't write anymore. It scrambled my brain."

"I'm sorry."

"It is what it is. Like they say, the Lord closes a door, he opens a window somewhere else. I can't put two words together now, but I can play piano like some kind of Art Tatum. Or at least it feels that way to me. Stop by Cherry Pocket for dinner some Friday. You can judge for yourself.

"I may do that." Cab added: "I suppose you can guess what I'd like to talk to you about."

"Sure. Ham Brock, Chuck Warren, Birch Fairmont, all that ugly stuff back then. You realize about a thousand cops have gone down this road before you."

"Well, do you mind going for a thousand and one?"

"I don't mind, but if it means giving up a source, even from a decade ago, I won't do that."

"Understood."

Twill pursed his lips. He glanced at his house and the surrounding woods, whose branches hung limply, as if they were wilting in the humid air. "How about we go out on the boat? My new toy. Let me just put Boots in his cage."

"Do you think your house is bugged?" Cab asked, with a small smile.

Twill didn't smile back. "You never know."

The former reporter turned on his heel and headed up the lawn toward his back door. He walked with a pronounced limp. He wasn't gone five minutes before he returned to the dock, with a six-pack of Bud Light dangling from one hand. He and Cab boarded the airboat. Twill took the seat beside the rudder stick, and Cab sat next to him. Twill fired up the caged propeller, which howled like a Boeing jet, and smoothly guided the flat-bottom boat onto the lake.

As they reached open water, Twill accelerated. A cooling wind blew back Cab's styled hair, and spray dampened his suit. Twill secured his Cubs cap low on his forehead. He raced all the way to the far shore, where a large field of grassy marshes grew out of the water. Twill slowed and turned the boat directly into the tall grass, and the airboat easily slipped inside the wetland, obscured from view. Cab could see the muddy bottom; the lake was only six inches deep here. Lily pads and green algae dotted the surface. Black flies buzzed the boat. He saw a full-size alligator—at least seven feet—sunning itself on a sandbar among the reeds.

Twill cut the motor and popped open a beer. He offered one to Cab, who shook his head.

"I do this every day. Not so bad, huh? I used to live in Orlando and work for a living. Who needs that? Guess there has to be a fringe benefit to nine weeks in a coma." He waved at the alligator. "How's it going today, Rex? Swallow up any tourists?" Twill chuckled and took a slug of beer. "So what kind of a name is Cab?" he asked.

"My mother was a big fan of the movie *Cabaret*," Cab said.

"With Liza?"

"Right."

"Hmm." Twill drank more beer, and then he pulled a joint out of his pocket. "You going to turn me in? It's medicinal. For the pain."

"Do what you have to do," Cab said.

Twill lit the joint and stretched out his legs. The marshland around them was a secluded nature preserve, walled off from the rest of the lake. Cab saw the walnut-sized head of a turtle poking out of the water. Nearby, a white heron darted its long neck into the ripples and emerged with a squirming fish.

"So when did it happen?" Cab asked.

Twill knew what he meant. "Nine years ago this Wednesday."

"The Fourth of July?"

"That's it. That also happens to be the day that Ham Brock and some of his buddies started serving their sentences for tax fraud, money laundering, and weapons violations. I guess their friends wanted to thank me for all the articles I'd done about the Alliance over the years. About six of them in hoods grabbed me out back of my apartment in Maitland. Took me in the trunk to a deserted section of the Ocala. I woke up in the hospital in September."

"I'm sorry." Cab didn't like that the Fourth of July—in three days—was an anniversary that had special meaning to Hamilton Brock and the members of the Liberty Empire Alliance.

"And here I am," Twill went on.

"Do you still keep an eye on the Alliance?" Cab asked.

"One eye is all I've got."

Cab winced. "Yes, of course."

"Never mind," Twill replied, grinning. "Sure I do. I never know when they might decide to come back and finish the job. I've got sources that keep me in the loop."

"I was wondering if you'd heard any rumors about the Alliance targeting Diane Fairmont," Cab said. He swatted away a particularly voracious fly. The heat was concentrated inside the grassy marsh, and he felt the sun cooking his long nose.

"Can't say as I have," Twill told him.

"Nothing at all?" Cab asked.

"You sound like you were expecting a different answer."

"I was."

"Well, something like that would be kept way under wraps. Just because it hasn't hit my ears doesn't mean it's not happening. What are you thinking? The Alliance got rid of Birch, so now that Diane is in the race, why not get rid of her, too? Kind of a revenge thing?"

"Something like that."

Twill rubbed the scar on his chin. He sucked on the joint, looking relaxed. "What makes you so sure they got rid of Birch?"

Cab was surprised. "You don't think the Alliance was involved? That's not what you said back then."

"Oh, I was on a rampage about hate groups in those days. Still am. People don't take these domestic terrorists seriously, but they're plenty dangerous. The Islamists don't have a monopoly on crazy. Ten years ago, you had politicians like Chuck Warren coddling these boys and calling them patriots. I held his feet to the fire over that, and it cost him the election."

"So what am I missing?" Cab asked. "The Alliance had a major grudge against Birch over his political policies. They came after you for writing about them. Why do you now think Hamilton Brock may be innocent?"

"I never said innocent. Him and his crowd, they're bad, bad boys. Did one of them also put on a hood and shoot up the Bok? The FBI says yes. Me, well, I'm not so sure anymore."

"What changed?"

Twill sighed and flicked the joint into the water. "Let's say I know there's a difference between assassination and murder," he replied.

Cab listened to the insects chattering. He began to understand why Twill preferred to talk in a place that was sheltered from electronic spies. "Are you saying that you think the motive wasn't political?"

"I'm saying that whoever pulled the trigger knew the hammer was going to fall on the Alliance. Maybe it was those boys, maybe it wasn't. Honestly, I don't really care either way. You won't find me shedding any tears over Ham Brock taking the fall."

"Except something must have put the idea in your head."

Twill yanked his tank top over his baseball cap. "Shit, it's hot. Ain't you roasting in that suit? Why do you wear something like that in Florida?"

"That's who I am," Cab said.

Twill called to the alligator. "It's who he is, Rex. You believe that? An idiot is who he is."

Cab couldn't decide if Twill was drunk or stoned or simply ducking the subject. "Somebody obviously told you something."

"Hey, why tell stories about the dead? Birch is gone, right? That's probably for the best. A lot of people knew he was a son of a bitch. He would have gone down in flames sooner or later. Even his insiders were onto him. Lyle Piper called me the Saturday before Labor Day. Said we needed to have a talk."

"About what?"

"I don't know. I was in the Keys that weekend. No phone. But I heard things after the murders that made me put two and two together."

"So help me do the math," Cab said.

Twill took a second beer can and rubbed the cool, damp aluminum over his chest. "Okay, look, I'm not saying it means anything.

People get mad, they blow off steam. You don't ruin somebody's life over that. That's why I never printed anything."

"Who are you talking about?"

Twill sighed. "You know that Diane had a son, right?"

"Drew," Cab said.

"Right. Drew. He had big problems, okay? Heavy into drugs. Hanging out with some really bad people. He killed himself not too long after the murders. Thing is, Drew hated Birch Fairmont. I mean, *hated* him."

"Who told you that?"

Twill put a finger on the side of his nose. "Sources. I can't name names."

"Okay, so Drew and Birch didn't get along. That's not exactly news when it comes to stepsons and stepdads."

"Oh, this was more than not getting along. Believe me. Look, I didn't go searching for this. I was a reporter, and I was convinced that Ham Brock and the Alliance had gone off the deep end. I was hunting for proof to put the bastards away. This gal I talked to, she didn't want to tell me anything. It kinda spilled out. I don't think she told the police either."

"Told them what?" Cab asked.

"A couple weeks before the murders, there was a problem at Birch's estate."

"What kind of problem?"

"She wouldn't say. Or maybe she didn't exactly know, but it sounded mean. What she did know is that Drew was so wild about it that he got dropped into rehab. Know when he got out? Right before Labor Day. Interesting, huh?"

"But you don't know what happened," Cab said.

"I don't. I looked for dirt, but nobody would talk. Even my original source got cold feet. She told me she didn't hear what she said she heard. Well, it ain't the kind of thing you're likely to make a mistake about."

"What did she hear?"

Twill leaned closer to Cab. The beer and pot were on his breath. "She told me she heard Drew screaming about how he was going to kill Birch Fairmont. This was right before he got shipped off to rehab. Quote unquote, he was going to blow his fucking head off."

Rufus Twill waited until the tall detective disappeared around the front of his house. He stayed in the boat, which bobbed gently in the waves beside the dock. He took off his baseball cap and rubbed his sweaty hands through his hair. When he was sure that he was alone, he popped another beer and dug a phone out of his pocket. He dialed a number with one hand.

"It's Rufus," he said.

"You shouldn't be calling me," Ogden Bush replied.

"Yeah? Well, I thought you'd want to know. Somebody else is poking into the old shit. A detective named Bolton. He says he's working for Common Way. Just wondering if you'd heard about that."

There was a long silence from the political operative. "Interesting."

"So they're keeping things from you, huh? Sounds like they don't necessarily trust you over there, Ogden."

"Shut up, Rufus."

"Hey, I didn't need to call. I'm doing you a favor."

"I know. I appreciate it."

"Yeah, well, appreciation don't come free. I like my new boat, but I was thinking, my truck's getting kind of old, too. Thought you might be able to do something about that."

He could almost hear Bush grinding his teeth. "I'll see what I can do. Now what did you tell the detective?"

"Oh, don't you worry about that," Twill replied. "I told him exactly what I told that kid Justin. Guess we'll see if Bolton winds up dead, too."

14

"You okay, hun?"

Peach looked up from her plate of fried shrimp, which she hadn't touched. She sat at a long table in a corner of The Crab Shack restaurant, next to a lovey-dovey couple feeding each other bites of crab across the table. The Sunday afternoon crowd was noisy, and Peach had a headache.

"What?" she said.

"Just wanted to make sure you're all right," the waitress repeated. "You're not eating."

Peach nibbled halfheartedly on a French fry. "Oh, yeah, thanks. I don't have much of an appetite. Could you package this to go?"

"Sure, hun." She added: "Where's your friend?"

"My friend?"

"You came in here once before with a real nice guy. Had one of those old-fashioned mustaches. You guys looked so cute together."

Peach tried to muster a smile. "He's busy."

The waitress put her hand on Peach's shoulder and gave her a just-us-girls look of sympathy, as if she'd blundered into the middle of a bad breakup. "I understand, hun. I'm real sorry."

Peach didn't say anything. All she could think about was that Justin wasn't here anymore. She could picture his face and hear his voice, but soon the memories would begin to fade. Like Lyle. Like her parents. She was holding on to a fraying lifeline, and eventually it would give way.

Justin on memory. *Everybody forgets everybody else. Fame doesn't buy you anything but a few years.*

When she'd paid her bill, Peach picked her way through the crowded tables and made her way outside. She stood near the entrance with the busy traffic on Gandy Boulevard roaring in both directions behind her. This was where she'd been standing in the photograph that Justin had tried to send her. She could picture herself with the silly grin on her face, her thumb jerking toward the door as if she were hitchhiking. It was nothing special, just one moment in the history of all of their moments.

Why would he want to send it to her again? Why on that night?

Justin always had a plan. She dug out her phone and opened the attachment she'd forwarded to herself. With the screen in front of her, she flicked her eyes back and forth between the photo and the funky décor of The Crab Shack. Everything was the same. The neon in the windows. The giant plastic blue crab. The ship's rope tied between old driftwood. The yellow surfboard. Nothing had changed.

Except—no. That wasn't true.

The street number of the restaurant was hung on a little sign above the windows. 11400. However, the photo on her phone showed a completely different number: 10761. Justin had edited the photo. It was a skillful job; no one would notice the alteration if they weren't standing in front of the building. He was sending her a message, but what was he trying to tell her?

Looking at the restaurant, she spotted another tiny change in the photo. Between the words *CRAB* and *SHACK* on the roof sign was a little white house that was shaped like an arrow. The house was tilted to the left as she stared at it, but in the picture on her phone, the house—the arrow—pointed right. The actual sign was angled toward an open, empty field beside the restaurant, but the sign in the photo pointed in the opposite direction, toward a side street leading away from Gandy Boulevard.

Suddenly, she could feel Justin guiding her. He wanted her to follow the arrow.

Peach jogged to the side street, which was San Fernando Drive. It was a nothing street, lined with telephone wires and crowded by palms and pines, but she stared at it now as if it were keeping secrets. She wandered down the middle of the street and found herself near a deserted industrial lot on the left. Everything was quiet, except for the shriek of birds. A quarter mile down the road, she passed two run-down bungalows on large, unkempt lots. Cars and boats were strewn across weedy lawns. Evergreens towered over the houses and threw needles across the gravel. She passed another intersection. More remote houses. More trees. Badly fenced yards with children's toys. Gardens growing nothing. It was a typical old Florida neighborhood, where progress had stopped in 1955.

Ahead of her, the road ended at a concrete barricade. She walked all the way to the fence and saw only an abandoned road overgrown with brush. There was nothing here and nowhere else to go. Frustrated, she turned around, and that was when she spotted the mailbox on the last house on the road.

The number on the box was 10761.

Peach felt herself breathing faster.

It was a tiny white house, no more than a few hundred square feet, behind a four-foot chain-link fence surrounding a big lot. The lawn was scrub and dandelions. The house had a matchbox screened porch on the right, which enclosed the front door. Six identical windows faced the street; all the blinds were closed. Flowering bushes had been planted underneath the windows, but the vines were shriveled and dead. A bushy oak tree loomed over the entire house.

She was alone. The road was deserted, and the house was isolated among the empty lots. If you wanted to hide where no one would see you or find you, this was the perfect place. She checked the mailbox, but it was empty. Even so, she knew she was where Justin wanted her to be.

Peach climbed the low fence. The driveway was cracked and furry with weeds. At the porch, she opened the swinging door, disturbing the web of a large spider. There was no furniture on the concrete slab. Despite the shade, the porch was stifling. She knocked on the door to the house, but she didn't expect an answer, and she didn't get one. When she turned the knob, she found that the door was open. She stepped cautiously into a small living room.

This was Justin's house. His safe house. She saw all of his antiques, all of his quirky collectibles. She'd been with him when he bought many of them. This was where he kept his personal life, where no one could find his secrets. Or so he'd believed.

He was wrong. Peach was too late.

Someone had found the place before her. Someone had beaten her to it. The house had been searched. Antiques that may have hidden anything lay in shards on the floor. Books had been ripped apart; so had the chairs and sofas. There were holes punched in the walls. If there had been anything to find, it was gone. She wanted to cry. It was almost worse, finding this corner of Justin's life that she had never seen before and realizing that a stranger had already violated it. Her breath came raggedly. Her eyes felt full. The house smelled like him, but he was gone.

Peach crossed from the living room to the house's single bedroom. It was dark even in the daylight. The wooden floor groaned under her feet. There was a twin bed, with a mattress that had been slashed, and a state-of-the-art desktop computer that had been disassembled to remove its hard drive, leaving a hole. The monitor was smashed, exposing its interior components. A file cabinet was pushed against the wall, its drawers open and empty. He'd had pictures on the wall, but they'd been ripped apart, exposing the rear of the frames.

Nothing. They'd left her nothing.

She saw a table near the bedroom's only window, which looked out on the sorry lawn. Outside, she saw the mature oak tree with a canvas chair beneath it. A ladder in the dirt. A push lawn mower that had long since rusted into disuse. Inside, there was a coffee mug on the table. She could imagine Justin here, sipping tea, staring at the lonely brush, working on—what?

A photo frame lay on the floor near the table, its glass broken. The photo was still inside the frame. It was her. It was the same photo of Peach standing outside The Crab Shack restaurant.

Another message?

If so, she didn't understand it, because this photograph didn't contain the edits she'd seen on her phone. Maybe the picture was simply a reminder that he'd been in love with her. He'd kept it in his bedroom. He'd stared at her when he was here.

She felt like crying all over again.

Peach took a long, deep breath of hot, dusty air. There was no evidence to find here, nothing that would help her. She'd reached another dead end. However, as she took a last look around the bedroom, she spotted a tiny triangle of paper peeking out from under the file cabinet. When she pushed the empty cabinet aside, she jumped as a three-inch lizard made a frantic escape. She bent down and retrieved the paper.

Someone—Justin?—had taken a close-up picture of a newspaper article that had been pinned to a cork bulletin board. It was impossible to tell where the photo had been taken. The article itself appeared to be nearly a decade old, copied from a Tampa newspaper.

The headline read: Frank Macy Gets Eight Years on Manslaughter Plea.

Only the opening paragraphs were legible in the photo:

Despite claims that the police had planted evidence against him, Tampa resident Frank Macy, 27, pled no contest to second-degree manslaughter charges today in the death of bartender Arnold White last February. Macy, who was already on probation for unrelated drug charges, was sentenced to eight years in prison.

White was assaulted in an alley behind The Spotted Dolphin, a bar in the Gulfside town of Pass-a-Grille on February 12. He later died of his injuries. One witness alleged that White had made sexual advances toward Macy on the night of the assault.

"This plea is a recognition of the fact that a jury trial would likely
have resulted in Mr. Macy's conviction of first-degree manslaughter,
resulting in a significantly longer sentence," said Ramona Cortes, Macy's
defense attorney. "We continue to believe that much of the evidence in
this case was manufactured by authorities in an attempt to . . .

Peach read the fragment of the article six times, but she didn't
understand it. She didn't know the name Frank Macy; she had never
heard of him or the victim. The only name she knew was Ramona
Cortes, who had been a high-profile defense attorney in Tampa before
winning her first statewide election for attorney general five years
earlier. Everyone at the Common Way Foundation knew Ramona,
because she and her Orlando firm had defended Hamilton Brock, too.
Now she was the GOP candidate for governor.

Why did Justin think this article was important?

She studied the police photograph of Frank Macy. He was a
stranger to her, not familiar at all, but he had an unusually soft, sensitive face. His dark hair was wavy and fell below his ears. He didn't
look like a thug. He didn't have a tattooed face and square chin, a flat
nose like a roadkill mouse, or mean dark eyes. Instead, he looked like
a refugee from a boy band. His bedroom brown eyes said: *Look at me,
little girl.* His skin just made you want to touch it. He looked lost.

Peach did some quick math in her head. Based on the date of the
article, and the sentence he received, Macy would have been released
from prison earlier this year. He was free.

It wasn't much, but it was something. She didn't know who Frank
Macy was, or what Justin wanted with him, but she was going to find
out.

15

The jungle-like garden in Diane Fairmont's Tampa estate was a mass of shadows. It was nine o'clock at night, but the summer days were long. Cab stood on the lawn, with the bone-white estate behind him. The air was ripe with dampness. A rabbit fed on the grass nearby, and gnats hovered in a cloud over the lily pond. He was procrastinating by not going inside. He felt nervous, like a twentysomething kid again. He'd avoided Diane for ten years, but he couldn't avoid her anymore.

What would they say to each other?

When the front door opened behind him, he shoved his hands in the pockets of his suit pants with unease. He expected to hear her voice, but instead, the voice was male and loud, breaking the silence like an earthmover on a weekend morning.

"Hey, detective!"

It was Garth Oakes. Fitness guru, masseur, would-be confidant and adviser to Diane. The man hopped down the steps and headed for Cab with an open-toed walk, his black ponytail swinging. He was dressed in pastels, as if *Miami Vice* had never gone off the air. White sport coat, collarless lavender shirt. The dusk made his skin as dark as a leather boot.

Garth thrust out his hand, and Cab shook it again.

"We met at the party on Friday," Oakes said. "Remember me?"

"Beat the Girth . . . With Garth," Cab commented.

"You remember! Yeah, I don't care how many times I see myself on TV at three in the morning, it's still a kick. You here to see Diane?"

Cab nodded.

"She's running late," Garth told him. "We just wrapped up a massage, and she wanted to take a shower."

"Okay."

"Hey, I hear you're looking into some of these threats against her, huh? Way to go. Can't be too careful. Me, I'm always prepared." Garth pulled aside the flap of his sport coat to reveal a ridiculously large automatic weapon holstered near his shoulder. "People figure I'm like the Hulk, you know? Beat 'em off with my bare hands. Except a fist isn't much good if the other guy is packing. Nobody messes with Garth, baby. You try, you eat some lead sushi."

Cab wasn't really listening, but he was pretty sure that Garth did say "lead sushi."

"I better get inside," Cab said.

"Oh, sure. Hey, the campaign's going well, huh? You see the latest poll numbers? Some folks are saying the governor may pack it in and get out of the race, but I don't think so. He probably figures the storm will give him a bump. Voters rally round the incumbent over that kind of thing."

"They do."

"He's going down, though." Garth pointed at the "Governor Diane" button pinned to his shirt. Or maybe it was pinned directly to the muscles on his chest. "She's a shoo-in. Unless they find some nasty dirt, I say she wins by seven or eight points."

"Dirt?" Cab asked.

"Well, politics ain't beanbag, right? You know they're out there looking."

"Is there anything to find?"

Garth shrugged. "There's *always* something to find. No saints and virgins in this business. I could tell you stories. Not that anyone could unzip my lips. You have to know how to keep secrets in my world."

"What happens on the massage table stays on the massage table?" Cab asked.

"Ha, that's funny! Right! Believe me, once somebody lets you run your hands over their naked body, they figure they can tell you just about anything."

"It's a good thing you're discreet."

Garth crossed his fingers and thumped his heart. "Believe it. People have tried to get crap out of me. Political people. Reporters, too. People know me and Diane are tight."

"That's right. You said you were at her place in Lake Wales a lot, didn't you?"

"Yeah, I'm still in Lake Wales all the time. Got a lot of clients there."

"What was it like at Birch's house back then?"

"Huh? Oh, ugly days. Ugly days."

"Because of the murders?"

Garth flinched. "Sure, of course. Because of the murders."

"And then with Drew's suicide," Cab added.

"Oh, yeah, even worse."

"It must have been difficult," Cab said, "with Drew going in and out of rehab all the time. An emotional roller coaster."

"You know it. That was super hard on Diane."

"My mother said that Drew spent time in rehab right before the murders," Cab went on.

"Oh, yeah. That was bad."

"What happened?" Cab asked. "I heard that Drew was really upset about something."

Garth looked like a train slamming on the brakes before a crossing. "Oh, well, who can tell with druggies, huh?"

"I heard he made threats."

"Threats?"

"Like he was going to blow Birch's head off," Cab said.

Garth laughed, which sounded like the nervous titter of a teenage girl. "Oh, that was nothing. Kid was worked up. No big deal."

"Except someone did shoot Birch," Cab pointed out.

"I know, crazy, right? What are the odds? It's a crazy world."

"Very crazy."

Garth checked his phone and fiddled impatiently with the buttons. "Well, I gotta run. I've got another rubdown tonight. One of the uniform chasers near MacDill. Here's my chance to find out the latest in air force secrets, right? Nice talking to you, detective."

"Same here," Cab replied.

The masseur saluted and shouldered off toward the estate's main gate at a brisk pace. He looked back and smiled nervously when he saw that Cab was still watching him. He gave a little wave, but Cab thought he couldn't get away fast enough.

Diane was waiting for him in the first-floor study. It was a man's room in a woman's house, with wine-colored wallpaper and heavy, dark walnut on a wall of built-in bookshelves. It had a fireplace and wet bar. The armchairs looked weathered and not particularly comfortable. An oil painting of Birch Fairmont above the fireplace made him look like a Rockefeller.

"Hello, Cab," Diane said.

He didn't know what to say, so he said nothing. He ran his fingers along the spines of the hardback books on the shelves. He could feel her eyes following him.

"Red or white?" she asked. She had two bottles of wine open on a silver tray. He didn't doubt that both were expensive.

"Red."

"That's what I prefer, too," Diane said, "but I have to drink white now because of the campaign."

Cab stopped and cocked his head, puzzled. She laughed and tapped a finger on her lips. "Teeth," she went on. "Red wine stains the teeth. Doesn't look good on television."

"Amazing," Cab said.

"Yes, it's a different world, but you know that. Your mother faced the same thing all those years."

"Yes, she did."

"Sit down, won't you?" Diane asked. "I don't bite."

There were two armchairs, decorated in a floral pattern, on either side of the antique table on which Diane placed the wine glasses. His was a large, gently fluted bowl glass, in which she'd poured two inches of Cabernet. Hers was a crystal tulip, and she'd filled it with sauvignon blanc. He sat down, and she sat down. The two chairs were angled toward each other, and Cab had to bend his long legs awkwardly so as not to touch her.

Finally, he looked at her. She wasn't wearing makeup, and her face was flushed from the shower. Or maybe it was flushed because she was remembering when they were last together. She was older now—her skin not as taut, her brunette hair scrubbed of gray—but she was still elegant and attractive. She was casually dressed, but to Diane, casual meant a rose blouse, white satin slacks, and heels. He'd changed into a beige suit and narrow tie.

They clinked their glasses in a silent toast and drank. The Heitz Cabernet was superb.

"Tarla doesn't know," Diane said. "That was your first question, wasn't it?"

He nodded, because she'd read his mind. He realized that Diane was different now. More confident and mature, more open. The Diane of ten years ago wouldn't have bulled her way into that particular china shop.

"Why didn't you tell her?" he asked.

"I figured you didn't want me to. I assume you didn't tell her yourself."

"You assume correctly."

"I hope you don't feel guilty about what happened between us," she said. "Or worse, ashamed."

"No."

"Good. You'll never know what that afternoon meant to me." After an awkward pause, she added: "Or how it changed my life."

There was nothing to say in reply, so again, he said nothing.

"Anyway, enough of that," she said. "It's over and done. We don't need to talk about it."

"Okay."

She glanced at the painting of Birch with emotions he couldn't read, and she drank more sauvignon blanc. "So."

"So."

"Tarla tells me she's trying to set you up with Caprice," Diane said.

Cab rolled his eyes. "Well, you know my mother."

"I do. You could do a lot worse, Cab. Caprice is brilliant, beautiful, driven. What we've done at Common Way is mostly thanks to her. Really, it should be her on the ticket, not me."

"I don't exactly see myself as a politician's courtesan," Cab said.

"Oh, with Caprice, I suspect you'd enjoy the experience," Diane replied, smiling. "However, it's your choice. You don't need all these middle-aged women interfering in your love life. Speaking of which, how is it for you having Tarla close to you again?"

"Challenging," Cab said.

"So I gather. She has some choice words for your girlfriend. What's her name? Wawa?"

"Lala," Cab said. "No, they don't exactly get along. Lala met us for breakfast after Mass a couple months ago. Tarla said the Catholic Church should change its name to IHOP. International House of Pedophiles."

"Your mother does speak her mind," Diane murmured.

"Yes, she does."

"She thinks you've spent your life running away from her."

"No, just running," Cab said, "but she has a point."

"So why do you do it?"

Cab sipped his wine. He had no intention of answering, but it was a good question. He usually avoided self-reflection the way he avoided yoga and Michael Bublé. He could have blamed Catch-a-Cab Bolton on Vivian Frost, the lover who'd betrayed him, the lover he'd killed; but the truth was, it had started long before her. He could have blamed Hollywood. He could have blamed Tarla, or his father, who didn't even exist for him. Any of those were easier than blaming himself.

"Are you planning to run away again?" Diane asked, when he ignored her question.

"My lieutenant in Naples would probably be happier if I did," Cab said, smiling.

"Hiding behind jokes. Just like your mother. She loves you, you know. You have no idea how abandoned you've made her feel. You two have only each other, yet you chose to keep yourself thousands of miles away from her for years."

Cab felt an urge to snap back at Diane. That was probably what she wanted. Instead, he tightened his grip on the wine glass and settled back into the chair. "It's really supposed to be me asking the questions here."

Diane laughed. "Sorry. There I go again. It's just that she's my best friend."

"I know. I love her, too, you realize."

"Of course you do."

"Unfortunately, for Tarla, being a part of my life means trying to control me."

"Well, rather than running away, you could try saying no."

Cab smiled. "Yes, I could."

Diane had already drained most of the wine in her glass, and she refilled it. He knew she was nervous, even if she didn't show it. She lifted the bottle of red, but he shook his head. After she took another swallow—a large one—she put down the glass and gripped the arms of the chair a little too tightly.

"Caprice tells me you're looking into threats against me," she said.

"That's right."

"Is this real, or just an excuse for her to seduce you?" she asked.

"I don't think she needs an excuse," Cab said. "As for whether it's real, I suppose she showed you the note."

Diane nodded. "She did. Am I supposed to take it seriously? I really can't believe the Liberty Empire Alliance would be so bold as to try this again. It's gracious of you, Cab, but I think you're wasting your time. I have security. We have a very able police force, not to mention the FBI. I'm sure if there were any genuine threat, they would know about it, and they'd be able to deal with it."

Cab felt as if he were being dismissed. "You may well be right."

"That's not to say I don't like having you around. I'm sure Caprice feels the same way."

Her words had gotten faster, as if she were racing for a conclusion she didn't want to admit openly. She wanted him to stop investigating. She wanted him to quit.

"I do have some questions," he said.

"Such as?"

"Do you really believe that the Liberty Empire Alliance killed Birch?"

Diane's jaw hardened. She looked offended. Or her offense was a convincing political act. "That's your question? I watched one of their *soldiers* murder three people. Including my husband. It could have been me, too, and it could have been your mother, in case you've forgotten."

"I haven't," Cab said.

"Then clearly, my answer is yes. I was there. I saw it happen."

"I'm sorry. I realize how horrible it was. If it's possible that the same person could be focused on you, then I want to follow any avenue to know who really pulled the trigger that night. That means finding out everything I can about the Labor Day murders."

Diane shrugged. Her body language wasn't designed to encourage him.

"I've tried to talk to Tarla about the shooting," he went on, "but she won't say anything. I think she's keeping something from me."

"Why do you think that?" Diane asked.

"I know my mother. Do you have any idea what it could be?"

"I don't. She and I don't talk about that night. We never have."

"Tarla's meeting me at the Bok sanctuary tomorrow afternoon," Cab added.

"Whatever for?"

"Sometimes being back in a place where something bad happened will jar memories."

"Maybe some memories are best left buried," Diane said. "I'd forget that night if I could."

"Tell me something, was Drew there with all of you that night?"

"Excuse me?"

"I was wondering if your son was on the dais, too."

"No, he wasn't."

"Where was he?" Cab asked.

"Drew? He was home. He wasn't well. What does this have to do with anything?"

"Nothing. I just wondered how the trauma affected him. Were he and Birch close?"

Diane frowned. "No."

"Stepfather and stepson. It's never easy."

She didn't respond well to his sympathy. "No, it's not."

"I heard that Drew had a bad episode shortly before the murders."

"My son had drug problems for most of his life, Cab."

"Yes, I know that. Was there anything that triggered that particular episode? Did something happen?"

Diane stood up, cutting him off. "Addicts don't need triggers, I'm afraid. Look, Cab, I hate to be abrupt, but can we cut this short? I'm tired. The campaign is exhausting. I really don't want to talk about this anymore."

"Of course."

"I'm sorry I can't be more help. It's nice to see you again. Really."

"It is." Cab stood up, too.

"As I said before, this whole thing is probably a waste of your time. Caprice's heart is in the right place, but I wish she'd talked to me before hiring you. I would have told her not to bother."

"I actually hope you're right about that," Cab said. "That would mean you're safe."

She led him to the front door, and the parting was awkward. They didn't embrace. They didn't shake hands. She acted as if she couldn't wait for him to be gone, and she closed the door immediately behind him.

He found himself alone in the garden. It was night now. At the base of the steps, golden lanterns on white pillars illuminated the sidewalk, leading him away from the house. He made his way to the main gate, which was elaborately sculpted in wrought iron, with designs of herons and tree branches. The security guard let him out. Cab noted with satisfaction that the man was observant and tough, but he was only one man, and there were plenty of ways to breach the wall.

Cab stood outside in the midst of the dark urban neighborhood. The weather forecast was right. The night had changed. A west wind was blowing, and the air pressure had dropped. He could taste rain on his lips. He'd lived in Florida long enough to know that a storm was coming.

He studied the houses around him and felt uneasy. Some had lights, others didn't. The yards were a maze of fences and mature trees, all black in the darkness. Cars were parked along the curbs, leaving wide spaces between them. He couldn't see far, but he spent several minutes waiting and listening.

Eventually, he crossed the street to his Corvette, but it didn't change what he felt.

Somewhere around him were the eyes of a stranger. He was being watched.

16

He put down his binoculars and melted into the cover of the trees. The cop was smart; the good ones had a sixth sense when someone was spying on them. He watched the red Corvette scream away from Diane Fairmont's estate, and he wondered if the cop was going to be a problem.

He didn't want more death, but sometimes it was necessary. Like the girl who'd broken into the foreclosure house. Tina. Young, pretty, sweet. After he cut her throat, he'd dumped her body in a park near the Gulf shore. Eventually, they would match the blood on the carpet in the house and realize she'd been there, but by then, it wouldn't matter anymore.

He only needed a few more days.

He thought about Justin Kiel. Justin was smart, too, like the cop. He'd put two and two together in a way that no one ever had. It could have been a disaster, but Justin had made the mistake of following him and trying to learn more. He was easy to spot, easy to trap.

All these years, his secret had been safe. Buried. Hidden. Until now. He should have expected it. Once the dirt was scraped off an old grave, there was always the risk that someone would stumble across it.

What's happening?

Why is there so much blood?

He squeezed his fists, pushing down his emotions. It was déjà vu. Ten years had changed nothing. All he could do was keep going.

He felt his throwaway phone vibrating in his pocket. He knew exactly who was on the other end of the line. He checked the neighborhood, and he was alone. He answered the phone: "Do you have it?"

The man replied: "Yes, I can get what you want. It isn't a problem."

"Good."

"This is serious firepower, friend," the man said.

"Yeah, so?"

"I want to make sure this doesn't come back to haunt me."

"Don't worry about that."

"I'm someone who worries. Do you have the money?"

"Yes."

There was a long pause. He could almost hear the calculations in the man's mind. Risk assessments. Greed. Eventually, greed always won out.

"Let's say Tuesday then," the man said. "The Picnic Island pier. After dark."

"I'll be there."

He hung up the phone. Everything was coming together now. Soon it would be Independence Day. Soon Chayla would roar like an animal across the land. The storm's violence would protect him. He would strike again, the way he had once before. And then they would finally have what they'd always wanted.

Power.

PART TWO

SOMETHING BAD

17

Cab expected the Pilot House at the Tampa Yacht Club to be crowded for Monday lunch. Instead, the room was empty. Attorney General Ramona Cortes sat alone at a table tucked into an oval cubbyhole at the back of the dining room. The walls around her were paneled in light oak and decorated with sailing flags. The bay windows were blocked by wooden shutters. Through the slats, he glimpsed the water.

Ramona put down her copy of the *Tribune* and got to her feet as he approached. "Cab," she said. "What a pleasure to see you again. Thank you for coming."

Cab smiled. "I didn't think it was optional."

"It wasn't. Not really."

"No campaign aides?" he asked. "Just us?"

"I like my privacy on certain matters." Ramona gestured at the empty dining room. "The restaurant is closed today, but they make an exception for me when I'm in town. I work out, and then I have lunch and dial for dollars. Fundraising is a never-ending process. Order whatever you want. I'm having tomato basil soup and grilled cheese."

"That sounds delicious."

A waiter hovered. Ramona held up two slim fingers, and he nodded and disappeared. A fresh iced latte sat in front of Cab's place setting. Apparently, his tastes were predictable. Ramona sipped club soda with a squeeze of lime from a highball glass.

The attorney general was polite, but with a no-nonsense demeanor. When she smiled, it was with her lips; she didn't grin. She was in her early forties, small, with delicate hands and a trim physique. If there was any gray in her bobbed black hair, she'd erased it. She had a V-pointed chin and hooked nose, and her dark eyes were sharp and confident. She wore a tailored charcoal suit, which looked every bit as expensive as the one Cab was wearing.

Ramona had been extremely successful in two careers. She'd started as a private attorney in one of the state's largest law firms and then made the transition to the rough-and-tumble world of Florida politics. She had money, she had intellect, and she had the courage of her convictions. However, Cab had seen her on television, and he knew that she wasn't a gifted campaigner. She appeared aloof in public. Detached. She relied for her appeal on no-nonsense toughness. Her campaign slogan reflected the kind of person she was: Ramona Cortes for a Strong Florida.

"How's Lala?" she asked.

"She's fine. Busy with an assignment."

"The two of you should visit me in Tallahassee sometime. A pool party around the holidays, maybe. Lala is my favorite cousin, you know."

Cab wondered if Ramona knew that his relationship with Lala was on shaky ground. Among the Cubans he'd met, family was everything, and secrets were few. If Lala had said anything to anyone, it would have sped along the grapevine.

"We should do that," he replied. He added with a smile: "Although won't you be busy running the state by then?"

"That's my plan." Ramona folded her hands neatly in front of her. "You're probably wondering why I wanted this meeting."

"I am."

"I won't beat around the bush, Cab. My sources tell me you've gotten into bed with the Common Way Foundation. Is this true?"

He wondered if Lala had called her. "I'm doing some work for them," he acknowledged.

"What kind of work?"

"Private work," he said.

Ramona studied him across the table. One of her index fingers tapped her other hand as precisely as a metronome. "Actually, I was just being polite. I know exactly what they've asked you to do. You're investigating threats against Diane Fairmont. You're trying to determine whether there might be a link to the Labor Day murders ten years ago."

"You're well informed."

"Does that surprise you?"

"No," Cab admitted.

"Let me tell you what's on my mind. I'd consider it a personal favor if you would resign from this investigation."

"Resign?"

"That's right. Terminate your contract with Common Way."

Before Cab could ask any of the dozens of questions that sprang into his head, Ramona was interrupted by a phone call. She excused herself and took the call, which turned out to be a long conversation. While the attorney general was talking, the waiter returned with bowls of soup and grilled cheese ciabatta sandwiches. Ramona gestured for him to eat, and he did.

He'd finished half his sandwich by the time she got off the phone.

"I'm very sorry."

"That's all right," Cab said.

"I'm sure you have questions, but I can't answer many of them. I'm sorry. You'll have to take it on faith."

Cab took a spoonful of soup. "When a politician asks me to take something on faith, I find myself becoming agnostic."

"I'm a lawyer, too," Ramona said with a ghost of a smile. "Does that help?"

"Even worse."

"Here's what I can tell you. I've been kept apprised of these so-called threats against Diane. The FBI doesn't believe they can substantiate their veracity."

"In other words, it's just a bunch of crackpots."

"That's one possibility," she said. "Another possibility is that people at the Common Way Party have manufactured the threats. They may not be real at all."

"You obviously don't like the people at Common Way," Cab said. "This couldn't have anything to do with the fact that Diane is pummeling you in the polls, could it?"

Ramona took a small bite of her sandwich and dabbed at her lips with the cloth napkin. She ate slowly, like a woman in no hurry. "If you read the papers, you know that the spread in the polls is no more than a few points. Hardly pummeling."

"Even so, I'm surprised you would take the threats lightly, given what happened to Birch Fairmont."

She took his measure, the way a woman sizes up a man. Solid or not solid. Fake or sincere. Deep or shallow. "May I speak confidentially, Cab?"

"By all means," he said.

"I'm sure you know that before I was elected, I was a criminal attorney. I built a statewide reputation by taking on high-profile cases that received a great deal of media attention. That included Hamilton Brock and the Liberty Empire Alliance. Not a case that my political enemies will allow me to forget. Obviously, I won't say anything about the specifics of the legal matters, but I will tell you my personal belief that the threat from the Alliance was overblown in the media. Ogden Bush oversold them as radical domestic terrorists, and he had a specific political purpose in mind—namely, helping the Democrats. However, Brock and his associates were mostly paranoid blowhards who loved guns and spouted off about imaginary government plots. We're talking about plumbers and Realtors. There were some thuggish characters among them perhaps, but not assassins."

Cab thought about Brock in prison. He wasn't convinced that the man was a paper tiger. He also thought about Rufus Twill, with his limp and his one eye. The Alliance wasn't afraid of violence.

"So who killed Birch Fairmont?" Cab asked.

"I have no idea."

"Then why do you assume the same person couldn't be targeting Diane?"

Ramona leaned across the table. "Honestly? Because I believe the Common Way Party would do *anything* to elect Diane Fairmont as governor. Including falsifying threats if it would churn up sympathy among the voters. It's no surprise that they're trotting out the Alliance again, given my own professional history with them. Believe me, Cab, I know these people. I know Diane. Hamilton Brock isn't the only client of mine who was on the wrong side with her. These people are ruthless and dirty, and you shouldn't be working with them. They'll sacrifice you in a minute if it suits their purposes."

Lala had told him the same thing. *You may find yourself in over your head with these people. Even you.* Chuck Warren had used similar language to describe the upstart party. Ruthless. Dirty.

One thing was certain. People were afraid of them.

"It's hard to believe that the Common Way Party could be any worse than what we've been getting from the other two parties for years," Cab said.

"I disagree."

"And you base this on what?"

Ramona shook her head. "I'm afraid I can't say anything about that."

"I've heard suggestions that Diane was somehow responsible for the scandal that enveloped the governor this year," Cab said. "The Common Way people set up his aide. Do you think that's possible?"

"Yes, I do. And believe me, I'm no fan of the governor."

Cab eyed the attorney general with surprise. "That's a serious accusation."

"We're under the cone of silence here. I'm telling you what I believe, not what I can prove. I really don't think that it's a coincidence that the governor found himself kneecapped this year. When the Common Way people face opposition, they mow them down. That's what they've done on policy issues for a decade. They've been shaping a legislature to their views by targeting candidates and destroying those that oppose them. Now it's time for Diane to march in and take over."

"Hamilton Brock called it a coup," Cab said.

"I'm not sure he's wrong about that."

"Do you think they've acted illegally? Or are you just complaining because they're better at the game than you are?"

"I think people complain about the government—as do I—but at least the actions of the government are largely transparent. There are watchdogs everywhere. An organization like Common Way has a huge endowment that allows them to wield influence behind the scenes with virtually no oversight. I think that kind of power offers an extraordinary temptation to cross the lines."

"If you believe that's true, shouldn't you be investigating them?" Cab asked.

"What makes you think I'm not?"

Cab nodded. He put down his napkin on the plate and stood up. "I appreciate the warning."

"Will you do what I asked? Will you quit?"

"No, not yet. Not solely on your say-so. I'm sorry."

Ramona stood up, too. She was a tiny dynamo next to him. "You're making a mistake, Cab."

"I'll tell you what I told them. If I discover that I'm being played, I'm out. Until then, I'm only interested in one thing. Making sure that Diane Fairmont doesn't suffer the same fate as her husband."

The attorney general frowned. "This isn't about being played," she said. "If it were just that, I wouldn't care."

"Then what is it?"

"A foundation employee named Justin Kiel was murdered recently," she told him. "The police concluded that the death was drug-related. I have reason to believe they are wrong."

"Why is that?"

"For the time being, I can't say," Ramona repeated. "I'm just suggesting that you be careful."

Cab shook his head. "I hope you're not implying that Diane is somehow involved in a murder. I don't believe that for a moment. I'm no fan of politicians, but how many of them would really kill to get elected?"

The attorney general sat down again and picked up her sandwich. "More than you think, Cab. More than you think."

18

"Frank Macy," Peach said.

Deacon's fingers stopped clicking on his keyboard. "Who?"

Peach slapped the paper she'd taken from Justin's safe house onto the desk in front of her brother. "This guy. He's got a long record. Drugs. Guns. Manslaughter. For some reason, Justin was interested in him. I'm betting there's a connection to his murder."

Deacon picked up the paper and studied it. "What is this? What does it have to do with Justin?"

"Justin kept a safe house for his computers and papers. Someone ransacked the place, but he missed this. I've been digging into Frank Macy all morning. He got out of jail earlier this year, but he's still in the area. He has an apartment near St. Pete Beach. I'm going to find him."

"Fruity, what the—" Deacon began. He stopped and stood up to look over the tops of the cubicle walls. When he sat down again, his voice was hushed. "Let's not talk about this here."

Her brother led them past the cubicle farm. She could see Ogden Bush's office on the far side of the building; the door was closed. Deacon guided her onto the street outside. It was a hot afternoon, but the wind had come alive, blowing garbage and dust around the pavement, making her blink. He walked quickly, and she struggled to keep up with him. They were in an area of derelict storefronts and barred windows. He led her three blocks to a small urban park that was little more than a square of dead grass and palm trees, with a row of green benches.

Deacon sat down. He was wearing an undersized gray T-shirt, jeans, and dusty boots. He slipped sunglasses over his face and scratched his rust-colored stubble. "Okay, you want to tell me what this is all about?"

"I want to know what really happened to Justin."

"I get that, but why? I know you guys worked together, but I don't understand what you're doing."

She took a breath. She was a private person, even around her brother, but she decided to tell him the truth. "It was more than that."

"What was?" Then Deacon tilted his head back and sighed. "Oh, man. Really? You and Justin?"

"We were in love."

"Hell's bells, why didn't you tell me, Fruity? No wonder you've been so upset."

"It was something just for us," Peach said. "We didn't tell anyone."

"Look, I'm sorry. I really am. I get it now, but I don't want you putting yourself in jeopardy over this. A murder investigation is for the police, not us."

"I can't stop." Peach felt her eyes welling with tears. She crumpled into her brother's shoulder and clung to his arm. The wind blew heat into her face like the open door of an oven. "It's just one more thing, you know? One more thing they took away from me."

He kissed the top of her head. "Yeah, I know."

"I loved Mom and Dad, and they died. I loved Lyle, and he died. I loved Justin, and he died. Maybe it's me."

"It's not you."

"Don't you get lonely without them?" she asked.

"Of course I do."

"I miss Lyle," she said. "With everything going on, all the talk about Labor Day, I've been thinking about him a lot."

"Me too." Deacon chuckled. "Except I also remember what an asshole he was."

"Don't say that!" Peach exclaimed.

"Hey, he's gone, and I'm really sorry, but I'm not going to pretend that he was something other than what he was. He didn't treat us well. Everything else in the world was more important than we were."

"He was responsible for us. That wasn't easy."

"I'm not saying it was, but you didn't see what he was like. You were a kid then, but I wasn't."

Peach frowned. In her heart of hearts, she knew Deacon was right, but she didn't like feeling that way. "No, I saw it," she said softly. "I just don't like to remember him like that."

"I get it. Remember him however you like. Believe me, I think about him every time I get into the Mercedes, but then I think: That car probably meant more to him than either of us did. I know that's harsh."

"Yeah." Peach sniffled.

"Now, you want to tell me what's going on? What have you been up to?"

Peach told him. She told him everything—about her late-night phone call from Curtis Clay, about her narrow escape from Justin's apartment with Annalie's help, about her late-night search of Ogden Bush's office, about her discovery of Justin's safe house, about the article she'd found about Frank Macy. It was a relief to say it out loud. To admit how much it meant to her to find the truth.

"Jesus," he said when she was finally done. "You've been busy."

She expected a lecture. Give it up. Let the police do their job. He didn't bother, because he knew she wouldn't listen.

"This guy in Justin's apartment, the one who claimed to be a cop," he said. "Who is he? Is there any way we can find him?"

Peach shook her head. "I didn't recognize him."

"He *sounds* like a private detective," Deacon said.

"Working for who?"

"I don't know, but I'll pull some state photo records for you to look through. Maybe we can ID him that way." Deacon hesitated, and he didn't look happy. "You know, there's something you have to think about. I know you won't like it."

"What?"

"This could still be all about drugs. Drug cases pull people out of the woodwork. Everybody smells money. This Curtis Clay, he could be hooked up with dealers looking for cash or dope."

"What about the photo I found? What about Frank Macy?"

"You said it yourself," Deacon reminded her. "Macy's got a long track record with drugs. If Justin was involved with someone like that, then it's possible that Macy or one of his allies took him out. I just want you to be prepared if the truth about Justin is something you're not happy with."

Peach was silent. She knew Deacon was right, but she didn't believe it. Then she said: "I need to get close to Macy."

"No way," Deacon said. "Doing research is one thing, but I don't want you going near this guy."

"I'm not going to walk up to him and start asking questions! I listen. Nobody knows I'm around. If I can get close enough, maybe he'll say something. This is humint, this is what I do."

"I know, and you're very good at what you do, but do you think this guy isn't? Don't believe his baby face. Criminals like Macy develop eyes in the back of their head."

"I get it, but I need to know why Justin was interested in him. If it's *not* about drugs, then there's something else. What could it be? Macy's been out of circulation for eight years."

Deacon hesitated. "Okay, look, don't read too much into this."

"Into what? Do you know something about him?"

"It's probably nothing, but I do know that Frank Macy has a connection to Diane. You may not remember. You were still pretty young."

"What's the connection?" Peach asked.

"Do you remember Diane's son, Drew?"

"A little," she said. "I know he killed himself."

Deacon nodded. "I only met Drew a couple times, but Lyle talked about him a lot. He was afraid that Drew's behavior would undermine

Birch's campaign. It's one thing that Birch's stepson had a big drug problem—that's bad enough—but he also hung out in Tampa clubs and got himself photographed in some compromising positions. And with the wrong kind of people."

The wrong kind of people.

"Are you saying Drew knew Frank Macy?" Peach asked.

"Yeah, he did," Deacon said. "Macy liked to hang out with rich kids. He knew how to hook them up with street people. Drew and Macy were together a lot. First in college, then in Tampa and Lake Wales. Macy was Drew's drug dealer."

19

Cab thought he'd become accustomed to the realities of fame, but it still surprised him that he couldn't go anywhere with his mother without her being recognized. Their afternoon at the Bok sanctuary was no different. Tarla wore a white summer dress—loose, sheer but not overtly sexy—with a leather belt tied in a knot at her slim waist. Her blond hair was casual and messy, and she wore big sunglasses and almost no makeup. Even so, people began to whisper as soon as she arrived.

At the welcome desk inside the interpretive center, a hostess in her early sixties finally screwed up the courage to say: "Are you—?"

Tarla smiled. Moments later, she was signing autographs.

He didn't have anything to do while Tarla hobnobbed with her movie fans, so he spent his time examining the displays about Edward Bok, the author and editor who had built the tower and gardens in the late 1920s. It was a supremely lovely, peaceful place, designed to embody Bok's philosophy: "Make you the world a bit better or more beautiful because you have lived in it."

He knew that Tarla had made the world a better place during her stay. Looking at the glow on the faces of those who recognized her, he realized how much she and her movies had touched lives. He doubted that he would ever be able to say the same thing. Never married. No children. Spending his days delving into dark hearts.

~~~~~~'t feel like much of a legacy.

"Well," Tarla said, appearing at his side again, slightly breathless. "That was fun, wasn't it?"

"Yes, someone told me how exciting it was to meet Naomi Watts in person," Cab replied.

"You're so funny, darling. Wicked but funny. You know, one of the women only had eyes for you. I may as well have been invisible."

"Excuse me?"

Tarla inclined her head toward the welcome desk with a flirty flick of her eyebrows. Cab glanced in that direction and saw a woman in denim overalls staring intently at him. When their eyes met, she turned away. He didn't know her, but she was about his age, black and skinny, with reddish cornrowed hair. The red T-shirt under her overalls advertised a local landscaping company.

"She looks quiet, but the quiet ones can surprise you," Tarla said.

"You don't say."

"I do say. I hear that librarians are ferocious in bed, for example."

"Where exactly did you hear that?" Cab asked.

"Oh, it's true. What they lack in uncorrected vision they make up for in voluptuous curiosity."

He knew better than to argue with his mother. He took a last look at the museum desk, where the black woman stared back at him again. Her puffy lips were pressed into a frown. She picked up a water tank as he watched her and headed outside to water the hanging flowers.

Cab offered Tarla his elbow, and she slung her arm through his as they left the welcome center and made their way uphill toward the tower. It was the top of the hour, and he heard carillon bells. The lawns around them were lush and manicured. Spanish moss swayed like a skeleton's arms as a stiff wind rustled the tree branches. Quivering red and pink flowers dotted the bushes. As they climbed, the concrete trail gave way to spongy dirt. Bamboo clusters leaned over the path. Where the ground leveled, they could see the pink stone tower and its elaborate metal grilles on the far side of an algae-laden pond.

They sat on a bench. The bells played a medieval carol. Tarla stared at the tower, which was full of memories for her, and the breezy self-assuredness in her face gave way to something more tentative. She could smile and make jokes, but she didn't want to be here.

"I know this is difficult for you," Cab said.

"More than I expected," Tarla admitted. "I never came back here. After."

"I'm not surprised."

"It's a shame, because this was one of my favorite places as a child. Diane and I spent hours here. There were days in Hollywood where I would sit and think about what was going on at the tower at that very moment. Who was there. What the weather was like. What music might be playing. It got me through tough times, remembering this place."

"Did you ever regret leaving home?" Cab asked.

"You mean, did I ever think about going back to Lake Wales? To my old life? Yes, many times. Even after I'd broken through, I had fantasies of going back. As soon as you leave something behind, you start to think of it as an easier, simpler time. Which it probably was."

"Why did you leave in the first place?"

"Oh, you know me, Cab. I wasn't cut out for small-town life. What would I have done here? I couldn't steal a rich man like Diane. I didn't have it in me. Probably, I would have been one of those women back at the welcome center. I'm sure they're very fulfilled, but me, I would always have been on a low simmer, wishing I'd done something else."

"How did Diane feel about your leaving?"

"She hated it. Hated me. At least for a while. However, when you chase a dream, you know you're giving something up. There's always a price. Your grandmother and I moved west, and a year later, she had a heart attack and died. I was alone. I really had no business making it on my own out there. I should have been ground into nothing. Most wannabes are. I was lucky. I never forget how lucky I was."

Cab frowned. Somehow, it was painful for him to think of his mother alone in Los Angeles, with nothing and no one to rely on for support. Tarla touched his sleeve. When he looked at her, she took his hand.

"May I ask you something, Cab?"

"Of course."

"Am I a bad mother?"

He was aware of the seriousness in her face and her fears over what he would say. "Why on earth would you ask me something like that?"

"Hollywood types are not exactly known for their parenting skills, my dear. We can't all be Brad and Angelina. I dragged you around the world. I threw you into crazy social situations with no preparation. I couldn't help but notice that as soon as you had the opportunity to get away from me, you did."

"I assumed you wanted me to follow in your footsteps," Cab said.

"Guilty," Tarla admitted. "Nepotism is the new black when it comes to actors. You could well have outshined me."

"I wanted to make my own footsteps, not follow yours. I was very much like you in that respect."

"And how is that working out for you?"

"Not altogether well," Cab admitted, smiling. "I guess your shoes are hard to fill."

Tarla laughed. "Mine? Minuscule, compared to yours. Not just those size thirteen feet of yours. Imagine me raising a son who would actually do something worthwhile with his life."

"Do you really mean that?" he asked.

His mother looked at him with genuine surprise. "Are you serious? Of course I mean it."

"Well, thank you," Cab said.

"I apologize if it seems that I'm trying to run your life, darling. I'm afraid it comes with the territory. I could promise to quit, but you wouldn't believe me."

"No, it's fine. As long as you don't mind when I pay no attention."

Tarla grinned. "Sooner or later, I'll wear you down. Which brings me to you and Caprice."

Cab held up his hand. "Enough."

"Well, you can't blame me for trying." She stood up and squared her shoulders. She waited as he got off the bench, too, and then added: "So are you planning to stay in Florida?"

"I guess I am," Cab said. "I'm not sure I'll stay with the police, but I need a home base. This is actually a lovely place. And, as much as it pains me to admit it, I sort of like having you close by."

"Well, you charmer you," Tarla said. "Come on, let's do this."

"Are you ready?"

"As ready as I will be."

They made their way to the tower, through the clutch of vines, past the webs of huge spiders, and finally broke onto the wide-open crest of the hillside. The bells above them had gone silent. The wind was loud and strong, like an ocean wave. He could see orange groves lining the land below them. That was where the killer had come from, an assassin in black marching through a cloud of citrus.

A wide path led from the tower itself, with soaring trees on either side, and ended in a broad swath of green lawn. "This is where they built the dais," Tarla said. "Diane and I were the first to be seated. She wasn't feeling well."

"Why not?"

Tarla shook her head. "I don't know. She didn't say."

"What about the assassin?"

"Nobody knew where he came from. However, we all knew what would happen when we saw him there. You could have asked anyone in the crowd. We knew people were going to die."

"Did he say anything?" Cab asked.

"No."

"Did anyone talk to him?"

"Birch swore at him before he was shot. Other than that, there was simply screaming."

"What did Diane do?"

"Diane? Nothing that I remember. She was frozen. In shock."

"Before the assassin shot Lyle, he turned toward Diane. You stood up and protected her."

Tarla sighed. "I told you, I don't remember that."

"You're here now. You've never been back before. Close your eyes."

She did, reluctantly. "Sorry, Cab, I don't—"

"Don't talk."

Tarla looked like a ghost, all in white with the wind mussing her blond hair. She inhaled, swelling her chest. The fabric of her dress fluttered. The two of them were alone, and except for the hillside breeze, the world was silent. No voices. No music. Sometimes it worked that way; sometimes the past could speak, if you invited it. He waited for her, and a minute passed, and then two minutes.

"I don't remember him," Tarla said, "but I remember what I felt."

"What was that?"

"I remember thinking he was an ordinary man. How odd that was. I was taller than him. He just didn't seem like—I don't know."

"A soldier?" Cab said softly.

Tarla opened her eyes. "No, he certainly didn't seem like a soldier."

"Do you remember anything else?"

"I'm afraid not."

"I wonder if you felt like you knew him," Cab said.

Tarla's face grew sharp. "Knew him? What are you talking about?"

"Is it possible he wasn't a stranger?"

"He was wearing a hood," she said. "And how could it be anyone I knew? Who would do something like this?"

Cab debated whether to say anything at all. Then he said: "Could it have been Drew?"

She reacted angrily. "Drew? That's ridiculous, Cab! No, it wasn't Drew."

"Someone overheard him threatening Birch shortly before Labor Day. He said he would kill him. Blow his head off."

"I don't care what he said. Drew did not do this. He was in the pool at home when we left."

"He could have gotten out of the pool."

"And driven there how? Do you think Diane left him with car keys? He was just out of rehab. He wasn't going anywhere."

She seemed certain of the truth, and he had to admit there was logic to what she said. He assumed that the FBI would have confirmed Drew's whereabouts as a standard check-a-box during their investigation. Even so, he wondered. Something made sense to him about Drew pulling the trigger. The whole affair felt personal.

Murder, not assassination.

"Why would Drew have threatened to kill Birch?" he asked.

"He was troubled, Cab. He was an addict. That doesn't make him a killer. He wasn't the type."

"No one ever seems like the type."

"I knew Drew. You didn't. I don't know why you're wasting your time with this, Cab. If you're trying to protect Diane, why aren't you back in Tampa? Whatever happened here was in the past. It's over, it's done. Why do you insist on reliving it?"

"Maybe because everyone tells me not to," Cab said.

"Yes, you're stubborn. I get it. You're my son. Just please tell me you didn't raise this nonsense with Diane."

"I asked where Drew was that night. That's all."

"And you don't think she's smart enough to leap from A to B? Cab, you disappoint me. She deserves better from you than foolish accusations. Let it go."

Cab felt slapped. He knew that when Tarla was asked to go places she didn't want to go, she blustered and got angry. He didn't know why the next words popped into his head. Maybe he just wanted to hurt his mother.

"We slept together," he told her.

Tarla stared at him. "What? Who?"

"Diane and I. That summer. We slept together. Once. I left the next day."

He did something he'd thought was impossible. He left his mother speechless. She opened her mouth, and it was as if she were staring at a blank cue card. She said nothing at all. The color drained from her beautiful face. This wasn't hurt; this was something much more profound. He'd damaged her in a way he couldn't comprehend.

She folded her arms across her chest. Head down, she stalked away from him.

"Wait," he called after her.

Tarla didn't stop.

"Let's talk about this."

His mother never looked back. She hurried down the trail to the tower and continued past it, where the downhill path swallowed her. She disappeared, and she wasn't coming back to him. He knew that.

He stared after her, utterly devastated.

It was an hour before Cab summoned the strength to leave the gardens. The clouds made it look darker and later than it was, but it was already early evening. He felt a hollowness in his stomach as he headed for his car.

"Mr. Bolton?"

Cab was outside the gates when he heard the voice behind him. He turned. The black woman in overalls who had been staring at him when they arrived hovered near the bushes. She spoke softly, as if hesitant about approaching him. Her fingers played with her cornrows.

"Yes?" he said.

"You are Cab Bolton, aren't you? You're a detective."

"I am."

"My name is Gladiola Croft. Rufus Twill told me about you. He said you were looking into what happened here. He and I, we know each other pretty well. I told him things."

"Things?" Cab asked.

"I used to work in Birch Fairmont's house," she said. "I was there that summer. Those murders? They didn't surprise me none. That man deserved what he got."

20

The waitress at the Starfish Grill in St. Pete Beach had the largest breasts that Peach had ever seen. They were like muskmelons over-flowing in brown flesh out of a low-cut orange T-shirt that was tight enough to be body paint. When the girl, who called herself Steffi, bent over her to put an O'Doul's on a salted napkin, Peach was pretty sure she could see all the way to China at the bottom of her cleavage.

"Fire wings'll be right out," Steffi told her with a toss of her blond hair. "You want anything else?"

Peach was distracted. "Uh, no, thanks."

"They're super big, huh?"

"What?"

Steffi pointed to the indie-rock magazine overturned on the table in front of Peach. The Dutch band Rats on Rafts was featured on the cover.

"Oh," Peach said, fighting the flush that crept onto her face. "Oh, yeah."

Steffi winked. She knew what Peach was thinking. "I love them. That what you're listening to?"

A headphone wire snaked from under the magazine and wound its way to Peach's ear. "No, Skynyrd."

"Hey, classic," Steffi said.

Peach nudged the magazine closer as the waitress disappeared. She wasn't listening to Skynyrd. The headphone was connected to a shotgun spy microphone and voice recorder hidden under the open pages. The microphone, pointed at a table nearest the white beach, amplified the conversation that Frank Macy was having with another man and two girls who didn't look much older than Peach. Frank and his male friend had pints of Guinness in front of them. The girls didn't look old enough to be drinking anything other than strawberry lemonade.

So far, they were talking about *Cosmopolitan* magazine and threesomes. Yuck.

Peach sipped her O'Doul's. She didn't drink, but she blended in readily enough at a beachside bar with a nonalcoholic beer in front of her. She'd taken her outfit from Harley Mannequin. Spiky black wig, streaked with red and blue. White *Road Warrior* tank top. Jean shorts with an oversized "American Rebel" belt buckle and fishnets down her legs. Black studded boots. She'd added thick blue eye shadow, a nose ring, and a fake tattoo of chains and flames on her forearm.

The bar was half a block from Gulf Boulevard at the southern end of the peninsula between the Gulf and Tampa Bay. Steps away, waves roared over the sand, crashing in foam. The patio umbrellas rattled and flapped in the wind. So did the palm trees. There was no sun, only layer after layer of dark clouds. On the beach, surfers rode in on the swells, and teenage girls had their hair swirled into birds' nests. The dust of blown sand coated everything, including her tongue.

"*One of my buddies has a place on the beach,*" Macy said. "*I think we should take the party there.*"

"*Does he have a hot tub?*" one of the girls asked.

"*Hey, it's a zoning requirement to have a hot tub when you live on the beach. Didn't you know that?*"

His joke was greeted with giggles. Frank Macy was a hit with the young girls. Macy, sexy and suave, looked like a male model. Wavy hair, long and deliberately greasy. A plain white tee under an unbuttoned checked short-sleeved shirt. Red European pants. Weirdly smart, innocent eyes. His companion, who was Asian and had mostly avoided the conversation, was tougher and less sophisticated. Muscle shirt. Tattoos. Wild, ragged hair with a shaved railroad track.

"*I bet my colleague here can get us all happy and relaxed,*" Macy said.

The Asian man didn't smile. He drank his beer, and his eyes were stone.

Peach spotted a familiar face near the entrance to the bar. Annalie Martine scanned the tables, eyeing the crowd, which was mostly swimmers with wet towels slung over the backs of the wooden chairs, and beach hipsters with dirty hair and chains. She hunted for Peach but didn't find her. Harley Mannequin had done her job.

Peach's phone vibrated on the table. She saw a text message.

Okay, I give up. Where are you?

Peach grinned and wiggled her fingers at Annalie across the bar. Her new friend picked her way through the tables, watched by most of the men, including Frank Macy. Annalie's hair was loose again. She was dressed in black, but her golden legs were shapely below the fringe of her Lycra shorts. Her biking shirt was a zipped sleeveless jersey. She wore fluorescent sneakers. She had a leather handbag, which she draped over the chair.

"One of these days, I'll spot you before you spot me," Annalie said. There was a burble of noise hanging over the bar, but Annalie kept her voice low. Only Peach could hear her.

"If you do, I'm slipping," Peach said.

Steffi thrust her immense breasts between them. Annalie ordered a Corona with lime.

"Wow, those things have to hurt," Annalie said as the waitress headed for the taps. She cast a dubious eye around the bar. "I didn't figure you for a boob 'n' lube kind of place. Big busts and tight short-shorts? Why are we here?"

"Work, not play," Peach said.

Annalie noted the overturned magazine and the wire feeding into Peach's ear. "So who are you after?"

Peach fingered the charm that dangled around Annalie's neck and smiled as if she were commenting on it. "Table nearest the sand, two guys, two teenagers."

Annalie cupped the charm in her palm. Her eyes swept the beach without her head turning toward the water. "The cute one or the nasty one?"

"The cute one."

"Who is he?"

"His name is Frank Macy," Peach said.

She explained what she'd found at the safe house and shared a folder on Macy for Annalie to study. While Annalie reviewed the research, Steffi brought a bottle of Corona, with a lime wedge stuffed in the neck, and a basket of spicy chicken wings. Annalie squeezed the lime inside and upended the bottle with her thumb over the top. She finished reading the snippet of the article about Macy shown in the photograph, and like Deacon, she didn't look happy.

"I know guys like him," Annalie said. "They float from suburban cocaine parties to downtown immigrant trafficking. A sweet face doesn't mean a thing. I've known sweet faces to pour boiling water down the throats of their competitors. Don't mess with him."

"I'm not messing. Just spying."

"What's he saying?" she asked, drinking from her bottle of Corona, slim fingers around its neck.

Peach listened.

"*Now that is a hot, hot woman,*" Macy told the table. He meant Annalie.

"*She's old,*" one of the girls protested. "*She must be thirty.*"

"*Are you kidding? You can tell by the shape of her mouth. She's born to give blow jobs.*"

"He likes your smile," Peach said.

"Nice. Exactly what are you hoping for? Do you think he's going to confess to Justin's murder between bites of fried pickles?"

"Maybe."

Annalie bit into a chicken wing and licked around her lips with her tongue. "I checked the reports on Justin's death. He was found at a dump of a motel next to the dog track, right? Three bullets in the head, execution-style. The police searched the room and found a brick of cocaine and ten thousand dollars squirreled away inside the guts of the microwave."

"I know."

"And now you're watching a known drug dealer."

"A drug dealer with ties to Ramona Cortes. And Diane and her son."

"Drugs are still the common denominator," Annalie said. "Are you sure Justin didn't have his fingers in the wrong pie?"

Peach opened her mouth to snap at Annalie, but she controlled herself. "Well, that's why I'm here. I need to know what Justin wanted with Macy. I don't care where it leads. I just want the truth."

"Even if the truth is what everyone says?" Annalie asked softly.

"Yeah, even that," Peach replied. She couldn't resist adding: "But it's not."

An hour passed slowly at the bar. Peach drank her O'Doul's. Annalie drank her Corona. When they were done, they ordered two more, and when they finished the wings, they ordered quesadillas. She kept listening and recording Macy's conversation, but he stuck to rappers, nightclubs, and sexual positions. He had nothing to say about politics, or Justin, or Diane Fairmont, and his hints at drugs were aimed at the girls. Annalie was right; he was too smart to say anything incriminating in public.

The beer was nonalcoholic, so maybe it was the wind and heat that made Peach feel buzzed. She and Annalie laughed and told jokes. She realized that she liked this woman, as different as they were. She felt comfortable around her. She didn't feel that way about many people. Hardly anyone, in fact.

Not knowing why she said it, she asked: "Do you think I'm weird?"

Annalie scrunched her forehead, but nothing she did made her less pretty. "Why would I think that?"

"I wear disguises. I'm a voyeur. I'm always listening to other people's business."

"It's your job."

"Well, yeah, but I'd probably do it anyway," Peach admitted.

"Still not really weird," Annalie said.

"I have mannequins at home. I collect them."

"Male or female?"

"Uh, female. I name them, too."

"Do you talk to them?" Annalie asked, grinning.

"No. Well, not in a long time."

"That's a little weird, but still pretty low on the scale. Do they talk to you?"

"No."

"Then you're good."

"There's more. I'm weird about sex, too."

Annalie smirked. "Do tell."

"I decided a long time ago that I wanted to be celibate."

"Okay. Not what I was expecting, but okay."

"I thought about it with Justin, but we never did."

"Well, it doesn't sound weird to me," Annalie said. "It sounds sweet. Someday you may feel differently, but until then, do what you want. Or don't do what you want."

"You have sex, right?" When Annalie hesitated, Peach added: "Sorry, I'm being too personal. I'm not good with boundaries."

"Don't worry about it. I'm not celibate, but I'm pretty conservative. I don't go jumping into bed. I have to be awfully close to a guy, and that hasn't happened a lot."

"Is it worth it? It seems like sex causes nothing but problems."

"You're right about that," Annalie said.

Their conversation was interrupted. Near the beach, the two teenagers at Frank Macy's table got up, grabbing purses, headed for the bathroom. When Macy was alone with his Asian companion, he leaned closer, whispering, and Peach tried to adjust the microphone. At the same moment, the wind gusted, blasting static into her ear. She scowled, because the conversation became mostly inaudible.

She thought she heard the word "gun."

And two words that sounded like: "Picnic Island."

The waitress, Steffi, appeared next to Macy with the check, and she murmured in his ear. He copped a discreet feel on her ass and gave her what looked like a hundred-dollar bill. Peach expected him to insert it in her cleavage. Macy and the Asian sauntered through the bar, passing so close to their table that she could smell his coconut body wash, and he gave Annalie an alluring, pretty-boy wink. He didn't seem to notice Peach.

"Did you get any of that?" Annalie asked when they were gone.

Peach rewound the recording. The words weren't any clearer the second, third, or fourth times. She told Annalie what she thought she'd heard, but she wasn't sure she was right, and she didn't know what any of it meant.

Annalie listened, too. "I can't make out a thing."

"No," Peach said unhappily.

They waited five minutes, then paid their own bill and exited the bar into the narrow parking lot. The dead-end street beside them led to a walkway across the grassy dunes and down to the beach. Peach wasn't parked in the restaurant lot, but in a more deserted lot on the other side of the street.

Annalie got into her Corolla. "See you tomorrow."

"Yeah, see you," Peach said. "And thanks."

She watched Annalie head toward Gulf Boulevard. She crossed the street, which was furrowed with cracked asphalt. The wind felt as if it would lift her off her feet. She walked with her head down, feeling oddly depressed. Her Thunderbird was near a Dumpster at the back of the lot. She came around the driver's side and swung the door open.

Like fireworks, the base of her skull erupted in pain and light.

She felt herself flying—thrown across the interior of the car—her face colliding with the passenger window, like a brick against her forehead. Her head ricocheted with a blinding jolt of pain, and then something heavy landed on her back, squeezing air out of her lungs. A fist grabbed her shoulder like a vise and spun her over. She gasped for breath.

Frank Macy was on top of her, in her face. She tasted blood in her mouth. When she blinked, she had double vision, seeing two of him. He looked as casually sexy as a lifeguard as he choked her with one hand and pressed the blade of a knife against her windpipe with the other.

"So who are you, little girl?" he demanded. "And why are you watching me?"

Her mouth moved, but no words came out. His hand came away from her throat, and she could suck in air. His fingers dug in her pockets, front and back. He opened the glove compartment. He grabbed her purse and spotted the voice recorder, phone, and microphone inside.

"You're not police," he said. "Who are you?"

He pricked her with the knife, breaking skin, drawing blood. Any deeper, and he would slice her throat open. She felt saliva and acid welling in her mouth.

"I need answers, little girl. You've got two seconds, or I slit that pretty neck."

He eased the pressure of the blade a tiny fraction, and she gagged and coughed. Sweat made her whole body wet. Tears leached from her eyes. She was going to tell him anything he wanted. Everything. She knew she would die anyway; he would suck out the truth, and then he would thrust in the knife. She felt dizzy with pain and terror; she saw flashes of bright color, like the afterimage of the sun. Her brain throbbed in and out with her heartbeat.

"I work for Diane Fairmont," she gasped.

Macy's face twisted in surprise. "Fairmont? Is that really true?"

She nodded, and he laughed. He actually laughed. His teeth were perfect. "All these years, and she's still scared of me."

Peach said nothing.

"You know what?" Macy went on. He nuzzled her ear. "*She should be.*"

His hand pawed her the way a lover's would. He massaged her breasts as if he expected to arouse her. She squeezed her eyes shut. He pulled at her clothes, separating the seams, exposing her. He found her belt buckle and popped it. Her zipper snickered down. Instinctively, she pressed her legs together. He was lean, but he was too strong for her. She tried to send her mind far away, but her mind had nowhere to go. His breath was sweet; he'd taken mints before assaulting her.

Someone screamed. It wasn't her own voice.

"*Let her go! Get off her!*"

Someone wrenched open the passenger door. Peach's torso spilled backward, and a hand caught her before she fell. She was conscious of Frank Macy rearing back, head banging on the hood as he ducked out of the other side of the car. Someone dragged her into the hot dusk, and in the swirling of pain and wind and color, she realized it was Annalie.

Annalie, holding her, propping her up.

Annalie, holding a gun that was trained on Frank Macy's face.

She heard the squeal of car tires. A black Lexus roared, appearing behind Macy. The driver's window was open, and Peach saw the Asian man from the bar, beckoning to Macy, a gun in his own hand. The two teenagers were in the backseat, looking terrified. It was a standoff. Annalie didn't fire. The Asian man didn't fire. Macy took a tentative step backward, grinned, then opened the rear door of the Lexus and dove inside.

The car tore off toward the strip of road that fronted the Gulf.

The screech of tires faded. They were alone, the two of them, Annalie murmuring at her—*are you okay, are you okay, are you okay.* She still held the gun. Somewhere behind them, the surf sounded angry and loud.

Peach's entire body turned to rubber. She felt herself melting, drowning in an ocean of relief. She let out a huge sob and collapsed into Annalie's arms.

21

Gladiola Croft lived in the poor section of Lake Wales, in the shadow of the water tower. The houses looked like army barracks, all of them the same square one-story design and the same buff-and-brown color, like watery puke. She didn't invite him inside. There were two lawn chairs by the front door, and he sat in one of them, hoping the fraying vinyl straps would hold him. A cracked flowerpot sat on the window ledge.

"You want some sweet tea?" she asked.

"I do."

She disappeared into the small house, letting out the electronic noise of a video game being played inside. Teenagers on the steps of the next row house eyed him, his suit, and his Corvette. Telephone wires criss-crossed over his head, and dark clouds ran across the evening sky.

Gladiola returned, two ice-filled plastic glasses in her hand. He took the wet glass and drank a swallow. "Excellent," he said.

She squinted as the wind blew dust in her face. "They say Chayla's gonna be bad."

"Yes."

"Wouldn't be too sorry to see this place blow away, but it's all we got."

"I understand."

She gave him a look that told him she really didn't think he understood at all. It was the look that someone with no money gave someone who had plenty. He was familiar with it, and he didn't feel guilty anymore. Life was a lottery. There were losing tickets and winning tickets.

"How do you know Rufus Twill?" Cab asked.

"He's my uncle."

Cab was surprised, but he could see the family resemblance when he looked at her face. "Did Rufus grow up around here?"

"Yeah, but he got out, went to college. Mama always said Uncle Rufus was smart. Sly smart, somebody who knew the score. He did well for himself, writin' stories that got politicians into trouble. Least until he let those boys get the drop on him. They messed him up."

"He says he plays the piano now. Have you heard him?"

Gladiola smiled. "Yeah, he ain't bad. Not as good as he thinks he is, but he ain't bad."

Cab wondered if people said the same thing about him. "Rufus told me he had a source who overheard Diane's son, Drew, threatening Birch Fairmont. Was that you?"

"Yeah, that was me."

"He said you took it back later."

"I did that, you're right. I didn't want to get anybody into trouble."

"So which is it?" Cab asked. "Which story was true?"

"Drew, he said it. Yes, he did. Big as life. Mr. Birch weren't there, though. It was just Drew and his mama and Mr. Muscles."

Cab cocked his head. "I'm sorry?"

"The massage guy. He was always there."

"Oh, Garth Oakes."

"Yeah, that's him. Not so bad to look at, I guess. I mean, you're a lot easier on the eyes than him, but the man did fill out a T-shirt."

"Garth was always there?"

"Oh, yeah. Some people like to rub shoulders with rich folks. Makes 'em feel special, I guess."

"What about you, Gladiola? Why were you there?"

"That's my job. Was. I came three times a week to clean the house. Started when I was sixteen."

Gladiola lit a cigarette. The wind took the smoke as soon as it escaped her lips. She was younger than Cab had first thought—maybe thirty—but she had a tired face. Her body was bony and small. As they sat in the lawn chairs, she kicked off her flat shoes and stretched her toes. She'd ditched her overalls inside, and she now wore plain cotton shorts below her red T-shirt.

Cab heard juvenile shouting inside the small house. "You have kids?" he asked.

"Ya think? I got three." Gladiola reached back and pounded on the door. "Hey, knock it off! Don't make me come in there!"

"What do they do when you're at work?"

"They go to school, and that's where their asses gonna stay. My sister watches 'em after. She's got three of her own."

"How long have you worked at the landscaping company?"

"A few years. When Ms. Fairmont moved to Tampa, I decided I was sick of scrubbing toilets and figured I'd do something else."

Cab finished his tea and put the plastic glass on the sidewalk next to his chair. He heard a bark and saw a wire-haired fox terrier scramble around the corner of the house. The dog eyed him suspiciously but then curled up next to Gladiola's legs. Its tongue lolled as it panted in the heat. The dog tentatively licked the side of Cab's damp glass, then knocked it over and dug a nose inside for the ice.

"So you spent a lot of time in the Fairmont house?" Cab asked.

"Sure did."

"What was it like?"

She pursed her big lips. "Weren't a real happy place."

"How so?"

"Nobody got along. Not Mr. Birch and his wife. Not Mr. Birch and her son. It was a marriage for show. I always had two bedrooms to clean, know what I mean?" She reached down and scratched the dog's head. "Didn't help that Mr. Birch was a first-class pussy hound. Liked to rub up against anything with tits and an ass."

"Did that include you?"

She swallowed tea and wiped her mouth. "Yeah, he grabbed what he could when nobody was looking. I didn't like it, but I didn't want to get fired. I never let him poke me, if that's what you're saying."

"Did Diane know what he was like?"

"Wives always know," Gladiola said.

Cab thought about himself and Diane. He wondered if husbands knew when the shoe was on the other foot. "Rufus said there was some kind of problem at the estate that summer."

Gladiola nodded.

"When was this?" Cab asked.

"Guess it was a couple weeks before Labor Day."

"And what happened?"

"It's not like I know the details," Gladiola said. "I wasn't in the room."

"You know something."

She played with her hair. Her eyes were tired. "It was a Saturday night. Ms. Fairmont had some kind of brunch thing on Sunday, so I was cleaning. The house was quiet. Most nights that summer, it was like a train station, people everywhere, 'cause of the campaign. But there was some money thing over in Tampa, and most of the campaign folks were there."

"So who was in the house?" Cab asked.

"Guess it was me and Mr. Birch and Ms. Fairmont. And the muscle man."

"Garth was there?"

"Oh, yeah. Like I said, he was always there."

"What about Drew?"

She shook her head. "He was off partying. Drinking. Drugs. Whatever he did in those days."

"So what happened?" he asked again.

"I was in the dining room, and I heard shouting. Real loud. Real angry. Mr. Birch and his wife, they were upstairs, and they were going at it."

"What were they saying?"

"Couldn't hear that. All I heard were their voices thumping in the walls. Must have been, I don't know, fifteen or twenty minutes. Then—"

"Then what?" Cab asked.

Gladiola eyed him and gave a little shiver. "Screaming."

"What was going on?" he asked.

"Weren't too hard to guess. Mr. Birch was walloping on his wife. It was something bad."

"What did you do?"

"I froze," she said. "I don't know how long it lasted, but then it went god-awful quiet. Few minutes later, Mr. Muscles came in, looking all white, told me to get the hell out, not to say a word to nobody. That's what I did."

"Did you tell anyone?" Cab asked.

"Nope."

"When were you next in the house?"

"Couple days, I guess. There weren't no brunch. They canceled it. I came around my usual day, and it was like nothing had happened. Ms. Fairmont went out of her way to say everything was fine. She didn't look fine, though. I mean, she sat in a chair and didn't get up once while I was there. In her bedroom, too, the sheets weren't the same. I always changed the sheets, but this time, somebody else did. Like I don't know, maybe there was something on them they didn't want nobody to see."

"Like what?"

"Like blood maybe."

Cab frowned. "What about Drew?"

"He stormed in while I was there. Practically foaming at the mouth. High as a kite, swearing up and down about what a bastard Mr. Birch was, how he was gonna blow his fucking head off. They got me out of there fast, but I heard what I heard. Oh, yeah."

"Except later you said you didn't," Cab said.

Gladiola looked nervously at her bare feet. "Like I said, why make trouble for people?"

"Did they pay you?"

"What?"

"Did they pay you not to say anything?"

Her lips scrunched up. "Yeah."

"Who paid?" Cab asked.

"Ms. Fairmont. After the murders, when all the police were nosing around."

"How much?"

"Thousand bucks. I shut my mouth fast."

Cab thought about it. The bribe may have been an innocent mistake on Diane's part. She was protecting her son from police scrutiny and a media frenzy. Even if Drew wasn't involved in the murders, the suspicion would have destroyed him. She was probably thinking about her fundraising efforts for the Common Way Foundation, too. A wife beater didn't make much of a martyr.

Diane was already becoming a very practical politician.

"And yet here you are," Cab said.

"Say what?"

"You're talking. Telling me what happened. Why?"

"Rufus said you was a detective," Gladiola said. "Figured somebody should know about this."

"Ten years later, you suddenly decide to spill your guts? While Diane Fairmont is in the middle of a campaign for governor? I find the timing of your crisis of conscience very convenient, Gladiola. Did you go to Diane looking for more money? Did she say no?"

Her face flashed with anger. "I didn't do that!"

"What about your uncle? Did Rufus give you money?"

She slapped the aluminum frame of the lawn chair, and the fox terrier yelped and bolted. "So what if he did? Rufus helps me out sometimes when he can. I got nothing!"

"So what will I find if I go inside? A new flat-screen? An Xbox?"

Gladiola said nothing, but he knew he was right.

"I like that brand-new airboat your uncle had, too," Cab went on. "Did Rufus think I wouldn't notice that?"

He stood up and smoothed his tie and slipped sunglasses over his face again, although it was nearly dark. "I really don't like people playing games with me, Gladiola. Rufus sent you after me like a drone strike. He and his friends are out to embarrass Diane Fairmont. Tell him I won't do his dirty work for him."

He headed for his Corvette across the mostly dead lawn.

"I wasn't lying!" Gladiola shouted after him, her voice a loud screech. "It happened just like I said."

He didn't look back. He jangled his keys on his finger.

"Ain't no game either," she went on, even louder. "You watch yourself, huh? That first boy, they killed him."

Cab stopped in his tracks. He pulled off his sunglasses. He slid his keys into his pocket, spun on his heels, and marched back up to Gladiola. She was small but defiant, staring up at him from the lawn chair.

"What did you say?" he asked.

"You heard me."

"Did you tell your story to someone else?"

"Sure did. 'Bout a month ago. Boy was asking questions about Mr. Fairmont and that last summer, just like you. I told him 'bout that weekend and what happened. He was real excited, he was. Said it could be something important. Now he's dead." She put a finger to her head and pulled the trigger.

"Who was he? What was his name?"

Gladiola folded her arms across her chest, and her jaw jutted out insolently on her face. "Twenty bucks. 'Cause you thought I was lying."

Cab took out his wallet and retrieved a fifty-dollar bill. He opened her hand, put it inside, and closed her warm fingers over it. He didn't say a word, but his eyebrows arched in anticipation.

Gladiola smirked, looking pleased with herself.

"Weird-looking boy," she said. "Funny little round hat and one of those curly mustaches. Said his name was Justin."

22

Peach waited with Annalie while she recovered from the assault by Frank Macy. The fear eased, and so did the nausea. Annalie disinfected the cut on her forehead. She was still in pain—her muscles ached, and her head throbbed—but now that she was safe, she wanted to be alone. Annalie, who'd come back after spotting a man in a red Cutlass staking out the parking lot, offered to stay with her. It took Peach until it was almost dark to convince her that she was fine.

When she headed north on Gulf Boulevard in her Thunderbird, she noticed Annalie following in her Corolla, all the way to the eastbound turnoff at Walsingham Road. Typically, Peach would have turned there, too, on her way back to Lake Seminole Park, but she didn't want to be followed anymore, and she wasn't ready to go home.

She kept driving through Indian Rocks Beach and finally turned east. She was still dizzy, and the pain got worse as she drove. Twenty minutes later, she found herself on the Frankenstein bridge headed back to Tampa. It was dark by the time she reached the city streets. The car, almost without her guiding it, took her to Diane Fairmont's estate. The dark water of the bay was on her left. Across the street, the house was invisible behind the wall and the overgrown trees.

She got out of the car. Her skin was bruised and tender. She crossed Bayshore, and it never even occurred to her to walk down the side street to the main gate. Instead, she pushed into the brush and found a gnarled oak whose branches hung over the wall. Like a monkey, she climbed, swinging her legs onto the lowest branch and pulling herself up, setting off a loud exodus of birds. Twelve feet above the ground, she found a limb sturdy enough to support her weight, and she inched along the bough with the wall below her. When she was clear, she let her body dangle, and then she dropped. The ground was soft.

There were no sirens or alarms. No running feet. She beat away the mosquitoes and stamped through the bushes until she reached the open grass. Garden lights sparkled like fairies. She heard the splashing water of a fountain. Something loud snuffled near the ground— a raccoon, which watched her with glowing eyes and a hunched back. Everything else around her was pitch black. The estate was fifty yards away, and Peach headed for the marble steps.

She rang the bell and heard rich Westminster chimes inside. A minute passed, and someone opened the door cautiously. She recognized Garth Oakes, who had his hand inside a coat, as if reaching for a gun. His clothes barely contained his muscles. His eyes pored over her and then narrowed with recognition.

"You're Deacon's sister, aren't you? What the hell are you doing here?"

"I want to see Ms. Fairmont."

"How'd you get inside?"

She didn't answer. Garth let her in, and she kicked off her shoes, rather than track mud along the hardwood floor. She felt small and dirty in her torn clothes. He led her to a corner room, brightly lit, with piano music playing softly from hidden speakers. A wall of windows looked out on the gardens, but the exterior was dark. Diane Fairmont was inside. So was Caprice. They sat on opposite sides of a round table with laptops in front of both of them.

Caprice assessed her condition with a single glance and got to her feet.

"Peach, what happened to you? Are you okay?"

Diane remained seated. She had half glasses on her face, and she studied Peach from over the tops of the frames as if she were looking at a homeless waif who had dropped into her parlor. Peach realized what she must look like in her bedraggled disguise. She tried to talk and couldn't. She felt overwhelmed. It had seemed so important to be here, and now she had no idea what to say.

"You're hurt," Caprice went on. "What's going on? Does Deacon know you're here?"

Peach shook her head mutely.

Garth and Diane traded looks across the room. "You want me to get her out of here?" he asked.

Caprice interrupted sharply. "Don't be stupid, Garth. This girl works for me. Peach, do you want to sit down?"

"No," she said finally. Looking around the elegant room, she decided that she didn't belong here. "No, he's right. I'll go. I don't know why I came."

"Something happened to you. What is it?"

"I just wanted to ask Ms. Fairmont something," she stuttered. She looked at Diane and found the question spilling out of her. "I wanted to know if Justin was working on a project for you when he was killed."

Peach didn't know what she expected. She didn't know what Diane would say. She had no idea how much it would hurt when Diane looked at her blankly and said, "Who?"

She didn't know who Justin was. He'd worked for her, he'd lived, he'd died, and he was still a stranger to her. To Peach, it was as bad as a slap in the face.

"Justin was part of our research group," Caprice explained softly. "He was killed recently. The police suspected drug trafficking was involved."

Diane's face tightened, as if blood and air had been sucked from her cheeks, and her eyes grew hard. "If he sold drugs, he's no loss to this world," she snapped, her voice bitter.

"They're wrong about him," Peach said. "I think his death had something to do with a man you know. Frank Macy."

Peach wasn't prepared for Diane's reaction. The woman shut the cover of her laptop so hard that it sounded like the crack of a gunshot. Her entire body shook with fury as she jabbed her finger at Peach. "*Frank Macy?* How dare you say that name to me? Do you know what that man did to me? To my son?"

Peach felt staggered. She wanted to turn and run. "He said you should be afraid of him. I thought I needed to tell—"

Diane slashed the air with her hand, cutting Peach off. Her face red, she stormed past Peach and left the room without a word. Like a servant, Garth followed on her heels. Peach and Caprice were alone. The piano music kept playing, oddly peaceful in the aftermath of Diane's outburst.

"I'm sorry," Peach murmured.

Caprice put an arm around her shoulder. "Frank Macy is a sensitive subject with Diane. You probably don't know about her son—"

"I do. I know."

"Then you can understand how she feels. And why drug dealers get no sympathy from her."

"Justin wasn't a drug dealer," Peach said. "I don't know what he had to do with Macy, but it wasn't drugs."

"Well, regardless, Macy is someone to stay away from, Peach. It's for your own safety, but it's for the campaign, too. You know how the media works. They'll grab things and turn them into stories. We can't have that."

"No."

"Should I call Deacon?" Caprice asked. "He can come get you."

"No, I can drive."

"Are you sure? You don't look good."

"I'm sure."

Caprice kept a protective arm around Peach's shoulder as she led her back to the hallway. At the door, Caprice followed her onto the porch. Peach stared into the gardens and found she was reluctant to go. Not yet. Not now. Reading her mind, Caprice gestured at a wrought-iron bench near the pond, and they both sat there, feeling the mist of the fountain. The breeze rustled Caprice's hair. Peach thought she was one

of the prettiest women she'd ever met. It was easy to understand why
Lyle had wanted to marry her.

"How are you, really, Peach?" Caprice asked. "We don't get much
chance to talk anymore. I feel bad about that."

"I'm okay. Lonely sometimes."

"After the campaign, I'll try to do better. I miss you. I see Deacon,
but not you."

"I know you're busy."

Peach knew that Caprice felt responsible for her. It wasn't her job,
but it was nice that she felt that way. If she and Lyle had married,
Caprice would have been her sister-in-law, but Lyle had wanted Peach
to think of Caprice as part-sister, part-mother, part-friend. She appreciated everything Caprice had done for her over the years, but she'd
never felt quite that close to her. Deacon was the one who had drunk
the Kool-Aid, signed on with Common Way, and devoted his life to
the cause. Peach had simply been swept up in his wake.

"How's your work?" Caprice asked.

"Okay, I guess."

"Deacon tells me you're very good at it."

"Thanks."

"I know it hasn't been easy for you," Caprice said. "Do you get out
much? Do you have friends?"

"Not really. I'm too busy most of the time. It's okay, I don't mind
being alone."

"It's easy to tell yourself that even when it's not true. You shouldn't
close yourself off. Lyle wouldn't like it."

"I know."

"Deacon says you've been thinking a lot about Lyle."

"Yeah. Some."

"I did that for a long time, too," Caprice said, "but there comes a
time when it's not healthy to dwell on the past."

"Oh, I just—I just wish I'd been nicer to him at the end. Things
were pretty rocky that summer for all of us. I feel bad about that."

"Don't. Lyle wouldn't want you to feel that way. You were just
a girl."

Peach smiled, even though the memory didn't cheer her up. "There was this one weekend. You probably don't even remember. I was so sick. Pneumonia. I had to go back home early from Tampa. Lyle was afraid I was going to throw up in his Mercedes. Actually, I think I did. Deacon took me to Mr. Fairmont's house that night."

"I do remember," Caprice said.

"Yeah. I was pretty delirious. It was really bad. All that blood."

Caprice cocked her head. "Blood?"

Peach looked at her. "What?"

"You said blood."

"Did I? That's weird." She shook her head. "No, phlegm. Nasty green stuff. Yuck. I was coughing up phlegm for days. That's what I meant to say."

23

Walter Fleming took a huge bite of fish taco and grabbed a paper napkin to wipe his mouth. He always stopped at the Taco Bus when he was in Tampa. He was parked under a tree at the back of the lot in his Chevy Tahoe, behind smoked windows. It was after midnight, but the Taco Bus—which literally dished out food from a renovated school bus—was open 24/7, and there was plenty of late-night traffic from urban kids lined up for carne asada.

Walter wore jeans and a black polo shirt. The baseball cap on his dashboard had a union logo, which was why he wasn't wearing it. He didn't want people remembering him.

The three-day union meeting at the downtown convention center was over. He'd stayed an extra day in the city, but he needed to head back to Tallahassee by morning. He wanted to be in the office before Chayla made landfall across the central coast. Storms were unpredictable, and nobody in politics liked events they couldn't control. That was how you lost elections.

He heard rapping on the window and unlocked the truck. The passenger door of the Tahoe opened, and Ogden Bush climbed in beside him. Walter cast a jaundiced eye on the man's two-thousand-dollar suit and the gold watch hugging his slim wrist. The cloud of the man's cologne made him want to crack the window. Bush looked dressed for a club in South Beach.

"That's what you wear, Ogden?" he said. "We're trying not to get noticed."

Bush shrugged. "I came straight from the Common Way office."

Walter grunted and took another big bite of swai fish, which was flaky and delicious. "Where's Curtis?" he asked, brushing crumbs out of his beard.

"He's in line. He wanted some *camarones.*"

Walter eyed the mirror. He spotted the fortysomething private detective at the food truck window, and he frowned, seeing the man chat up three teenage girls. Curtis Ritchie's car, a red Cutlass, was parked nearby. Walter was paranoid about being seen—or, worse, taped or photographed—but as a rule, he insisted on in-person meetings when he needed to talk about political business. Phones, computers, e-mails, tablets, they all scared the hell out of him. You could never delete any of it. Sooner or later, someone would dig up the bits and bytes, and it would be all over the news. Besides, he liked seeing people's faces. You could read a lot in faces about who was scared and who was lying.

"How's the governor?" Bush asked him.

"Nervous."

"Yeah, he should be."

"Are there any surprises coming that I should know about?" Walter asked.

Bush shook his head. "No. They're watching him and his people, but so far, there aren't any new shitstorms." He added: "One of their spies caught you and Brent talking at the convention. That could have been bad. Good thing you covered for me."

Walter shrugged. He knew who it was. The girl in the elevator. Damn, those people were smart. He'd warned Reed about underestimating Common Way. "Don't worry, nobody knows about our arrangement," he said. "Not even the governor. Not yet."

"Let's keep it that way," Bush replied. "If people find out I'm play-ing both sides of the street in this race, that's bad for business."

"We're the ones who have everything to lose, Ogden. For you it's just about money."

Bush smiled, and even in the darkness of the car, his teeth were white. He brushed lint from his lapel. "Not true. I want back in, you know that."

Walter finished his taco and crushed the paper wrapper into a ball. He didn't like Ogden Bush. He didn't like dealing with double agents and moles, but that was the price of the political game. The ends jus-tified the means. Young people got into the game with high-minded ideals, but sooner or later, the smart ones realized that winning dirty was a hell of a lot better than losing clean. There was no prize—and no power—for the ones who came in second.

His relationship with Ogden Bush went back more than a decade. In those days, Bush was a newcomer. Smart, ambitious, but young and untested. When the Twelfth District incumbent dropped dead that year, Bush bucked the party establishment by helping a far-left state senator win the primary. He did it by trashing Walter's own handpicked candidate, but Walter didn't hold grudges. He respected brass-knuckle tactics and people who took risks. Bush would have been a pariah if his candidate had lost, and they both knew it. Instead, Labor Day happened, and Bush hung the Liberty Empire Alliance like an albatross around Chuck Warren's neck. The Dem won. Bush became a star.

Even so, Walter knew that Bush's arrogance would catch up with him sooner or later. Two years ago, Bush backed a black Senate can-didate who was forced out of the race over allegations of cocaine use. Bush called it racism, and his accusations split the party and cost them the election. Party leaders excommunicated him. His business dried up.

Walter knew how badly Bush wanted to get back inside the party after two years in the wilderness. That gave him leverage. When Bush wormed his way into Diane's campaign, Walter approached him with a deal he couldn't refuse: Become a spy. Pass along dirt they could use against Diane. If the governor won, Walter would make sure that Bush got taken off the party shit list. If Diane won anyway, Bush could grab credit for steering the campaign.

Politics.

"What's their plan for Chayla?" Walter asked.

"Lay low. Ride out the storm. They'll have Diane show up at Red Cross sites and hand out soup and cookies. Lots of photographs. It'll be a wait-and-see thing on the government response. If things go smoothly, they'll congratulate the governor—you know, this is no time for partisan divisions. If things go badly, they'll let surrogates roast him for incompetence."

Walter nodded. He'd expected all of that.

The back door of the Tahoe opened. Curtis Ritchie climbed inside, carrying an order of spicy shrimp, which he peeled awkwardly with one hand. He leaned between the front seats, carrying an aroma of garlic and cayenne, mixed with the cigarette smoke clinging to his clothes.

"Shit, these are good. I wanted a taco, but the girls said these were better."

Walter twisted far enough to see the detective's face. Ritchie carried a heavy load of blond stubble, and his unruly hair looked as if it hadn't been washed in a couple days. "You want to flirt with teenagers, Curtis, do it on someone else's time."

"I'm divorced. I'm a free man again. I like to shop around."

Walter snorted. "Like those *chicas* would give you the time of day."

Walter had been married for almost five decades. He still appreciated the appeal of young girls, but to him, they were like something you admired in a museum. He'd seen too many middle-aged politicians self-destruct over affairs with pretty aides. Sometimes he thought every man who ran for office should be castrated first. There would be fewer distractions, and they might actually get something done.

"So what do we know?" Walter asked. "Tell me something."

Ritchie popped a shrimp into his mouth and licked his fingers. "My alter ego, Detective Curtis Clay of the St. Pete police, is still asking questions. You can't rush these things."

Walter held up a hand to stop him. "Knock it off about that. I'm sure you're kidding, because if you were really doing anything illegal, like impersonating a cop, I'd have to shut this operation down and get your license pulled. Right? I asked Ogden to make it damn clear that we were paying for investigative services only. If I'm ever asked to put my hand on a Bible in court, that's what I'm going to say."

Ritchie smirked. "Yeah, of course, I was kidding. I'm a kidder."

"So what do we know?" Walter repeated.

"So far, nothing much," Ritchie said. "You wanted real dirt. That takes time."

Walter shook his head in frustration. He'd told Brent Reed to be patient, but patience wasn't one of his own virtues. His blood pressure was always high, no matter how much medicine he took.

"Look, Walter," Bush said, taking a shrimp from Ritchie's basket, "we both know what the people at Common Way are like. You can't win as often as they do without crossing the line. I don't know if it's bribes or wiretapping or what, but there's something to find. I can't dig into it myself, because we can't have anyone finding out about our special relationship. That's why we have Curtis here."

"Yeah, and what is Curtis here doing besides eating shrimp?"

Ritchie grinned. "It's really good shrimp."

"What about this kid Justin you told me about?" Walter asked. "What's the deal with him?"

"Rufus tipped me off that Justin Kiel was asking questions about the Labor Day murders," Bush replied. "I asked Justin why, but he clammed up. I told Curtis to start checking him out, but somebody shot the kid in the head before we could figure out what he was doing."

"Who did it?" Walter asked, staring at Curtis Ritchie.

Ritchie's brow furrowed. "Don't know. I was following him, but the kid was smart. I think he made me. He went underground, and I lost him."

"The police think the murder was a drug thing, but it smells funny," Bush added. "He's asking about Birch Fairmont, and then he gets popped? Makes you wonder."

"Is there something hinky about the Labor Day murders?" Walter asked. "Something the FBI missed?"

Bush shrugged. "Hard to say. Rufus has it in his head that Diane's son was involved. If he was, and she knew, that's huge. Back then, I wanted everyone focused on Chuck Warren and Ham Brock, because we needed to crush Chuck in the polls. Now? It wouldn't hurt to have some ugly rumors about Diane and Drew."

"Sounds risky to me," Walter said. "Her son killed himself. We don't need to generate any more sympathy for her."

"Common Way's got someone looking into this, too," Bush added. "His name's Cab Bolton. He's a Naples cop. Caprice went around me and hired him herself."

"Why would she do that?"

"Supposedly, there are threats against Diane, and he's trying to track down the source. Of course, Caprice is smart. She may be trying to make sure there are no unexploded bombs in Diane's past. Like Drew."

Walter jabbed a finger at Curtis Ritchie. "If there are any bombs like that, it's your job to find them, so we can blow them up ourselves."

"Hey, I'm on it," Ritchie assured him. "I've been keeping an eye on one of their researchers. Peach Piper. She's been digging into whatever happened to Justin, too."

"Piper? As in Lyle's sister?"

"That's her. I was following her earlier today, and she led me to somebody interesting. She's been tracking a drug dealer named Frank Macy. Smooth character but a real whack job. He got out of prison on a manslaughter gig earlier this year."

Walter shrugged. "Macy. Is that name supposed to mean something to me?"

Bush leaned across the seat and grinned. "I looked him up. Frank Macy sold drugs to Diane's son, Drew, ten years ago. Small world, huh? As a little bonus, guess who his lawyer was? Ramona Cortes."

That was the first thing Walter had heard in days that put him in a better mood. "I like it," he said. "I like it a lot."

Ritchie finished the last of his shrimp. "Yeah, we figured you would. Macy could be our missing link to all sorts of shit. With any luck, he'll beat a path right back to Diane and Ramona. Maybe we can take down both of those bitches."

24

"Do you always carry a gun?" Peach asked.

Annalie punched the pause button on the remote control. The play-back on the sixty-inch television in the Common Way conference room froze, leaving the governor with his mouth open in front of the electricians at the union convention. It was Tuesday morning, and the two of them were reviewing hours of video footage gathered at campaign events, hunting for gaffes that could be used in campaign ads.

"It's Florida," Annalie said. She hefted her purse up and down as if she were working out with weights. "Even Mickey Mouse probably carries a piece."

"Well, I'm glad you came back to check on me. Thanks."

"No problem. I didn't want to take any chances. That guy in the red Cutlass was watching you. I don't know if he was connected to Macy or not, but he definitely had his eyes on you."

Peach got up and paced. Inside the conference room, the stale cold air made her shiver. Outside, the building rocked, and the walls groaned. She wondered who the man in the Cutlass was. She was a spy, and she didn't like being spied upon herself.

"I talked to one of my contacts about Macy," Annalie added. "There's not much buzz about him, but he had eight years in prison to make connections. He could be into anything."

"Yeah."

"What exactly did Diane say when you mentioned him?"

"She got furious. She thinks Macy was the one who got Drew hooked on drugs. Though I don't know why that would matter to Justin."

Peach sat down again. Annalie said nothing.

"And then there's Alison," Peach went on. "Justin wrote her name in the poetry book. He must have wanted me to find it. She must be important, too."

"You don't know who she is?"

"Deacon thought she might be a lawyer for the foundation, but I can't find evidence that Justin ever contacted her." She added after a pause: "You would have liked Justin. There was something deep about him that you don't find in a lot of people."

Annalie brushed her raven hair out of her eyes. "Well, if you liked him, I'm sure I would have liked him, too. You seem to be a pretty good judge of people."

"No, I don't think I know people at all," Peach said. "I keep them away. Caprice says I'm too closed off."

"You've been through a lot."

"Yeah. It's hard to get close to people. And even harder to trust people." She dragged words out of herself. "I mean, I don't really know you, do I? I like you, but I don't know anything about you."

Annalie smiled, as if she knew it was hard for Peach to say something like that. "What do you want to know?"

"I don't know. Where'd you grow up?"

"Near Bonita Springs."

"Are your parents alive?"

"Yes."

Peach nodded. "People think it's odd when I ask that, but I don't really know what that's like, you know? To have parents."

"I know."

"Did you go to college?"

"UCF."

"I never wanted to go to college," Peach said. "What did you do after you graduated?"

"Partied. Ran up debt. Experienced the joys of minimum wage."

They both laughed. Most Florida grads could tell the same story, spending the decade after school as beach bums and Parrotheads. Even so, Peach watched Annalie fiddle with a pen on the table, and an unwelcome thought leaped into her head: *You're lying to me.* She had no idea why Annalie would lie about her past, or what she was hiding from her. Or maybe she was just being Peach Paranoid again.

"Well, like I said, you would have liked Justin. He would have liked you, too."

"That's sweet."

They were silent. Annalie looked uneasy.

"So Justin never said anything to you about Frank Macy?" she continued. "The name never came up?"

Peach shook her head. "No."

"Show me the photo again," Annalie told her. "The one you found in Justin's safe house. Do you still have it?"

Peach slid the paper from her pocket and unfolded it. Annalie studied it carefully, and she pointed to the edges of the picture.

"Here's what I don't understand. This isn't a copy of the article itself. The article was pinned up somewhere. See the cork paneling on the side? That looks like a bulletin board."

Peach had seen that, too. "So?"

"So where was this taken?"

"I have no idea."

"You were in Justin's safe house and his apartment," Annalie said. "Could it have been in there?"

"I don't think so. Maybe this was inside Frank Macy's apartment. I could get in and search it."

"No, you will *not* do that," Annalie told her firmly. "If anyone goes in there, it's me. I'm the one with the gun, remember?"

"Yeah, okay," Peach said, but she seethed with frustration. She needed a direction. She needed to do something. It was as if Justin were in the corner of the drab conference room, his arms folded, shaking his head at her in disappointment underneath his porkpie hat. *Hey, come on, Peach, I'm counting on you.*

The phone in the conference room rang. Peach knew she should get it, but she couldn't move. She stared at Justin in the corner as if he were real, with that I-know-everything smirk on his face. In her imagination, he winked at her and jabbed a finger at the phone as if he were pointing a gun.

You're going to want to take that call, Peach.

Annalie reached across the table and grabbed the receiver.

"Hello?" And then: "What's his name?"

Annalie hung up the phone, her features dark with concern. "What is it?" Peach asked.

"There's a detective out front who wants to talk to you about Justin."

"Is it Curtis Clay?" Peach asked. "The fake cop?"

Annalie shook her head. "No, this one's real. His name is Cab Bolton."

25

Cab sized up the young woman in front of him. She was pretty in a Carey Mulligan way, with pageboy blond hair and freckles. Her tiny mouth was constantly changing expressions, and her blue eyes had a luminous intensity. Her expression was severe and suspicious, like a yipper dog growling to protect its turf. She obviously had a paranoid streak, because he didn't think anyone had ever studied his identification more carefully. After holding it up to the light and comparing his photograph, she called the Naples police to get a description of him.

Finally, she hung up.

Cab smiled at her. "So? Am I me?"

"They said if my head came up higher than your neck, it wasn't you."

"I hope they mentioned the earring, too. And the hair gel."

"They said it was a pomade from London."

"They obviously know me too well," Cab said. "So now that you know who I am, how about you tell me who you are."

She sat on the other side of the conference table with her hands folded in front of her. The oversized armchair made her look small. "Peach Piper."

Cab heard the name and made the connection. "As in Lyle Piper?"

"My brother."

"I'm sorry."

Peach shrugged. "What do you want, Detective Bolton?"

Cab didn't answer immediately. His eyes wandered around the conference room. He spotted the frozen video on the television, and as he did, Peach reached for the remote control and shut it off. The governor's face disappeared. He glanced out the window behind him at the cubicle farm and saw dozens of earnest workers in their twenties with bad haircuts. The room hummed with the white noise of air-conditioning.

He noted the arrangement of papers around him and realized that Peach hadn't been alone in the conference room. Someone had been here with her, but whoever it was had left quickly.

"What exactly do you people do here?" he asked. "This place is kind of shabby for a big-name foundation, isn't it?"

"We do research."

"What kind of research?"

"Political research," Peach said.

Cab nodded. The girl didn't want to give him details. "I get it. Secret, world-changing stuff, huh? You could tell me, but then you'd have to kill me?"

"Something like that," Peach replied.

"I thought opposition research was about catching politicians saying stupid things. How tough can that be? It's like shooting fish in a barrel, isn't it?"

Peach didn't reply, but her lips twitched with the tiniest of smiles, as if she were finally succumbing to his charm. "You still haven't told me what you want."

Cab didn't answer right away. He liked to meander with witnesses, which usually made them nervous and anxious to talk. Silence made people uncomfortable, especially around cops. However, as young as this girl was, she didn't rattle easily or open her mouth. Behind her paranoia, Peach was obviously smart.

"I asked at the desk to talk to someone who knew Justin Kiel," he told her. "They sent me to you."

"Why are you interested in Justin?"

"I think you know why. He was murdered."

Peach played with the television remote control in her hand. "Well, yes, he was, detective, but he wasn't murdered in Naples. The crime took place in St. Petersburg. So how does this involve you?"

Cab smiled again. No doubt about it—she was smart.

"I'm not actually investigating the murder itself," Cab admitted. "Not for the police, anyway."

"So you're a private citizen, and I'm a private citizen. That means I don't have to answer any of your questions, right?"

"Yes, you're right. Then again, I'm also working for your boss."

Peach hesitated. "Ms. Fairmont?"

"And Caprice Dean," Cab said.

"What did they hire you to do?"

Cab said nothing, and the girl nodded at the irony. "Yeah, okay, you could tell me, but then you'd have to kill me," she said.

"Something like that," Cab replied.

"Why do you care about Justin? The police say he was killed in some kind of drug deal gone bad."

"Do you believe that?" Cab asked.

"Do you?"

Cab studied the girl's defiant face. He'd come in here expecting to play cop games with her, but instead, she was playing cop games with him. He decided to be honest and see how she dealt with the truth. "No," he said.

Peach couldn't hide the intensity of her reaction. It wasn't surprise or curiosity. It was *exhilaration*. With one word, he had changed something inside her. She leaned forward with a strange excitement, as if, suddenly, she knew her place in the world. She'd been vindicated.

"If it wasn't drugs, what was it?" Peach asked.

"You tell me."

She was silent. Around them, the walls shook with the wind. "I have no idea," she said finally.

Peach was lying. As always, lies told him more than the truth. She knew more than she was letting on, but whatever she knew, she was reluctant to tell him. He was a stranger.

"How well did you know Justin?" he asked.

"We worked together, that's all."

Cab heard the translation in his head: *We were close. Very close.* He wondered exactly how close. Were they friends? Were they lovers? He thought that her skin flushed at the very sound of his name.

"What did you two work on?"

"Research."

"Oh, right. Your lips are sealed. I know you have to be careful about telling people what you do, but we're on the same team, Peach. I'm not the enemy. If you and Justin were digging into something that got him killed, you should tell me."

"Justin and I weren't working together before he was killed," Peach said. "I can't tell you anything."

"What about computer records?"

"The police took everything. You'd have to talk to them."

"Is there anyone else in the office who would know something?"

"Ogden Bush is the liaison to the campaign. You could talk to him."

"Is he here?"

"No."

"Then I guess I'm talking to you," Cab said.

"I already said I can't help you."

Peach gathered her files around her, as if the conversation was over. Cab thought about who this girl was. Peach Piper, sister of Lyle Piper. A decade earlier, she would have been a child, grieving the loss of her brother. The summer when Birch Fairmont was assassinated had changed her life profoundly. It had to be in her consciousness every day.

"One more question," he said. "This one's not about Justin."

She was suspicious. "Okay."

"Who killed your brother?" Cab asked.

Peach stared at him. "What kind of question is that?"

"I imagine it's a question you think about all the time. Who do you think murdered Birch Fairmont and Lyle Piper?"

"I don't know who pulled the trigger. It was some right-wing fanatic from the Liberty Empire Alliance. Maybe it was Ham Brock himself."

"You believe that's what happened?" Cab said.

"Of course. That's why I'm here."

"That's very noble."

"Don't patronize me," Peach snapped. "You wouldn't be sarcastic if someone from your family had been murdered."

"I wasn't being sarcastic, I was being sincere. And I nearly did lose a family member that day, although I know that isn't the same thing."

Peach's eyes narrowed with recognition. "Bolton? You're related to Tarla Bolton?"

"I'm her son."

Her face softened. "I'm sorry. I didn't realize."

"That's okay. I usually don't advertise it."

"Everybody says your mother saved Ms. Fairmont that day. She was very brave."

"Well, my mother rarely thinks before she acts," Cab said. "Sometimes the results are better than others."

"It was a terrible day," Peach said.

"Were you there?"

"No. Thank God. I couldn't have handled seeing it happen."

Cab leaned across the conference table, which meant he was almost in Peach's face. She looked very young. "Did you spend a lot of time at Birch Fairmont's estate that summer?"

"Sure. Lyle was there all the time because of the campaign."

"What do you remember?"

"Not much. Deacon and I spent a lot of time in the pool. I read a lot. I was just a kid."

"You strike me as a kid who would notice things," Cab said.

"Like what?"

"Like something bad happening."

"I don't know what you mean," Peach replied.

"Do you remember anything about Birch and Diane?"

"No. They weren't together a lot. Birch was on the road. Ms. Fairmont was alone."

"Did you talk to her much?"

"Oh, no, hardly ever."

"What about Diane's son? Drew?"

He saw a slight tic in Peach's face. "What about him?"

"Did you know him?"

Peach shook her head. "Why are you asking about him?"

"No reason."

He let the silence linger. Staring at her, he thought she was telling the truth this time. She didn't know Drew. Even so, something about Drew's name had elicited a reaction, and she was obviously curious about why he'd brought it up. It was the same message as before: *I could tell you things, but I won't.*

She didn't trust him. Not yet.

Cab thought about Gladiola Croft's story. Something had happened two weeks before Labor Day between Birch and Diane. An argument. A fight. Maybe it didn't mean anything at all; maybe Drew's threat to kill his stepfather was just twentysomething angst. Or maybe this was all a game by Rufus Twill—and the shadowy people pulling strings behind him—to create a scandal that would tarnish Diane's campaign.

He would have been willing to believe the story was just a convenient lie, except for one thing.

Justin Kiel was dead. That was real.

"Two weeks before Labor Day, something very ugly happened at Birch's estate," Cab told Peach. "Do you know anything about that? It was a Saturday night."

"No, if it's the weekend I'm thinking about, I was sick. Pneumonia. I don't remember much. I'm sorry."

"I'm asking because of Justin," he told her.

"How does this involve Justin?"

Definitely friends, Cab thought, watching her face. *Probably lovers.*

"Justin was in Lake Wales shortly before he was killed. He was asking questions about the Labor Day murders."

"*What?* No, that can't be right."

"You didn't know? He didn't tell you about it?"

"No, he didn't," Peach said. She looked dazed, as if a wave had washed her away. "He didn't say anything like that."

He lowered his voice, but he held her blue eyes with his own. "You understand why I'm worried, don't you? Someone killed Justin. It happened *two weeks ago*. Maybe the police are right, and this was a drug-related murder, but I don't like coincidences. I don't like the fact that Justin was looking into Birch's murder, only to wind up dead himself. I want to know what he found, because if it was enough to get him killed, then something is going on. Something is going on *right here and now*."

Peach stood up. "Stop," she said. "Just stop. Please."

"Peach, if you know anything—"

"I don't," she insisted.

"I need you to trust me."

"I don't know you," she said.

"Listen to me. Someone killed Lyle and Birch. Someone killed Justin. They may not be finished yet."

"I have to go. I'm sorry."

Peach held up her hands and backed away from him. He may as well have been holding a gun. Like a spooked deer, she bolted from the office without another word, leaving him alone.

Cab eased back in the reclining chair, frustrated, and let out his breath in a sigh. He didn't like walking away with nothing. He'd learned to trust his instincts, and his instincts told him that Peach knew more about the past than she'd told him. She probably knew more than she really understood.

He wished he had Lala with him. Lala had a way of connecting with young women that Cab never had.

His eyes scanned the conference room table. Peach had left her files behind her. He had no interest in spying on the inner workings of the Common Way Foundation, but he noticed a half-folded piece of paper on the desk, tented and face down, as if Peach had been looking at it before he arrived. Curious, he used a fingertip to slide the paper toward him.

Cab unfolded it and read it. He didn't understand what the photograph showed him, but by instinct, he didn't like it. Something about this single piece of paper in his hand felt dangerous. And important.

He saw a name he didn't recognize. Frank Macy.

And a name he did. Ramona Cortes.

26

Peach knew where she needed to go. Lake Wales.

She drove inland. Interstate 4 was jammed with cars. There had been no evacuation ordered for Chayla's landfall, but some coastal residents weren't taking any chances with the storm.

It took her twice as long as it usually would to reach the exit at Lakeland, where she headed southeast toward Bartow. The farther she drove into the backcountry on the quiet two-lane highway, the more she retreated into her past. The land between towns was untouched by time. Flat, empty green fields. Fruit stands selling mesh bags of oranges out of barrels. Billboards advertising gun shows. The sky was a depressing charcoal overhead.

She thought about what Cab Bolton had told her.

Justin had been in Lake Wales before he was killed. They'd been there together barely a month earlier, and then he'd *gone back* without saying a word about it. He'd started asking questions about the Labor Day murders. That was his secret.

Why?

Part of her was angry at him. He'd lied and kept her in the dark. Their trip to Lake Wales was supposed to be a chance to talk about who they were, about life, love, sex, and the future. Their future. She'd even thought about breaking her vow that weekend and letting him take her virginity, but in the end, he'd been the one to say no, and she loved him even more for it.

She wondered how that same man could have deceived her. She wondered if he'd had an ulterior motive about the trip from the beginning.

When she'd left Lake Wales with Deacon years earlier, she had never wanted to see the town again. Justin had been the one to persuade her to return with him, but with each mile they drove, emotions rushed back. Memories flooded her, disconnected images that made no sense and left her deeply anxious. She was haunted by grief, loneliness, and loss. Through it all, Justin was there beside her.

Now she was going back again. Alone. She needed answers.

Ten miles outside town, when the first spatter of rain struck her windshield, she saw a cross in the long grass by the highway shoulder. Flowers decorated it, and the paint was fresh. Someone still honored whoever had died there. It was nice to think you could die and not be forgotten.

That had been her marker. That was where she'd pulled off the road with Justin.

"Why are we stopping?" he asked.

Peach didn't answer. She let the dust settle before climbing out of the car into the humid morning. They were alone here, early on Sunday, with nothing but the buzz of crickets rising from the fields and the black splotches of hawks circling in the blue sky.

She sat on the hood of the car. The metal was hot underneath her jeans. Justin came and joined her.

"See the little white cross?" she told him. "You have to be careful when you drive here."

Justin nodded, but he didn't understand.

"It's terrible how you see them everywhere," she went on, "and you know that every cross means somebody was lost."

Peach breathed in the moist air. The sun was merciless. She realized that all her muscles were wound up into tight little knots. Her knees drummed relentlessly, making the car shake. She didn't want to go home again. She didn't want to be back in Lake Wales.

"We don't have to do this," Justin murmured.

"I know."

The world was absolutely still. She stared past the sagging telephone wires. Brown and white dots of cattle interrupted the green fields. Trees of uneven height lined the horizon. Some looked as tall as giants.

"You'd think I'd remember everything, wouldn't you?" she said. "I don't. It's more like photographs in my head."

"What do you remember?" he asked.

Peach took his hand and squeezed it tightly. "A policewoman broke the news to me. I was at Birch's estate. I'd spent the evening there in one of the spare bedrooms, and I'd fallen asleep. They were all supposed to come back later. Lyle, Caprice, Birch, Ms. Fairmont, her friend Tarla, the movie star. Instead, none of them did. The police woke me up. They were all over the house. She told me that Lyle—she told me he was gone. So was Birch. I turned on the television, and that was all anyone could talk about."

"You were alone?" Justin asked.

"Deacon was at our apartment, but he came and joined me. It was hours before anyone else got back, and they didn't talk to us. That was it. That's how your whole life changes."

He took her hand, and he kissed each of her fingertips. She wanted to cry, but she had no tears.

"It was supposed to be a treat for me. I'd been so sick, and now that I was feeling better, Lyle said I could stay up for the party when they came home. I think he felt bad. He'd been angry for weeks. Me, Deacon, Caprice, he was yelling at all of us. This was a way to make it up to me."

"Why was he so mad?"

She shrugged. "That was Lyle. He had a temper. I understand campaigns now better than I did then. All the intensity. All the pressure. And that was the very first campaign for the Common Way Party. Lyle had everything riding on that race. He and Caprice had been planning it for years."

A truck passed them on the rural highway. It was so big and fast that the vibration nearly slid them off the hood of the car. The truck carried fruit; she smelled a wave of citrus in its wake.

"People drive so fast," Peach said, shaking her head. She closed her eyes. "Poor Lyle, that last month was a nightmare."

"How so?"

"Oh, it was my fault," Peach said, with a tiny laugh. "There was some big political fundraiser in Tampa in August, and Lyle had to go. He took me and Deacon with him. I really, really wanted to see the city. Deacon wound up like a babysitter, which he didn't like, and Lyle didn't have five minutes to spend with us. Then I got sick on Saturday night. Puking, hacking, burning up. It was really bad. Lyle acted like I was doing it just to annoy him. I wanted to go back home, and I was screaming and crying about it, and Lyle told Deacon to take the car and drive me back to Lake Wales. Deacon wanted to stay, so they yelled at each other, and then I yelled at both of them. Real nice. Anyway, Deacon finally drove me back, but that was a mess, too, because he hit a deer, which banged up Lyle's precious Mercedes. By the time we got back, I was so sick I was almost delirious, and Deacon was so rattled he could hardly walk straight. So he took me to Birch's estate to get help."

She was quiet.

Justin said, "Peach?"

And then: "Are you okay?"

"Yeah." She shrugged. "Yeah."

"What is it?"

"We walked into the middle of something there," she said.

"What?"

"I don't know. My doctor was already at the estate when we arrived. Dr. Smeltz. He said it was pneumonia, that it was lucky we got there when we did. I think my fever was like a hundred and four. Deacon was freaked out about the car, so he wasn't any help. I remember Caprice putting me to bed and kissing my head. She was very sweet. I woke up two days later, I think, or that's how it felt. Lyle was there when I did."

"What did he say?"

"Nothing. I said I was sorry about being sick, I was sorry about the car, but he didn't say anything. I felt horrible, like I'd caused all the problems. I mean, I was twelve, I didn't know any better . . . except . . ."

"Except what?" Justin asked.

"I don't know. Something had changed."

"I don't understand."

"I'm not sure I do, either. Everyone was different. It's like I went to sleep that Saturday night, and when I woke up, nobody was the same. Lyle hardly talked to anyone. I'm not sure he ever slept. Ms. Fairmont, I didn't see her at all. She was practically invisible. Birch drank all the time. There was this weird blackness hanging over everyone in the house. It felt like . . . it felt like something was going to happen. And then it did. I know that sounds crazy, but when the policewoman woke me up that night, it's like I already knew. I was expecting it."

"You couldn't have been expecting anything like that," Justin said.

"You wouldn't think so, would you? But she didn't have to say a word. I had this premonition. I think I even said it out loud before she did."

"Said what?"

Peach frowned. "I said, 'They're dead, aren't they?'"

Finally, she drove into Lake Wales. Its deserted downtown streets felt like echoes of a ghost town. She saw no one. She drove past the Walesbilt Hotel, painted sea-foam green. It had once been a glamorous destination, but it was abandoned now, a fenced-off ruin with broken and boarded-up windows and deep cracks riddling the stucco. She and Justin had thought about breaking in at night, like urban explorers. Instead, they'd sat outside, eating fried chicken in her car and studying the destruction wrought by marauders and storms.

She'd thought she would always remember that weekend with Justin as one of the great moments of her life. It had felt like the beginning of something, but instead, it was the end. A few weeks later, he was gone. Now she wondered whether their romantic getaway had been nothing but a cover for whatever he was hiding from her.

Days later, he went back to Lake Wales.

Days later, he started digging into the past of a killer named Frank Macy.

He'd kept secrets from her all along. It made her feel bitter; it made her feel like a child.

And yet—*and yet*—he'd left clues for her, too. Just for her. Bread-crumbs that no one else could find. Part of her whispered that he was trying to protect her.

Part of her whispered that he had done it all for her. That he was trying to answer the question that had haunted her for ten years.

27

"Cab," Caprice said. "What an unexpected treat."

She got up from behind her desk at the headquarters of the Common Way Foundation, which was on the other side of downtown from the shabby building that housed the foundation's research department. Her corner office was located near the pencil top of the SunTrust tower. Floor-to-ceiling windows looked out on the skyline in two directions. Westward, he could see the cloud mass marking the fringe of Chayla as it marched toward the coast. It was a dark day. The building swayed almost imperceptibly with the gusts.

Caprice's brunette hair was pulled tightly back, and her white skin and soft face were emphasized by amber teardrop earrings. She wore a gray business suit, with a skirt that fell just below her knees. Her heels were tall. Her serious eyes became flirtatious as she leaned in and kissed him on the cheek.

"To what do I owe the pleasure?" she asked.

"I have questions," Cab said.

Caprice smiled. "Of course you do. You are just full of questions."

He strolled on the plush carpet to the windows overlooking the city. Caprice stood next to him, close enough that her hips brushed against his. He was very conscious of her presence.

"The storm will be here soon," Caprice said. Her eyes were on him, not the sky.

"Yes, it will."

He sat at a round glass table near the window. Caprice took the chair next to him. She smiled, waiting for him to start. The toes of her shoe casually rubbed his pant leg. She knew she made him uncomfortable, and he was pretty sure she liked the power she held.

"I just met Peach Piper," Cab told her.

"Did you? Peach is a sweet girl, but don't underestimate her. She's wicked smart. You could sit right next to her and not even realize it because of her disguises."

"She was telling me about a foundation employee named Justin Kiel," he said.

"I'm not surprised. Deacon says that Peach was quite sweet on Justin."

"I'm wondering why you didn't tell me about Justin yourself. A member of your research team was murdered two weeks ago. You didn't think that was useful information in evaluating potential threats against Diane?"

"The police didn't raise any security concerns about the crime," Caprice replied. "They said it was drug-related. One dealer shoots another. Honestly, I wanted it kept under the radar as much as possible. It's not a great campaign story when an employee of the foundation turns out to be connected to drug trafficking."

"I'm not sure it's that simple," Cab said. "Justin was looking into the Labor Day murders before he was killed."

Caprice's brow furrowed with concern. "Are you sure about that?"

"I am. Was he working for you?"

"No, of course not."

"I thought maybe you hired him before you hired me."

She shook her head. "I didn't."

"If he was killed because he was asking questions about Birch's death, then the threat against Diane is real and serious. I think you should increase security around her."

Caprice nodded. "I will. Do you know if Justin discovered any-thing that would help you?"

"Not yet." He added: "I'm not the only one interested in Justin's death. Ramona Cortes asked to see me. She mentioned Justin, too. She doesn't think his murder was drug-related."

"Ramona," Caprice said, shaking her head. "Well, I doubt she knows anything more about the case than you or me. She's just stirring the pot. Anything that might embarrass Diane would draw Ramona like a magnet."

"Do you know her personally?"

"Of course. Remember, I'm a lawyer, not just a pretty face. We go back a long way. Lyle and Ramona were classmates in law school, before their political paths diverged. She's very ambitious. People think the attorney general is supposed to be above politics, when in fact, it's one of the most political positions in any state. It's no surprise that so many top elected officials started out as AGs. You have the power of prosecution, and you have a platform to get lots of publicity for what you do. Believe me, Ramona wants Diane out of the race any way she can, because she thinks she can beat the governor head to head."

"She tried to talk me out of working for you," Cab said.

"I bet she did."

"She has a pretty Machiavellian view of Common Way. She thinks you're not above using ruthless political tactics."

Caprice smiled. "We're not."

"Within the law?"

"Naturally within the law, but we play to win. I don't apologize for that. The other parties are simply upset that we're getting bet-ter at the game than they are. Don't let sour grapes from Ramona concern you."

Cab didn't doubt that Caprice was right about Ramona. In dealing with politicians, every word, every smile, every truth, every lie, was layered with motives. He didn't need to ask who was trying to play him, because everyone was. They all had their own agendas.

"Does the name Frank Macy mean anything to you?" Cab asked. "He was an old client of Ramona's who went to prison on manslaughter charges a few years ago."

"Did Peach tell you about him?" Caprice asked.

"Not directly, but she had some information about him with her."

"Yes, Peach showed up at Diane's last night, talking about Macy. Diane didn't take it well. Drew hung out with Frank Macy in college. He was a drug dealer, one of those street-smart scholarship students who know how to capitalize on rich friends by using their urban contacts. Smart but tough. On some level, I think Diane always blamed Macy for Drew's death. Peach thought that Justin was interested in Macy, too."

Cab's expression hardened. "Justin was looking at Frank Macy? Macy was Drew's drug dealer? And you still didn't call me about any of this?"

Caprice reacted with obvious annoyance. "You don't get it, do you, Cab? We are running a statewide political campaign. Drug killings do not help us. Someone like Frank Macy is poison. If his name is linked to Diane's in the media, our poll numbers drop. So no, I don't want you looking at him. I don't want Frank Macy within ten miles of anyone from Common Way. Was he involved in Justin's death? I have no idea. Frankly, I don't care, but if you want my political opinion, think about this. If Ramona Cortes wanted to attack Diane, an old client like Frank Macy would be a great way to do it. Macy wouldn't need to be connected to the murder at all. Just planting his name would hurt us. Has it occurred to you that Ramona might be behind all of this? That she might be manipulating you and Peach to sabotage Diane?"

"It has," Cab said.

"Then maybe you should stop listening to her and focus on what I hired you to do."

Caprice showed the sharpness of her teeth for the first time. She was a dominatrix, accustomed to getting what she wanted. He felt the allure. He knew exactly what a relationship with her would be like. He had no illusions that he would be the one in charge. She could take a strong man and drive him mad.

"Sorry," she said, putting her smile back on. "That's my passion coming through."

"I realize that."

"Remember, politics means nothing to you, but it's everything to me."

"I realize that, too."

She was the coquette again. "Forgive me?"

Cab smiled. "Of course."

"I didn't mean to treat you like an employee. It's a bad habit of mine. Honestly, I have to confess, I was thinking about other things when I hired you. I wanted to get to know you better. Not that you're not good at what you do, but you're very attractive."

"The feeling is mutual."

"It sounds callous, but I don't really care about your girlfriend. If she can't keep you, that's her problem. I'd like to see more of you."

"Believe me, I'm tempted," he said, "but it will have to wait until this business is done."

"Because you work for me?" she asked, her eyes gleaming. "Are you afraid of sexual harassment?"

"Not at all."

"Maybe you should be."

"I'm not worried," Cab explained, "because I don't work for you anymore."

He watched Caprice inhale sharply, her nostrils flaring with anger. "Is this a joke, Cab? Because it's not funny."

"It's not a joke. I have a new client."

"Who?" she demanded. "So help me, if Ramona Cortes—"

"It's not Ramona."

"Then what is this about?"

"I guess you could say my client is Justin Kiel."

Caprice leaned across the table, pointing a blood-red fingernail in his direction. "Oh, come on, Cab, what kind of nonsense is this? I asked you to help Diane. She's your mother's best friend. Do you care so little about her?"

"On the contrary. I care about her a great deal. If Justin Kiel was killed because he was asking questions about the Labor Day murders, then I need to know exactly what he found, because I want to protect Diane. But I can't do that if I have to be concerned with how my investigation fits into your political calculations."

"I said I was sorry," Caprice snapped.

"I know you did, but you're not sorry in the least. That's okay. You have your priorities. I have mine."

Caprice frowned. "So what does this mean? You keep working on the case, but I don't have to pay you for it?"

"Pretty much. Think of it as a sound business deal."

"How can I argue with that?" she asked.

"You can't."

"Then I guess we're done," she concluded.

"Not quite. Now you're a witness."

"Excuse me?"

"Justin wanted to know what happened ten years ago. So do I. Let's start with a fight between Birch and Diane a couple weeks before Labor Day. It was a Saturday night. It was so bad that Drew ended up threatening Birch's life, and he wound up in rehab. He got out of rehab just days before the murders. I'd like to know exactly what went on in that house."

"I don't know," Caprice replied.

"I think you do. Peach said you were there."

She was silent for a moment. "Diane would not want you looking into this, Cab," she said softly.

"Maybe not, but I have no choice. I'm heading back to Lake Wales right now. I'm going to find out what's going on sooner or later. You might as well tell me."

"I'm asking you to drop it. Please. As a friend, not as an employer."

"I can't do that. I'm sorry. I don't care what this does to the campaign."

"Well, I do care. So does Diane."

"What really happened that Saturday night, Caprice? What are you people hiding?"

She stood up languidly from her chair. Every movement she made had grace; her body was a seamless extension of her sexuality. She leaned toward him, close enough to engulf him in a sweet breath of perfume. With a little smirk, she took his earlobe in her mouth and bit him.

"Go to hell, Cab," she whispered.

28

The rain lashed the windshield of her Thunderbird. An ash tree bowing over the roof of the Lake Wales Public Library twisted in the wind like a drunken dancer. Peach opened the car door, which wrenched out of her hand. She ran for the library entrance, and in the doorway, safe from the downpour, she smoothed her hair, adjusted her fake black glasses, and made sure that her tan blouse was properly tucked into her brown skirt.

She looked like a librarian. Everyone was more comfortable talking to people who looked like they did.

Peach knew that Justin would have come here first. He always said that libraries held the answers to every question that could be asked in the world. If he was digging into the events in Lake Wales, he would have started at the Lake Wales Public Library. Someone was bound to remember him.

Inside, the thump of rain on the roof was as loud as thunder. The building was mostly empty. She saw a lone librarian at the registration desk eyeing the oversized front windows as they shook in the wind. The woman was in her fifties, plump, with strawberry hair and a round face.

Peach gave her a shy smile. "Hello."

"Can I help you?" The woman's voice had a trace of a German accent.

"Oh, well, I don't know. It's personal."

"Yes?"

"My boyfriend was here a few weeks ago," Peach said. "I was hoping someone here talked to him."

The librarian came up to the counter. "And what is this about?"

Peach displayed a photograph on her phone of her and Justin near the lake just blocks from the library. Arms around one another; big smiles. "See, that's us," she said.

The woman squinted. The picture softened her, because it was two young people who were obviously in love. Peach could also tell from her expression that she remembered Justin, with his weird mustache and hat.

"You saw him, didn't you?" Peach asked.

"Well, yes, I do remember him," the librarian admitted. "A young person with an old-fashioned mustache like that, so unusual. He was funny, too. He had a lot to say about life. I liked him."

Peach nodded. Her eyes stung with tears, which she didn't need to fake at all. "He was a philosopher."

"Oh, dear," the librarian replied immediately. "Did something happen?"

"He died."

The woman grabbed her hand. "I'm so sorry, how awful for you! He was just a boy. How can I help you?"

"Well, you can't, probably. Justin was a writer, like me. He was doing a story for an Orlando magazine about the tenth anniversary of the Labor Day murders—you know, with Diane Fairmont running for governor now. I'd like to finish the article for him, but I can't make heads or tails of his notes, so I'm trying to follow in his footsteps. Re-create his research. That's why I'm here."

"I see."

It wasn't entirely a lie, and Peach sold it with the sweetness of her face. "Anything you can tell me would be such a help," she said.

"Well, yes, he said he was doing a story about those terrible murders," the woman said. "He asked me if I lived here back then, but I'm afraid I only came to town five years ago, so I couldn't help him."

"Did he talk to anyone else?"

"Maybe a couple of our volunteers, but they're not here today."

"Oh. I understand."

"He was in the library for a long time," the librarian told her. "He spent much of it in our microfiche section. I think he was going through all of the newspapers from back then. He made a lot of copies."

"You don't know what he copied, I suppose."

"No, I'm sorry, patrons make their own copies. I can show you our newspapers, however, if you'd like."

"Yes, okay," Peach said.

The librarian guided her to a row of carrels stocked with microfiche readers, near the windows that looked out on the fierce rain. She pulled out a drawer in a nearby file cabinet. With a quick glance, she took a box from the back of the drawer and opened it to show her a stack of oversized negatives.

"These are the Lake Wales papers from August and September of that year. I believe that's where your young man started."

Peach nodded. "Thank you."

"Do you need help with the machines?"

"No, I'm fine. Thank you so much. I appreciate your help."

Peach sat down alone at a microfiche reader, and she quickly found the newspaper reports for the day after Labor Day. When she saw the headlines and photographs, her eyes blurred with tears, and her stomach squirmed, as if a great hole had opened up inside it. Instead of reading, she stared out the windows, hypnotized by the beat of the rain. She was glad there was no one else around.

It didn't really help her to know that Justin had studied the newspapers from ten years ago, other than to confirm that Cab Bolton was right. She didn't know what Justin would have learned, or what she hoped to discover by revisiting events that she had spent a long time trying to forget.

Her phone rang. She was grateful for the interruption.

"Fruity," her brother said when she answered. The connection was bad; the storm was already eroding the quality of the signal.

"Hey."

"I'm in the office, where are you?"

Peach hesitated. She didn't want to admit what she was doing. "The library," she said.

"Caprice told me about last night."

"Yeah, I figured."

There was a long pause. The connection flitted in and out, making him stutter. "I am pretty pissed, you know that, right? Caprice said you made contact with Macy. Do you know what kind of man he is? He may look like Leo DiCaprio, but he's not."

"I'm sorry. I didn't go there alone. Annalie was with me—"

"You could have gotten her killed, too!"

Peach felt like crying again. "Don't yell at me, Deacon."

Her brother went quiet. She thought for a moment that she'd lost the call, but then she could hear him breathing. "I know. I'm sorry. Look, do you think I ignored what you said? I started investigating Macy myself as soon as you told me about him."

"What did you find?" Peach asked.

"I hooked up with some of my contacts who know the Liberty Empire Alliance pretty well. Word is, their recruitment efforts are strong in the state prison system. If Macy spent eight years there, maybe they got to him."

"You think he's tied in to Ham Brock?"

"I don't know. I'm still asking around."

"Ramona Cortes represented both of them."

"Yeah, I know. Interesting, huh? Look, I'm going to try to follow—"

He stopped talking.

"Deacon?"

And then again: "Deacon?"

She looked at her phone. The call was gone. She tried dialing his number, but she had no signal.

Peach fidgeted impatiently. Suddenly, Lake Wales felt far away from everything. She didn't know what she was doing here. She spent half an hour pretending to study the newspapers and hoping Deacon would call back, but when he didn't, she decided she should go. She put the box of microfiche on the shelf to be refiled. She headed for the exit door, but the librarian called to her.

"Did you find what you needed?"

Peach stopped at the desk and gave her a weak smile. "Oh, yes, thanks. It was very helpful."

"I'm so sorry again about your boyfriend."

"Thank you."

"You be careful in the storm, okay? The best thing to do is find somewhere to hole up and let it all blow over."

"Yes, you're right," Peach said. She turned away, but as she did, she thought of another question. "Oh, there's one other thing, if you don't mind. I was wondering, did Justin ask you anything about someone named Alison?"

The librarian stared at her. "Alison? I don't think so. Do you have a last name?"

"I don't."

"Do you know anything else about her?"

"I'm afraid not. Just the name Alison."

Peach thought the woman looked suspicious, as if now this was all about exposing a boyfriend's affair.

"Well, he didn't say anything about that," she said, her voice clipped.

"Okay. Thank you again." She added: "I appreciate your help. I'm sorry to bother you. Sometimes it's just nice to talk to someone who met him, even a stranger. It makes him feel not so far away."

The woman's face lost its ice. "Of course. You know, I do remember something. I didn't think about it at first, because your young man asked one of the other staff members about it, not me. I simply over-heard him. He was looking for someone."

"Do you remember who?"

The woman's brow furrowed. "A doctor, I think. He was looking for a doctor who practiced around here ten years ago, and he was wondering if he was still in town. My associate looked it up for him."

"What was his name?"

"Let me think. Wills? Wells? I'm sorry, I wish I'd paid more attention, but I didn't."

"That's okay."

Peach was disappointed, but then, with a strange little chill, she reached into her past and pulled out a name. It made no sense. It couldn't be him. Why would Justin want to know anything about him?

"Smeltz?" she murmured. "Reuben Smeltz?"

The librarian's eyes widened with recognition. "Why, yes! That was it! I'm sure that was his name."

"And is he still alive? Is he still in town?"

"Let me check." The woman tapped keys on her keyboard, and not even ten seconds later, she beamed. "Yes indeed. Dr. Smeltz has an office—"

"On East Park Avenue downtown," Peach said. "Near the old clock tower."

She raised her eyebrows. "You're right. That's exactly where it is. Do you know him?"

Peach didn't answer her, but yes, she knew Dr. Reuben Smeltz. He was the man who treated her for pneumonia that night at Birch Fairmont's estate. He was her own doctor.

29

Garth Oakes jogged down the steps of the sprawling lakefront home in Lake Wales. He wore a form-fitting white T-shirt and baggy red nylon pants over his tree-trunk legs, and he carried a large nylon backpack. His black ponytail bobbed as he ran to his Subaru Outback. He dumped the pack in the rear and took a quick, hungry glance at the red Corvette parked immediately behind him. The rain was too heavy for Garth to see through the windshield, so Cab flashed his headlights at him.

Garth squinted, and then he ran for the passenger side of the Corvette and clambered into the sports car. He shook himself like a wet dog, releasing a spray of rain and an aroma of rosemary oil.

"Well, hey!" he said. "Detective! This is a small world."

"Not so small," Cab admitted. "I called your assistant. He said this is where you were."

"Oh, cool, okay. Hope you weren't waiting too long."

"Not long at all," Cab said.

A gust of wind rattled the car. Wet leaves and garlands of Spanish moss blew across the chassis. A hundred yards away, the surface of the lake was dappled by the relentless downpour.

"Woo, what a storm, huh?" Garth exulted. "And this is only the teaser. I've got to get back to Tampa before the roads get too bad."

"I won't take a lot of your time."

"Oh, don't worry about it, I'm fine." The trainer nodded at the house across the street, which had manicured hedges and white columns adorning a long front porch. "Been doing weekly massages for that lady for fifteen years. Hundred-dollar tip every time, but wow, it's like rubbing one of them shar-pei dogs, know what I mean? Wrinkles everywhere. People think the massage biz is glamorous, like you spend your days oiling up women who look like Beyoncé. I mean, I'm not saying you don't get a hot twentysomething now and then, but they're never the ones who spread their legs and ask if you can give an *all-over* massage, know what I mean?"

Whenever Garth talked, Cab found himself practicing Transcendental Meditation to see if he could crowd out whatever the man was saying.

"Hey, want a power bar?" Garth asked, digging in his pocket and pulling out a chocolate protein bar. Cab shook his head, and Garth unwrapped it and took a big, chewy bite. "Anyway, it's a living. I'd love to give up most of my personal clients and focus on my training videos, but I'm not there yet. Who knows, Diane gets in, maybe I get a publicity bump, you know?"

"Beat the Girth . . . With the Gov?" Cab asked.

Garth laughed, spitting granola onto the dashboard. His teeth were oddly purple against his Coppertone face. He'd been drinking wine, and he seemed a little drunk. "I love it! I love it!"

Cab studied the wet, muscle-bound masseur. A hanger-on, that was how Gladiola Croft described him. Garth stayed close to Diane for the perks it brought him. Money. Access. Clients. Gladiola said he was always around that summer, and ten years later, he was still a fixture in Diane's life. Cab didn't think it was sexual. The vibe that Garth gave off was overtly gay. Even so, he appeared to be Diane's secret keeper.

"Listen, Garth, I need your help with something," Cab said.

The masseur nodded. "Yeah, sure, what ya got?"

"Someone connected to the Common Way Foundation was murdered last month."

"Oh, is this the guy that this chick Peach was talking about? I heard about that last night."

"Justin Kiel," Cab said.

"Okay, yeah, what about him?"

"Did you know who he was? Did you ever talk to him?"

Garth shook his head. "Nope, never did."

"Did anyone mention him to you? Did Diane?"

"No, she didn't even know who he was," Garth said.

"What about a man named Frank Macy?" Cab asked.

Garth whistled. "Oh, yeah, him I know. Don't mention him to Diane, she'll go crazy."

"Because of Drew?" Cab said.

"Right."

"What was their relationship?"

"Oh, it was complicated."

"How so?" Cab asked.

Garth finished his power bar, crumpled the wrapper, and shoved it into Cab's ashtray. "Well, you gotta remember what Drew was like. I mean, here's a kid who grew up with nothing. Mom's dirt poor. Hardly any food on the table. Then she marries a rich entrepreneur, and next thing you know, the kid's living in high so-ci-ety. Some kids can't adjust to that."

Cab waited.

"Not that Drew was a bad kid," Garth went on. "I liked him. He just never had his head together."

"How so?"

"Well, for starters, Drew was gay. He came to me for advice, because he couldn't deal with it. I mean, it's one thing to be a gay guy like me, buff and all. Nobody's going to mess around with me, hear what I'm saying?" He winked at Cab. "Guess I'm not telling you anything about me that you haven't already figured out, huh?"

Cab smiled. "No."

"Don't suppose you play for the men's team."

"Sorry."

"Never hurts to ask. Anyway, Drew was skinny and shy. Kids in school tormented him. Vicious stuff. So did his stepdad."

"Birch did?" Cab asked, frowning.

"Oh, yeah. Never in front of Diane, but Drew told me that Birch called him queer and fag and all sorts of other shit behind Diane's back. Kid *hated* Birch. Can't say as I blame him."

"What about Frank Macy?"

"Drew met Macy in college. Lower-class background, but brainy, suave, and ruthless. Badass package. Drew used to bring him to the estate in Lake Wales, like they were buddies. I think he liked the idea of hanging out with somebody who was cool and streetwise, you know? If I had to guess, Drew was probably super-attracted to Macy, too."

"Macy's gay?" Cab asked.

"Doubt it. Even if he was, he wouldn't have looked twice at Drew. But there are plenty of so-called straight guys who don't mind having another guy suck their dick. As long as they're not the one on their knees, they figure it doesn't count. You ask me, Macy wouldn't have minded Drew taking the shine off when he didn't have any girls around. I think that would have messed with Drew's head in a big way."

"Did Diane know any of this? Did you talk to her about it?"

"Later. Much later. After Drew ate that gun. It wasn't just the drugs that did him in. Drew told me that he and Macy had a falling-out. Macy said he was done with him. I'm thinking he was pretty cruel about it. That was the final straw for Drew, who was fragile to start with. It wasn't long after that he killed himself."

Cab shook his head. This was worse than he thought. And more deadly. "Did Macy and Drew hang out together that summer before the Labor Day murders?"

Garth nodded. "Sure. I mean, it was a pretty sweet deal for Macy, huh? Rich kid always in need of a fix, plus an estate with a swimming pool and free booze. What's not to love?"

"Birch couldn't have been too happy about that during the campaign."

"No shit. Lyle went ballistic about it, too. They were afraid the press was going to get wind of Macy. Birch and Diane argued about it, and Birch told Drew he never wanted Macy in his house again. Drew didn't care."

"One more question, Garth. Birch and Diane. Two weeks before Labor Day. What really happened?"

The man's tanned face lost a couple shades of color. "Hey, I really shouldn't talk about that."

"If you think you're protecting Diane, you're not."

"Yeah, but still. I've said too much."

Cab leaned across the seat. "There was an argument. Screaming. You came and told the maid to get out. Why? What did Birch do?"

"Look, I wasn't in the room," Garth said. "I assume the son of a bitch got rough with her."

"How rough?"

"Rough enough that he told me to call a doctor and get him there fast. Then he told me to get the maid out of the house and get myself out, too."

"What did you do?"

"Exactly what he said."

"You didn't check on Diane?"

"I wanted to, but I didn't know what Birch would do. It was the worst I'd ever seen him. The guy had murder in his eyes."

"Who else was in the house?" Cab asked.

"Nobody."

"Who else knows about this?"

"Hardly anyone," Garth said. "I figure Lyle and Caprice found out, but they weren't going to tell anybody. Guess that's about all. Oh, and the doc. Reuben Smeltz. He was Diane's doctor."

Cab made a note of the name.

"And Drew," Cab said.

"Yeah, I don't know if Diane told him everything, but Drew could see she was hurt bad. She didn't appear in public again until Labor Day. People were starting to talk about it."

"The stress drove Drew into rehab?"

Garth nodded. "Yeah, he nearly killed himself with an overdose. Smeltz saved his life and got him back into treatment."

"Do you think Drew was serious?" Cab asked.

"About what?"

"Killing Birch," Cab said.

He expected a flat denial, but the masseur worked his mouth unhappily, like he was chewing something he couldn't swallow. "Does it matter? Birch is dead. So's Drew."

"It matters. Someone murdered Justin Kiel because he was asking the same questions."

"Hey, I knew Drew," Garth insisted. "The kid wasn't up to something like that. Bad enough to gun down Birch, but those other people, too? No way he did that himself."

"Okay. If he didn't pull the trigger himself, maybe he had help."

"Like who?"

"Like Frank Macy," Cab said. He saw a shadow in Garth's face as the masseur put two and two together. "Come on, Garth. Is there something you're not telling me?"

"It's nothing," he said. "I saw something, but it's not important."

"You obviously don't think that's true. What was it?"

Garth was silent, and he squirmed uncomfortably in his seat. The wine had loosened his tongue, but not enough to get him to spill his secrets. Cab was losing patience.

"Look, Garth, I'm trying to protect Diane. Justin's dead. She may be at risk. I need your help if I'm going to keep her safe." He didn't bother to add that if something happened to Diane, the gravy train ended for Garth. No more parties. No more hanging out in the mansion. No publicity bump for his exercise videos. Garth could connect the dots for himself.

"There's probably no connection," the masseur finally replied. "This happened weeks before Labor Day. Way back in July, I think."

"What did?"

Garth hesitated. "I heard gunshots."

"Where?"

"In the orange groves near the estate. I checked it out. Drew had a gun. He was firing into the trees. Blasting away the fruit. I don't know, he might have been high. It wasn't a good scene, you know?"

"You never told anyone about this?"

"Are you kidding? No way. I didn't even tell Diane until later in the summer. I didn't want to get the kid in trouble."

"Was Drew alone?" Cab asked.

Garth shook his head. He swallowed hard. "No. No, he wasn't alone. That's the thing. Frank Macy was with him. It was Macy's gun."

30

The knife was warm, heated by the dying man's severed entrails.

When he finally withdrew it from the body at his feet, torrents of rain poured into the wound. The rain spattered the blade, washing pink watery blood over his hands and onto the stone pier. The body below him twitched. The dying man's breath hacked and foamed; his heart still had a minute or two to beat, spurting rivulets that oozed into the bay.

The man with the knife breathed heavily. It had gone as planned, but it was never easy. First a blow from the flashlight to the other man's forehead, dizzying him. A jab to the throat. Ankle around ankle, driving him backward to the ground, his skull cracking on stone. And then the knife, opening him up, letting him bleed out.

The storm blotted out everything around him. He could barely see the beach, which was fifty yards away. The industrial buildings bordering the park were dark, deserted shapes. The agitated water slurped against the Picnic Island pier like a noisy blow job. Out in the channel, white lights outlined a giant ore tanker headed for safe harbor, but the ship appeared as disembodied as a ghost floating in darkness.

Below him, the man's eyes were fixed, like gray stones. It was almost over. He would spend eternity that way, with that same look of impotent, furious surprise. His mouth was stuck open. The blood no longer pulsed from the giant gash. The dead man's fingers were still curled around the aluminum pistol case, so he peeled them away, taking the handle of the case in his own hand. He had what he needed now. Everything was ready.

He pushed himself to his feet, staring at the body.

"Don't move!" a voice called to him above the rain.

Instinctively, he flicked up the heavy flashlight toward the sound. He saw a gun, twenty feet away, pointed at his chest. The man holding the gun squinted into the bright light. He was bulky, with blond hair plastered to his face. He wore a sport coat, dress pants, and sneakers. He looked middle-aged and soft.

This wasn't a moment for panic or fear, just cold calculations. Twenty feet wasn't an easy shot in the driving rain, but if he charged, he was dead. The man was a stranger, but his appearance was no accident. One of them had been followed. Himself or the dead man at his feet. It was bad either way.

The man with the gun came closer, rubbing his eyes. The rain was like a waterfall. The gun wobbled as he pointed it. "He dead?" the man shouted, nodding at the body on the pier. "That took balls!"

He didn't reply. The man had seen the murder play out. That was no good. He watched the man try to keep the gun steady and keep water out of his eyes. The flashlight was bright; it had to be a fat orange blob on his retinas now. The downpour made the man gulp and swallow.

"Looks like a gun case!" the man called, gesturing at the aluminum case. "You planning on shooting somebody?"

"You," he hollered over the howl of the storm.

The man's eyes widened nervously, but then his stubbly, fleshy face relaxed, and he chortled. He came even closer, until they were almost chest to chest. "That's funny."

"It's no joke. Who are you?"

"The name's Ritchie."

"Better get the hell out of here, Ritchie."

The man with the gun grinned at the hollow threat. "Yeah? Maybe you haven't noticed, but your gun's inside a metal case, and mine's pointed at your chest. Now get on your knees."

He assessed his options. There was a four-foot railing on one side of the pier. On the other side, the pier was open, inches above the swirling water. He didn't know how deep it was or what debris littered the bottom. As they confronted each other, the wind tore into both of their bodies, shoving them off balance. Rain threatened to drown them where they stood.

"Get on your knees!" Ritchie shouted again. "Put the pistol case down."

He squatted and put the aluminum case in front of him. Ritchie knelt down, and his blurred eyes, soaked by rain, flicked toward the pier as he groped for the handle of the case. The barrel of Ritchie's gun dipped sideways.

That was the moment he needed.

With Ritchie off balance, he corkscrewed sideways, throwing himself off the pier. Ritchie's gun cracked above the storm. The bullet singed the flesh of his arm, but in the next moment, the water engulfed him, and he sank below the surface. The bay was warm and black. He kicked through the water, putting distance between himself and where he'd entered the bay. Somewhere above him, Ritchie fired again, and then again, but he knew the man was blind, seeing the afterimage of the flashlight as if he'd been staring into the sun.

He felt the bottom; it wasn't deep. His head and then his torso rose out of the water like a sea monster. Ritchie was immediately above him. He seized the man's right ankle with both hands and levered his leg into the air. Ritchie toppled backward. The gun blasted harmlessly toward the sky. Ritchie landed hard on the concrete pier, and he slithered out of the water and threw himself on top of the man, wrestling for the gun. He pinned Ritchie's wrist; the gun fired again, loud and hot. Ritchie landed a haymaker on the side of his skull, shunting him sideways, making the world spin. Heavy and strong, Ritchie rolled on top of him. The rain poured over their bodies.

The gun fired again, so close now that the explosion made his ear bleed. A bullet ricocheted on stone and metal, and something sharp cut his face. He grabbed Ritchie's wrist again, but the man outweighed him, and he could see the gun barrel push toward his face. He felt something in his pocket. Something sharp and solid. In a single seamless motion, he yanked out his knife and drove it sideways into the flesh of Ritchie's neck, until the hilt collided with cartilage and bone.

Ritchie howled. His fingers loosened. The gun fell.

He dislodged the big man with a heave of his fists, and Ritchie flopped over on his back, grabbing at the knife in his neck with both hands. The knife oozed out of his body, wet and slippery, and clattered onto the pier. Ritchie gagged and clambered to his knees, pawing the ground for his gun, but it wasn't there. The killer already had the gun in his hand.

He watched Ritchie, who was choking on the blood that rose in his throat. The man scuttled on his hands and knees like a giant crab, limbs twitching, head jerking as torn nerves fired randomly at his brain. He put the hot barrel against Ritchie's skull and fired into his head. One shot, expelling bone, brain, and blood in a cloud. Ritchie became dead weight, collapsing. The second dead man on the pier. The second man he'd killed tonight.

He was soaked with bay water, rain, and sweat, but he had to move. He shoved Ritchie's gun into his belt. Bending over, he grabbed Ritchie's body with both hands and rolled him toward the edge of the pier, until the dead man fell free and splashed into the dark water and sank. He straightened up, his whole body aching. The bullet that grazed his arm had left a burn on his skin. He was still alone, surrounded by the tumult of the storm, but the noise was muffled in his ears. He stared into the bay, unable to see anything below the surface. They would find Ritchie eventually, but that didn't matter to him.

The other body was the one he needed.

He grabbed the dead man's ankles and dragged him toward the beach, letting the storm clean away the trail of blood.

PART THREE

CHAYLA

31

"You work late," Cab said.

Dr. Reuben Smeltz snorted. "Paperwork," he said. "That's what medicine is about today. A thousand insurance companies with ten thousand forms and a hundred thousand codes. I delivered a baby last week. By the time I get the paperwork done, he'll be trying out for his sixth-grade soccer team."

"I guess the profession has changed a lot."

"Profession? We're just mechanics now. Paid by the hour." Smeltz slugged coffee from a foam cup and grimaced.

"It's still better than being a lawyer, though, right?" Cab asked.

Smeltz smiled. "You do know how to look on the bright side of life, detective."

"That's what people tell me." Cab glanced at the water-stained drop ceiling as the fluorescent lights flickered. A gust of wind rocked the windowless office. "Anyway, I appreciate your seeing me. You must be anxious to get home."

The doctor shrugged. "Storms are storms. I've seen a lot worse than this."

Smeltz was in his late sixties, medium-height and overweight. His hair was brown, but it was thinning, combed back and greased down to lie flat on his head. He had a jowly face and tiny circular glasses. He wore a pressed shirt and tie, and his white coat was hung on a rack near the office door. Papers were spread out in front of him, and he took occasional bites from a chicken-and-pear salad along with sips of his coffee.

He sat behind a weathered oak desk. His leather armchair had splits in the seams where bits of yellow foam were escaping. Cab sat in front of the desk in an uncomfortable wooden chair that didn't encourage visitors to stay longer than necessary. The doctor had diplomas and photographs of patients on the wall behind him, reflecting a practice in Lakes Wales that dated back decades. The wall on Cab's right was lined with file cabinets, and each drawer was hand-labeled with letters of the alphabet.

The other wall, which had fake wood paneling, included a long table with a 1980s-era coffeemaker, a potted poinsettia, a bowl of round multicolored mints, and a surprisingly modern laser printer. A heavy door at the end of the wall featured a sophisticated combination lock.

"So you're from Naples?" Smeltz asked between bites of salad.

"Yes, I am."

"My wife likes Naples. She thinks we should retire there. Get one of those high-rise condos."

"They're very nice," Cab said.

"Yes, except then all the seniors find out you're a doctor and they want free advice on everything from shingles to melanoma. For that, I may as well stay here." He speared a piece of romaine lettuce with his fork. "People ever tell you that you don't look much like a detective?"

"Regularly."

"Cop or not, you realize I can't say a word about my patients."

"Of course," Cab said.

The rain on the roof sounded like a firing range. A drop of water squeezed through the ceiling and squished onto the carpet. The doctor got up and retrieved a large orange bucket, which he positioned under the leak.

"Old building," he explained. "I keep putting off replacing the roof."

Another drop fell, making a loud *chunk* in the bucket.

"So you've got concerns about Diane Fairmont's safety," Smeltz went on. "True or not, that doesn't change anything. Diane was my patient, which means my lips are sealed, at least until she tells me otherwise. If you think you can weasel something out of me, don't try. That just annoys me. People have played those games with me for years."

Smeltz grabbed a tissue and blew his potato-like nose. He crumpled the tissue, threw it away, and pumped a blob of alcohol sanitizer into his hand.

"Who's been asking you questions about Diane?" Cab asked.

The doctor chuckled. "Oh, she's a popular topic. Sometimes it's reporters. Sometimes it's political types. Last month I had a man in here who was obviously a private detective. He hinted he would make it worth my while if I spilled some secrets. God knows who he was working for. The whole thing is a pretty sorry business, if you ask me, all these spies looking for dirt."

"Diane's in the same business, isn't she? Common Way isn't shy about looking for dirt on its political opponents."

"Maybe, but the lady has my vote."

"You like her."

"I do. Always have."

"You mentioned reporters knocking on your door. Did one of them happen to be Rufus Twill?"

Smeltz smiled wide enough to show a row of aging teeth. He leaned back in his chair, which squealed in protest. "Oh, sure, Rufus talked to me. He was a patient growing up, and I suppose he figured he could wheedle something out of me. I sent him packing without so much as a 'No comment.'"

"What did Rufus want to know about Diane?"

"I suspect you already know, detective, but if you don't, I'm not going to tell you. I'm sorry. I have a broad definition of privilege. I don't talk about my patients, and I don't talk about what other people say about my patients."

Cab nodded. "I imagine it had something to do with an incident between Birch and Diane shortly before the Labor Day murders."

The doctor's face darkened. The bucket on the floor went *chunk* again. "I told you, I have nothing to say."

"Was Birch your patient, too?"

"No."

"So he doesn't enjoy privilege."

"That makes no difference," Smeltz said.

"I just want to know what kind of man Birch was."

The doctor rubbed the layer of fat gathered under his chin. "If you're asking whether I cried when Birch was killed, I didn't."

"I heard he was a bully and a son of a bitch."

"I won't dispute that characterization," Smeltz said.

"Were you surprised when he was killed?"

"Of course. Nobody expects terrorists to strike in their own backyard."

"Some people think Birch's death was personal, not political."

Smeltz narrowed his eyes. "What are you implying?"

"I have a witness who overheard Diane's son, Drew, threatening to blow Birch's head off. He was seen with a gun that summer. And he got out of a stint in rehab just days before the murders."

"You can't honestly believe that Drew—" Smeltz exclaimed, but he stopped in mid-sentence. "You're not going to goad me into saying anything, detective. Drew was my patient, too. I'm not discussing him."

"He's dead."

"That doesn't change my obligations."

Cab dug in his suit coat pocket for a piece of paper. "You mentioned someone visiting you last month who looked like a private detective. Was this the man?"

He showed Smeltz a photograph of Justin Kiel taken from a newspaper article about his murder.

The doctor took the paper and shook his head. "No, not even close. The man I spoke to was older and heavier." Smeltz was about to hand the paper back to Cab when he looked at the photograph again. He didn't look happy. "Wait a minute."

"Do you know him?"

"Well, I recognize him, yes. He showed up when I was working late a few weeks ago. He works for a computer repair company. Apparently, my assistant called and said we were having problems with our computer. I'm always having problems with this damn thing."

Cab nodded. Justin was clever. "Did you leave him alone in your office?"

Smeltz thought about it. "Actually, I did. Someone knocked on the outside door while he was working on the printer. It was a very annoying foreign person who was looking for directions and didn't seem to understand anything I was saying." The doctor frowned and tapped the paper with a thick finger. "Who is he? Are you saying this man was some kind of spy?"

"Yes, he was. Of a sort."

Smeltz pounded his desk in annoyance. "Was this about Diane again? If you find this man, I want to press charges."

"I'm afraid you won't be able to do that. He was murdered."

"Oh my God!" Smeltz exclaimed.

Two drops fell from the ceiling in quick succession. *Chunk chunk.*

"His death is one of the reasons I'm concerned about Diane."

The doctor looked flustered. "Well . . . I hate to hear that, but I still can't tell you anything more than I have."

"I appreciate your privacy concerns," Cab went on, "but if this man—Justin Kiel—was in your office, it's possible that he found something that contributed to his murder. Something in your files. I know that you want to protect your patients, but if Justin learned a secret about Diane or Drew—"

Smeltz shook his head. "He didn't."

"How can you be sure?"

"There's nothing about Diane or Drew on my computer. My computerized records don't go back that far."

"What about hard copy files?" Cab asked, nodding at the row of file cabinets in the office.

"The files aren't there either," Smeltz told him. "I'm not a fool, detective. Too many people have expressed interest in Diane for me to keep her papers in my ordinary files. Believe me, this man was only alone in my office for five minutes at most. He didn't find them. Nobody would find them."

When Cab got back to the deserted main street of Lake Wales, the rain stung his face like a swarm of bees. He wore a black Burberry trench coat with the collar up and the belt tied at his waist. His wet blond hair lay messy and flat on his head. He endured the assault like a statue, frozen and tall. The night was black, and the wind carried a faint smell of oranges. He crossed the street beside the old marble clock tower and got into his Corvette, which was parked diagonally in front of the Lake Wales News building. He was opposite a small plaza dotted with waving trees and a checkerboard sidewalk.

The downtown street wasn't a hive of activity in the best of times, but in the storm, it was eerily quiet. Clouds of rain whipped between the old storefronts, taking on shapes like giant skeletons.. The only light was the glow from the doctor's office, and as he watched, the light went black. Dr. Smeltz was going home.

Cab turned on his engine. He didn't feel like making the long drive back to the coast. He decided to get a motel room, even though he knew the storm would be worse by morning. The rain, as bad as it was, was simply a preview of coming attractions. The real danger would begin tomorrow when the swirling body of Chayla nudged over land.

Tomorrow. The Fourth of July. Independence Day.

He backed out of the parking place and switched on his headlights. The beams captured the sheeting rain and the gray stone of the clock tower. He squinted. Just for an instant, he saw someone standing in the plaza. It was a young woman, alone, buffeted by the downpour. Water pooled like a lake at her feet. She was skinny, and without a coat she was soaked to the bone. He couldn't see well

enough to recognize her face, but there was something oddly familiar about her. He thought she was staring at him and that she knew
who he was.

The wind gusted, the girl turned, and she vanished behind a curtain of rain. It was as if she'd never been there at all.

32

Peach waited until Dr. Smeltz left his office.

She recognized the doctor's lumpy profile. He hadn't changed in the years since she'd seen him as a child. She had always liked him. He was gruff but had a sweet soul, and he had a special weakness for kids. Her appointments with him had always taken a long time, because he had Lego dinosaurs and Disney action figures for her, and he seemed to enjoy playing with them as much as she did. Or maybe that was just his way of making her feel at ease in a scary place.

Dr. Smeltz bounded across the plaza, his multiple chins tucked against the rain, his brimmed hat dripping like a waterfall. He passed within ten feet of Peach, but he didn't see her. The doctor got into an Audi and drove away, his tires throwing up a wave of water. She figured he was going home to his house by the lake, with the huge front yard that stretched to the beach. Lyle had taken her there once. It was one of the last things they'd done together. He'd said she needed a follow-up visit for her pneumonia, but he didn't take her to the medical office. When they got to the doctor's house, Dr. Smeltz didn't even examine her at all. Instead, she played on the lawn with Google, the doctor's Westie puppy, while Lyle and Dr. Smeltz talked inside.

Lyle had never told her what they talked about, but afterward, he'd gone to see a lawyer in Orlando.

Peach stood in the rain. The Gulf storm was warm, but she felt chilled. The plaza was empty. So was the main street, now that the two men had left. She saw no traffic, but she kept an eye open for police cars stalking the downtown area. The doctor's building, which was low and built of tan brick and stucco, was deserted. The three tall windows facing the plaza were black. The wind nearly picked her up and carried her away. She hugged the trunk of a palm tree.

She thought about Cab Bolton. She'd spotted his car on the street, and she wanted to know where he was going. He'd seen her when he left the office, but she doubted that he would have recognized her in her disguise. She wondered what he wanted with Dr. Smeltz. Him and Justin both. They had plucked this man from her past, and she didn't understand why.

Or did she?

Staring at the clinic where she had gone dozens of times as a child, she realized that she knew exactly what they were looking for. She heard Cab's voice in her head earlier that day. *Two weeks before Labor Day, something very ugly happened at Birch's estate.*

And then another voice. Her own voice. Talking to Justin. *We walked into the middle of something.*

Deacon had driven her to Birch's estate on that awful Saturday night. The night of sickness and delirium. The night when they hit the deer. The night when her body was burning up and the nicest thing in the world was to have Caprice carry her to that lavish guest bedroom that smelled of vanilla and coconut and to see, hovering behind her, that smiling, fleshy, familiar face. Dr. Smeltz. Her doctor. He would make everything better.

My doctor was already at the estate when we arrived.

That was the connection she'd failed to make all these years. Why would a child give it a second thought? He'd already been called to the house. Not for her. For something else entirely.

Something bad.

Justin must have found out, and Justin was dead. Had Cab Bolton found out, too? Had Dr. Smeltz told him? It didn't matter. She needed to know for herself.

Peach shut off her phone and checked the downtown street. Awnings on the storefronts flapped madly, like baseball cards in a bicycle spoke. The trees bent down as if they were praying. Branches, leaves, and dirt spat through the air. She knelt in the plaza, which was lined with loose red bricks. It was easy enough to dig her fingers into the gaps and pry them free. She uprooted the bricks and scattered them around the plaza the way the storm would. Gusts of wind could lift up rocks and hurl them like javelins.

She took one brick and walked ten more feet to the edge of the plaza, where she stood in front of the three floor-to-ceiling windows that looked in on the lobby of the clinic. *I'm sorry, Dr. Smeltz.*

Peach hurled the brick into the center window. The glass shattered, caving inward, leaving shards on every side that looked like a shark's teeth. The crash banged loudly in her ears, but the howling wind drowned it out. No alarm sounded. No strobe lights flashed. She kicked some of the glass teeth out of the frame with the toe of her shoe and carefully squeezed through the hole into the building.

Rain flooded inside, pooling on the floor. The brick lay in the middle of the sandstone tile, surrounded by fragments that crunched under her feet. The water made the floor slippery, and she stumbled. Her skirt tore, and a gash opened on her knee. When she touched it, the cut stung, and her fingers came away with blood. She sucked them clean.

The waiting room was small. It smelled of antiseptic cleaner. Behind the receptionist's desk, she saw a door that led to the rest of the clinic. She'd been here many times, heard the young nurse call her name, and followed the woman nervously to the examining rooms in the back. Peach pushed through the wooden door, the way she had as a kid. When she closed it behind her, the hallway was black. She fumbled for a light switch and found it, and fluorescent lights flickered to life overhead. There were no windows; no one outside would see.

Most of the doors in the hallway were open. They led to different examining rooms. She saw cushioned tables on which she'd sat as a child, pedaling her legs. The doctor's little wheely chair. The cabinets where he'd grabbed bottles and needles. In one of the rooms, she saw green Legos that had been made into an alligator, and she smiled. Some things didn't change.

Dr. Smeltz's name was on a plaque in the middle of one door. She opened it, stepped inside, and closed the door behind her, turning on the lights. The office smelled of Dr. Smeltz, which meant it smelled of coffee and those little chocolate mints he kept for patients, but which he mostly ate himself. Peach saw a bowl of them on a table near his computer. She couldn't resist taking one and biting down on the candy shell. The taste brought a wave of memories.

Something in the office made a loud *chunk*, and she had to cover her mouth to keep from screaming. When it happened again, she saw rainwater dripping from the ceiling into an orange bucket. She giggled at her overreaction, but it reminded her that she had broken into an office building and was mounting an illegal search. She couldn't waste time.

She spotted the doctor's locked steel file cabinets. Like she had in Ogden Bush's office, she did a search of the desk, and it took her less than five minutes to find a key. She unlocked the file cabinet on the wall and opened the middle drawer, which was labeled with a handwritten "D–F."

Peach pawed through bulging folders. The files were squeezed together so tightly that she could barely separate them. Dr. Smeltz had been practicing in Lake Wales since the 1970s, and the spidery ink on some of the folders had faded. Papers were yellowed. The alphabetizing wasn't always perfect. Peach went from front to back, checking each folder, but found no files on Diane Fairmont. The name Fairmont didn't appear at all.

Ms. Fairmont's maiden name was Hempl. Dr. Smeltz had probably treated her before she married Birch. Peach repeated her search on the drawer labeled "G–I," but again, the effort was fruitless. She began to feel frustrated, and her nervousness grew as time passed. The last cabinet on the wall had three unlabeled drawers. She checked them, but they were empty except for unmarked file folders and a box of markers. Finally, she unlocked the other file cabinets on the wall and began to search all of the remaining drawers.

She expected to find her own medical file, but she never got there. She had reached the M files when she heard voices.

Peach froze, and her heartbeat soared with fear. Someone had spotted the broken window. She remembered that she'd left the outer hallway light on, which was *stupid, stupid, stupid*. She closed the drawer where she was searching and locked the cabinets with soft clicks. Her eyes traveled the room for a hiding place. She dove for the light switch, flicked off the office light, and groped her way to the desk. Finding it, she felt for the doctor's armchair and nudged it backward. The casters squeaked. Peach folded herself inside the small space under the desk, then pulled the chair as tightly against herself as she could. She held her breath.

She wondered if she'd been dripping on the floor, leaving a trail.

The office door opened, and the overhead lights came on again, harsh and bright. The voices got louder. There were two men. She heard their footsteps. At least one of them had a body odor problem.

"I'm telling you, the storm broke the window," said one.

"Yeah? Did the storm turn the light on, too?" The second man had a Spanish accent.

"They probably forgot."

The footsteps moved around the office. One of the men came up to the desk; she could see the shadow of his legs. He walked behind the desk; he was next to the chair. If he bent down, he would see her. She could have reached out and pulled up his sock, which had fallen to reveal a bare ankle.

"Nobody," said the first man.

The second man grunted. He was the one who was close to her. "Check the drug cabinet."

"It's locked."

"The book says always check the closet if there's an alarm. The combination is 0630."

The second man moved away from the desk. Peach let out her breath in a slow, silent hiss. She heard the clicking of metal buttons, and the door to the supply closet opened. The floor was concrete; she could hear the difference in the sound of their footsteps.

"All clear here. Man, he's got a stash, huh?"

"He's a doctor, what do you expect?"

The two men returned to the office and locked the supply closet door.

"That it?" said the first man.

"We have to call Dr. Smeltz," his colleague replied.

"He's not going to be happy coming out in the storm."

"He's not going to be happy seeing his window broken and his lobby looking like it's in the middle of Crooked Lake."

"We hanging around?" asked the first man.

"You are. I'll go to the next call. I'll swing back and pick you up after the doc arrives."

The first man muttered unhappily under his breath. Moments later, the office light went off. Peach waited, not moving. She heard footsteps receding in the hallway. The voices continued, muffled and distant, and then they went silent. She heard a door open and close.

Immediately afterward, a radio blared in the waiting room. Loud, hip-hop music. She wasn't alone. The first man had stayed behind, waiting for Dr. Smeltz. She knew that the doctor would only need ten or fifteen minutes to make his way back to the clinic. She needed to be gone before he arrived.

Peach scrambled out from under the desk. She could still smell the mildewed aroma of sweat the men had left behind. Her instinct was to make an immediate break for the rear exit that led to the alley, but she still hadn't found a file for Diane Fairmont. Dr. Smeltz didn't keep her file with his other patient records, but she realized that was no surprise. He would keep the records separate and secure. Even so, she didn't think he would keep the file off-site, in case he needed to access the information. There was only one room in the building that had a heavy door and a secure lock. That was the drug closet ten feet away from her.

The lock that opened with the combination 0630.

Peach wasted no time. She turned on the office light again and quickly keyed the buttons to gain access to the supply closet. Inside, with a quick review of the room, she found herself disappointed. There were no file cabinets. No lockboxes. The room was lined with metal shelves that were stocked with pharmaceuticals and medical supplies. She saw nowhere to hide files. Her face fell. The clock was ticking, and she needed to go.

Then she spotted a red metal chest shoved into a corner. It was two feet by two feet and twelve inches high. She'd almost missed it, because boxes of gauze and bagged patient gowns had been stacked on top of the lid. A small padlock latched the chest shut, and a hand-written sign had been taped to the front. The sign read, in bold black letters: **BIO-HAZARD**.

She stared at it, frowning. Why would a hazardous-materials chest be covered up with supplies? Why a handwritten sign? She knew Dr. Smeltz. He wasn't fussy about a lot of things, but he was particular when it came to the safety of his practice.

Peach crossed the room and used a hairpin to pop the tiny padlock. She shifted the clutter off the chest, undid the latch, and opened the heavy metal lid. There were no used needles or contaminated waste inside. Instead, the chest was empty except for two thick file folders.

One folder was labeled **DIANE (HEMPL) FAIRMONT**.

The second was labeled **DREW HEMPL**.

Peach stared at the folders and thought: *This is wrong.* However, she'd already left the line between right and wrong far behind her.

She gathered the files into her arms. Quickly, she relocked the chest and replaced the supplies, so it looked as if nothing had been disturbed. She hoped Dr. Smeltz didn't look too carefully. Glancing at the clock on the wall, she shut the supply closet door again.

Music thumped from the waiting room. It was Nicki Minaj. Peach switched off the lights and inched the office door open. The hallway lights were dark, but she pushed her face out to peek down the hallway, and she saw that the lobby door was open. A male voice rose above the music; the first man was on his cell phone. As she watched, he wandered into view, his back to her. He was tall and meaty, wearing a tight gray uniform.

Peach slipped into the hallway. A red exit sign glowed at the end of the corridor to her left. The medical files were snug under her right arm. Rain drummed on the roof above her. She backed up, keeping her eyes on the man in the lobby. Nicki sang about "Beez in the Trap," and the security guard did the worst white man's dance Peach had ever seen. He was still on the phone.

"Are you kidding? No way I'm apologizing to her. Okay, so I yelled at her kid. Big deal. She's lucky I didn't put my foot up his ass. Little twit was sticking peanut butter in my Blu-ray player! Is that supposed to be funny? I mean, the thing's completely f—"

He spun around, still dancing, and then he stopped dead.

Peach was a shadow halfway down the hallway, but he stared right at her. Their eyes met across the dark space. His mouth fell open in surprise.

"HEY!" he bellowed.

Peach turned and sprinted. Footsteps pounded behind her, but a scream and crash intervened as the man slipped in the pooled water and wiped out. She stole a look behind her; he was struggling to get up. He shouted curses after her, but she widened the gap and hit the emergency exit door with her shoulder. It flew open, and she bolted into the storm. Her heart was thumping, her mouth open, swallowing water that sprayed into her face. It was night, and the rainfall was a black shroud.

She was across the plaza before the man made it out of the building. She raced into the darkness and disappeared.

33

Cab perched his long legs on the motel bed, which took up most of the room. The motel had a musty, old-cigarette smell. He sat by the window with an open bottle of red wine in front of him. The hammering of rain on the glass was hypnotic. The wine was delicious; he always kept a bottle of Stags' Leap in the rear of the Corvette, in case of emergency.

Sitting alone in a cheap motel room in the middle of a storm definitely counted as an emergency. He was on his second glass.

He thought about what he had discovered so far and what it all meant.

Ten years ago, Birch Fairmont committed some unspeakable act that Diane and the people around her had kept a closely guarded secret to this day. Only two weeks later, an unidentified assassin shot three people at the Bok sanctuary, including Birch. Back then, no one made a connection between the two events. Instead, the Liberty Empire Alliance got the blame for painting a target on Birch's chest. Hamilton Brock went to prison but claimed he was set up by a mole inside the Alliance. Chuck Warren lost the election but saw a conspiracy orchestrated by the Democrats and the media.

Conspiracy or not, the crime went unsolved.

Fast forward to now.

Rufus Twill, who had led the media wolf pack going after the Liberty Empire Alliance ten years ago, was singing a different song. So was his niece, a former employee at the Fairmont household. They were both spreading rumors that Diane's son, Drew, hated Birch and wanted him dead. Drew also had a relationship with a hip, violent young drug dealer named Frank Macy. If Cab connected the dots, then maybe Birch's death wasn't what everyone originally believed. Or maybe he was being played, and this was just a new political conspiracy aimed at Diane.

Rufus Twill had an agenda in pointing a finger at Drew after all these years. That was obvious. He wasn't the kingpin; someone else was orchestrating the rumors. Money had changed hands. It felt like the usual election-year games—but Justin Kiel's death wasn't a game. He'd been executed.

Justin had found something that made him a mortal threat. He'd been asking questions about Birch's murder. He'd searched the office of Dr. Reuben Smeltz. He'd followed the trail of Drew's drug dealer, Frank Macy. And he wound up with a bullet in his brain.

Definitely not a game.

Cab knew the least about Frank Macy of any of the players in this drama, but what he did know troubled him. Macy had a criminal record and access to guns. He also had connections to a woman who would very much like to see Diane's downfall. The attorney general and Republican gubernatorial candidate, Ramona Cortes.

Cab didn't know what to believe anymore. He was in a shadow play, where he couldn't trust what his eyes told him. The wine swam in his head. His clothes were still wet; he was cold. The rain fired at the motel window like a machine gun. He picked up his cell phone and did what he always did when he couldn't sort out what was real and what was not.

He called Lala.

Signal was weak as the storm fought the satellites. He didn't expect an answer, but this time, on the second static-filled ring, he heard her voice.

"Hello, Cab."

He almost forgot to say anything. Then he recovered. "The storm's bad. Are you safe?"

"Yes."

"Are you alone?"

God, what a stupid thing to say. He could hear her smile. "Shouldn't I be asking you that question?"

"I have no interest in Caprice Dean," he said.

"Liar."

"Well, I have interest, but I'm taking your advice to heart."

"Good."

She was quiet and far away. The storm felt as if it were coming between them. He expected the call to drop and split them apart. He felt the physical distance and the desire for her body; it had been weeks since they'd made love. More than that, he felt ungrounded without her.

"Where are you?" she asked. "At Tarla's place?"

"No, I'm in Lake Wales."

"Because of Diane Fairmont?"

"Yes."

Her words broke up. He held the phone near the window. "What? I didn't hear that."

"I asked if you'd found out anything."

"Only that you were right. I'm swimming with sharks."

"Well, your teeth are pretty sharp, too," Lala said. "I should know."

Cab grinned. "Nice memory for a man alone in a motel room. Tarla says we should try phone sex."

"Yes, because sexual suggestions from your mother really turn me on."

"You too?"

He heard her laugh. He could always make her laugh. Then, as the silence drew out, he remembered where he was. "Honestly?" he told her. "I'm worried."

"About what?"

"I have this feeling that the past is about to repeat itself, and I'm not going to be able to stop it."

She didn't answer. He thought he'd lost her again. He wondered if she realized he'd been drinking.

"Lala?"

"Cab, if you find *anything at all*, I want you to call me."

He was surprised by the intensity in her voice. "I haven't. I have puzzle pieces that don't fit together. I have motives layered upon motives. None of it tells me who really killed Birch Fairmont. None of it tells me whether Diane is really in jeopardy."

He waited for an answer, but didn't get one.

"I'm not working for Caprice anymore," he went on. "I want to know what's going on, but I can't do that with politicians trying to manipulate me."

"I know how you feel. Really, I do."

"Caprice wasn't happy. I think she wanted a detective boy toy."

He heard her laugh again. "I hope you didn't quit because of me."

"Partly."

"I feel guilty about that. I don't own you."

"Don't worry about it," he said. "I do have a problem, though."

The static swallowed her voice again. When she spoke, she said, "What problem?"

"I'm anticipating the return of Catch-a-Cab Bolton."

"Oh." Lala knew what his nickname meant. It was a symbol of his jackrabbit past. Never staying in one place. Never staying in one job. He was always chasing something or being chased. "So are you going to leave Florida? Tarla won't be happy."

"What about you?"

"This is about you, not me."

"I didn't say I wanted to leave town. I'm saying I like the idea of working for myself. My vacation from the Naples police is likely to become permanent. I don't think I was born to be part of a bureaucracy."

"Okay."

"I just want to make sure you understand that it has nothing whatsoever to do with you and me."

"Okay."

But he didn't think she believed him.

"Happy Independence Day," he said.

"What?"

"It's past midnight. It's the Fourth of July."

"You're right."

"No fireworks this year. Chayla's spoiling the party."

"I guess so."

"Did you know that Independence Day is the anniversary of Hamilton Brock going to prison?" he asked.

"I didn't."

"That bothers me. Anniversaries like that are dangerous. Except now I'm starting to wonder whether the Liberty Empire Alliance was involved in Birch's murder at all."

He heard a knocking on his motel room door.

"I have to go," he said. "I ordered a pizza."

"You?"

"Yes, me. There aren't many options here this late."

"Pizza Hut doesn't put Brie and spinach on their pies, you know."

"So they told me," Cab said.

"Listen, Cab, there's something you should know."

"What?"

She didn't answer right away. He thought of a thousand different things she might say, and he wasn't sure how to reply to any of them.

"Nothing," she went on.

"Are you sure?"

"I'm sure. Enjoy your pizza. But remember what I said. If you discover anything that doesn't feel right, I want you to call me right away."

"Okay."

"I mean it. Call me."

"Yes, mother."

"Oh, that is so not funny."

"Sure it is," he said.

Cab hung up and put down his wine glass. He felt bad about bringing a pizza delivery guy out in the storm, but he was hungry, and the kid would like the tip. He couldn't believe they didn't put Brie on their pizzas.

He grabbed his wallet out of his pocket and opened the motel room door, ushering in a wave of silver rain. It wasn't a teenager delivering his pizza.

Peach Piper stood on the doorstep.

34

"Well," Cab Bolton said, as he ushered her into the motel room and closed the door. "It's Peach, isn't it?"

"Yes."

She watched the gangly detective slump into a chair by the window. He looked amused, rather than surprised, to see her here. He held up a half-empty bottle of wine. "Want a glass? It's excellent, I promise."

"I don't drink."

"I have a pizza coming, if you're hungry."

"Is it vegetarian?"

"It is, actually."

She shrugged. "I could eat."

Peach shifted uncomfortably, dripping on the carpet. The room was dark. He noticed her glance at the light switch, and he leaned over with long arms and turned on the lamp. He gestured at the bed. "You can sit down for the same price."

"Okay."

"I was about to swear that I have no evil intentions, but since you're the one who showed up in my motel room, shouldn't that be your line?"

Her lips twitched in a small smile. It was hard not to like this man. She sat primly on the end of the bed and put the two damp medical files next to her. His eyes studied the files curiously, but he didn't ask about them.

"You're soaked," he said. "I have an extra blanket in my trunk. Do you want it?"

"No, I'm okay. Thanks, though."

Cab eased back into the chair and picked up his glass of wine. "So."

She knew he was waiting for her to explain. She didn't know what to say or even why she'd decided to come here. The arrival of the pizza gave her more time. Cab answered the door, paid the boy with what looked like a fifty-dollar bill—no change—and propped open the white box on the table in front of him. He put a triangular slice on a paper plate and handed it to her, and when she took a bite, she decided she was ravenous. They finished more than half the pizza in silence.

He watched her the whole time, but his curious stare didn't bother her. His blue eyes were smart and ironic; so was his funny little grin. He was unusually handsome. Being so much younger than he was—at least ten years, probably fifteen—she didn't feel any attraction to him, but that didn't mean she couldn't appreciate a man who was very cute. It wasn't just his movie-star looks. He projected an aura of being utterly comfortable in his own skin. As if he took the world seriously and himself not at all.

Of all the things she had to say, she finally said: "So how tall are you?"

Cab threw back his head and laughed. She had the impression that he liked her, too. "When I wear three-inch stilettos, I'm six-foot-nine," he said.

She giggled. "Well, you're tall even without them."

"A little."

"I suppose you're wondering—"

"Why you're here? Yes."

"I saw your car from the highway," she said.

"And so you just decided to say hi?"

"Not exactly," she admitted.

He smiled at her. "Let's see, that was you in the plaza near Dr. Smeltz's office, right? I imagine you saw my Corvette in the parking lot at the foundation office today. So after you broke into the doctor's office to steal Diane Fairmont's medical file, you decided we were both after the same thing, and you made a leap of faith to trust me enough to share it with me. How am I doing?"

Peach's eyes widened. "I—um—"

"By the way, I'm not psychic," Cab told her. "Dr. Smeltz called me. He assumed I stole the file myself. He wasn't happy about his broken window, but he felt better when I offered to pay for the damage."

"You did?"

"I did."

"Oh." Peach took a glance at the files. "Did you tell him it was me?"

"I didn't know it was you, not until you showed up. By the way, you realize that what you did is against the law, right? If I were a cop, I would have to arrest you, but fortunately, I'm in the process of reevaluating my career plans."

"Oh," she said again.

"Since you're not in cuffs, do you want to tell me why it was so important to get your hands on those files?"

He handed her another slice of pizza, but Peach wasn't hungry anymore. She was starting to feel young and stupid. "I want to know what happened to Justin."

"So do I."

"He was looking for Dr. Smeltz. I figured that he wanted what you did. He was trying to find out what happened between Mr. and Mrs. Fairmont."

"And now you know," Cab said. "You've looked at the files, right?"

She nodded. "It's really awful."

"Tell me."

Peach got up from the bed. She paced, her fingers laced together in front of her. She wasn't in disguise now. The rain had washed off her makeup. She'd changed back into her own oversized T-shirt and red jeans. It made her feel exposed. She didn't like anyone seeing who she really was.

Even so, she'd realized immediately that she couldn't keep the files to herself. Not when she saw what was in them.

"Dr. Smeltz wrote it all down. He should have gone to the police, but Ms. Fairmont begged him not to. She knew it would destroy her husband. It would have been the end of his campaign. It would have been the end of the Common Way Party. She didn't want that."

Cab waited. She was grateful that he didn't rush her. Peach grazed the top of the file with her fingertips, as if it could burn her.

"Birch had been drinking. A lot."

"That's usually how it starts," Cab said.

"He knew that Ms. Fairmont had been unfaithful. She'd had an affair."

Cab said nothing, but Peach saw discomfort cross his face.

"They argued. There was a lot of shouting. Then he got physical. He started punching her. Kicking her. It was vicious. There was blood everywhere."

Peach stopped and felt a sudden wave of nausea that was so strong it almost dropped her to her knees. She backed up to the wall and covered her mouth with her hand. Her eyes squeezed shut. She could smell her own panic and fear.

"Are you all right?" Cab asked, concerned.

"Yeah. It's just—so horrible that he could do that. She never said a word."

"Even strong women sometimes stay silent," Cab said.

"Drew found out," Peach went on. "He went crazy. He wanted to kill Birch. He was completely out of control. Dr. Smeltz put him in rehab."

"He got out right before Labor Day," Cab said.

"Yes."

"Still burning for revenge."

"Yes." Peach stared at Cab and whispered: "Do you think Drew killed Birch? And my brother?"

"I don't know, Peach, but it's possible."

She tried to imagine the horror Drew must have felt. The fury. He would have been about the same age then that Peach was now. An adult, but still tethered to his childhood.

"It was terrible, but I'm not sure I can bring myself to blame him," she said. "Birch nearly killed his mother. He murdered her unborn child. It must have driven Drew insane. How do you live with something like that?"

The room fell silent, except for the roaring of the rain, which was like a furious heartbeat. Peach stared at the floor, thinking of loss. Her loss. Ms. Fairmont's loss. Things that couldn't be undone. She kept thinking about Ms. Fairmont and felt a kinship with her that she'd never felt before. Knowing what she'd endured, she felt they were joined somehow.

Peach felt a chill from somewhere and realized it was Cab. When she looked at him, he was suddenly a stranger. He'd stood up from the chair, ghostly white, his handsome face stripped of life. She could see him trembling with an emotion that had opened up like a fissure in the earth. Anger. Or grief. Something inconsolable. He was not the same man he'd been moments earlier.

"What did you say?" he asked. "Birch murdered her *child*?"

Peach realized she hadn't told him the worst part of the story. It was as if she could barely say it out loud. "Yes, Ms. Fairmont was pregnant," she explained. "It was in her medical file. That was what started everything. Birch knew the baby wasn't his. That's when he started kicking her and when she started screaming. He was punishing her for what she'd done. By the time he stopped, she'd miscarried. She lost the baby."

35

Tarla answered the door in a black silk nightgown and robe. Her feet were bare. Her bed hair was mussed. She was beautiful, but he could see a hint of age in her face, as if it were the first time he'd noticed that she was growing older. He hadn't seen her since their fight at the Bok sanctuary, but her lips bent into a smile that was very much like his own. She was about to make a joke. Then she saw his expression, and everything changed. She knew, the way a mother always knows, that her son was in grievous pain.

"What is it, Cab?"

He pushed past her into the apartment, which was lit only by the kitchen light. The patio doors were opaque with rain. He was exhausted. The two-hour drive from Lake Wales to Clearwater in the storm, with his mind swirling, had left him numb. He wasn't able to cry.

"Did you know?" he asked.

Tarla stared at him. It was in her eyes: She knew exactly what was going on. She said nothing, because she was afraid of anything she might say. This was one of those fragile moments. Play it wrong, and the world would shatter. She was all too familiar with their history. She didn't want him to run away from her again.

"*Did you know?*" he repeated, harsh and demanding.

"Only when you told me about you and Diane," Tarla replied calmly. "Then I guessed."

"But you knew she was pregnant. You knew she lost the child."

Tarla put her palms together in front of her lips, as if she were praying, which he knew she was not. She didn't try to embrace him. They weren't touchy-feely like that, and she was smart enough to realize that this wasn't a situation that could be fixed with a hug. She sat down on the plush white sofa in the semidarkness. "Sit down, Cab," she murmured.

"I'll stand."

"Oh, for God's sake, sit down," she snapped, but then she shook her head in annoyance with herself. "I'm sorry, darling."

Cab sat down in an armchair across from her. He leaned forward, his elbows on his knees.

"I found out much later," Tarla told him. "I didn't know back then. I knew something was wrong—I knew she'd been injured in some way—but I had no idea what had happened. She didn't say a word. How did you find out, Cab?"

"It doesn't matter."

"I don't imagine Diane told you," Tarla said.

"She didn't. When did she tell you?"

"After Drew killed himself. I'm not sure she meant to, but it spilled out with her grief."

Cab nodded. "What did she say?"

Tarla clenched her fists in anger. "Birch assaulted her brutally. That monster. Honestly, I wish I'd known, I would have killed him myself. Imagine the two faces you need to do something like that to your wife and then stand up and proclaim yourself a political savior."

"What else did she tell you?" he asked.

"She realized she was pregnant in July. It was a shock, of course. I gather she'd stopped bothering with protection. You get to your mid-forties without another child, and you start to assume—"

"Did she say who—?"

"She only told me it wasn't Birch," Tarla replied. "They hadn't had sex in months. You have to believe me, Cab, she did *not* tell me who the father really was. I asked, of course, but she said she hadn't told him, and she said she would never tell anyone. She said—" Tarla stopped. "Do you really want to hear what she said about it, darling?"

"I do."

"She told me it was a one-time affair. Literally one time. She said it was born out of her great need, and it was with a man who made her feel special for the first time in a long time."

"And who ran away and avoided her for a decade," Cab said bitterly.

"Well, what did you plan to do, Cab? Marry her? You may recall, she was already married at the time."

"Is that supposed to make me feel better?" he asked. "I'm angry at myself, but I'm angry at her, too. She never told me. Don't you think I had a right to know? The baby was mine, too." It was strange how devastating those words were as he heard them on his lips.

"I understand, darling, but consider her situation. A married woman whose husband is running a political campaign? She finds herself pregnant by another man? Most women in her situation would have ended it. She didn't. She wanted the baby."

"Was it a boy or a girl?" he asked quietly.

"I'm sorry, I don't know."

A son or a daughter. That was the kind of question a single man didn't take much time to think about. He felt a wave of rage directed at Birch Fairmont. The man had murdered his child. If he'd known the truth back then, he might have killed Birch himself.

He had to remind himself: *Someone did.*

"She couldn't have expected to keep it a secret forever," Cab said. "Sooner or later, people were going to notice."

"I think for a while she simply couldn't face it. She kept it from everyone as long as she could. I was her best friend, but she never told me. Birch was so caught up in the campaign, I doubt he saw what was happening to her. On the other hand, you're right, it couldn't last forever. So she decided to tell him."

Cab knew how it went from there.

She told Birch that weekend. That Saturday night.

It was bad.

"That was when he assaulted her," Cab murmured.

"Yes. The man cheated on her constantly, but let her have one affair and he couldn't handle it. She didn't want a divorce—that was the last thing she wanted. She told Birch the real father didn't know and never would. She said no one would ever think that the baby wasn't his. They could announce it. It would be a *boost* to his campaign. A little late-in-life miracle. Voters would love the idea." Tarla carefully brushed a tear from each of her eyes. "Well, you know how Birch reacted."

Cab wanted to cry, but he felt empty. He had nothing inside.

"I'm so sorry, darling," Tarla said. "Really I am. If I had known, I would have told you. You deserved the truth."

"It wouldn't have changed anything."

"I suppose not." His mother studied his sunken face and said: "Does Diane know that you've found out about this?"

"No."

"Are you going to tell her?"

"Do you think I should?" Cab asked.

"Yes, I do. I'm going over to Diane's place tomorrow to ride out Chayla with her. I could talk to her myself, but I think it's something you need to do. You have questions, and she's the only one who can answer them."

"I have questions, but she won't like them," Cab said.

"What do you mean?"

"She kept the story hidden. I need to know why."

"Can you blame her?" Tarla asked. "The media would have been incredibly hurtful. She deserved to grieve in her own way, not have her life blown up by scandal. That's still true today, Cab. Common Way is her life. Regardless of whether you're angry at her, you have no right to expose what happened and put everything she's worked for in jeopardy."

"I'm not sure the secret is about politics. I'm not sure it ever was."

"What on earth are you talking about?"

"Drew," Cab said.

Tarla sprang to her feet. "Oh, honestly, Cab, this again?"

The silk of her nightclothes swished as she padded to the windows and stared out at the rain. The Gulf was invisible. He came up behind her and put a hand gently on his mother's shoulder.

"Drew threatened to kill Birch," he said. "Now I know he had a very powerful motive to do so."

"I told you, he didn't do it. Leave it alone. What do you hope to accomplish?"

"Sometimes the truth is enough," Cab said.

Tarla spun around, and strands of golden hair flew across her eyes. Her face was flushed as she shouted at him. "Do you always have to be a fucking *policeman*?"

Cab was calm, but his mother looked embarrassed by her profane outburst. She turned back to the window and leaned against the cold glass with her forehead. He could see, in the blurry reflection, that her eyes were closed.

"Does it really even matter?" she murmured. "Does it really matter after all these years? It's over. It's in the past."

"Even if that were true, yes, it does matter. Birch wasn't the only one who was killed that night. Lyle Piper didn't deserve to die. The citrus farmer who tried to intervene, he didn't deserve to die."

Tarla turned around, and she looked chastened. "You're right, of course."

"And I don't think it is over. Someone named Justin Kiel was murdered last month. I think it's because he was asking questions about the Labor Day killings."

"How could that be?" Tarla asked. "Even if Drew was involved, he died years ago."

"Drew may have turned to someone else for help. Someone who is still alive. Someone who's trying to cover his tracks. Drew had a relationship with a drug dealer named Frank Macy, and he might have used Macy as part of the plot."

Cab stopped as Tarla's face tensed with recognition. She was an actress and recovered almost immediately, but he didn't miss it. The name Frank Macy meant something to her. She knew who he was.

"Mother?" he asked. "What do you know about Frank Macy?"

"Only that he was a friend of Drew's. I remember meeting him that summer."

She shrank from the hardness in his eyes.

"What else?" he asked.

"Oh, darling, drop it. I got enough interrogations when I guest-starred on *Law & Order*. That Sam Waterston, he is yummy."

"You're hiding something," Cab said. "You've been hiding something from me all along. What is it? Did you recognize the gunman? Was it Macy?"

"I told you, I don't remember a thing about that night."

He took her chin gently between two fingers. "Mother, this is not a game. This is not one of your movies. Innocent people have died, and they are still dying. You can't hide what you know. Not anymore."

Tarla blinked back tears, and she wasn't acting. She was genuinely distressed. "I can't say anything. Not to you. Don't you understand? You are a cop, darling. Whatever I tell you, I know you will have to act upon, and I can't allow that."

Cab reached into his suit coat pocket. He pulled out his badge, and he put it in his mother's hand and closed her fingers around it. "This is me resigning. I'm no longer a police officer. I'm a private citizen."

"Cab, it isn't that simple."

"It is. You *need* to tell me."

Tarla turned away with his badge still clutched in her hand. She looked as if she would rather open the patio door and jump than to open her mouth.

"I had no idea what I was seeing," she said. "I didn't give it any thought at all. It was only afterward that I wondered. I never said anything, but I've always wondered about it."

"Was this on Labor Day?"

She shook her head. "It was two days before."

"Mother, what did you see?"

"That man," Tarla replied. "Frank Macy. I recognized him. It was in the garden of the estate, near a road coming out of the orange groves. I was taking a walk, and they didn't see me. They had no idea

I was there. I saw an exchange of money between them. It was a large amount of money."

Cab closed his eyes. He felt as if the pieces had finally come together. Two days before Labor Day, Drew paid Macy. This wasn't for drugs. This was for murder. Drew paid Frank Macy to kill Birch Fairmont, and Macy chose to make it look like an act of domestic terrorism. And the dominoes began to fall.

"I wish you'd told me before," he said quietly. "This changes everything. Drew may be dead, but Frank Macy isn't. He's alive, and he's dangerous."

Tarla shook her head. She looked stricken. "You don't understand."

"What?"

"It wasn't Drew," she said. "I didn't see Drew pay the money to Frank Macy. It was Diane."

36

Peach left her T-Bird in Lake Seminole Park, the way she always did. It was three in the morning, and with each hour, the storm got worse.

Cab Bolton had said almost nothing when he left her at the motel in Lake Wales. No explanations. No excuses. *"I have to get back to Tampa right now. You can stay if you'd like. The room's paid for."* Then he sped away in his Corvette as if his entire life depended on it.

Peach had no desire to stay the night in Lake Wales. Instead, she went home. She'd followed Justin's trail, but now it had led her back where she started. She still had only one name circled in her brain, like a target. Frank Macy. He was closer than ever to the heart of everything. Somehow, Justin had made the mistake of getting in Macy's way.

Then she realized she had one more name that troubled her. The name she didn't understand at all. Alison.

Peach pulled a phone from her pocket. It was off; she'd turned it off before she went inside Dr. Smeltz's office. When she turned it on, the phone was slow to reacquire signal. She finally was able to open her mobile browser and hunt for the name of the lawyer that Deacon had given her. Alison Kuipers. She found an entry for the woman at the Tampa law firm used by the Common Way Foundation, and she dialed the lawyer's direct number.

"*This is Alison Kuipers. Please leave a message . . .*"

Peach wasn't sure what to say. When she heard the beep, she left her number but no name. Then she added: "Call me as soon as you can. It's about Justin Kiel."

She hung up. As she did, her phone let out a noise like a wolf whistle. She had voice mail. When she checked her phone records, she saw that her brother Deacon had called while her phone was off. The call was three hours old.

She played the voice mail message and heard his voice, but it was muffled and strange. He was whispering.

"*Fruity, it's me. Hey, listen . . . I got a call back from someone in state corrections. He says Frank Macy spent two years inside with a roommate named Truc. Vietnamese, gang affiliations in LA. Truc is back on the street, and word is, he's involved in gun trafficking. High-capacity assault weapons. Give me a call as soon as you get this message, okay? There's something you should know about Macy and Diane, too . . .*"

There was silence, and Peach thought that Deacon had hung up, but a moment later, he went on.

"*Listen, if Macy really is involved in something, chances are he's not alone. Don't trust anybody.*"

Peach climbed out of her car and was immediately drenched. She didn't run to dodge the rain; she didn't have the energy, and her twisted ankle throbbed. She felt carried by the wind at her back. She squished through loose mud to the hole in the fence and made her way to Ninety-Eighth Street. Their house was black. Deacon's Mercedes was parked in the driveway. He was home.

She kicked through running water in the street. It was dark brown with dirt and littered with pine needles, and it was already deep enough to carry debris from neighboring yards. She opened the gate in the warped fence—NO TRESPASSING, BEWARE OF DOG—and headed for the front door.

Give me a call as soon as you get this message, okay?

Ten feet away, she froze. Their front door was wide open.

The driving rain drowned out every other noise around her. Her eyes flicked to the windows, but she saw no movement behind the ratty curtains. Instinctively, she glanced over her shoulder. She was alone outside the house, but she didn't feel less afraid.

Peach had never owned a gun. She had never even held a gun in her hand, but she wished she had one now. Or she wished Annalie was with her, pointing her own gun at the open door.

She approached slowly. The door was broken just above the doorknob. The frame was splintered, and the strike plate had been torn off. Someone had kicked their way into the house. Gusts of wind carried rain across the tiled foyer. She peered inside, but all she could see was a silver sheen reflecting on the floor. She reached around the doorframe to flip the light switch, but the power was off.

Peach took two steps into the foyer. In the living room on her left, she could distinguish the stark white shape of Sexpot Mannequin, who was where she'd left her, in lingerie, strong arm cocked behind her head. Nothing looked disturbed. The timbers of the house shook. With the noise of the storm muffled, she listened again. She didn't think anyone was here, but the Mercedes was parked in the driveway. Her anxiety soared.

She called: "Deacon!"

Her brother didn't answer.

She tiptoed toward his bedroom. The rainwater followed her, moving like a snake. The air was stale and still. She retrieved the tiny penlight on her keychain and cast a weak beam in front of her. She sweated under her wet clothes. Her hand trembled. The fluttering light illuminated the open door of Deacon's bedroom, and she saw something smeared across the wood. Getting closer, she touched it, and her finger came away sticky and red.

Blood.

"Oh, no," she whispered. "Oh, no, no, no, no."

The flashlight lit up the bedroom. She moved it around to the bed, to the floor, to the bathroom. The room was empty, but she saw evidence of a fight. The sheets had been torn off the bed, and she saw more blood on the white mattress. She clasped both hands over her head in frustration and pulled at her hair. She bit her lip so hard that it split between her teeth.

She took her phone and dialed Deacon's number. There was no answer.

She dialed again. And again. Each time she heard the call go to voice mail.

Peach ran from the house, leaving the broken door open behind her. She blinked, barely able to see through rain and tears. She held up her arms against the wind in her face, as if she could keep the gusts from blowing her away. Tree branches snapped and fell around her. She stumbled forward into the street, which was swollen with two inches of water, nearly knocking her off her feet.

She fought to the park and clambered inside her car. Her face was streaked with dirt. She was spattered with mud.

What to do, what to do, what to do.

Peach dialed 911. The circuits were overloaded, and the call failed. Half the city was declaring an emergency. Even if she got through, the police weren't coming. Not now. Not in the storm. She was on her own, and she needed help. *Don't trust anybody.* That was what Deacon had told her, but she couldn't listen to him now.

Peach dialed the phone.

"Annalie, it's me," she said when she got voice mail. "Deacon's missing. I need to see you right away. Please. Meet me at the office whenever you get this message. I'm going there now."

37

Cab couldn't sleep.

He lay with his eyes open, staring at the ceiling. He was mostly undressed, on top of the duvet and sheets. The storm howled on the other side of the wall. The placid Gulf had become a monster, lashing the coast. Dawn was two hours away, but there would be no sun and barely any light when morning came. It was a dark day. Independence Day.

Boy or girl. He found himself going back to that question over and over. He'd lost a child, and he didn't even know if it had been a boy or a girl. Each wave of emotion that washed over him became something else as it retreated. His fury at Birch. His anger that Diane had kept the secret from him. His sympathy for her and what she'd suffered. His pain at the thought of how far she might have gone to avenge what her husband had done to her.

Cab felt responsible. He'd been the trigger. He'd set everything in motion. That one week, that one afternoon, had rippled far beyond the moment. A child had died. His child. And then others had been killed.

His fault.

He wondered how things might have been different. If Diane had carried the baby to term, would he still be in the dark? Would Birch be alive? He imagined himself seeing a ten-year-old boy—or girl—with ocean-blue eyes, taller than he or she had any right to be. Would the thought have flitted across his mind? Would there have been some kind of kinship, some connection, between the two of them?

Not that he would ever know. All he could do was speculate.

He had never thought about wanting children. He'd grown up as Tarla's only child, so he never spent time around babies. He'd never known his father, so he didn't know what that relationship could be like. In the early days with Vivian Frost in Barcelona, he had fanta-sized about a life with her, and maybe in the back of his mind that life had included kids. Her death—her betrayal—had hollowed out his desires for a long-term relationship. He couldn't imagine himself as a husband, let alone a father. A child never entered his consciousness.

Boy or girl.

Cab got out of bed and headed into the living room in his briefs. He thought about pouring himself a drink, but he already had a head-ache from the wine in Lake Wales. He watched wind and rain flood-ing through the halo of lights far below him. In the other high-rises, he could see a handful of apartments where the owners were awake, like him.

It was easier to think about work. About the puzzle. He knew what he had to do in the morning. He needed to talk to Caprice about Birch and Diane and the violence between them. He needed to see Diane, too.

He needed to hear about their child from her lips.

Cab turned in surprise as the doorbell chime rang through the condo. He noticed the clock and assumed it was Tarla. This was the guest apartment; Tarla lived in her own place next door. He really didn't want to talk to his mother again. They'd shared enough anger and secrets for one night. Even so, he went to the door and peered through the spyhole. It wasn't Tarla.

He opened the door.

Lala, her face wet from the rain and wet from crying, came through the door, closed it softly, and put her arms around him. She didn't say a word. She knew the truth, and her own heart was breaking. That was when he finally cried, too. He didn't sob; he didn't have the strength. Instead, tears welled in his eyes and spilled onto his cheeks in a slow trickle. She held him tightly, and he put his arms around her, too, and they stayed like that in a kind of bubble.

When she pulled away, she put her hands on his cheeks, which were damp.

"I'm so sorry."

"How did you—" he asked, but there was only one answer. A very surprising answer.

"Tarla called me," Lala said. "She told me you were here. She told me—what you found out."

Tarla. Just when he thought he couldn't stand his mother for one more day, she went and reminded him that she loved him.

"Is it possible that she really likes you?" Cab asked.

"It's possible that she knows you needed someone. Even me."

He took her hand. It had been a long time since they'd held hands. Her grip was strong. She wanted him to feel her. It was a reminder to him that his attraction to Caprice was nothing but physical. Lala was different. Lala was more. That was what made her so attractive and so terrifying to him. That was why their relationship was in jeopardy. It could be deep, or it could be nothing at all, but it couldn't be something casual.

He didn't know what he wanted, and she knew it, but she didn't expect him to choose now.

"What did she tell you?" he asked.

"Just that Diane lost a child. Your child. That's all I needed to know."

"There's more. I don't think the Labor Day murders were what everyone believed they were. Diane paid—"

Lala put a finger on his lips. She shook her head. "Not now. Tomorrow, but not now. You have to let yourself grieve. Give yourself one night."

"I never thought something like this would hit me so hard," Cab admitted. He tried to smile and make a joke. "Me as a father? It's a horrifying thought."

"You do yourself a disservice to talk like that," Lala said. "I mean it, Cab. I don't want to hear that from you."

He realized that he couldn't escape her seriousness. Nothing he did or said would make the situation less tragic. She could accept that reality, and he couldn't. She was the Mass-every-Sunday Catholic. She was a branch on a sprawling Cuban family tree. She had a community, and he had nothing except his mother, who was a loner like him. To Lala, loss like this was a part of life you faced and accepted, because more loss was always on the way. To him, it moved the earth.

He took her, and he held her.

She knew he needed her. She could feel his arousal blooming out of his grief. He touched her golden face, and her skin felt hot. Her black hair was wet and in disarray, and the messiness of it made him want to touch it and run his fingers through it, which he did. She took two steps backward and took the fringe of her black Door County tank top in her hands. He'd bought it for her months earlier; he was pleased that she was wearing it. She peeled it up her taut stomach and pulled it over her head, baring her full breasts for him. His hands were on her.

They came together, kissing. The time apart, the distance, the arguments, melted away. He knelt in front of her and removed the rest of her clothes. He kissed her stomach, kissed up her body to her face. Her fingers, with sharp nails, pushed his shorts down. They were naked; they were pressed together. It was the Fourth of July, and fireworks lit up their eyes. He had never needed a woman so much.

She led him to the bedroom. They lay facing each other, touching, but then she pulled him on top of her. Her knees bent, and her legs separated. He was trapped between her thighs; he was inside her. Everything else in the world finally fled his mind, and the only things left were her skin, breath, and wetness.

The storm raging outside sounded distant and unimportant, nothing but a summer rain.

Cab awoke two hours later. It was a short night, but he felt as if he'd slept forever.

It wasn't light outside. He could barely see. He stretched out a hand to the warm indentation on the mattress, but the bed was empty. Lala was gone. There was no note and no message on his phone. He pushed himself up, propped against a pillow. Through the doorway to the living room, he could see that her clothes were gone, too. The sensation of their lovemaking lingered with a satisfying ache on his body, but if it hadn't been for the faint essence of her perfume in the sheets, he wouldn't have been able to swear she had ever been there.

38

Annalie rapped her knuckles on the window of the Thunderbird, and Peach bolted awake. She shook herself, reached across the car, and unlocked the passenger door. Her friend scrambled inside out of the rain.

Peach stared at the downtown streets. It was early. Tampa was a ghost town. She was in her usual parking place, spot 52 in the lot outside the Common Way research office. Around them, the storm felt like a living thing. The lot was filling up like a lake, and if the water got much deeper, she was afraid that her car would float away.

Peach gave her a quick, earnest hug. "I was afraid you wouldn't be able to get here."

"We don't have a lot of time," Annalie replied. "In another three or four hours, everything on the coast will be impassable. You should be home, Peach, not here. It's not safe. What's going on? Your message said something about Deacon."

"He's gone. They took him."

"Who did?"

Peach took a breath and explained everything. She played his voice mail for Annalie, who frowned as Deacon talked about gun trafficking.

"You saw blood?" Annalie said quietly.

Peach nodded.

"You've tried calling him?"

"Over and over. No answer."

Annalie was silent. The wind roared.

"If he was asking questions about Frank Macy, it's possible that Macy heard about it," Annalie said finally. "Someone could have tipped him off."

"But what is Macy doing?" Peach asked. "What's he up to?"

Annalie stared through the windshield. Drips of rain slid down her face. "Whatever it is, it's not good."

Peach folded her hands tightly together. "You think he killed Deacon, don't you?"

"I have no idea, Peach," Annalie said. "I hope not."

"We need to find Macy."

Annalie grabbed her wrist. "*We* don't need to do anything. Not you."

"I can't just sit here."

"Go into the office. Go through Justin's e-mails. Go through Deacon's e-mails. See if you can find anything that would tell us what Macy is doing or where we can find him."

Peach felt her face flush, and she opened her mouth to complain, but Annalie interrupted her. "Listen to me, Peach. Please. You're emotionally involved. You're out of control. I don't blame you, but that's the way you make mistakes. Let me worry about Frank Macy. Let me find him. If you find anything that would help, you call me right away. Okay?"

Peach wanted to scream, but she knew Annalie was right. "Yeah, okay. Keep me posted. Don't leave me in the dark."

"I won't."

Annalie got out of the car and ran to her Corolla. A few seconds later, she drove away, carving out waves of water as if she were parting the seas.

The more time Peach spent in the office, the more her frustration grew.

The foundation was closed for the holiday, but even if the office had been open, the storm would have kept everyone away. She worked in peace, listening to the walls rock. Her fingers flew on the keyboard, but she learned nothing. She went back through Justin's e-mails but didn't find anything that would explain what he had discovered. She knew Deacon's password, and she studied his e-mails, too, but there was nothing other than his usual campaign research.

She checked her brother's office voice mail. There was one new message from Caprice, which had come in the previous evening.

"Deacon, it's me. Tried your cell phone, but couldn't reach you. Give me a call in the morning. I'm going over to Diane's, and we'll ride out the storm there. If you need me, I should be at the house by ten a.m. or so."

No one had been able to reach Deacon. No one knew where he was.

She didn't know what to do next. She logged in to Justin's account again and opened up the edited photograph taken outside The Crab Shack. He'd used the picture to guide her to his hideaway, but there was nothing left inside the house except the article about Frank Macy poking out from under a file cabinet. Whatever he wanted her to find, someone else had already found it and stolen it.

Then she remembered the photograph in the broken frame on the floor of the bedroom. It was the same photograph of herself that was attached to the e-mail. When she'd found the article about Frank Macy, she'd forgotten all about the photograph on the floor. If Justin wanted a picture of her in his hideaway, he had plenty of others to choose, but he'd used that one. She didn't think it was an accident.

He was trying to tell her something more.

She decided to go back to Justin's safe house. It was empty. No one would be there. She couldn't stay in the office any longer, doing nothing.

Before she logged out, however, she took another look at Justin's messages and saw the other e-mail he'd failed to send. The one to Ogden Bush.

I need to see you.

She grabbed her coat, but instead of leaving, she headed down the empty office corridor to Bush's office. She let herself inside, the way she had two days before, and unlocked the man's file cabinets again. The file on Justin was still missing. She remembered a file on Birch Fairmont in another drawer, and that file suddenly took on new significance for her. She opened the other drawer, but the file on Birch was gone, too.

Bush had cleaned house.

She relocked the file cabinets and did a search of the man's desk. She reviewed pink handwritten phone messages, copies of research reports that been gathered and written by the employees in the office, lists of media contacts around the state, and drafts of Diane's events calendar for the week ahead. Nothing looked unusual or suspicious. Bush wouldn't leave anything lying around that he didn't want someone to see. It was a dead end.

Then she saw that his voice mail light was flashing.

With only the slightest hesitation, Peach punched the speakerphone, and she heard a voice with a faint Southern drawl fill the office. "*I need to talk to you right now. It's urgent.*"

It was a short message, but the voice was familiar. She'd heard it before. For a moment, she struggled to place it, and then she knew. The recognition washed over her. The voice belonged to the man who called himself Curtis Clay, the man who'd pretended to be a St. Petersburg cop. The man who had held a gun on her and tried to put her in handcuffs in Justin's apartment.

That man. That fraud. He was in bed with Ogden Bush.

She clicked off the phone, but as she did, a silky voice called to her from the office doorway.

"What are you doing here, Peach?"

Ogden Bush had his hands on his hips. He wore a wet fedora. His raincoat dripped on the floor, and she could see a tailored black suit underneath it. His face was dark and curious, but he didn't sound angry. He was too smooth to blow up at her, and that made her trust him even less.

"You're a spy," she said.

"Excuse me?"

"You're a spy. You've been spying on *me*."

Bush's face melted into a politician's smile. He sat down in the guest chair and made no attempt to dislodge Peach from behind his desk. He crossed his legs, displaying wet shined shoes, and smoothed the creased lines of his suit pants.

"We're all spies at this place, Peach. Isn't that what you're doing, too? You didn't need to sneak in here. If you wanted answers about something, you could have talked to me. Exactly what do you want?"

Peach stabbed the button on Bush's phone. The short message played on the speakerphone. "Who is he?" she asked.

"He's a contact of mine," Bush said.

"He works for you."

"Lots of people work for me. You work for me, too."

"No, I work for Diane Fairmont."

"We both do," Bush said.

"That man calls himself Curtis Clay," Peach went on. "He called my home and pretended to be a cop. I caught him in Justin's apartment."

"What were *you* doing in Justin's apartment?" Bush asked with a wink. "You see? I told you, we're all spies. None of us is innocent."

"Who is he?" she repeated.

Bush picked up a small pewter replica of the Bok tower from his desk and played with it between his fingers. He didn't answer. She smelled his cologne, and she watched his ruby ring glint under the light. His face was a mask, but she knew he was thinking fast. Looking for a way out.

"What do you know about Justin's death?" Peach asked.

"I only know what the police tell me, Peach."

"I don't believe you. You kept a file on Justin. He wanted to talk to you the night before he was killed. Why did he want to see you?"

"I have no idea," Bush told her calmly. "We never spoke. This is the first I'm hearing about it. I think you should go home, Peach. The storm is getting bad. The office is closed. You shouldn't be here."

"My next call is to Ms. Fairmont. I'm going to tell her everything."

Bush shrugged. "She knows what I'm doing."

"We'll see."

Peach watched the man's face. She wasn't a poker player, but she knew a bluff when she saw it. She picked up the phone and punched the number for Ms. Fairmont's house. Ringing buzzed through the speakerphone. Before there was an answer, Bush leaned casually across the desk and depressed the button on the receiver to cut off the call.

"All right, I think we can arrive at a compromise," he said. "The fact is, there are things that Diane is better off not knowing. Candidates think they want to know everything, but really, they don't. It's what we call plausible deniability."

"I call it lying," Peach said.

"Whatever. Okay, you want to know who that man is? His name is Curtis Ritchie. He's a private investigator, and yes, I use him from time to time. There's nothing unusual about it. It's common practice. I asked him to gather some information for me on Justin's activities."

"He told me he was a St. Petersburg cop."

"I told Curtis to stay within the bounds of the law," Bush said, "but he's ex-police. Sometimes he forgets where the lines are drawn now that he's on his own."

"Why were you spying on Justin?"

Bush continued to twist the pewter model between his graceful fingers. "I found out that Justin was asking questions that were outside his job responsibilities here at the foundation. I was curious. I wanted to know why."

"About the Labor Day murders."

The man's eyebrows rose, as if she knew more than he expected. "Yes."

"Why do you care?"

"The only things that scare me in political campaigns are things I don't know."

"Were you afraid something might come out that would make Ms. Fairmont look bad?"

"If there was anything like that," Bush said, "I wanted to find out about it before our enemies did."

Staring at him, Peach realized for the first time that she no longer had any idea who their enemies were. Once everything had seemed clear to her. Now she was caught in a labyrinth of ulterior motives. She didn't know whom to trust.

Deacon had already told her: *Don't trust anybody.*

"What did Curtis Ritchie find out?" Peach asked. "He called you last night. His message said it was urgent."

"I never reached him."

"What was he doing?"

"He was following someone that you led him to," Bush admitted. "An unpleasant character named Frank Macy."

Peach wanted to jump across the desk. "*Where?* Where is Macy?"

"I don't know. The last time I talked to Curtis, he said that Macy was in the industrial docks area, heading toward the Picnic Island pier. He thought Macy might be meeting someone. I haven't been able to reach him since then."

39

Cab pulled into the cobblestoned driveway of Diane's estate. The wrought-iron gate ahead of him, sculpted with herons and vine leaves, was closed. He turned off the Corvette's engine. Rain gushed horizontally across the windshield. He saw no security staffing the gate or patrolling inside the wall. He didn't like that the exterior of the estate was deserted. The wall was built for privacy, not protection, and an intruder could easily get to the house without being challenged. He would have preferred to see men with guns outside.

His phone rang, and he saw the caller ID for Caprice Dean on the line.

"Good morning, Cab," she said. "What a beautiful day."

"Is it?"

"Oh, you're not scared off by a little storm, are you?"

He could hear the grin on her lips as she teased him. He was disappointed that he still felt a physical reaction to the undercurrents in her voice. There were some women like that, women you had to work to resist.

"Apparently, the storm scared off the security at Diane's estate," he replied.

A sheen of ice returned to her voice. "Where are you?"

"In her driveway."

"Cab, really? Do you have to bother Diane today?"

"I do," he said.

He knew she wanted to snap at him, but was restraining her temper. "Well, I'm going to be over there myself in a couple of hours. If you're still there, I'm going to kick you out. Unless you can play nice and forget about work and just have cocktails with us, that is."

"Not today, I'm afraid."

"Your mother's coming, too."

"Yes, she told me." He added: "You said you were going to increase security here at the house."

"I did. We should have two men inside right now."

"Inside," Cab said.

"Yes, inside. Maybe you haven't noticed the torrential rain and sixty-mile-an-hour winds. Do you really expect me to have people standing outside in the storm?"

Cab frowned. "No."

"Well, good, can you get off my back? Not that I would typically complain about you being on my back."

He didn't take the bait. "What do you want, Caprice?"

"I wanted to apologize for yesterday."

"That's not necessary."

"I overreacted," she went on. "I'm not used to people telling me no. Actually, I enjoyed having you stand up to me. It makes me even more interested in you, personally and professionally."

"Professionally, I'm in charge of solving crimes, and you're in charge of protecting your pretty political ass."

"That sounds about right. And personally?"

"Personally, nothing is going to happen."

She sounded disappointed. "Don't I have a chance to persuade you? I can be very persuasive if you give me an opportunity. I'm not looking for a commitment. Neither one of us wants the white picket fence, do we? We're not signing up for marriage and kids."

Kids. Cab thought again: *Boy or girl*. No, he didn't want a commitment, but he wanted more than he would find in bed with Caprice.

"I was going to call you today," he said. "I found out what happened between Birch and Diane."

"No comment," she said.

"I want to know if you and Lyle knew about it. I want to know *who else* knew."

"And I repeat: No comment."

"Fine. You won't talk. Let me tell you what I think. You and Lyle found out what happened that Saturday night. You knew exactly what Birch did to Diane. You knew you were running a monster on the ballot."

Caprice's voice tensed with frustration. "Cab, you are playing with fire here. This kind of scandal is exactly what Diane's enemies want, and it will do nothing to protect her. Do you really want to be a tool for Ramona Cortes?"

"You're talking about politics, Caprice, but I'm talking about murder. People died. Your *fiancé* died. Don't you care what really happened?"

"How dare you say something like that to me!" she exploded at him. "I don't need you to lecture me about what I owe to those people. I know what happened. I know who was responsible for it."

"Last chance. Did you and Lyle know what Birch did?"

"Yes, *of course* we knew!" Caprice hissed at him. "Do you think we're idiots? Do you think we could spend all that time with a candidate and not realize he's a self-absorbed, cheating, abusive son of a bitch? News flash for you, Cab. So are half the politicians in Washington and Tallahassee. Birch would have fit right in."

"Maybe so, but he never would have been elected if the truth had come out back then. He would have been crucified for what he did to Diane. It would have been the end of the Common Way Party before it even started."

"You're right. That's true. It's true today, too. Why the hell do you think we kept it a secret? Why do you think it's *still* a secret? People like heroes and martyrs, Cab. They want the image, they don't want reality. Do you think anyone would thank you if you exposed what Birch did? That's not what they want to hear. The person you'd be hurting is Diane, because *victims* don't get elected governor."

"But sometimes victims kill their abusers," Cab said.

Caprice was silent. Then she said: "What on earth are you talking about?"

"Diane paid money to Frank Macy two days before the murders. What was that money for?"

The silence dragged out again, even longer this time. "I can't believe you'd even suggest something like that."

"Diane was seen with Macy."

"I don't care who saw what. Diane did not have Birch killed."

"Are you sure?"

"Cab, do you think we could have kept what Birch did out of the press without Diane being involved? I talked to her personally. Just her and me, woman to woman. It was *her* choice to keep it a secret. It was her choice to go on with the campaign. You may find this hard to imagine, but she believes in Common Way, and she believed in it back then. She chose to stay silent about Birch because she wanted him to win despite everything else. Do you think she would turn around and have him murdered?"

"Do you have another explanation?"

"I don't," Caprice said, "but I know Diane. She wouldn't do that. Besides, we're not just talking about Birch. Can you honestly tell me that you think Diane would let innocent people die?"

"Not if she knew what was going to happen. Maybe she didn't know."

"You think she paid Frank Macy, but she didn't know what he was going to do?" Caprice asked.

"Macy's not an idiot. He's smart. He'd protect himself. Murder Birch, and people wonder why. They ask uncomfortable questions. But *assassinate* Birch and make it look like domestic terrorism? Now it's a political crime. Now there are fall guys. Ham Brock. Chuck Warren. The Liberty Empire Alliance."

"You're wrong," she said. "Frank Macy sold drugs to Drew. Diane blames him for Drew's death. That's all I know. If she paid him, it wasn't for the reasons you think. It was something else. Maybe she just wanted him to go away." She paused, and then she added harshly: "And I'll tell you another thing. It's no accident that this is coming out now. Whatever went on between Macy and Diane, I'm certain that Ramona Cortes knows what it is. Ramona was Macy's lawyer. She wants it exposed, and she wants your fingerprints on this, not hers."

"I still have to talk to Diane. I have to know what happened."

"Do whatever you need to do, but I'm begging you to be discreet. The suspicion alone will destroy Diane if it becomes public."

"You think I don't know that?" Cab asked.

"I think you do, but you don't seem to care."

Cab wondered if that was true. Tarla had accused him more than once of being obsessed with answers, regardless of who got hurt. After Vivian Frost's betrayal, he'd come to believe that anyone in the world was capable of evil. He took it personally when people lied to him.

Maybe that was the problem. This was personal. Diane had never told him about the loss of his child, and he wanted to hurt her as a kind of revenge. He was ready to believe she was guilty of something terrible. He was ready to ruin her.

"I care about this more than you think," Cab told her. "I hate what Birch did to Diane."

He waited for an answer but heard only thunder. "Caprice?"

And then again: "Caprice?"

Finally, she came back on the line. Her voice was different. She didn't sound like a politician anymore. "Cab, we have a problem."

"What is it?"

"Ogden Bush just called me on my other line. Peach was in his office a few minutes ago."

"Peach? Why?"

"Apparently, someone broke into her house last night," Caprice told him. "Her brother Deacon is missing. Peach says Deacon was talking to his prison contacts about Frank Macy before he disappeared. Cab, I don't know exactly what happened ten years ago, but right now, I don't care. I'm more concerned with what's happening today. Get inside, and check on Diane."

40

Peach's Thunderbird crept along the scrub-lined gravel road through the docklands area. The pavement was invisible under the rippling water. Pebbles and sand cracked on her windshield like bullets shot by the fierce gales. Her wipers fought a losing battle against the rain, and she leaned forward, trying to see. A quarter mile ahead, the road split. A dead end led toward the port, where she could see a mammoth tanker docked in the water. To her left, a sign pointed toward Picnic Island Park. She headed that way, thudding across railroad tracks and driving slowly, unsure of the depth of the water underneath her tires. Ahead of her, palm trees and evergreens bowed toward the east, as if to say: Run. Run that way. Run fast.

The road ended at a crescent beach adjoining the bay.

The sprawling waterside park was the heel on the boot that made up the Tampa peninsula. Facing west, she stared at the narrowest point of the channel leading into Old Tampa Bay, across the water from the city of St. Petersburg. The low-lying park was webbed with marshes and creeks. It was mostly wild and unkempt, matted with sea grass. Fuel tanks and mountains of crushed sandstone loomed in the industrial area bordering the park. A concrete pier jutted into the water beside a boat launch. Angry waves threw themselves over the pier, sending up twelve-foot clouds of spray.

She turned off the engine. The sky was black, like night. She could barely open her car door into the wind. When she stepped into three inches of water, she felt herself thrown backward by the force of the gusts. Her clothes were sodden. The rain pelleted her face; she had to shield her eyes. The noise of the storm was deafening, a shrieking chorus of water and wind.

At first, she thought the parking lot was empty, but then she spotted a car hidden inside a grove of trees. It was a burgundy Cutlass, heavily dinged with years of abuse. The car was littered with wet leaves and had obviously been stranded here for hours. She staggered in a zigzag across the lot. Something slimy brushed her ankle, and she realized it was a fish, swept from the bay into the shallow lake that now covered the parkland. Better a fish than an alligator. She splashed forward onto spongy mud that sucked at her sneakers, and when she reached the abandoned Cutlass, she yanked open the door and piled inside.

The car smelled of smoke and French fries, despite an old pine air freshener dangling from the mirror. Its torn leather seats were buried under crumpled food wrappers and newspapers. A GPS navigator was suctioned to the dashboard. She spotted an old gallon milk jug one-third filled with a yellowish liquid, and her lip wrinkled in disgust.

Peach looked into the backseat. She saw a pair of binoculars and realized they were made for night vision. She spotted the corner of a laptop poking out from under a *Penthouse* magazine, and she needed two hands to lift the machine into the front seat. The laptop was a Toughbook, made for rugged use. She traced a USB cable plugged into one of the computer ports to a digital camera.

This was a stakeout car. A spy car.

She opened the glove compartment, which was crammed with electronic charger cables and receipts. She rifled through the pile of papers but didn't find any insurance information or owner records. She lifted the lid of the laptop and pushed the power button, but the battery was dead.

Peach flipped down the sun visor. She found a stack of more than a dozen identification cards tucked under an elastic strap. She pulled out the laminated cards and flipped through them. The card issuers were all different. State and county agencies. Trade associations. Corporations. Banks. The cards were fake, using a variety of aliases, but several of the cards included a photograph, and she recognized the man in the pictures.

It was Curtis Ritchie. Ogden Bush's private investigator. The man she knew as Curtis Clay.

Peach slid her phone from her pocket and called Annalie, and she was grateful when the woman answered. The connection was intermittent and ripped with static, but she could hear her.

"Peach, what is it? Are you okay?"

"I'm fine. I'm over in Picnic Island Park."

Annalie's unhappiness cut through the line. "I told you to stay in the office. What are you doing there?"

"The man who was following me in the red Cutlass, he's a PI named Curtis Ritchie. He works for Ogden Bush. Bush said that Ritchie was following Frank Macy last night, and the trail led here. I found the car, but he's nowhere around."

"You should get out of there," Annalie said. "Right now."

"There's no one here—"

"It doesn't matter. Someone may be coming back to get that car."

"I need to see you," Peach said.

"It's not safe to travel. The storm's getting worse."

"*Please*. I'm going to Justin's safe house. Can you meet me there?"

There was a long pause, and she thought Annalie might say no. Then the woman replied: "All right. It will take me an hour. Be careful."

Peach hung up the phone.

She gathered up Ritchie's Toughbook and digital camera, and she grabbed the charger cables from the glove compartment, hoping they matched the devices. She shoved the equipment under her shirt, which provided meager protection against the storm. The hardened plastic shells were cold on her damp skin. She opened the door and ducked out into the rain and kicked the door shut behind her.

Clutching the equipment against her body, Peach struggled back to her Thunderbird. She was nearly blind. Twice, the wind literally blew her to her knees. Pine needles whipped around her face, stinging like razors. The water at her feet swirled in foamy whirlpools, keeping her off balance. At her car, she dumped everything onto the passenger seat and heaved herself inside. She was shivering. She turned on the engine and blasted heat into the interior. The wipers shot back and forth.

She examined the electronic equipment, hoping it wasn't permanently damaged by the storm. When she checked the cables, she found a car charger with an adapter end that fit the laptop. She plugged it in and connected the power end to the car's cigarette lighter. The AC indicator on the damp machine turned green.

"Yes," she murmured to herself.

Then she jumped so high her head struck the roof.

Someone rapped sharply on the driver's-side window. Peach saw a man completely wrapped in a yellow slicker. His face was flushed and wet, and he looked as young as she was, with a pimply face. His hood was pushed down, and he wore a security officer's cap, robed in plastic. Behind him, ten yards away, she spotted a white SUV labeled PARK RANGER. The lights were on. The engine was running.

Automatically, Peach hit the lock on the car doors. The park policeman rapped on the window again. She lowered the window an inch, and he pressed his lips close to the gap and shouted to be heard.

"Ma'am, the park is closed."

She smiled and shouted back. "I was just leaving!"

"Are you okay? I saw you fall."

"I'm fine! Thank you!"

His eyes traveled to the laptop and camera, and then he looked across the roof of the car to the border of the parking lot, where he spotted the Cutlass. She watched his eyes squint with suspicion.

"Ma'am, what are you doing down here?"

"What?" She pretended not to hear.

"Does that equipment belong to you, ma'am?" he demanded, pointing at the Toughbook on the seat.

"You mean the laptop? Of course."

He frowned. "Can you show me some identification, ma'am?"

"Is this necessary? I need to get home. I'm sorry—I didn't know the park was closed."

"Your ID, ma'am," he repeated.

Peach sighed and dug in her back pocket for her wallet. She slid out her driver's license and passed it through the crack in the window. Rain flooded down the glass inside the car.

"Turn off your car please, ma'am."

"Look, officer, I'm cold and wet. I wasn't doing anything wrong. Can I please just have my license back?"

He didn't return her license. Instead, he pushed through the flooded park toward the Cutlass. She saw him peer inside and make a circuit around the vehicle. He opened the door, seeing what she saw: the clutter of a man who lived much of his life in his car. He popped the trunk release, checked it, and slammed it shut. He climbed inside the vehicle, and she remembered that she'd left Curtis Ritchie's roster of fake ID cards on the passenger seat in full view.

It didn't take long. The officer was smart enough to know that something was very wrong. He reemerged into the storm, his face grim. He retreated from the car and headed straight for her. Peach knew where she was headed next. A prison holding cell.

She watched him come closer. As she debated what to do, she saw the park policeman pitch forward into the green water. He'd tripped on something snagged on the trunk of a palm tree. Whatever it was jutted above the surface like the back of a turtle. As he pushed himself up, the officer's arm disappeared under the water, and Peach watched with a weird sense of horror as his hand reappeared a second later, holding something at the end of his fingers.

It took her a moment, through the wild rain, to see that the policeman was clutching a fistful of hair. He was holding a head. A head, white and pale and dead, connected to a body.

She knew that face. It was Curtis Ritchie.

Peach screamed.

She shoved the Thunderbird into reverse and shot backward, spinning the wheel. The car spun, as if she were riding a Tilt-a-Whirl. It turned, kicking up spray, its tires grinding on gravel and water. The engine coughed once and then roared. She shoved the gear down again, and she sped out of the park without looking back.

41

A bodyguard met Cab at the front door of Diane's estate. The man wasn't tall, but he was heavily muscled, and his brown eyes moved constantly, surveying Cab from head to toe and studying the estate's empty porch, where a curtain of rain spilled from the roof. He seemed competent. But he was one man, and it was a big house: he couldn't be everywhere at once.

"Where is she?" Cab asked.

"The sunroom."

"Alone?"

"No, Garth Oakes is with her."

"Do you have a partner here?" he asked the bodyguard.

The man shook his head. "He was in an accident on his way up from Bradenton. I'm on my own."

Cab frowned. One man.

"Stay alert," he told him.

He hung up his Burberry trench coat and followed the bodyguard down the wood floor of the hallway. The house was warm. The sconce lights on the walls flickered. At the end of the hall, a wide oak door opened into an airy sunroom, but there was no sun. The room, on the corner of the house, featured a wall of floor-to-ceiling windows, including two patio doors leading out into the garden. The glass was silver with rain.

Chocolate-brown frieze decorated the floor, but the carpet ended twelve feet from the patio doors, where Italian marble took over. The wall on Cab's left was white, with stylized square panels and gold molding. A chandelier dripped crystal from the ceiling and was bright against the darkness of the morning. A claw-foot settee, with Tiffany table lamps on either end, was positioned on the wall on Cab's right. The room also included a breakfast nook near the tall windows.

Diane lay facedown on a massage table that had been erected in the center of the room. She was naked, with a towel discreetly draped across her backside. Garth, his hands glistening with oil, kneaded the muscles in her neck with his thumbs, under the fringe of her bobbed brown hair. The sound of the door made Diane open her eyes. She saw Cab and didn't look surprised. Her eyes closed again.

"Give us a few minutes, will you, Garth?" she murmured.

"Oh, sure, of course."

Garth wiped his hands on a towel. His tanned skin looked almost orange under the chandelier. He wore a silk lavender polo shirt, black-striped Zubaz, and Crocs that matched his shirt. He'd swapped his ponytail for a hair knot on top of his head.

"Hey," he said to Cab.

The masseur was subdued. He grabbed a sport coat, which sagged with weight. Cab figured that the man's gun was shoved into one of the pockets. The masseur brushed by him as he left the room. Cab turned away to give Diane privacy, and he avoided the reflections in the windows. He heard her climb off the massage table and listened to the swish of fabric as she covered herself with a robe.

"I'm decent," she murmured.

She sat in the breakfast nook near the patio windows. Her long fingers cradled a champagne flute, filled with a mimosa. She watched the storm assault the windows, and her face looked far away.

Cab took a seat across from her. "It's not safe sitting so close to the windows."

She shrugged. "They're reinforced for storms."

"Not for bullets," he said.

She gave him a strange look. "Is there a threat?"

"There may be."

Diane showed no concern for her safety. She gave the French doors a curious look, as if seeing a gunman outside would be as interesting as seeing a lost doe. She was distracted, and he wondered if Tarla had called her. He wouldn't put it past his mother to give her best friend a warning. *Cab's coming. He knows.* As if reading his mind, Diane said: "Dr. Smeltz talked to me."

"Ah."

"Someone stole my medical files. He says it was you."

"No, it wasn't me, but I was able to retrieve them. They're safe. You won't be reading anything in the papers."

Diane didn't look comforted. Her face tightened with fury. "Do you have any idea how violated I feel?"

"I think I do."

Diane tugged the flaps of her robe tighter below her neck. Something about the gesture gave him a vivid and unwanted memory of their two bodies together. He wondered if the same image was in her head. It had felt right at the time, but almost immediately, it had gone wrong.

"So," she said. "You know."

"Yes, I know."

She leaned her head back and stared at the ceiling. She was a powerful woman who looked powerless. "I told you that afternoon changed my life."

He said nothing.

"I suppose you're going to ask how I could have kept this from you," she went on. "It's a fair question. I've thought about it myself a great deal. Then and now."

Cab shook his head. "Obviously, I understand. I don't like it, but I understand."

"Still, she was your child, too."

He wasn't prepared for how that one sentence cut open his heart and left him bleeding. *She.* A girl. He'd been summoning his courage to ask the question, and now she had answered it for him. She recognized what she'd done, and her face filled with sincere distress. "I'm sorry," she continued. "I didn't mean to break it like that, but I thought you would have seen it in my file."

"I didn't look that closely."

"Well, yes. She. A daughter."

He shrugged. The gesture was false. "A daughter I never would have known anyway. I suppose it doesn't matter."

"Of course it matters, Cab!" Diane exclaimed. "And for what it's worth, I apologize. Back then, I had no choice but to hide the truth from you, and from Tarla, too. It doesn't make it right, but you can appreciate the situation I was in. After that, well, I have no excuses to give you. You deserved the truth, but I never sought out the right moment. I didn't want to revisit what happened. Even so, a day doesn't go by that I don't think about her."

His emotions betrayed him. Whatever he wanted to say lodged in his throat and went nowhere. His eyes felt wet.

"I never thought it compromised a strong man to cry," she told him. "I've had years to deal with this. It's new to you."

Cab wanted to ask what he needed to ask and then escape. He cleared his throat. "There are things I need to know."

"I'm sure. It changes everything, doesn't it, knowing what a sick son of a bitch my husband was? Why do you think I've worked so hard to keep the truth hidden? I'd like to tell you that Birch was sorry for what he'd done. Maybe for a day or two, he was, but then he went back to being the man I knew. Utterly self-absorbed. Utterly heartless."

"And yet—"

"And yet I covered for him. That's right. Was I weak? Back then, yes, I probably was. I thought it was my fault. That's the way victims are programmed to think. Besides, I was the one who invited you into my bed. I had to accept the consequences."

"Not those consequences," Cab said.

"No. Looking back, I was a fool about a lot of things. Some lessons are hard to learn."

"Diane, I need to ask you about the murders," he told her.

"It was *not* Drew," she snapped. "There's simply no way he was involved. Yes, I told my son what happened to me. Yes, he hated Birch. Did he want to kill him? I'm sure he did, but Drew didn't have the inner strength to do something like that. You're wrong, Cab."

"I believe you. Drew wasn't the shooter. Whoever pulled the trigger had a calculating mind. He knew exactly what he was doing."

"Then what else can I tell you?" Diane asked.

"Drew doesn't fit the profile of the murderer," Cab went on, "but Frank Macy does."

Diane cocked her head in surprise. He tried to read her eyes to see whether the surprise was genuine or an act, but whatever she felt was quickly subsumed by her bitterness toward the man. Her knuckles tightened around the crystal glass in her hand.

"Why on earth would Macy kill Birch?"

"Maybe because someone paid him," Cab said.

Diane slowly put down the glass. She closed her eyes for a long second. He could see her chest swell with a deep breath. She pushed back her chair and got up, and she wandered into the dead center of the room, directly below the chandelier. She crossed her arms and stared at the floor. Her feet were bare on the brown carpet.

"Tarla saw us," she said. "She saw me with Macy, didn't she?"

"Yes, she did."

"I thought I caught a glimpse of her on the trail. That poor dear. All these years, she wondered if I arranged to have Birch killed, and she never said a word to me about it. She never asked me for the truth."

"She knew what Birch did to you."

"Still, that's a true friend." She looked up at Cab. "I wasn't paying off Macy to commit murder. That's not what the money was for."

"It was two days before Labor Day, Diane."

"I know. I can understand your suspicion."

"Then explain it to me. Why did you pay Frank Macy?"

He wasn't prepared for her answer.

"I wanted him to get me a gun," Diane replied.

"A gun? Why?"

Diane sat down on the settee. She looked small with the windows framed behind her. "That's a good question. I'm not entirely sure I know the answer. At the time, I planned to kill myself. I can't tell you the kind of despair I felt. I couldn't admit publicly what Birch had done to me, but I wasn't sure I could go on living with him. Knowing what he'd taken from me. I had visions of putting that gun in my mouth, but—"

"But what?" Cab asked.

"I have to be honest. I thought about killing Birch, too. Maybe I would have killed him and then killed myself. I don't know. However, I'd be lying if I said I wasn't thinking about murdering my husband." She shook her head. "Despite that, I didn't kill him. Maybe with a few more days, I would have screwed up the courage and done it, but someone beat me to it."

Cab could read her face. He knew she was telling him the truth. "Did Macy get you the gun?"

"He did."

"Do you still have it?"

A tear slipped down her cheek. "No. Drew found it. It was the gun that he—"

Cab nodded. "I'm sorry."

"I blame Frank Macy for his death, but in the end, I have to blame myself, too."

"Who else knows that Macy sold you a gun?" Cab asked.

"Only Macy and me, I assume. And now you and Tarla. Macy could have told someone, but it wouldn't have been in his interest to admit it. I'm sure the gun wasn't legally obtained."

"What about Ramona Cortes?" he asked. "Did she contact you? Did she try to use your transaction with Macy as leverage? Defense attorneys will use any ammunition available to them to get their client a better deal."

"Indeed they will."

"Did she?" he repeated.

Diane trembled, like a sapling caught in the storm. "I don't know why you're asking about this. There's no reason to think Macy had anything to do with Birch's death. You should just drop it."

Cab got up and walked over to her. The black windows felt dangerous. He knelt in front of the settee.

"Maybe Macy didn't kill Birch. Or maybe we're simply missing something. Either way, Macy is in the middle of whatever's going on right now. Justin was looking at him, and now Justin's dead. Deacon Piper is missing. The question is why."

"*Deacon?*" Her face turned ashen. "Deacon is missing? When? What happened?"

"Caprice says someone took him from his house last night."

Diane's hand flew to her mouth. "Oh my God."

She leaned forward and put her arms tightly around him. He could feel the curves of her body pressing on him through the thin robe. It was awkward; they felt like strangers. Strangers who had slept together. Who had conceived a child.

"What's going on, Diane?" he asked.

She took a deep breath. He had to remind himself who she was and what this meant to her. She was a candidate for the most powerful office in the state. There were people who would do anything to bring her down. And here he was, asking for her worst secrets.

"I did something illegal," she murmured, as if speaking softly would make her innocent. As if the truth would still be hidden.

He gently eased her away from him. "What did you do?"

"You have to understand my situation," she said. "After Drew died, I went crazy. I'd lost everything. I needed to blame someone. I became obsessed with Frank Macy. I wanted him punished, but nobody could stop him. I worked with the police to get drug charges filed, but he walked away with probation. All I could think about was getting him behind bars. It was like I couldn't go on with my life until I'd avenged Drew's death. I was willing to do anything in my power to put Macy away. And you know—by then—I had a lot of power. A lot of money. It made me think I could do whatever I wanted, and there would be no consequences."

"What happened?" Cab asked quietly.

"There was a killing in the town of Pass-a-Grille. A bartender was assaulted and died of his injuries. There were no witnesses. It was in a bar that Frank Macy frequented. Macy *knew* the bartender. Don't you see, this was my chance. Finally, I *had* him. So I arranged to have DNA evidence planted in the alley and in Macy's apartment. Macy had no alibi. He was selling drugs that night. You have to love the irony, don't you? He must have suspected I was behind it. Ramona called me, and she didn't say it outright, but she made it clear that she thought I'd paid someone on the police to make sure Macy was framed. However, even she couldn't make this one go away. Macy took a plea and did eight years. Less than he deserved for what he did to Drew, but at least I had a measure of justice."

Cab closed his eyes. "Diane—"

"I know. It was wrong. You have to remember, I'm in politics. I convinced myself that the ends justified the means."

"You didn't do this alone," he said.

"No."

"Who helped you? Was it someone with the police?" Then Cab realized that he already knew the answer. "Deacon Piper," he said softly. "It was Deacon, wasn't it? He planted the evidence."

Diane nodded. "I needed a spy, you see. Someone I could trust. Deacon knew how to do these things. He handled everything for me. It was a private thing between the two of us. But if he really is missing—"

"Then it means Frank Macy knows what happened," Cab said. "He's out for revenge. On both of you."

42

Dead eyes stared at him from inside the trunk of the car.

Through the overnight hours, rigor had made the body stiff, like an alabaster statue in a museum, fingers frozen into claws. He saw the webbed purple bruise on the forehead where the corner of the flashlight had fractured the skull. Hungry black bugs had already swarmed the hole in his abdomen and begun to feed. Pieces of intestine peeked between their wriggling bodies like a messy plate of pasta.

He grabbed the aluminum pistol case and blew two hitchhiking insects onto the garage floor with a puff of breath. He opened the case and retrieved the gun, which was cradled in gray foam. Checked it. Readied it. The butt felt smooth and sure in his gloved hand. As it had once before.

Ten years ago.

It felt as if he were back in the orange grove. He could feel himself marching in the sandy soil. The crickets chattered warnings that no one else understood. Each hot breath under the hood rebounded in his face. He remembered the sense of freedom as he broke into the clearing. Saw the lights beckoning him. Heard the swell of voices.

He remembered odd things from that night. The first to die, the citrus farmer, had crumbs in his mustache from something he'd eaten.

No one had said a thing to him about it, and so he died with pastry on his face. What was his name? He didn't know; he hadn't even read the news reports. They say you always remember the first, the look on the face, the sounds of dying, the way the soul gets ready to flee the body. All of that was true, but of course, the man on the dais wasn't his first.

He remembered his first. He remembered Alison.

He replaced the pistol case in the car and shut the trunk, obscuring the body. When he checked the clock on his phone, he saw that it was ten o'clock. His nerves frayed. Acid rose in his throat. It was soon. It was almost time. Chayla was a bonus, as if the devil had a sense of humor.

He rehearsed everything that would happen next. Walk two blocks to the estate. Head for the lights of the sunroom, where they would be waiting for him, unaware. That was the most important part of what he needed to do, and yet it would take the least time. The hood. The explosions of the gun. The bodies falling. All of that would be over and done in seconds, and he would be on his way. He knew how it would go, because he had done it before.

Back to the foreclosure house for the last time. Take the car. Drive. Drive south, through the storm, on the deserted highways; drive all the way to the Everglades, the wilderness where bodies became food for the alligators. He could dump him there, and it would be over. His work would be done.

He stared at the newspaper articles thumbtacked to the bulletin board. His collection of greatest hits.

FAIRMONT TO ENTER GOVERNOR'S RACE

**ONE YEAR LATER, MORE TRAGEDY:
FAIRMONT STUNNED BY SON'S SUICIDE**

**FRANK MACY GETS EIGHT YEARS
ON MANSLAUGHTER PLEA**

**COMMON WAY FOUNDATION INFLUENCE
GROWS—AND SO DOES CONTROVERSY**

He'd thought about leaving the articles behind to taunt the police, but he didn't think it was necessary now. They would know where the trail led. They would know, but just like ten years ago, they would find only roads that led nowhere.

He shoved the gun into his belt and removed a cigarette lighter from his pocket. With a flick of his thumb, he lit a flame, and then he yanked the first article from the wall, leaving behind a torn scrap of paper. He held a corner to the flame and watched the fire catch, running and spreading, incinerating the pulp to gray ash. As the fire neared his fingers, he let it fall to the floor, where he kicked at the ash with his toe and watched the fragments float. He pulled another article and burned it, and then another and another, and finally, the garage was redolent of smoke and fire, and the bulletin board was empty except for the one article on which he'd scrawled a single word.

REVENGE.

"Ashes to ashes," said a voice from the doorway.

43

Peach clenched the wheel as she flew across the Gandy Bridge.

She felt as if the wind under her tires would lift her like a Cessna and pitch her into the bay. Despite her efforts to keep the car straight, the heavy Thunderbird zigzagged back and forth between the lanes. She was alone heading west, with no more than a few stray headlights shining in the opposite direction as people escaped the Gulf. The rain belched from the sky, looking like a tsunami carrying the sea into her face. Individual drops sped like fleeing dots of light across her windshield. The normally placid bay surged with white foam, and waves as high as houses spewed across the low-lying bridge.

She breathed a sigh of relief when the causeway crossed back onto land. The storm surge had overrun the beaches, and she could see surf pawing at the shoulders of the highway. Justin's safe house was less than a mile west. When she spotted The Crab Shack restaurant, she turned left, splashing through four inches of rippling water as she drove to the very end of the deserted road.

No one else was around. She didn't see a light or a car anywhere. It was just her and the storm.

When she got out of the car, the water was up to her ankles. The limbs of the oak tree hanging over the house groaned with the wind.

She mounted the fence with Curtis Ritchie's equipment bundled in her arms, and then she kicked her way toward the porch. The air was full of brine. Her lips tasted of salt. She wrenched open the screen door and watched a snake slither in panic down the concrete steps into the water.

Inside, dampness hung in the living room. She could see patches of black mold growing near the air vents. Cockroaches shot for the walls as she stood in the middle of the room, dripping on the carpet. Everything was as she remembered it, cluttered with the debris left by whoever had searched this place. She didn't think anyone had been here since her last visit. She checked the clock on her phone and wondered when Annalie would arrive.

Peach deposited Curtis Ritchie's laptop and digital camera on a bruised antique coffee table, marred with circular water stains. She studied the compact house and wondered if there was really anything to find here. The search had been thorough. She eyed the ceiling, but there was no crawlspace overhead. The drawers and cabinets in the kitchen were wide open. So was the refrigerator, which had been raided by bugs. The room smelled of spoiled meat.

She returned to Justin's bedroom, where she'd found the newspaper article that had led her to Frank Macy. It had been hidden under the file cabinet. She toppled the file cabinet with a crash, scattering more roaches. She'd thought there might be papers taped to the underside, but she was wrong. Frustrated, she sat on the ruins of Justin's mattress.

"You should have told me what you were doing," she said aloud.

The photograph of herself in front of The Crab Shack restaurant was on the floor in its small broken frame. She bent down and retrieved it. Pieces of glass sprinkled to the carpet like jewels. She removed the photograph from the frame, but nothing was hidden behind it, and nothing was written on the back of the photo paper. It was a print he'd made at Walgreens. She examined the details in the photo, noting that this was the original, unlike the attachment he'd planned to send in his e-mail. The restaurant number was unaltered. So was the arrow on the roof.

She returned the photo to the frame and carefully picked away the remaining glass. She put it back on the little table in front of the window, the way Justin would have had it. He would have been able to stare it as he worked on his computer. She hoped that looking at her made him smile, but it wasn't a particularly flattering picture, with that big goofy smile on her face, hair greasy and unwashed, arm high in the air with her thumb pointing behind her. She remembered telling Justin that all she needed were checkered overalls, and she could have been standing outside a Bob's Big Boy restaurant.

Peach got up and went to Justin's laminate desk. The dismembered computer was unusable. So was the smashed monitor. She sat in his chair, which faced the window. If he'd left her something, it might have been small, like a flash drive, but she found nothing but dusty cables inside the desk drawers. She knew that whoever had been inside the house had stripped the place long before she got here.

The photo mocked her, as if she were laughing at herself. Then she noticed something unusual. In the photo, she was pointing backward with her thumb. The gesture highlighted the restaurant behind her, but as she stared at the photo from Justin's desk, she realized that she was pointing out the window. Outside. Not inside the house.

Peach got up from the desk. Ignoring the flood of rain, she unlocked the window and threw it open. She jutted her face outside, squinting into the downpour. She saw a lake surrounding the house, rather than the grass and weeds of the yard. The thick, decades-old oak tree was on her left, sprouting huge limbs over the roof. On her right was an old propane tank. Scrub brush in the nearby vacant land grew right up to the edge of the chain-link fence.

She climbed out the window and dropped into the water. The ground was mud under her feet. The bark of the old oak tree was furrowed with seams and knots, and she examined the larger gaps with her fingers to see if anything was shoved inside. When that proved fruitless, she picked up the empty propane tank, but it was no more than rusted debris. There was almost nothing else in the yard, except a telescoping ladder lying against the foundation. She dragged it out of the water and examined the underside of each step, but Justin hadn't hidden anything for her there.

It was another dead end.

The photograph was just a photograph, not a message.

Peach returned to the house and shut the window, but it caught on the frame and stayed open half an inch. She was soaked, and she knew she smelled like a wet dog. When she checked her phone again, she saw that Annalie was late. It had been almost ninety minutes since their phone call. When she returned to the living room, she peered through the blinds, hoping to see Annalie's Corolla arrive outside, but she saw only her own T-Bird parked out front. She dialed her friend's number on the phone again, but there was no answer. She didn't leave another message.

She sat on the torn cushions of the sofa. Drips of water splattered on the carpet. The broken antiques of Justin's life were in ruins around her. A baroque gold clock with cherubs. A child's rocking horse with chipped paint. A tapered, rose-colored bottle made of delicate glass. A laughing Buddha with a well-rubbed stomach. Nothing matched anything else. Justin had never cared about a theme for his collection; he simply bought pieces that spoke to him.

His books were scattered across the floor. Biographies of classical composers like Brahms and Haydn. Eclectic science books covering everything from astronomy to microbiology. Novels and essays from the eighteenth century. *Joseph Andrews. Rasselas. Gulliver's Travels.* There were titles in French that she didn't understand. It was all so . . . Justin.

One book caught her eye. She'd missed it before, because it was mostly covered under a record album of Bruno Walter conducting Beethoven's *Fidelio*. Sitting on the sofa, she spotted the green cloth cover of a small book of poetry. It was the same book—the same edition—of poetry by William Blake that she'd purchased for him as a birthday present. She frowned to think he'd already owned a copy, but he had never said a word about that when she gave it to him.

Peach got up from the sofa and picked up the volume. Without even thinking about it, she flipped to the page for "The Tyger."

He'd written something there, just as he had in the copy she'd found in his apartment. The handwriting was the same. She knew it all too well. This message was no more helpful than the name—*Alison*—she'd found on the same page in the book she'd given him.

The message said: **YOU ALREADY KNOW THE TRUTH**.

Peach shook her head. "No, I don't know," she said aloud. "Justin, I really don't know anything."

In frustration, she threw the book against the wall, where the binding broke and yellow pages floated to the floor. She was sick of his mysteries. She was sick of his enigmas and codes. He hadn't trusted her enough to tell her what he was doing, and now she was left to pick up the pieces.

She sat down on the sofa again and opened the cover of Curtis Ritchie's laptop. She booted it up on battery power. The thumbnail for Ritchie's username on the login screen was a close-up photograph of a woman's breast. That pig. Frowning, she clicked on the thumbnail, and it asked her for a password. Peach swore. She knew nothing about the man, and she had no idea what he might have used as his password. Randomly, she picked things out of her head. 12345. ABCDEF. 00000. After ten unsuccessful tries, she slapped the lid shut.

This was getting her nowhere. She wondered again: Where was Annalie? She glanced toward the lonely street, which was drowning under the assault of the storm. A finger of worry crept up her spine.

She grabbed Ritchie's digital camera. There was only a single bar of power left on the battery indicator; she didn't have much time to examine it. She opened the file of photographs on the microSD card, which consisted of hundreds of pictures, and scrolled to the beginning.

The first picture she saw was of Justin.

He was on the beach behind his condominium. He wore ridiculously long swim trunks, and his feet were in the calm surf. He wore headphones connected to a white iPod in his hand. Probably listening to Mozart. Peach clicked to the next photograph. Justin again. And again. Ritchie had been stalking Justin everywhere he went. She saw Justin getting into his car in the office parking lot. Justin eating a Cuban sandwich at the Kooky Coconut. Justin at a St. Pete antique mall. She saw herself, too. Ritchie had plenty of photographs of the two of them together. It made her heart ache, because scrolling through the pictures was like looking at a travel album of the final weeks they'd spent together.

It was also hugely invasive. Ritchie had photographed the two of them inside her house. He'd crept up to the window like a voyeur and snapped shots into her darkened living room. She saw the two of them snuggled together on her sofa. Justin clowning with Harley Mannequin. Herself, laughing, with her hands over her ears, as he made her listen to a Strauss opera. They were moments frozen into her memory, but she felt cheated now, realizing she had shared them with someone else. Someone who was watching their every move.

She clicked through the rest of the photographs. Justin had successfully kept one aspect of his life secret. There were no pictures of his safe house. There was nothing to suggest that Ritchie knew where this house was, which meant that he hadn't been the one to search it. She wondered how Justin had concealed the location; he'd obviously come here often, and yet somehow he'd made sure that he wasn't followed. That was one advantage of being paranoid. You took precautions.

And yet everywhere else Justin had been, Curtis Ritchie had been there, too. She flipped forward and backward, going faster and faster, hypnotized by everything she saw. For a few brief moments, Justin was alive again.

Justin in Starbucks.

Justin in the produce aisle at Publix.

Justin on the sponge docks in Tarpon Springs.

Justin in Starbucks again.

Justin in Lake Wales. She recognized the environs. Ritchie had followed Justin on the secret trip he made to Lake Wales without her. She saw him at the library. At the Bok sanctuary. Out on a deserted stretch of highway. Walking out of Dr. Smeltz's office with a backpack slung over his arm.

The next photograph showed Justin in a parking lot near the doctor's office. He had something in his hand that looked like the same kind of medical file that Peach had retrieved from the locked supply closet.

What was the file? And where was it now? Whoever had searched his safe house must have found it and removed it.

She kept flipping through the pictures. The camera flashed a warning that the battery was almost dead. It would go black soon. When the camera died, she knew she would feel alone again. Looking at the pictures made her feel that Justin was with her.

Justin at The Pier.

Justin in an antiquarian bookstore.

Justin in Starbucks again.

He'd been in Starbucks a lot, which wasn't unusual, but something about the picture attracted her eyes. The photo was taken from outside, through the shop window. Justin was at a table with his back to the camera, but he wasn't alone. Someone else sat across from him, but all Peach could see when she zoomed in was an arm. A female arm. Justin was meeting a woman at the coffee shop.

Who?

She clicked to the next photograph, which was taken at the same Starbucks on the same day. Ritchie was inside now, at the counter. The angle was reversed. The off-kilter photo showed Justin from the front, and his companion's back was to the camera. Peach stared at the back of a woman's head. Stared at luscious, long dark hair.

Peach began to hear every breath in her chest. She felt dizzy. The throb of a headache split open her forehead. She didn't want to see the next photograph, but she had no choice. She knew what she would see, because she recognized the woman now. She watched the picture fill the small screen, and there she was.

Annalie.

Annalie was at the table with Justin.

PART FOUR

HIT AND RUN

44

The receptionist at the police department in St. Pete Beach laughed at Cab over the phone. "I'm sorry, could you say that again, detective? I really want to be sure I heard you correctly."

"You've got an ex-con named Frank Macy whose driver's license record indicates that he has an apartment in St. Pete Beach," he repeated. "I'd like you to roll a couple uniforms over there to see if he's in his apartment now."

"You want us to bring some bagels or scones over there with us?" the receptionist asked.

"That's funny," Cab said. "I appreciate your sense of humor. I know my timing isn't exactly perfect—"

"Perfect? Detective, maybe you haven't looked outside your window recently, but we have a tropical storm on top of our heads right now. If you look west, you'll probably see Dorothy and Toto blowing past you any minute. So as hard as you may find this to believe, we're not just sitting around the station watching repeats of *Burn Notice*. We're a little busy out here. And we don't have time to send our officers on babysitting detail for some ex-con."

"I just want to know if he's *there*," Cab insisted.

"Then I suggest you drive out here yourself and knock on his door," she snapped. "Now I've got about a hundred other calls on hold, and some of them may actually be important. Happy Fourth of July, detective."

She hung up.

Cab didn't blame her. Nothing would get attention today other than the storm.

He threw his phone on the passenger seat of the Corvette. He was still parked outside the wrought-iron gate of Diane's estate. The neighborhood around him was empty. Some of the residents had probably left town ahead of Chayla, and all the others were inside, cursing the fact that the storm had landed on a summer holiday. As he watched, the lights glowing in the palatial homes went dark. He didn't see lights anywhere now. Not on the street. Not inside Diane's estate. The power was out. The morning was already grim under the black sky, and the outage seemed to extinguish the last glimmer of life.

Cab got out of the car. Despite his black trench coat, he was already wet to his skin where the rain streamed under his collar. He shoved his hands in his pockets and studied the dense foliage closing in around the estate. The brick walls were overgrown with ivy. Trees knelt down and stretched out their branches on both sides of the walls.

He walked to the end of Coachman Avenue, where the elegant cobblestones ended. He followed the wall of Diane's estate, avoiding the rivers overflowing out of the curbs. Flying leaves made a kind of green snow in the air. Where the road turned, he found a row of compact bungalows on a tree-lined street. There were no cars anywhere. Everyone had pulled their vehicles inside the safety of their garages. He saw no lights here, either. The outage covered the entire block.

Turning in the opposite direction, he followed Richards Court to where it ended two hundred yards later at Asbury Place. Nothing was different here. The area felt equally desolate and dark. No cars on the street in either direction. No power. He glanced at a house on the north side of the T intersection that was obviously deserted, with boarded-up windows and NO TRESPASSING signs posted on the front door. Another foreclosure house among thousands in Florida.

Cab walked toward the bay, where the houses got larger again. He could see the wild panorama ahead of him, besieged by the storm. The thin trunks of the palm trees were bent over like question marks. A spiny frond slapped his face so hard that it felt like the cut of a knife, and when he touched his hand to his cheek, it came away with blood that was quickly washed clean by the driving rain. It was growing more and more unsafe to be outside in the storm. There were no perceptible threats in the neighborhood around him, but that didn't make him feel better. The threats that bothered him were the ones he couldn't see.

Cab returned along the sidewalk of Bayshore Boulevard to the corner of Diane's sprawling estate. He didn't see anyone on the streets. When he climbed into his Corvette, he realized that the sheer pounding of the storm had left his muscles aching and stifled his hearing. He glanced in the mirror and saw that the cut on his cheek had stopped bleeding. His blond hair lay flat on his head.

He grabbed his phone.

He scrolled through his recent calls and found the number from which Ramona Cortes had invited him to lunch. He dialed the number, but there was no answer on her private cell phone. He left a message asking her to call him, and then he found the number for the offices of the attorney general in Tallahassee. It was a public holiday, but he suspected that the office would be staffed while Chayla was assaulting the Gulf Coast in the middle of a statewide campaign. Three transfers later, he found himself connected to a senior aide to Ramona Cortes.

"I'm very sorry, detective," she told him, "but Attorney General Cortes isn't in the Tallahassee office today."

"I understand. It's important that I talk to her soon. We had lunch on Monday, and she asked me to stay in touch on an investigation I'm running." That was partly true, so he didn't feel guilty about fudging the facts.

"Let me see what I can do, detective."

Cab hung up, but before he could decide on his next move, his phone rang again. Not more than five minutes had passed.

"Detective Bolton? It's Jaci Muzamel. I'm Ramona's personal assistant. I understand you're trying to reach her."

"I am."

"I have instructions to put you through if you call. Ramona is still in Tampa for the campaign, but unfortunately, she's not reachable right now."

Cab was surprised that Ramona had anticipated that he might call her again—and that she would consider it a priority to take his call. "It would be helpful if I could talk to her as soon as possible," Cab said. "I know the storm is causing problems everywhere."

"It is, but the storm's not really the issue. Ramona is very regimented about her workout routine. I'm not even sure a hurricane would keep her away from the club. She always turns off her phone. It's the one hour of the day she keeps to herself."

Cab glanced up the street toward Bayshore Boulevard. "Is that the Tampa Yacht Club? That's where I met her for lunch."

"Actually, it is."

"Well, I'm not far away from there," Cab said. "Would she mind if I drove over and met her in person?"

"I think that would be fine. She was adamant that she wanted to talk to you if you tried to reach her. I'll call ahead to the club and have them let you in."

"I appreciate it," Cab said.

He put down the phone and headed out on the deserted streets. The Tampa Yacht Club was only a mile away. He wondered if Ramona would still be happy to talk to him when she found out that he wanted to ask questions about an old client named Frank Macy.

45

Annalie.

Annalie had lied to her. She'd lied from the very beginning. She knew Justin.

Peach checked the date of the photograph on Curtis Ritchie's camera and saw that the picture had been taken only a week before Justin was killed. A week—just before he dropped off the radar. Annalie was part of the plot. Either she had killed Justin herself, or she knew who did. Then she'd wormed her way into a job at Common Way in order to find out what Justin knew.

Part of her mission was deceiving Peach. Pretending to protect her. Pretending to be her friend. All the while, Annalie had tracked everything that Peach was doing, and like a fool, Peach had played right into her game.

She thought about Deacon's message.

If Macy really is involved in something, chances are he's not alone. Don't trust anybody.

She thought about Annalie's odd reticence in sharing details about her past. She'd written it off to her own paranoia, because she needed a friend. She'd overlooked all the signs that this woman knew more about Justin—and about herself—than someone from the outside should ever have known. She'd trusted Annalie.

A mistake. She stared at the living room in Justin's safe house, which had been searched from top to bottom, and she thought: *Annalie was the one who searched the house.*

And now Peach had invited her back here. Annalie—who always carried a gun and had shoved that gun into Frank Macy's face, as if they were strangers.

They weren't strangers. They were partners. Working together.

Peach had to get out of the house. She didn't want to be here when Annalie arrived. Her emotions would betray her. Annalie would take one look at Peach's face, and she would realize that Peach *knew*. If it were about anything else, she could wear a disguise, but this was about Justin. She couldn't stare at this woman and cover up her rage.

She grabbed Ritchie's digital camera and Toughbook. Before she left, she hurried back into the bedroom, grabbed the photo of herself out of the frame on the small table, and shoved it into her back pocket. That was private. That was between her and Justin, and she didn't want to leave it for anyone else to find.

It was time to go, but when she returned to the living room, she saw that she was too late. Blurred headlights flashed through the rain and cut across the walls. Through the blinds, she saw Annalie's Corolla pulling up in front of the house. Peach froze. The car door swung open, and Annalie ducked into the storm.

Peach stood in the middle of the living room, watching and waiting. Annalie hoisted one leg over the low fence, then the other, and she dropped into the rain-speckled lake surrounding the house. She examined the place with both hands on her hips. Her long black hair was plastered to her face and neck.

There was nowhere to hide. Annalie would see her if she tried to make a run for her Thunderbird. She also realized that she didn't want to run. Not now. Not from this woman. She wanted to confront her about what she'd done. She wanted to know who else was involved. She wanted answers.

Annalie headed for the porch, and Peach finally sprang into action. Looking around for something to defend herself with, she scooped up a pink glass bottle from the floor and clutched the neck in her fist. She stepped lightly to the bedroom and hid behind the open door. She held her breath, listening.

The wooden screen door opened and slammed shut on rusted hinges. Footsteps climbed the front steps. She heard the knob turning on the front door, and then the storm grew louder, as if it were inside the house with her.

Annalie called out: "Peach? It's me."

Her voice sounded normal. Friendly. When Peach didn't answer, Annalie called again, but her tone was deeper and more cautious. "Peach? Are you here? Are you okay?"

Peach's fingers were slippery with sweat. The glass bottle was hard to hold. The storm hammered the roof above her, and the bedroom felt damp and hot. A cockroach crept up the wall near her face. She had to take a breath, and she tried to do it silently, but her chest felt tight with fear.

A sharp metallic click snapped the silence from the other room. She knew that sound, because she'd heard it often enough when Deacon was manipulating his own weapon. It was the slide of a semiautomatic handgun being racked. Annalie had her pistol in her hand and a round in the chamber. It was ready to fire.

"Peach?" she called again.

Annalie headed for the bedroom where Peach was hiding. Her squishy footprints sank into the wet carpet, one after another. At the doorway, she stopped. Peach couldn't see her, but she was so close that Peach could hear water dripping from her hair. The window was cracked open, causing the wind to whistle and moan. Rain spat through the gap.

Peach hoisted the bottle over her head.

Half of Annalie's body appeared beyond the door. Annalie faced the window, looking outside, not looking behind her. Her bare arm was cocked at the elbow, gun in her hand, her index finger bent on the trigger. Peach saw golden skin on the curve of her jaw. She recognized Annalie's beautiful face, and something flinched inside her. She didn't want to believe that this woman was her enemy.

Don't trust anybody.

She didn't have time to second-guess herself. Annalie felt the presence behind her and began to turn, and in the same moment, Peach swung the bottle down hard. The elegant glass cut awkwardly through the air and landed on Annalie's skull, breaking into pieces. The woman took a staggering step in pain and surprise. Her hand tensed; the gun went off, blasting a bullet into the bedroom wall, which erupted in dust and plaster. Annalie's eyes closed, and she crumpled, knees buckling. She pitched to the floor. The gun spilled from her hand.

She lay in the middle of the bedroom, limbs splayed, not moving. Glass shards surrounded her.

Peach rushed forward and grabbed the gun. Annalie's eyes blinked, and her breathing was loud. A wave of fury washed over Peach. Annalie was alive, and Justin was dead. She felt no sympathy for her. She didn't care what happened next, to either of them. Grabbing Annalie's arm and leg, she roughly shoved the woman over on her back. Peach stood over her, kicking away glass.

"Who are you? Tell me who you are! Tell me what you did to Justin!"

Peach crouched over Annalie. She jerked one hand back and slapped the woman sharply across the face, leaving a bloom of red. "Tell me what you did! You bitch! You liar!"

A low moan rumbled from Annalie's throat as she tried to focus. Peach slapped her again, even harder.

"I saw you! You were with him! Did you kill him? Was it you? Tell me, *was it you?* If you were the one, so help me, I will pull this trigger right now. I will! I'll kill you myself!"

Annalie's jaw moved. Her eyes opened and closed. Staring at her, all Peach could see was Justin's face and then the photograph of the two of them together. Annalie and Justin. A week before he was murdered.

"Do you think I won't kill you? Do you think I'm just a kid? You played me from day one. Did you laugh at how easy it was to get me to trust you?"

Peach aimed away from Annalie's head, and she jerked on the trigger, too quickly, too heavily. The gun fired wildly into the floor, and the recoil forced her arm back and nearly made her fall. She cringed with the violence of the explosion. The bullet blew up splinters from the floorboards. Annalie's head rocked in agony as the shock waves cracked in her skull.

Peach knelt over Annalie, a knee on her chest. She held her tightly down.

"I'll do it," she vowed. "I will. I don't care."

Annalie's breath stuttered. Her eyes blinked into narrow slits. The world had to be spinning, a hurricane of noise and light, but Annalie's mouth moved soundlessly, and a choked word gasped from her throat.

"*Peach.*"

Peach screamed at her again. "You killed Justin! You bitch, you killed him! Did you kill Deacon, too? Are you the one?"

"Peach," Annalie repeated, unable to say anything more.

"It was you!" Peach shouted. She couldn't stop herself. She couldn't think about right and wrong. The words bubbled out with spit and foam. "It was you, it was you, it was you, it was you!"

Annalie tried to talk again, but Peach shoved the gun into the woman's open mouth. Between her red lips and her perfect teeth.

"This is what you did to Justin! *You blew his head off, and that's what I'm going to do you!*"

She slid her finger over the trigger. Nothing made sense anymore. Not the past. Not the future. There was only right now, her and Annalie and the gun. There was nothing in her world but the rain and the heat of this moment. Pull the trigger, and she was dead, and Justin was avenged, and maybe, maybe, she could have peace after everyone she had lost.

Pull the trigger. Pull the trigger.

She began to feel the pressure on her skin. The trigger pushed back at her finger. They did a little dance together. Finger and trigger. Pull. Pull. Pull.

That was when music interrupted her. Wildly improbable music. Gloria Estefan sang "Rhythm Is Gonna Get You."

Annalie's phone was ringing.

46

Cab sat at a multi-station weight machine in the fitness room at the Tampa Yacht Club. His trench coat and suit coat hung from a lat bar. His leather shoes were a lost cause. The club still had electrical power, and several flat-screen televisions in the empty room were tuned to CNN. He saw live reports of the ferocious surf hitting the Gulf near Clearwater. He wondered where his mother was and where Lala was.

He checked his phone. Fifteen minutes had passed. Ramona Cortes still hadn't arrived.

One of the club employees served him a bear claw and a bottle of water. The sugar helped keep him awake. His ears still rang from the noise of the storm. When he finished the pastry, he got up and went to the mirrored wall and adjusted the knot in his tie.

Over his shoulder, he saw the attorney general join him in the fitness room. She was wet from the rain.

"Hello, Cab," Ramona said. "A little overdressed for Pilates, aren't you?"

"I'm more of a Zumba man."

"I'd like to see that," she said, chuckling. "Do you mind if I run while we talk?"

"Not at all."

"This hour is sacred. Regardless of what else you do, you need to respect your body. As it is, I had to cancel my massage today, and I never miss that. My masseur is unavailable."

Ramona was dressed in running shorts and a tank top. She had a towel draped around her neck, and she wore pink Nikes. She was a small woman, but her legs were muscled and shapely under the snug Lycra. Her arms looked strong. She climbed onto a treadmill and set it at a slow pace. Gracefully, she jogged along with the moving platform.

"So I hear you quit," she called over the noise of the machine. "Caprice must not be happy. She's a stubborn woman. She's accustomed to getting what she wants."

"Funny, she says the same thing about you," Cab said.

"I'm sure she does, and she's right. Anyway, I'm glad you took my advice."

"Well, I decided I would live a happier life not working for politicians."

"Astute choice," Ramona said. She increased the speed of the machine, until she was running, not jogging.

"I'm still investigating the threat against Diane," Cab said. "I'm convinced it's real and imminent."

Ramona gave him a sideways glance. "Why do you think that?"

"Because I'm looking into someone with a considerable motive to harm Diane. He's someone from your past. A client named Frank Macy."

If she found the name unexpected, she didn't show it. "Frank? I really don't think you need to worry about him."

"When did you last talk to him?"

"It's been several years. I severed ties to prior clients when I was elected. I knew he was released not too long ago, but that's all. Mind you, I know Frank, and it wouldn't surprise me if he's up to his old tricks again. Drugs. Guns. He likes having money to throw at the girls on the beach."

"Frank had close ties to Diane's son. Drew Hempl. And he has a history with Diane, too."

Ramona's lips pursed into a frown, but the speed of her run didn't change. "Yes, I know he does."

"What do you know about Frank's relationship with her?"

"Quite a lot, actually."

Cab wondered how far to go. How much to say. "Enough to get Diane into political trouble?"

"Yes," she acknowledged. "Probably enough to ruin her."

"And yet nothing has been exposed. You're showing remarkable restraint when it comes to a political opponent."

Ramona switched off the machine and slowed to a stop. She wiped her forehead with the towel. "What are you suggesting, Cab?"

"Caprice suspects you're behind everything that's going on. She thinks you know damaging secrets about Diane and Frank Macy. You can't release anything about it yourself, so you're using me to bring it out into the open. Destroying Diane's political ambitions and furthering yours at the same time."

"Do you believe her?"

"I don't believe any politician. That includes you."

She chuckled. "Well, you're right. For a politician, the agenda comes first. Ahead of friends, if we're lucky enough to have any. Even ahead of family, as much as it pains me to say so. As long as we get what we want, the ends justify the means."

"That's what everyone tells me," Cab said. "Does that mean you'd jump at an opportunity to wipe out a political enemy? An opportunity with Frank Macy's name on it?"

Ramona sighed and pointed at Cab's bottle of water. She waggled her fingers at him, and he handed it over. She took a sip. "Look, Cab, I'm not asking you to trust me. I'm asking you to look at it from my perspective, which is political self-interest. Frank Macy was my client, and any communication between him and me is still governed by attorney-client privilege. If I were to violate that privilege, I could be disbarred, which would be something of a political liability for the attorney general of the state of Florida."

Cab smiled. "True enough."

"Even if I wanted to find a way around privilege—say, by using a rich, handsome, ridiculously tall investigator to do my dirty work for me—I would still be putting my head on the chopping block. My connection to Frank Macy is a matter of public record. As soon as his name starts popping up in the media, so does mine. That's not politically helpful. So as much as Diane wants to keep her interactions with Frank a secret, you can be assured that I want to keep my name away from him, too."

"Maybe so," Cab said, "but Frank's still a threat to Diane."

Ramona climbed off the treadmill. She continued to drink Cab's water. "Why are you so sure? You have no reason to think he was involved in the Labor Day murders, do you?"

"I thought I did, but apparently I was wrong about that," Cab admitted.

"Ah." Ramona chose her words carefully. "In other words, you suspected that Diane or her son might have used the services of a third party to resolve the problem of an abusive husband."

Cab's eyebrows rose. "You know a lot."

"It's an ongoing investigation, and I'm up to speed on all aspects of it. Our special agent friends have their flaws, but they did examine that angle in considerable detail back then and concluded there was nothing to it. It was kept out of the media out of deference to the family."

"I see."

"So that's why I consider Frank Macy to be a nonissue."

Cab shook his head. "There's more. Justin Kiel had a newspaper article in his safe house about Macy's manslaughter plea. So it appears that Justin was looking at Frank before he was killed. In addition, as of last night, Deacon Piper is missing. Someone broke into his house. He was talking to sources about Frank Macy earlier in the day."

Ramona frowned. "You're sure about Justin?"

"Yes."

"That surprises me, but it's still a big leap to think that Frank was involved in his death. Or in Deacon's disappearance. What's the connection?"

Cab hesitated. He was handing Ramona a political bombshell by saying anything. "Hypothetically?"

"If you wish."

"Okay. Let's assume that you and Macy were correct that fraudulent evidence was used to implicate him in that manslaughter case in Pass-a-Grille. Let's also assume that if Diane was involved in planting evidence, she had help from someone inside Common Way. Someone like Deacon Piper. If Frank Macy suspected that Diane and Deacon stole eight years of his life, don't you think he'd do something about it?"

Ramona's eyes grew smoky. "I knew I was right about Diane. I can't believe the arrogance of those people."

"I'm speaking hypothetically."

She shrugged. "Yes, of course."

"You see why I'm trying to find Macy. If Deacon is gone, Diane is next. I'd like you to pull strings to help me locate him."

"Look, Cab, Frank is certainly capable of violence. I don't wear rose-colored glasses about some of my old clients. However, I don't see him targeting Diane or Deacon. He's not that foolish. He likes his breezy life too much to put it in jeopardy over a crazy scheme for revenge. And the situation with Justin Kiel is much more complicated than you realize."

Cab stared at her. "Why?"

"I can't say."

"If this is about politics—"

"It's not," she said. "I can't discuss an ongoing criminal investigation."

"Ramona, I need your help. If I'm right, time is very short."

She frowned. "This is extremely delicate. I need your assurance that nothing I say will make its way back to Common Way."

"You have it," Cab said.

Ramona sat on the edge of the treadmill. "The fact is, I've long suspected that Common Way has engaged in illegal activity behind the scenes. Espionage. Blackmail. Maybe worse. What I've never been able to do is prove it. However, a few months ago, an employee in what I call the black ops area of Common Way approached my office."

"An employee?" Cab asked. Then he said: "Justin Kiel."

Ramona nodded. "Justin didn't like what was going on there. He had the same suspicions that I did. He believed that Common Way was illegally influencing legislative policy, candidate selection, elections, whatever. They were using money—and probably other criminal tactics—to get their way. Justin offered to be a double agent for me. To dig into the foundation's secrets. It all had to be handled with absolute confidentiality. I couldn't be directly involved. If Diane Fairmont discovered that I was using someone inside her organization to spy on her, the blowback would have thrown me out of the campaign and probably out of office altogether. So I recruited someone to serve as a go-between with Justin. I needed someone I could trust implicitly. And we began to gather information."

"What did you find?" Cab asked.

"Plenty to be suspicious about, but no proof that would lead to indictments. We couldn't proceed without rock-solid evidence, and we didn't have it. And then a few weeks ago, Justin contacted his go-between to say that he had urgent new information. He didn't explain what it was—and he was murdered before he had a chance to share it."

"His new information could have been about Frank Macy," Cab said. "Justin may have come across Macy's plans regarding Deacon and Diane."

"Maybe, but I don't think so. I know you've been listening to this girl Peach Piper, but she was emotionally involved with Justin. It clouds her judgment. I'm sympathetic, but I think she's on the wrong track about Frank."

Cab's eyes narrowed. "How do you know so much about Peach and her investigation into Justin's death?"

"Because Justin was my own agent," Ramona replied calmly. "Do you think I would sit here and do nothing? He worked for me, and I want to know who killed him. I arranged to get another mole inside Common Way to investigate his death. I used Justin's go-between to work undercover. She was highly motivated, because she knew him. They were friends. She wanted to catch his killer as much as I did."

"A mole," Cab said. "Undercover."

"That's right."

There was only one person Ramona would have used for a mission like that.

I needed someone I could trust implicitly.

Ramona said nothing more, but she didn't need to say a word. Cab knew exactly who it was. When you can't trust your friends, you turn to your family.

"Lala," he said. "You put Lala inside Common Way."

He grabbed his phone and dialed.

47

Gloria Estefan sang, and Peach stared at the caller ID on Annalie's phone. What she saw made no sense at all.

Cab Bolton was calling Annalie.

She pushed herself to her feet, standing over Annalie's prone body. Her first paranoid thought was that Cab was part of the conspiracy, but she'd checked his identification. She'd called the Naples police. He really was a detective. He really was one of the good guys.

Or was he?

Don't trust anybody.

"Hello?" she said.

There was a pause before he answered. When he did, she recognized his voice. "Who is this?"

She tried to think, but confusion overwhelmed her. She said nothing.

"Hello?" Cab continued. "Who's there?"

"It's Peach," she murmured.

"Peach? How did you get this phone?"

"Why are you calling Annalie?" she asked.

"She's a friend of mine. Peach, is she there? Can I talk to her?"

Peach stared at the woman on the floor. Her eyes were open now, and her lips were moving, but Peach couldn't understand the words. "She killed Justin," Peach said into the phone.

"What? No, she didn't, Peach. She *didn't*. I promise you."

"I have her gun."

"Peach, let me talk to her. Please."

"You people took Justin away from me, but you're done. It's over. You can't stop me."

His voice grew urgent. "Peach, *listen to me*."

"No, you listen!" she shouted, losing control. "I'm sick of people lying to me. Justin lied! He shut me out, and he lied! Now Annalie lied to me, too. Do you hear me? I'm sick of it! You're not going to get away with it anymore."

"Peach, stop," Annalie murmured at her feet.

"Peach, stop," Cab told her, like an echo.

She pointed the gun at Annalie's head again. "Why should I? Why shouldn't I just shoot her?"

Cab's words tumbled over the phone line. "Peach, the woman that you know as Annalie is actually a police investigator named Lala Mosqueda. She is *not* part of any conspiracy. She did *not* kill Justin. She's been working undercover for the attorney general to find out what really happened to him."

Peach blinked. "What?"

"She is not the enemy. She is on your side."

"You're lying," Peach said. "You're all lying to me."

"Peach," whispered the woman at her feet. The stranger at her feet. "I'm sorry. It's true. I'm a cop. I was working with Justin."

Peach still held the gun in her hand. It was pointed at Annalie's head. Except Annalie wasn't Annalie.

"Why should I believe you?" she demanded.

The woman on the floor braced herself on her hands, her elbows bent. The barrel of the gun was an inch from her dark eyes. "Because Justin was my friend, too. Because I want to catch whoever killed him as much as you do."

Cab's voice came through the phone. "She's telling you the truth, Peach."

"I don't—I don't know—"

"My name is Lala," the woman said to her. "Is that Cab on the phone?"

Peach nodded mutely.

"Okay, listen to me. Slowly point my gun toward the wall. Please. Nice and steady. Don't make any sudden movements with it."

Peach looked inside her heart. Annalie was Lala, and she didn't know who Lala was, but she realized that nothing had changed. She liked her. She didn't want to hurt her. She wanted to trust her—and Cab Bolton, too. Her whole arm trembled as she thought about what she'd been ready to do. The gun in her hand felt ugly and lethal. She could hardly hold it, and she swung her whole body in order to point the barrel at the wall.

"That's good. Give me the phone, okay?"

Peach handed the phone to her. The gun was still in her other hand.

"You know how to rack the slide," Lala told her. "Keep your finger off the trigger."

Peach yanked the slide of the gun back and forth, and a gold cartridge popped from the barrel like a jack-in-the-box and fell to the floor. Lala closed her eyes and breathed easier. As Peach watched, Lala spoke into the phone.

"Cab Bolton," she said. "Get your ass over here."

Cab squatted in front of Peach, who sat on the floor with her back against the wall and her arms wrapped tightly around her knees. Her eyes stared out the window at the storm. She looked even younger than she was.

"Don't be hard on yourself," he said. "You had no way of knowing. I didn't know, either."

Lala winced as she held an ice pack to the back of her head. "I wanted to tell you, Peach. Really. I'm sorry."

"I almost killed you," Peach murmured.

"Well, you didn't. Anyway, I understand how you must have felt, seeing me in those pictures. I feel stupid that Curtis Ritchie was able to get those photos without me realizing it."

Cab got to his feet. "Are you sure you're okay?" he asked Lala.

"I think so. It's just a nasty bump. I was woozy, but I didn't black out."

"Still." He took her face in his hand and moved his finger left and right in front of her nose to make sure that her eyes were properly focused. She stuck out her tongue at him, and then he leaned in and kissed her lips. "I didn't have a chance to do that this morning," he said.

"I said good-bye," Lala told him, "but you were asleep. Guess I wore you out."

"I guess you did."

Peach stared at them. "So are you two—"

"I keep him in my life to drive myself crazy," Lala replied.

"I keep her in my life to drive my mother crazy," Cab added.

Cab watched a little smile play across Peach's face. She found them funny.

"So why are we here, Peach?" Cab asked. "You said this was Justin's hidey-hole, but you didn't know about this place until after he was killed?"

Peach shook her head. "I knew he had a safe house, but he never told me where it was."

Cab looked at Lala. "What about you? Did you know about it?"

"No."

He studied the wreckage of the house. "Well, someone found it."

"I don't think it was Curtis Ritchie," Peach said. "There were no pictures of this place on his camera. The trouble is, whoever searched it took everything. There's nothing left to tell us anything. It's a dead end."

"How did *you* find this place?" Cab asked her.

He listened to Peach explain about the photograph attached to a draft e-mail from Justin and about the edits in the picture that had led her down San Fernando Drive to this house. She pulled a hard copy of the photograph from her back pocket and showed it to him.

"See? Justin kept this picture in a frame by the window. I thought maybe he was sending me another message, but I guess I was wrong. I couldn't find anything."

"You said the photo in the e-mail was edited," Cab said. "What about this one?"

"I don't think so. The street number is the same now. So's the little house on the restaurant sign."

"What about other changes?"

"I—I'm not sure I really looked."

"Do you still have the original?" Cab asked.

Peach nodded. "It's on my phone."

She scrolled through her camera roll, clicked on a picture, and handed the phone to Cab. He stared at the image on the camera screen, then at the printed photo in his hand. He went back and forth several times, and at first he thought Peach was correct. The photos were identical.

Except—

"The vent," Cab said.

Lala looked at him. "What?"

"Justin added an exhaust vent on the roof of the restaurant. It's right above Peach. It's in the hard copy print here, but the vent's not in the original photograph."

Cab didn't have time to say anything more before Peach was on her feet and over to the bedroom window. She threw up the sash and practically jumped through the cramped space into the flooded yard. She pushed through the standing water until she could see the roof of the house, and then she pointed and screamed.

"There's a vent above the bedroom. Right above the bedroom! That can't be right!"

Peach ran for the side of the house, and Cab saw her struggling to mount a telescoping ladder against the frame. It fought her in the storm like a reluctant dance partner. When she finally slapped it under the roofline, he reached out through the open window with both hands and grabbed the ladder to steady it. The lightweight aluminum bucked and swayed as the wind tried to rip it out of his grasp.

"Be careful, Peach," he called. "I can't hold it."

She climbed past him. He could see her legs and feet immediately in front of him as she pulled herself up onto the house's low roof. Her body thumped on the shingles over their heads. She shouted something he couldn't understand, and then a tortured twisting of metal screeched from above them. Cab saw an aluminum vent hood sail like a Frisbee across the yard. Peach's body reappeared in front of him. He hugged the ladder, but when she was halfway to the ground, a gust of wind wrenched it from his hands and threw it backward. Peach flew, landing flat on her back in the water.

"Peach!" Cab shouted.

He started to climb through the window himself, but she pushed herself to her feet. "I'm okay, I'm okay! I've got something!"

She had a large, plastic-covered package tucked snugly under her arm.

He helped her through the window back into the bedroom. She looked immensely pleased with herself, and he realized that the importance of this discovery wasn't about anything they might find inside the package. It was about her and Justin. In the end, he'd trusted her. He'd left something for her to find. Not anyone else. Her. He was still the young man she'd loved.

Peach reached out her arms and handed the package to Lala. "You look," she said.

The package was approximately twelve inches by fifteen inches, wrapped in heavy plastic and sealed with duct tape. It was damp with spray but otherwise undamaged. Cab could see a thick sheaf of papers and manila folders inside. Lala took the package to the mattress and used her fingernails to pick at the duct tape and peel the folds of plastic apart.

Cab saw a stack of photographs that had been produced on a home printer. He recognized the first page; it was a match for the article on Frank Macy that Peach had found under the file cabinet. Justin was no fool. He'd anticipated that things might come to a bad end, and he'd made a backup of everything he'd discovered.

Lala didn't flip through the rest of the photographs immediately. Instead, she removed a thick manila folder, similar to the records that Peach had stolen from Dr. Smeltz's office. Peach recognized it, too.

"Is that a medical file?" she asked Lala.

Cab saw Lala's brow wrinkle in confusion. "Yes, it is."

"Curtis Ritchie had a photograph of Justin outside Dr. Smeltz's office," Peach said. "He'd stolen someone's file. Is it a duplicate of what I found? Is it Ms. Fairmont's file?"

She shook her head. "No, it's not hers."

"Then whose is it?"

Lala looked at Peach. "Yours," she said.

48

Tarla tipped her champagne glass into the circle with Caprice and Diane. Their crystal glasses clinked together.

"To Governor Diane," Tarla said with a smile.

Caprice repeated the toast, but Diane said nothing. Her smile was forced. They drank, and then Diane turned away toward the windows looking out on the garden. Candles lit the room, flickering and throwing shadows on the walls. The power was out.

Caprice leaned close to Tarla's ear. "Do you know where Cab is?"

"No, I haven't talked to him."

"You know how much I like him, Tarla, but he's going to ruin Diane's campaign if he's not more careful. He doesn't seem to appreciate the collateral damage we could face if certain things are exposed."

"My son never met a sleeping dog he didn't want to wake up," Tarla commented.

"Well, I'd still feel better with him in the house today."

"Does Cab believe there's a serious threat?" Tarla asked.

"He can't be sure, but some bad things happened overnight. I'm worried."

Tarla nodded and sipped champagne. Caprice wandered away to an armchair in the corner of the sunroom, where she tried to get storm updates on her cell phone. Signal came and went.

The threat of violence didn't feel real to Tarla. Something so foreign never felt real until it happened. It made her think about the warm Labor Day night ten years ago. A holiday then, a holiday now. Her only concerns then had been Diane's health, and her annoyance with Birch, and her frustration with Cab shutting her out of his life. Then, in the blink of an eye, blood had been spilled. People had died. A man who smelled of sweat and fear had shoved the barrel of a gun in her face.

She didn't believe something like that could happen again. Could it?

She studied Diane, who was unusually quiet. They hadn't had any real chance to talk, and the unspoken things hung between them. Tarla felt guilty about what she'd told Cab. The money changing hands between Diane and Frank Macy. She felt angry, too, that Diane had never told her that the baby she'd lost had been fathered by Cab. Even between good friends, there were secrets that could cost everything.

Tarla approached Diane by the floor-to-ceiling windows and put a hand on her shoulder. Her friend looked back and acknowledged her. The silence between them seemed to carry all of their apologies, as if nothing else was needed. Each of them knew what the other was thinking. Sometimes it was strange to recall that they had been friends for more than four decades, ever since they were ten-year-olds lying side by side on the open lawns of the Bok sanctuary and fantasizing about their futures. Neither of them could have imagined how the future would really turn out.

"Don't tell Caprice," Diane murmured.

Tarla was concerned. "What?"

Diane looked at her aide, whose back was to them on the other side of the sunroom. "When the storm is past, I'm getting out of the race."

"No! Why do that? You were born for this."

"I've done things," Diane whispered. "Things that can't be undone." She saw Tarla's face and added: "Not Birch. Other things. If I'm going to ask people to trust me as governor, I have to be able to trust myself."

"You're making a mistake," Tarla told her. "The past doesn't matter. I know who you really are."

"Do you? I don't even know myself anymore. Maybe it happens to every politician. I'm becoming the mask that I despise in every candidate from the other parties. We need someone authentic."

Tarla squeezed her hand. "Don't do anything rash. Give it time."

Caprice called to them from a chair in the corner. "You're on the air, Diane."

She'd found a live stream on her phone. The local network superimposed a photograph of Diane over footage of surf pounding the beaches, and they played a voice-over of a phone interview she'd conducted earlier in the morning.

"No, I'll be right here in Tampa. I'm not going anywhere. The important thing is to put safety first, and that means supporting the first responders who are putting themselves at risk and going without sleep to help everyone in central Florida. If you don't need to be outside, stay home, and let those good people do their jobs."

"Nice," Caprice said.

The screen shifted to a shot of the governor outside the capitol building in Tallahassee. He had a similar message of support, pledging every available state resource to protecting the area and rebuilding from any storm-related damage. It was impossible not to notice that the sun was shining in the Panhandle. He was a long way from Chayla.

"Not so much as an umbrella," Caprice added. "That's going to hurt him. He can talk about not getting in the way of rescue efforts all he wants, but people will remember that you were here, and he wasn't."

Diane said nothing, as if she were sick of political intrigue. She turned back to the windows. Behind them, Caprice muted her phone again, restoring silence except for the beat of the storm. Tarla could see their reflections against the glass in the darkness of the morning. The light of the candles aged both of them. They were two middle-aged women, at that stage of life when they had to decide if they could forgive themselves for their mistakes.

"I told Cab things I probably shouldn't have," Tarla admitted. "I'm sorry."

Diane's lips creased into something like a smile. "Well, I didn't tell Cab things that I probably should have. I guess that makes us even."

"You could have told me. I wouldn't have judged either of you."

"Keeping secrets is a hard habit to break," Diane said.

Tarla heard her phone ringing in her purse on the breakfast table. She retrieved it and saw that her son was calling. "Speak of the devil," she told Diane. And then into the phone: "Hello, darling. We were just talking about you. Are you going to join us?"

"Soon," Cab said, but his voice crackled with static, as if he were far away. "Is everything okay over there?"

"Perfectly fine. Just three lonely women against the world. The power's out, but we're making do."

"You're alone?" Cab asked. "Where's security?"

She struggled to hear him. "Oh, I'm sure there are men with guns wandering around somewhere. And of course we have Garth, in case there's a massage emergency."

"I'll be there in less than an hour," he told her. Before he hung up, he added: "Mother, I don't say this often, but be careful. If anything at all unusual happens, call 911, and then call me."

"You are so dramatic. I really wish you'd gone into acting."

"I'm serious."

She lowered her voice. "I know you are, darling. I hear you. Get here soon."

She hung up. Diane was watching her. "What did he say?" she asked.

"He's on his way."

Diane nodded. She took her empty champagne glass to the table and refilled it from a pitcher of mimosas. As she sipped from the glass, she looked around the sunroom, and she seemed to notice for the first time that it was just the three women keeping vigil against the storm.

"Where's Garth?" she asked.

Cab put down the phone. "There are no problems at Diane's place for now," he said.

Peach wasn't listening. She held her medical records in her hands, and she slowly pawed through the pages without looking at what was written there. "Why would Justin take this?" she asked Cab. "Why would he care? And why hide it with these other things?"

"I don't know," Cab told her. "Sometimes boyfriends get curious about things they should leave alone."

Peach shook her head. "Not Justin. If he wanted to know something, he would have asked me. Plus, he meant for me to find this. He wanted me to see it."

Cab couldn't pretend to understand. It was a piece of the puzzle that didn't fit, but he didn't have time to worry about it. Lala looked up from the other papers that Justin had hidden away inside the false vent on the roof. "We may have bigger problems. Cab, take a look at this."

Cab sat next to her on the bed. Lala showed him a copy of the photograph that he'd already seen, displaying the article about Frank Macy's manslaughter plea. Then she turned over more pages. There were other copies of newspaper articles, all of them dealing with Diane Fairmont and her son and the Common Way Foundation. It was like an obsession, but it wasn't the articles themselves that bothered him. These weren't copies made from a newspaper. Someone had made copies of these articles and posted them on a wall like a macabre collection of trophies. Like warnings. It was the kind of collage he'd sometimes found after a stalker struck his victim.

He saw more photographs. These were taken inside an empty garage. The bulletin board was in the background, against a foreground of an oil-stained floor. And then more photographs, inside what appeared to be an abandoned house.

"What is this?" Cab asked, but he knew what it looked like. A staging ground. The lair of a killer.

He realized that he was staring at the reason that Justin had been murdered. Somehow, Justin had found this place. A place that no one was supposed to know about. Not until after more people had died.

"The bigger question is *where*," Lala said. She could read his thoughts. She knew what these pictures meant.

She put the last photograph in front of him. It was an exterior shot of a dilapidated chocolate-brown house at a T intersection, with a BANK SALE sign posted in the front yard. The branches of an old elm tree brushed the roof. The windows were boarded over with plywood.

"We need to go," Cab told her, getting up.

"Do you know where it is?"

"I was just there," he said. "I saw it this morning. It's two blocks from Diane's estate."

49

Garth checked every room on the first floor of the estate, but the security guard wasn't there. He'd seen him fifteen minutes earlier in the kitchen, with his gun on the table and a croissant in front of him. Now the croissant was half-eaten, and the security guard and his gun had both vanished. Candle wax oozed across a plate, but the candle had gone out, and he could smell smoke in the air.

When he checked his phone, Garth saw that he had zero bars of signal. He held it in the air and shook it, but the cell towers had finally gone down. He picked up the house phone and heard nothing. No dial tone.

They were an island now. Cut off.

He opened the front door and shouldered onto the porch. The storm wailed. The wind hurtled debris across the yard. He shouted the guard's name, but his own voice was like a whisper. The garden lights were off. It may as well have been the middle of the night.

Garth grabbed an oilskin slicker from the hall closet and shrugged his beefy torso into it. Before he zipped it, he removed his gun from his shoulder holster and shoved it inside one of the raincoat pockets. The coat had a hood, which he yanked over his head and tied with a knot under his chin. He shoved his feet into rubber boots. When he jogged down the steps into the deep water, he felt as if the bay had overrun the land and turned it all into a vast sea. The animal sculptures in the garden seemed to be drowning.

He bowed his head against the wind and pushed toward the back of the estate. The paths were invisible except for the humps of land jutting out of the water like the undulating tail of a monster. He left the open lawn and found himself in dense foliage. Trees fired leaves at him. Grit got in his mouth. The rain squirmed inside his slicker. The sheer force of the water in his face made it hard to breathe.

"Screw this!" Garth said aloud.

He turned around, using one arm to shield his face from the branches that whipped through the air like knife blades. He followed the fence hugging the border of the estate and then veered into the gardens. Mud sucked at his boots under the water, and he kept losing his balance, because he couldn't see the ruts of the ground below his feet. Finally, he felt hard cobblestones as he reached the driveway. He headed toward the house.

That was when he heard the shot.

It came from outside the property. The sharp bang was barely audible over the wail of Chayla screaming at him. He reversed course and ran toward the wrought-iron gate at the street. The two halves of the gate slammed wildly back and forth, open and closed, closed and open. Garth had to dive out of the way when one of the metal panels took aim at him like a baseball bat. When both halves swung open again, he hustled onto the street. He was outside the grounds now, and he saw the storm roaring out of the bay. The waves of rain came and came and came. The wind picked up everything in its path and swept it toward him.

He squinted, trying to see. He had no idea where the gunshot had come from. Ahead. Behind. Was it really a shot? Maybe someone had set off a firecracker for the Fourth of July.

No, it was definitely a shot.

Garth pulled his gun from his pocket. He splashed down the street, carried by the wind at his back.

"I don't hear sirens," Cab said. "I don't see any lights."

Lala nodded in agreement. "There's nobody coming."

They were alone on Bayshore Boulevard. Waves crashed in twenty-foot surges that swept from the bay on their right and flooded through both lanes toward the houses that fronted the opposite side of the street. The sports car rode on water, not pavement.

"Try the security guard again," Cab said.

Lala shook her head. "No signal."

The street was black. There was no light anywhere. He slowed in the deep water to keep the car from stalling, and he felt the tires bump up on the curb as he swerved, unable to keep a straight path. When he spotted the cross street that led to the abandoned house, he swung the wheel left, and the Corvette fishtailed. He shot down the narrow cobblestoned street. Where the road ended, he parked on a soft shoulder. The brown roof of the foreclosed property was barely visible beyond a swath of mature elm trees. Cab got out, and Lala got out on the other side. They both had their guns in their hands.

A chain-link fence marked the eastern edge of the lot. Squat hedgerows grew beside it, giving them shelter. They stayed low. In the rain, they could barely see. He felt as if he were a passenger on the Maid of the Mist, engulfed by the spray of Niagara Falls. They crept close to the rust-stained stucco wall of the house. The front windows were nailed shut with plywood, and kids had spray-painted the boards with graffiti.

They reached the front door. It was locked.

Cab cupped his hands over Lala's ear. "The garage," he said.

He led her along the front sidewalk. Panicked lizards leaped from the bushes and skittered up the wall. Water cascaded down the slanted roof of the garage and sluiced over their heads. They slogged into the driveway, where they stood in front of a tan double-wide garage door. Cab pointed at Lala's gun, and she held it straight and ready as he bent down to yank the chrome handle. The door slid upward on its tracks with a bang.

A black Lexus sedan was parked in the middle of the concrete floor, facing the street. Cab approached on the left side of the car, and Lala shadowed him on the right. They met at the rear of the sedan. The garage was deserted.

"I know this car," Lala murmured. "It's Frank Macy's."

Cab slid a penlight from his pocket and cast a beam around the garage. He spotted the cork bulletin board on the east wall and recognized it from the photographs Justin had taken. When he examined the bulletin board, he saw that only one article remained, thumbtacked in the very center. He recognized a gauzy picture of Diane, and he saw the message written across the paper in red marker.

REVENGE.

Gray ash lay at his feet. With the garage door open, the wind scattered the ash into a cloud. He bent down and could still see burned fragments of paper that had survived the char. When he caught one, it was fresh and warm.

"Cab," Lala said.

She crouched near the trunk of the car. He came closer, and he said, "Yeah, I smell it, too."

Cab opened the driver's door of the sedan and pulled the trunk-release lever. The trunk popped open with a soft click. He heard Lala suck in her breath, and he knew what she'd found.

"Is it Deacon?" he asked.

Lala shook her head. Her face was screwed up in puzzlement.

He came around the back of the car. The first thing he saw was an aluminum pistol case, which was open and empty, with a slot in the foam where the gun had been. The next thing he saw were bugs crawling across a large sheet of plastic wrap, feeding on the belly of the body that stared up at him. He recognized the face.

It was Frank Macy.

50

Peach felt abandoned.

She'd wanted to go with Cab and Lala, but they had refused to let her join them in Tampa. They told her to go home, but she couldn't bear to set foot inside her own house. She couldn't stay here either, not when everything in this place reminded her of Justin. Cab had given her a key to his mother's condominium in Clearwater, but she didn't want to head west into the teeth of the storm. So she perched on Justin's sofa as stiffly as one of her mannequins, listening to Chayla beat on the house like a hip-hop singer.

Justin on hip-hop. *If Beethoven were alive today, he'd probably be a rapper. I think I'm glad he's dead.*

Justin.

Her medical file sat on the table in front of her, unopened. Her records. Her history. *Everything* about her was in there. Dr. Smeltz had been her doctor from the day she was born, and he had been her doctor until she and Deacon moved to the Gulf. Really, he was still her doctor. She had never chosen a new physician; she hadn't seen a doctor in years. Other girls went to the doctor to deal with birth control, but that wasn't an issue for her.

Everything.

Like the time, after her parents died, when she'd gone crazy with a razor blade and cut herself on her stomach. Lyle had found her bleeding and rushed her to the hospital. She still had the scars. They'd made her see a psychiatrist, but she hated the man's questions and his annoying, patient voice. Couldn't he see that all she needed was for her parents to come back from their trip? When were they coming home?

Around that time, she found a mannequin sticking out of a Dumpster behind a Kohl's department store. Her first. Ditty. She'd called her that because she kept hearing that John Mellencamp song in her head—the one with the little ditty about Jack and Diane. She'd rescued Ditty from the garbage and taken her home, and Ditty had been a better therapist than any of the real live people who wanted to help her. She'd spent hours talking to the mannequin in her bedroom.

Everything.

Her mind. Her body. Her life.

"Why did you take my file?" she asked Justin.

You already know the truth.

Peach picked up the thick folder and left it in her lap. It took her a while to open it. When she finally did, she turned to pages in the middle. Somewhere around age six, she'd broken two bones in her right wrist. Funny, she didn't even remember it. She waved her right hand as if she were a beauty queen in a parade, but her wrist worked fine, and she'd never noticed any pain there. Kids heal. She saw her mother's signature on release forms for X-rays. Thinking about it, she had a vague memory of wearing a cast and of Deacon writing FRUITY on it.

More pages. Physicals. She remembered the cold steel of a stethoscope on her chest and how she squealed. The wooden stick on her tongue. Ahhhhh. Dr. Smeltz poking her in the belly button. "You're as fit as a fiddle with a hole in your middle." Herself, giggling every time.

Weird rash. "You shouldn't touch those plants, sweetie, they're poisonous."

Prescription for Amoxicillin for a bad ear infection.

Chicken pox. "I've seen lots of tots with spots."

Diarrhea.

Burn on her pinkie from touching a hot stove. She still had a whitish patch of skin there.

Pneumonia.

The notes on pneumonia were near the front of the file, because it was one of the last times she'd seen Dr. Smeltz. She remembered getting sick in Tampa and Lyle and Deacon screaming at each other. She remembered the long drive home at night, the loud music, the weird sweet smell in the car, and then herself throwing up all over the backseat. Deacon, shouting at her.

The soft bed at Diane Fairmont's house. Dr. Smeltz in the bedroom. "You're lucky I was here, young lady. You are very sick, but I'm going to make you better. Okay?"

She removed a page from the doctor's notes. His handwriting was awful. *Fever at 104. Taking immediate steps to bring temperature down. Delirium. Girl keeps repeating: Why is there so much blood?*

Peach blinked and read that sentence again.

Girl keeps repeating: Why is there so much blood?

She heard a voice in her head, but it was her own voice.

"What are you doing?"

"What's happening? I'm scared."

"Why is there so much blood?"

Peach snapped the file shut. She stared at her hands and saw that they were trembling like leaves afraid to fall. She put the file back on the table in front of her, and she never wanted to open it again, never wanted to see it again. *You already know the truth.*

She closed her eyes. The thump of the storm became a thumping inside her head, pressing on the walls of her skull. She felt herself go somewhere else, somewhere long ago and far away. It was night. She was on a road, the world spinning. And then her brain, sounding like the kindly voice of Dr. Smeltz, interrupted and pulled her back: *Don't you go there, young lady.*

Peach thought about Justin in the library at Lake Wales. She imagined him at the reception desk, smiling, being charming, asking the librarian to find a local address for Dr. Smeltz. Before that, he'd spent hours among the microfiche carrels, copying pages from the newspapers ten years ago. She saw a stack of pages he'd left for her. Articles he'd copied from the microfiche.

Those pages looked scary to her now. She didn't want to see them, but she picked them up anyway. Most of the copies were from newspapers printed the day after Labor Day, featuring ugly black headlines about the murders. But not all. As she dug through the pages, she saw that Justin had gone further back, to the weekend when things began to go bad. When everything was different. When nobody was the same.

She saw an article about a political fundraiser in Tampa.

"Oh, Lyle, can I go, too? I want to see the city! And the zoo! Please please please please please."

She remembered Lyle: stressed, angry, driving her and Deacon in the Mercedes to Tampa. Another argument. Deacon sulked the whole ride. He didn't want to go, not with his twelve-year-old sister, not as a babysitter. Lyle left them alone in the city; he had things to do, important people to talk to. She and Deacon went to Busch Gardens. She took rides; he smoked funny-smelling cigarettes and said not to tell Lyle about it.

On one of the rides, she noticed that her throat had begun to hurt.

By evening, she was in the hotel room in bed, burning up. Coughing. Sweating. Sobbing: "I just want to go home, please take me home, I want to go home!"

Lyle shouting at their brother: *"Goddamn it, Deacon, for once in your life, stop thinking about yourself, and do what I tell you! Get in the car, and drive your sister back home right now!"*

Peach picked up another article from the stack of copies Justin had made. She read the headline:

SEARCH CONTINUES FOR MISSING TEENAGER

Police and community volunteers scoured the woods surrounding Lake Wales yesterday, continuing the search for Alison Garner, 14, who was reported missing by her parents late Saturday evening.

No evidence of the girl's whereabouts have been discovered so far, and no witnesses have come forward with information about the disappearance.

Alison was believed to be riding her bicycle when she left the family home, which is located on Old Bartow Road in West Lake Wales. She was last seen wearing red nylon shorts and a white tank top . . .

No matter how many times Peach tried to read the article, she couldn't finish. She simply saw one name over and over.

Alison. Alison. Alison.

There was one page left that she hadn't seen. One more article that Justin had copied. She didn't want to pick it up, because she knew exactly what it would say. She knew how the story ended.

You already know the truth.

She turned over the paper.

TEENAGER BELIEVED VICTIM OF HIT AND RUN

The search for missing teenager Alison Garner came to a tragic end late yesterday, when two migrant workers found the girl's body hidden in a gully off the shoulder of Highway 60.

Police have concluded that the girl was struck by a vehicle on the highway while she was riding her bicycle, which was also found hidden near the body. The coroner reported that Garner was apparently alive for some time after the accident and might well have been saved if emergency personnel had been alerted.

"That's the terrible thing about this case," said Lake Wales Police Chief Thomas Cappelman in yesterday's press conference. "Whoever hit this girl simply dragged her off the road and let her die. He hit her, and then he hid her body and didn't tell a soul. This wasn't just an accident. This was murder. When we find the driver, that individual is going to prison for the rest of his life. I promise you that."

"See the little white cross?" Peach had told Justin. *"You have to be careful when you drive here."*

51

Frank Macy looked surprised.

That was what Cab thought as he studied the dead man's eyes. Surprised that he had been conned. Surprised that a man who was smart, cool, and lethal could be played for a fool. Surprised that anyone would try to make him famous for a series of murders he didn't commit.

"Someone wants Macy to take the fall. That was the plan all along." Cab pointed at the empty pistol case. "Macy's prints are going to be on the gun and the clip," he said.

He stared at the article pinned to the bulletin board and the message scrawled across it. All fake. This was never about revenge. It was all about misdirection. They'd been led down the garden path, led toward Frank Macy from day one. Someone wanted them to believe that history was about to repeat itself.

And it was. It was.

"Macy would have taken the blame for the Labor Day murders, too," Lala said. "No one would ever have found his body. Biggest manhunt since Booth, and all the while he would have been sitting inside some alligator's stomach."

"He's in the house right now," Cab said. "He's going to kill Diane. That's the final play."

Cab thought: *My mother's in there, too.*

The rain washed inside the open garage door like a wavy curtain. The wind was a loud, incessant whistle. He turned toward the door, but whatever was going to happen had already begun. Not even a block away, he heard the first bang, and then in rapid succession, he heard four more bangs, muffled but sharp. Gunshots.

Cab sprinted. The storm hit him in the face, as if he'd struck a wall. It nearly knocked him backward off his feet. Lala ran, too, but he didn't wait for her. His feet punched through the standing water, down the driveway, onto the street. It was like running through molasses, the water grabbing his ankles, the slick mud making him slip. He was in slow motion, battling the wind.

He could barely see, not in the daytime darkness, not with his eyes slitted against the downpour. He couldn't hear anything except the storm roaring in his ears, as fierce and loud as a lion. He ran by feel, his fist clenched around his gun.

Fifty yards from Diane's estate, he spotted a lump in the water, like a whale breaching. When he knelt down, he saw a body face down near the sidewalk. Cab felt the man's neck, but there was no pulse. He grabbed his shoulder and turned him over, and he recognized the face of the estate's security guard, with a bullet hole like a third eye squarely in his forehead.

Whoever had pulled the trigger was already on his way, heading for Diane. And Tarla.

Lala caught up to him. She tugged on his sleeve, pulling him to his feet. "Come on," she shouted. "Cab, come on!"

They left the dead guard where he was. They kept running.

Cab charged toward the vine-covered walls surrounding Diane's house. The mop heads of the palm trees shot spikes through the air, forcing him to duck. The bay seemed to be coming for them, like an entire ocean slouching down the street. He reached the iron gates of the estate, which swung wildly, bouncing open and then snapping shut like the jaws of a giant turtle. He and Lala waited. When the wind split the gates apart, Cab grabbed Lala's hand and dragged her through the gap just before the heavy wind reversed course and took aim at them with the speed of a train.

They bolted up the cobblestoned driveway, but someone was in their path, blocking their way. A man waited for them on his knees. His arms drooped at his side, and when the man's fist emerged from the water, it held a gun. He didn't point it at them. Instead, the man's torso swayed, and the gun fell from his hand. His whole body sank sideways, and he went limp.

Cab and Lala ran forward. It was Garth.

The masseur's tanned face looked pale for the first time in his life, and watery blood pulsed from a scorched bullet hole near his shoulder. His brow and bulbous nose were contorted in pain, but he relaxed when he saw Cab.

"I chased him back here," Garth mumbled. "Bastard killed the guard. He got me, but I think I got him, too."

"I'll stay with you," Lala said.

"Forget me. He's heading inside."

"Just one?" Cab asked.

"Just one guy. One guy with a big gun. Déjà vu, huh?"

The storm raged. The house shook.

Tarla and Diane sat on opposite sides of the sofa on the north wall. Caprice stood in front of the floor-to-ceiling windows, staring out at the garden. "You'd think the eye of the storm would be coming across soon," she said.

Tarla hoped that was true. They needed a break where the wind died and the rain stopped. Chayla seemed to become more violent as the hours passed. They felt as if they were in a cage, with zoo animals roaming free just beyond the black glass.

The room smelled of cranberry, like Christmas, an oddly comforting aroma in the hot summer. A fat, scented candle burned unevenly on the table near the patio doors, and its liquid pool of wax glistened.

A tapered white candle flickered in front of them, casting a shimmery glow on Diane's face. Otherwise, they were in the dark. With the power off, the air had grown hot and heavy.

"What's happening?" Diane asked. "And where's Garth? How long has he been gone?"

"Do you want me to go look for him?" Tarla asked.

Near the doors, Caprice shook her head. "I don't think we should go anywhere alone."

Tarla wondered where Cab was. She told herself that soon enough, he would be here. Everything would be fine. He would stroll in, wet, smiling, hair spiky, and he would make a joke. There was nothing to worry about.

"Damn the phones," she said when she tried to call him. No signal. She wanted to hear her son's reassuring voice.

Blown sand rapped on the glass, as if it were knocking, asking to come in. Tap tap tap, like a Morse code. Leaves slapped on the doors and stuck there. Water squeezed its way onto the tile floor in tiny puddles. Wind got inside the walls and wailed like a ghost pining for a lost love. Tarla experienced a strange sensation, and she didn't know what it was. It had been such a long time she'd felt anything like it, but something nameless wrapped itself around her body like a damp fog. And then she understood. It was fear. She was scared to death.

Tap tap tap, said the sand.

Slap slap slap, said the leaves.

My love, my love, my love, said the ghost in the attic.

Bang bang bang.

Tarla stood up immediately, her body tense. "What was that? Did you hear that?"

Diane stared at her. "I didn't hear anything."

"That wasn't the storm," Tarla said.

Caprice eyed the invisible garden. She went and got a candle from the table and held it near the glass, its light like a beacon. The storm assaulted the window, inches from her face. "I don't see anything," she said.

Caprice turned around to face them. She still held the candle.

Tarla looked over Caprice's shoulder, past the dancing light, which reflected in the glass. One moment, nothing was there, and the next moment, something took shape outside the doors.

A man. A man in a hood.

Tarla screamed.

52

Peach drove.

She didn't care about the storm. She didn't care that everyone else had closeted themselves inside their homes to steer clear of the worst, furious hours. The wind threw her heavy car like a toy around the highway, but she drove and drove, past the beaches, across the bridge, into the desolate heart of Tampa. She wasn't aware of time passing or of debris pounding her windows or of her engine coughing out warnings as the water threatened to flood it. The bay could have swallowed her whole, and she wouldn't have flinched; she would have stared sightlessly ahead as she vanished under the waves.

She drove.

Her mind was a child again. Chayla was in the future. Her past rose out of the bay like a sea monster, winding its fingers around her throat. She remembered.

She remembered everything she'd buried for ten years.

The accident threw her body forward.

She was already dizzy from the sickness in her chest. Her clothes were glued to her clammy skin. She'd thrown up twice in a plastic garbage bag, but where she'd missed, she'd spit up over the backseat of Lyle's Mercedes.

The car smelled like her puke, mixed with the nasty sweetness of whatever Deacon was smoking in the front seat.

She lay there, stretched out in the back, coughing, gagging, her chest hurting, wondering if she were going to die.

Then she was airborne. Metal hit metal. Tires squealed. She flew, rolling and slamming into the back of the front seat. Her head hurt. Her mouth bled. She found herself on the floor, staring at the roof of the car.

Deacon murmured something, like a curse or a prayer. "Oh my God."

He got out and left her. She heard his running footsteps on the highway. She was alone. She hacked, and phlegm caught in her throat and bubbled onto her lips. She had vomit in her hair. She was scared, and she wanted to be home.

"Deacon?" she called plaintively, but he didn't answer. "Deacon!"

She heard strange noises on the road, like when they were camping and Lyle scraped a shovel over dirt to cover up a fire. She pushed out her tiny hands, feeling for the door handle. When she pulled the lever, the door unlatched, and she dragged herself into the humid night. Her brain spun when she stood up. She thought she would throw up again.

Peach looked for her brother. It was as if he had disappeared—but no, there he was, behind the car, twenty yards away. The moon made him look like a ghost. The highway was empty, and empty highways made her think of wolves and owls and alligators and other things that had teeth and claws.

"Deacon? What are you doing?"

She shuffled toward him. Her feet were bare. The rocky shoulder poked at her skin. She wore only her little white nightgown, which flapped in the summer breeze.

"What's happening? I'm scared."

He didn't notice her at all. She got up really close to him, close enough to see his wild eyes and his mouth hanging open like a dog's. He was breathing loud and sweating. He clenched and unclenched his fists. His hands were dirty.

"Deacon?"

She looked down. Splatters of red shined near his feet, like a map broken up by lakes. A big lake and smaller lakes. They made a trail along the asphalt and the dirt shoulder and down into the thick grass of the gully.

"Why is there so much blood?"

Her brother saw her for the first time, and his eyes widened. He sucked in his breath and bellowed at her. "FRUITY, GET BACK IN THE CAR!"

She shriveled in fear. "But Deacon, I—"

"GET BACK IN THE CAR AND SHUT UP!"

Peach ran to the Mercedes over the rocky ground and practically dove into the backseat. She took a fleece blanket she'd used and threw it over her head. She curled into a corner, hugging herself so tightly she thought she could squeeze herself into a ball and roll away. She waited, and she had no idea how much time passed before Deacon got into the front seat again.

She could feel him looking at her, even though she couldn't see him.

"I'm sorry," he murmured. "I apologize for yelling at you."

She didn't dare say a word.

"We hit a deer. I freaked out."

Peach let the blanket slip off part of her face, enough to free her eyes. Her voice muffled, she spoke into the fleece. "Did it die?"

"Yes, it died."

"Oh, no. Oh, was it a big deer or a little deer?"

"It was a big deer. It lived a long life. Don't be sad."

"But what do we do—"

"We don't do anything," Deacon told her. "It didn't happen. Do you understand me? It never happened." He leaned way far back, until his body was almost over the seats, and he was practically in her face. "I mean it, Fruity. You never tell a soul about this. It's our secret. Okay? Promise me."

"I promise," Peach told him.

It was the promise of a scared little twelve-year-old girl, but she kept her word. She never told anyone. After a while, she even stopped telling herself. The accident became a kind of odd little dream from her pneumonia, something that might have been real and might have been a fantasy. It wasn't even until she and Justin drove to Lake Wales again, and she came upon that isolated section of Highway 60, that she even remembered that anything had happened.

Deacon hit a deer. Right there in that dangerous section of road. It had nothing to do with the little white cross.

Peach drove. She might as well have been flying, with Chayla lifting her on its wings. She kept hearing an echo of voices, as if they were stuck in the clouds, raining from the sky. Deacon's voice. And Lyle's voice, too. Arguing. They always argued, but this was much worse.

"*I can't protect you anymore,*" Lyle shouted. He didn't know Peach could hear them from her sickbed. That she was listening to things that made no sense.

Deacon: "*You're supposed to be my brother. This is my whole life!*"

"*Blame yourself, not me,*" Lyle told him. "*You didn't give me any choice. I'm sorry, but you have to face what you did. I talked to a lawyer. She says there's no way to escape this.*"

Except there was an escape.

With Lyle dead, it all went away.

Peach drove. And drove. She knew where she was going and who she had to see. She knew where Chayla was taking her, carried along by the winds at her back.

53

The patio door was locked.

The man raised his gun and fired two shots into the floor-to-ceiling window beside the door. The glass around the bullet holes became white frost, and cracks wriggled outward like lightning bolts. Wind punched loudly through the two holes, increasing the pressure on the weakened frame, and when he fired again, the window exploded inward in a hail of diamonds.

Tarla squeezed her eyes shut. Glass rained down on her hair. Her ears rang with the explosions. The air in the sunroom smelled burned, and Sheetrock dust made a cloud where the three bullets tunneled into the rear wall.

He stepped through the shattered window past jagged teeth clinging to the frame. The storm came with him, loud and uncontrolled. Curtains on both ends of the wall of glass began to dance. Ten feet away, Tarla felt spray soaking her face. With the window broken, the zoo cage had swung open, and wild animals poured inside.

The man with the gun was dressed as he had been ten years earlier, all in black. The hood covered his face, but seeing him, Tarla knew it was the same man. This time, she knew she wouldn't walk away alive, waking up in a hospital days later. None of them would. She had a vague curiosity about what it would feel like when he shot her, how much it would hurt, how long it would take her to die. She tried to swallow her regrets, which were numerous. Cab's smile filled her mind, as it had the first time.

Caprice stood next to her, stiff as a corpse. Her hair sparkled with fragments of glass. Her eyes were dark little stones, and her jaw was set, fiercely determined. She looked like a cat on the hunt, ready to pounce. Tarla wanted to catch her eye and say: *You won't win.*

Diane hadn't moved. This man had come for her, but she looked serene, as if the Chopin funeral march were playing calmly in her head, a piano serenade for the soon-to-be dead. For the first time in a long time, Tarla thought that her friend looked free. She realized it had been a terrible mistake for Diane ever to enter the election campaign. Politics changed you. It made you worse than you were. Now, with that burden lifted, she could simply be Diane again, if only for a few more moments.

Time hung in the air, the way a bubble floats, but every bubble has to pop eventually. The man took a step toward the three of them. He couldn't miss, not at this distance. Even so, he was hurt. His free hand clutched his side. Tarla could see a tear in the fabric, drenched red with blood.

"You don't need to hide this time," she said. "Who are you?"

He stopped, and it was as if, finally, he wanted them to know who he was. He took his gloved hand from his wound and grabbed a fistful of nylon above his forehead and slid the hood off his face. His red hair was flat and wet. His skin flickered with dark shadows from the candles. He was handsome and rugged, the kind of man who drew second looks wherever he went. To Tarla, he was so, so young—not even thirty—which meant that ten years earlier he had truly been no more than a boy. An eighteen-year-old, slaying his brother, like Cain killing Abel. Tarla realized that it was *youth* she had sensed behind the hood back then. Youth, that foolish time when emotion means everything, and consequences don't exist.

Diane said: "*Deacon?*"

"I'm sorry," Deacon Piper said to her.

Tarla was close enough to see his face clearly. He wasn't sorry. He wasn't necessarily a killer in his heart, but he wasn't sorry. He was a man with a mission, who wouldn't stop until he was done.

"Why?" Diane murmured. As if it were nothing but idle curiosity. As if she were talking about the choice of paint on a wall. "Why do this?"

"I have no choice," Deacon replied.

"Don't tell me you're some kind of closet Nazi," Tarla interrupted loudly. Somewhere in her mother-of-a-policeman brain, she thought: *Play for time.* Time made all things possible. Even rescue. "One of those awful Alliance members out to make the world safe for fascism? That would be very disappointing."

"I can do this, or I can go to prison for the rest of my life. That was my choice then. It still is." He added: "I don't take any pleasure in it."

"Well, that makes me feel so much better," Tarla said.

"Don't toy with us!" Caprice hissed, speaking for the first time. "If this is who you are, then you have to live with yourself. If you think you can do this, then screw up your courage and do it."

Deacon pointed the gun at Caprice. "Do you want me to kill you first?"

"I don't care what you do."

Deacon stared at her and said, "Bang"—but he didn't fire. He swung the gun back to Diane, who showed no fear. She watched Deacon and the black barrel of the gun with a peculiar fascination. Deacon limped closer, arm outstretched, ready to shoot. No regrets or doubts. No hesitation. No second thoughts.

Tarla stepped in front of him.

She blocked his way, a human shield between him and Diane. She wasn't going to let him kill her friend, not then, not now. "I think we've been in this position before," she reminded him.

"Yes, we have," Deacon replied.

"I'm curious. Why didn't you kill me ten years ago?"

"Honestly? You were too beautiful to kill."

"And now?"

Deacon actually smiled. "You're still beautiful."

He pointed the gun at her lovely face.

She thought: *So it's like this.*

A voice from the broken window interrupted them. It was Cab's voice, calm and deadly. It wasn't in her head; it was real. "Deacon, put your gun down right now."

Cab stood in the window between the sharp jaws of glass. Clouds of rain swarmed around him. He had both hands on the butt of his gun, his finger on the trigger. The wind made it hard to aim, but he fought the gales as he stepped through the wreckage of the window into the sunroom. He didn't blink as he stared Deacon down. Behind him, silently, Lala slid inside the house too, her own gun also directed at Deacon's face. Two against one.

Deacon eyed them quietly, but he didn't lower his weapon.

"It's over," Cab told him. "Kneel down, and lay the gun on the floor."

Deacon still didn't move. He was a game player, analyzing his options, deciding if there was a way to win.

"That's my mother," Cab went on. "If you kill her, I'll be forced to kill you."

"Maybe that's what I want," Deacon said.

"No, I don't think so. I don't think you're suicidal."

Lala spoke to Deacon. Her voice was soft. "We already found Frank Macy's body. We know you were planning to frame him. The plot's done. You've lost. More killing won't change that."

Deacon gave the barest shrug. He turned away from Tarla and squatted and laid the gun at his feet. When he straightened up, he lifted his hands in the air. "What now?" he said.

"Lace your fingers on your head," Cab told him. "Turn around. Walk backward toward me slowly."

Deacon did as he was told. He turned around. He took a step backward.

At that moment, with wicked timing, Chayla intervened.

The locked patio door shuddered. The sixty-mile-an-hour wind knocked on the door and then smashed it in, throwing the door on its hinges. It swung like a missile into Cab's back, kicking him sideways into Lala like a bowling pin. They both toppled; their guns skidded along the wet floor.

Deacon immediately bent down to scoop up his gun. He pivoted to aim at Cab, but Caprice dove across the short space, colliding with Deacon, who tumbled backward and rolled. Dizzied, he scrambled to his feet with his gun in his hand. Caprice grabbed Cab's gun from the floor, and together, simultaneously, they pointed the weapons at each other.

Deacon backed toward the open window. He held his side, which was bleeding profusely. "Have you ever fired a gun?" he asked Caprice.

"No."

He took a sideways glance at Cab and Lala, who were crawling on the slippery tile, trying to regain their balance. "Do you really think you can?"

"Watch me."

"You'll die, too," he said.

"Maybe."

Deacon took her measure, deciding if she was serious.

He tilted the gun barrel down as if to surrender, but then, with a smirk, he turned and ran. Caprice fired repeatedly after him. The bullets were like little bombs blasting between the walls. Windows cascaded outward, breaking and falling. The storm howled as if Caprice were firing into its belly. She kept shooting wildly as Deacon vanished, until the gun was empty and each new pull of the trigger ended in an impotent click.

Deacon was gone. Chayla folded him up into her furious heart.

Cab, who was still reeling from the impact of the door, jumped through the window in pursuit.

54

A searing pain burned like a lit cigarette on Deacon's back and made a trail of fire through his soft insides. As the bullet exited through the taut muscles of his stomach, he realized with a sense of wild surprise: *She shot me.* The impact kicked him forward, stumbling, but he righted himself. He put a hand on his abdomen, which was warm and wet, and pressed hard, feeling blood squirm between his fingers.

He was invisible in black. Behind him, silhouetted against the pinpoints of candles, he saw Cab Bolton scanning the grounds. The gardens hid Deacon. He lifted his gun and fired from the trees, and Cab ducked. He didn't think he'd hit him.

The distance to the foreclosure house felt like miles. He knew he wouldn't make it. He headed away from the main gate, following the vine-draped north wall through dense bushes that whipped into his face. The house loomed to his right, nothing but a black shape.

Escape was impossible. He understood that. He was dying from the hole in his abdomen, but it didn't stop him from using his last breath to get away. If he could get to the estate's garage, if he could steal a car, there was hope. As long as blood pumped, then his heart was beating, and he was alive. He'd learned that lesson a long time ago.

Why is there so much blood?

That one night, that one moment on the road, never left his head. He could still feel the bitterness gripping his stomach as he made the nighttime drive from Tampa. He could feel his head swim with each joint, but the pot didn't relax him; it just fed his impatience. That night, he was an eighteen-year-old boy, hating the world, hating his domineering brother, hating his little sister puking in the backseat, hating his parents who had died. All of that rage made its way into his foot, dead-heavy on the accelerator. Seventy miles an hour. Eighty.

He was alone on the highway, and then he wasn't alone. Alison was with him.

Alison, who was nothing but a flash of blond hair in his headlights. Alison, who flew when the bumper of Lyle's Mercedes clipped her bicycle tire, whose head landed like a falling meteor on the asphalt.

He remembered the panic he felt. His body was bathed in sweat. His fogged head went around and around. He remembered running from the car to where she lay. He remembered staring at her on the ground, so small and limp, blood flowing, her eyes closed. He knew what to do. Call an ambulance, wait with her, hold her hand, whisper in her ear that everything would be okay. That was what he planned to do, even as he took her sneakered feet and dragged her off the road into the damp gully. He could imagine himself explaining the accident on the phone and giving the police his location, even as he covered her still-breathing body with dirt and leaves, even as he shoved her mangled bicycle under the cover of a flowering bush. *There's a girl, she's hurt,* he heard himself say, even as he screamed at Peach to get back in the car, as he told her never to say a word to anyone about what had happened.

He hit a deer. That was all. That became the truth.

If Lyle had left it at that, if he had let Deacon take the car to Jacksonville for repair, maybe his brother would still be alive. Lyle was no fool. He'd seen the headlines; he'd seen through the lie. And so he had to die. Strange, how simple the calculation was. He could talk to a lawyer and plead guilty and give up his life, or he could put a bullet in his brother's brain. Strange, how easy it was to do that. How good it actually felt, silencing that awful, judgmental voice forever.

He wasn't sorry. He hated Lyle. He only wished he could have told his brother to his face who the man of the family really was. Lyle was a coward who wanted big things but blinked at what it took to get them, who never understood that the ends justified the means. Not like Deacon. He wished his brother had known the truth. Then again, maybe he did. Maybe in that final instant, he knew who was putting that gun to his head.

Deacon emerged, bent and weak, from the trees. He staggered for the garage's rear wall and collapsed against it, breathing heavily. When he twisted the doorknob, it was locked, but he pressed his gun against the bolt and fired, busting the door inward. He fell inside. The three-car garage was sticky and dark, and he could see vehicles in each stall. He limped beyond the cars and threw open one of the big doors. Turning back, he spotted a door leading inside the house, and next to it were three sets of hooks, which glistened with car keys. He dragged himself across the concrete floor, trailing blood. He grabbed the keys and threw himself inside the closest vehicle, which was a monstrously sized ebony Cadillac Escalade.

He tried the first set of keys. They didn't fit. The second set made the engine growl to life. He shot backward, weaving, dinging the side of the Audi in the adjoining space. The rain swirled down as he backed into the cobblestoned turnaround, spilling over onto mud and brush. He gripped the wheel with one hand like a vise. His insides were a blowtorch that didn't cool when he shoved his other hand into the wound. He had to remind his brain what to do next.

He shoved the gear into drive. His foot jammed the accelerator, and the truck fishtailed. He couldn't keep straight. He fingered the dashboard and found the switch for the headlights, and the bright beams lit up the driveway like searchlights. Through the driving rain, he caught a glimpse of Cab Bolton running toward him across the estate's sodden lawn. Deacon headed for the iron gates, which snapped open and shut, and he crashed through them, tearing them off their hinges, skipping them like beach stones onto the street.

He was free. He swerved down the neighborhood street, throwing up waves, barely clearing the trees on either side. Debris clung to his windshield. He squinted to see. He felt the way he had a decade earlier, bitter, his head swirling, going faster and faster.

And then there she was. In the middle of the street. In his headlights.

Just like back then. An innocent girl, about to be thrown aside, crushed by the tons of steel. His foot lurched to the brake, and he heard a voice screaming in his head: *Stop stop stop stop stop stop.*

It wasn't Alison. He was in the present, not the past.

It was Peach.

She saw him coming, and she knew it was her brother. There was no doubt in her mind. He drove wildly, like a man trying to escape his crimes. The headlights of the SUV were dragon's eyes. The truck bore down on her, but she stood in the middle of the street, her hands at her sides, the storm punishing her body, and she didn't move. She made no attempt to dive clear. She heard the whine of brakes, heard the tires slipping in the water, saw the back of the truck skid.

The Escalade lurched to a stop inches from her body.

She had to shield her eyes, but she could see him behind the headlights. The driver's door opened, and he climbed out. He clung to the window with one hand to keep himself upright, and he screamed at her.

"Fruity! Get out of the way!"

Peach simply shook her head and didn't move. The lights bathed her, making her feel small. Small, which was how she'd felt ten years ago, wandering in a haze onto the deserted highway. Deacon had screamed the same way then, in desperate terror, telling her to get back in the car.

He was the same man. Her brother.

"This isn't about you!" he shouted.

She walked around the corner of the SUV. She came close to the driver's door, and she could see that he was badly wounded. "Not about me?" she said, but the storm was louder than she was. Hearing it try to drown her out, she raised her voice and shouted back. She was no longer a child.

"Not about me? You killed Lyle, didn't you? You killed Justin, too. It was you!"

Deacon raised his other hand. There was a gun in it, pointed at her head. "Fruity, get out of here!"

"Sure, kill me! That's what you do, Deacon. You kill people."

"I'm not kidding!"

Peach walked closer, until the gun was a beast in her eyes. Wild wind, wild rain plunged from the sky. "Neither am I! Do it!"

He was the young one now. He was still eighteen. His voice screeched. "Goddamn it, Fruity! Don't make me!"

"I don't care! Do you think I don't know what you did? I remember the accident. I remember *Alison*. So now you have to kill me, too, just like everyone else, right? So pull the trigger!"

Deacon shoved the barrel against her forehead. It was hot; it burned. Over his shoulder, beyond the car, she could barely make out two people sprinting through the storm. They were fifty yards away, but they were getting closer. Two people. Cab. Lala.

Deacon glanced back and saw them, too. He pushed the gun into her face again, so hard it made her stumble.

"Go away! Just go away! I don't want to hurt you!"

Peach took both hands and wrapped them around the gun. His hand was cold against her warm fingers. His blood smeared her face. Their eyes found each other, and his eyes were lost and lonely. His skin was bone white, his red hair matted on his head. His whole body trembled.

"*Deacon, stop!*" Cab shouted.

Deacon wrenched away, ripping the gun from her grasp. He threw it into the gutter, where the weapon vanished under the rushing water. Slamming the door, pushing past her, he ran, but it was not a run at all. He tottered like a dirty drunk. Six steps later, he lurched to a stop, and his knees crumbled. He went down, sinking to all fours, and then his left side gave way, and he sprawled onto his back, twitching, spread-eagled. A river washed over him, deep enough nearly to cover his body.

Peach's breath stuttered in her chest, and she splashed toward him. She got on her knees and slid an arm under his limp neck and held him. His eyes were open but gray. His lips frothed with blood. She was vaguely aware of Cab and Lala drawing close, of them standing over her and touching her shoulder, but she didn't move. She waited, because the end was near.

She stared into his face, but it wasn't him she saw. He seemed to become everyone else she'd lost, everyone she'd never had a chance to hold. Her mother. Her father. Lyle. And Justin. Justin, with his pork-pie hat swirling away in the water, his mustache drooping, but still with that grin, teasing her, loving her. She wanted to hold on to all of them forever. Keep them here. Keep them alive for another second.

But the man in her arms was none of those people. He was her brother. He was a killer.

"Oh, Deacon," she said, but his eyes had already closed.

55

Chayla had fled.

The clouds scurried after her, leaving the detritus of the storm—cars pushed around like toys, trees downed, roofs torn away—to glitter wetly under a perfect sun. Steam rose from standing pools of water. Fish rotted on streets and sidewalks half a mile inland from the Gulf and the bay. The rumble of backhoes and dump trucks made a whine in the background as the cleanup of the region began.

The elegant landscaping of Diane's garden had been torn apart. A fallen palm tree lay across the grass, its shaggy top half-submerged in the duck pond. A stone flamingo had been beheaded. Bushes were uprooted, and when the mild wind blew, they rolled like tumbleweeds. The floor of the gazebo, where Diane and Cab sat, was dirty with mud and branches.

They'd cleaned off chairs, and they sat with china mugs of pomegranate oolong tea. Diane didn't look at him; instead, she studied the disarray in the foliage, as if plotting its rebirth. She picked up a long strand of weeping willow that lay across the ledge of the gazebo. It was like seaweed plucked from the beach. She tried to bend it into a circle, but it didn't bend, and so she dropped it back to the earth behind the shelter.

"I haven't thanked you for saving our lives," she told him.

"Thanks aren't necessary," Cab replied. "I'm sorry you were placed in such a frightening situation."

"Well, nevertheless. I'm very grateful. I'm sure Tarla is, too."

Cab smiled. "I believe her exact words were, 'Did you have to wait until the last second like this was the eighteenth sequel to *Die Hard*?'"

"That does sound like Tarla," Diane said.

"She also mentioned that McTiernan wanted her in the original movie instead of Bonnie Bedelia, but she couldn't stand Bruce Willis."

"So she's coping well with her second brush with death."

"She is."

Diane picked up her cup of tea, but then she put it down again, as if it had lost interest for her. "I'm still shocked about Deacon. I do feel bad for him, despite everything. And for his sister."

"Peach is strong. I like her. If it weren't for her, Deacon's plan might well have succeeded. Frank Macy's body would have disappeared into some deserted part of the Everglades. Deacon used the gun he got from Macy at Picnic Island, so Macy's prints would have been on it. All the evidence would have pointed toward Macy, not just now but for the Labor Day murders, too."

"And toward me," Diane added. "Or Drew."

"Yes, a lot of people would have believed that you or your son paid Macy to kill Birch back then. Neither of you would have been alive to protest. Meanwhile, Deacon would have reappeared a couple days later, having 'escaped' from wherever Macy and his friends had been hiding him after he was supposedly abducted."

"What about that young man Justin? Why was he killed?"

"Justin obviously put two and two together," Cab told her. "He connected Alison's death to Deacon and realized that Lyle was the real target of the assassination on Labor Day. Justin must have started following Deacon, and that led him to the foreclosure house. After being inside, he probably guessed what Deacon was planning, but Deacon got to him before he could tell anyone."

"The real mystery is why, isn't it?" Diane asked. "Why did Deacon take it so far? Why kill me now?"

Cab nodded. "Yes, that's the unanswered question. The FBI has been digging through his house and his computer records, but it doesn't look like he left much of a trail regarding his motive. For now, they suspect he was afraid of being exposed for his role in the original murders."

"Do you believe that?" Diane asked.

Cab rubbed his suntanned chin. "Oh, I'm sure that was part of it."

"But?"

"But I think there's more to the story," Cab said. "The police discovered something curious. About six months ago, Deacon visited Hamilton Brock in prison."

"Brock? Why?"

"No one knows. Brock isn't talking. He claims it's another conspiracy theory aimed at pinning a murder charge on him."

"Are you suggesting that Deacon was secretly a member of the Liberty Empire Alliance?"

"Well, there was nothing in his personal effects to suggest he was harboring a radical ideology, and it's hard to believe he could have kept it hidden from Peach and others all this time. On the other hand, Deacon would have been a prime candidate for recruitment. An angry teenage boy. Parents dead. Disaffected. Maybe when he decided to kill his brother, he thought he could strike a blow for the Alliance by killing Birch, too."

Diane looked thoughtful. "Do you think we'll ever know the truth?"

"The investigation will continue, but no one in the Alliance has an incentive to talk." He added: "What about you? I saw the headlines. I saw the crush of press outside. You've dropped out of the race."

Diane nodded.

"You've got a perfect excuse for doing so," Cab said, "after what you've been through."

"Yes, but I'm not interested in excuses. I did something wrong. I've hired an attorney to negotiate a plea to cover my actions involving Frank Macy. I imagine I may see some time in Club Fed. Or not, depending on whether they take mercy on a distraught mother."

"And on whether that bartender's death in Pass-a-Grille was really a coincidence," Cab said. "Some of my friends in the police think you and Deacon planned the whole thing to bring Frank Macy down."

"I realize that. For what it's worth, it's not true. If Deacon killed him, he did it on his own, without telling me. I never would have been involved in murder."

"I believe you."

"Even so, this is the end of my public life. I'm out of politics. I'm resigning from the foundation, too. I told Tarla that she and I should take a long cruise somewhere, if I'm not playing solitaire in a women's jail."

"She mentioned that. Somewhere with nubile brown men. She said once Garth is on his feet again, he could come along to apply the tanning butter."

"Oh, Tarla," Diane replied, shaking her head.

"I guess this means Ramona Cortes will get what she's always wanted," Cab went on. "With you out, it's a two-person race for governor. She's ahead in the polls. Everyone says she's going to win."

"That's what they say," Diane agreed. He saw a peculiar smile flit across her lips.

"You don't think so?" Cab asked.

Diane went back to her tea, even though it was cold now. "I think the election is still four months away," she said. "Anything can happen."

Walter Fleming nursed his Budweiser, which he drank from a long-necked bottle. The union boss had half a dozen more bottles soaking in ice in a silver bucket beside his deck chair. The blistering noon sun turned his high forehead pink. He wore an ugly yellow-striped bathing suit that he'd owned for years. His flip-flops lay in the sand at his feet. He wore black Ray-Bans that looked a lot like the sunglasses his father wore in the 1950s. Everything old was new again.

He sat in the sand behind his retirement home, which was near Carrabelle on the panhandle. The ground was flat, and the water hardly moved. A few teenagers splashed in the water, but this place was too boring for most of the kids. He spent weekends here with his wife. She lived in the house permanently, while Walter spent his weekdays in Tallahassee and in union halls around the state.

It was Monday, but he didn't feel like working. He was in a foul mood. His mood didn't get better when he saw Ogden Bush strolling toward him from the deck of his house. Ogden wore a dress suit and a fedora, which made him stand out like a politician shaking hands at a state fair. His black skin glowed with sweat, but he sported a cool grin, which nothing ever erased. He had a tan envelope scrunched in one of his slim hands.

Bush took off his hat and wiped his bald head. He stood on the beach, admiring the girls in the surf. "Aren't you worried about skin cancer, Walter?"

"You're the only mole that bothers me, Ogden," Walter replied.

Bush chuckled. "Funny. That's funny."

Walter took a swig of beer and wiped his beard with his sweaty forearm. Beside him, Bush settled into an empty chair. Without being asked, the political spy grabbed one of Walter's beers from the icy bucket, twisted off the cap, and drank half of it in a single swallow.

"Quiet around here," Bush said. "You really want to retire in this place? It would drive me crazy."

"I like quiet. I don't get much of it."

Both men finished their beers in silence. Walter flicked at a bee that buzzed around his head. His lips drooped downward in a perpetual frown.

"You look like Grumpy Cat, Walter," Bush told him. "What's with the gloom and doom?"

Walter dropped his empty bottle into the bucket. "You've seen the polls?"

"Sure. They suck."

"They suck all right. The governor got no bump from the smooth response to Chayla. All the headlines have gone to Ramona Cortes talking about law and order and political corruption. She sits there and lumps the governor's scandal in with the Common Way shit like it's a symptom of some bigger problem, and the national media eat it up. She's up ten points. Ten."

"Cheer up," Ogden told him. "It's not the end of the world."

Walter stripped off his sunglasses and jabbed them at Bush. "See, that's what I hate about consultants. It's all a game to you. You win some, you lose some. At the end of the day, you don't care. Me, I think about a right-winger like Ramona Cortes sitting in the governor's office, and it makes me sick. It's a fricking disaster."

"You'd rather Diane Fairmont?" he asked.

"Between the two of them? Yeah, I'd take Diane over Ramona, but that's not going to happen."

"Nope," Bush agreed. "Diane's toast. She managed to look noble stepping down, though. People see her as a victim again. Lots of sympathy."

Walter snorted. "So what are you doing here, Ogden? You need a job?"

Bush shrugged. "Yeah, kinda ironic, huh? Diane's out, so am I."

"We're not hiring."

"No? We've got a deal, Walter. I expect you to live up to it. I kept my end of the bargain. I was your spy."

"A spy who couldn't deliver," Walter snapped.

"Oh, don't be so sure. You're going to want to see what I brought you. Of course, if you'd prefer, I can simply burn it, and you can spend the next four years dealing with Governor Cortes."

Walter's eyes narrowed. "What are you talking about?"

Bush waved the tan envelope in the air. "I have a little parting gift from our friends at Common Way."

"Like what?"

"Like a nuclear bomb," Bush said.

Walter frowned. "What is it? Where did you get it?"

"It showed up on my desk. I don't know who left it there, but I can guess. Fact is, I think they suspected my divided loyalties. As for what it is—well, see for yourself."

He handed the envelope to Walter, who dug out a pair of reading glasses from a canvas bag beside his deck chair. Walter undid the hook on the envelope and slid out a single sheet of paper. It was a copy of a ten-year-old invoice from an Orlando law firm, and the services rendered were described simply as: "Consultation."

Walter recognized the name of the firm. It was an old-line white-shoe law firm with political connections and a practice that spanned corporate and criminal matters. He also recognized the name of the man to whom the bill was addressed.

Lyle Piper.

"What the hell is this?" Walter asked.

"Check out the date of the consultation."

Walter did. The two-hour discussion between Lyle Piper and his lawyer took place a week before the Labor Day murders. "Okay, so? I'm being dense here, but I still don't get it. It doesn't look like a bombshell to me."

"Do the math, Walter," Bush told him. "Deacon Piper hit a girl in Lyle's Mercedes and dragged her off the road and left her to die, right? His brother figured it out. So he consulted a criminal attorney, because he wanted Deacon to turn himself in. This is the invoice."

"Yeah, I know the story," Walter said.

"Okay, but do you know who was a partner in criminal law at that Orlando firm ten years ago? And do you know who was also a friend of Lyle Piper's going back to their law school days?"

Walter's brow wrinkled in confusion, and then his confusion washed away like footsteps in the wet sand. He realized that Bush was right. The paper he was holding in his hand was radioactive. "Son of a bitch," he murmured. "Ramona Cortes."

Bush tapped his nose with his index finger. "You got it."

Ramona Cortes.

Walter shook his head in disbelief. "She knew. She knew what Deacon Piper did to that girl. She knew it ten years ago."

"Yeah, pretty convenient, huh? Ramona had Deacon Piper's whole life in her hands. One word from her, and he'd be behind bars for thirty years. Talk about having leverage over somebody."

"She'll deny everything," Walter said. "The invoice doesn't list her name. It doesn't say anything about the nature of the consultation. We'll never be able to prove that she was involved in the plot."

Bush shrugged. "Who cares? Let her deny it all she wants. She'll spend the next four months answering questions about what she knew and when she knew it. The allegation alone will destroy her."

That was true. This piece of paper would change the race. Ramona would lose. The governor would win.

Or would he?

"Why would Common Way give this to you?" Walter asked.

"Obviously, they don't want their fingerprints on it."

"So what's their game? Nothing's free with those slippery bastards."

"They don't like Ramona. She's out to destroy the foundation. If they can't have Diane in Tallahassee, they'd rather see the governor reelected than a sworn enemy like Ramona."

"I don't buy it," Walter said. "They're up to something. They're still trying to fix the race. You know what Ramona's going to do if this comes out. She'll throw it back in our faces and say this is another dirty trick from the governor's campaign. It'll be ugly street warfare. That's what Common Way wants, isn't it? Let us pound each other for a few weeks, drive both of our numbers down, and then they step in and find a new candidate who vaults into the lead."

"Maybe so," Bush said, "but do we have a choice? Without this dirt, there's no race at all. Ramona wins."

Walter didn't like being between a rock and a hard place. He liked being the rock, banging on everybody else. Even so, he couldn't say no. He didn't trust Common Way, but sometimes you had to give your enemies what they wanted and hope you could still screw them tomorrow. "Yeah, okay," he said.

"We go nuclear?"

"We go nuclear," Walter agreed.

"The rollout has to be handled delicately," Bush told him. "It can't come from any of our usual sources. We've got to stay ten miles away from this. Everybody will suspect it comes from us, but we can't let anyone prove it."

"Do you think I don't know that?" Walter asked. "Don't worry. I know guys. We'll get the story planted. This thing will land like Pearl Harbor in Ramona's camp."

Ogden stood up and laced his hands behind his neck, relishing the sun. "Excellent. It's always a pleasure doing business with you, Walter."

Walter didn't return the compliment. He studied the paper in his hand and took no pleasure in it. He was already anticipating the fall-out, imagining the headlines, the press conferences, the claims and counterclaims. It would be a bloodbath, but elections usually were.

"So what do you think, Ogden?"

"About what?"

Walter nodded at the piece of paper. "You think Ramona really did this? She was ready to have Deacon Piper commit murder to put her in the governor's chair? I can't stand the lady, but I just wonder if it's true."

Bush's lips folded into an amused smile. "Walter, you surprise me. This is politics. What the hell does truth have to do with anything?"

56

"Hello, Alison."

Peach stared at the little white cross that was pushed into the ground near the highway shoulder. Pink flowers decorated it. Someone had slung rosary beads around the cross. It wasn't a grave, but if a ghost had to pick a place to haunt, this was a pretty spot. By all rights, Chayla should have unearthed the fragile memorial and trampled it, but God had made an exception for Alison. The cross had come through the storm unscathed.

She sat cross-legged in front of it. The ground was dry. Her Thunderbird was parked twenty yards away. A truck passed on the lonely highway, and the driver gave her a short toot of his horn. Paying respects.

Alison Garner. Fourteen years old. She was two years older than Peach had been that night, but two years was nothing.

"My name is Peach," she said. "You don't know me, but I was there. It was my brother who hit you. I mean, wherever you are, you probably already know that. I guess I knew it, too, but I never wanted to admit it to myself. It's funny what the brain can do. Anyway, I wanted to say I'm sorry. You should have had a life, and you didn't."

Peach waited. She wasn't expecting an answer, but it was polite to let your words sink in. She'd always done the same thing with her mannequins. Talk to them, and then let them think about it. Annalie—Lala—would have said she didn't need to worry unless they started talking back.

"I saw your parents," she went on. "They miss you a lot, but they seem happy. I was afraid they would yell at me or something, but they cried and hugged me, and I started crying, too. They said I should stay for dinner, but I didn't want to impose. I asked to see some of your things, though. They still have a lot of them. You were a Britney fan, huh? I saw you had a concert program. She was never one of my favorites, but I could see where you would like her. They had a video of you, too, singing in church. You had a pretty voice. Me, I can't sing at all."

Peach looked up at the sky. Birds flitted and called to each other in the trees. A month had passed, and the storm was a fading memory.

"I've been trying to decide whether my brother was a bad person," she went on. "I mean, I know he was. You probably hate him, right? It was weird talking to your parents, because I figured they would hate him, too, but they said Christians believe in forgiveness. They told me how sorry they were for me and how I must miss Deacon. They said they know how hard it is to lose someone you love, no matter how it happens. And the thing is, they're right. I do miss him. I still love him. I hope you won't think badly of me for that."

She brushed a tear from her eye. Another one followed, and then there were too many to wipe from her face, so she let them flow.

"I hear you had a boyfriend. I saw a picture of you two going to a dance. Did he kiss you? Boys are funny about that when they're young. I never had a boyfriend until this year, and he's—well, he's gone now. We kissed. We never did more than that, because it's just not my thing. Sex just gets in the way. I liked kissing, though. I liked holding him and having him hold me. I miss him, too. I miss him a lot. I don't know, sometimes I think it's me. People who get close to me die. I don't really have anyone now. Nobody's left."

Through her tears, she managed to laugh at herself. She'd never been a fan of self-pity. Things were what they were. Even so, here she was, with another imaginary friend. She was twenty-two years old, and she talked to mannequins and ghosts.

"Sorry," she said. "I'm making this all about me, when you're the one who's dead. Except, who knows, maybe you're already back. Or I don't know, maybe it takes a while. I think there are old souls and new souls. Do you know what I mean? Some people seem like they've been around for centuries even when they're young. Justin was like that. Other people feel like this is their first go-round. Oh well, I don't know. I probably sound crazy to you. Anyway, if you're back, and you see me, give me a wink, okay? I don't know what I'm going to do next. I quit my job. I'm sick of politics. But I'll be around."

Peach got up from the highway shoulder and brushed the dirt off her pants. She dug in her back pocket and pulled out a slim volume of poetry. It was the book she'd found in Justin's safe house—the duplicate of the volume she'd given him of poetry by William Blake. She'd wrapped the book in plastic. She put it on the ground and propped it against the cross.

"I don't know how things work where you are," she said. "If you can read, I thought you might like this. If you see Justin, maybe he can read some of them to you. He was good at that."

A gust of wind rose up and rattled the trees. To Peach, that felt like an answer from somewhere.

"Well, I should go," she went on. "I have a dinner party to go to. With a movie star. Can you believe that? Me! I guess that means I should change clothes." She turned to walk away, but then she stopped. She bent down again, rubbing one of the flowers adorning the cross. "Take care of yourself, Alison."

She walked back to her Thunderbird, did a U-turn, and headed back toward Tampa.

57

"Do you think she's okay?" Lala asked.

Cab followed Lala's eyes to Peach, who stood on the balcony of his mother's condominium. The young girl leaned against the railing, staring out at the calm waters of the Gulf. For as young as she was, she looked older now. An old soul. He'd grown very fond of her, in the way a man does who has lost a daughter. She was quirky, but so was he. She had strange New Age ideas, and she was altogether too serious, but for someone who had lost as much as she had, she dealt with it well.

"Actually, I think she's fine," Cab said. He added: "It helps her to have a friend like you."

Lala smiled. "Are you being charming?"

"Always."

She tipped her wine glass against his. He didn't think she'd ever looked more elegant. Lala, who lived in her black jeans and black T-shirts, wore a fuchsia cocktail dress that barely reached to her knees. A deeper crimson sash circled her waist, with a flowered brooch in the middle. The dress was sleeveless, showing off her lean, strong arms. Her tumbling black hair ended in broad curls below her shoulders.

"Did I mention you look beautiful?" Cab added.

"Tarla said formal."

"She'll be jealous. She's not used to being outdazzled."

"Smooth talker," Lala said, but he knew she was pleased. "Do I need to compliment you, too?"

"Yes, because I am so insecure about my looks," Cab said.

"Very."

He grinned. "You'll stay the night?"

"You just want to see this dress in a pool at my feet."

"I do."

"We'll see," she said. "Some of us work for a living, you know."

"Sounds dreary," he replied.

He knew she had to be back home in the morning. It was an August weekend. Lala had joined him in Clearwater late on Friday, and it was Sunday now. Tarla had made herself discreetly absent for most of that time, but his mother had insisted on a dinner party before Lala returned to Naples. He suspected it was really more of a spying mission on his relationship with Lala.

"What about you?" she asked.

He understood the question. When would he come home? He lived on the beach in Naples, but he'd stayed here in the apartment next to his mother for more than a month. Lala was starting to wonder if he'd ever return or if he was now permanently under Tarla's thumb. There was no job to pull him home anymore. He'd already made good on his promise to resign from the Naples police. He was a free man, for whatever that was worth. He didn't know exactly what freedom entailed. So far, he wasn't in a hurry to find out.

"Maybe I'll come home with you tomorrow," he said.

"Really?"

"I do miss my place. Plus, I should probably feed the cat, right?"

"You don't have a cat."

"Well, that's lucky."

She smiled at him. A smile deserved a kiss, so he bent down and kissed her. They were bad at some things together, and good at others, and they were good at kissing.

"Won't Tarla miss you if you go?" Lala asked.

"She misses me already. She misses me when I'm here."

"Where is she, by the way?"

"Picking up Caprice." He waited for her face to erupt with displeasure, and then he said quickly: "Kidding. Kidding. You really don't like Caprice, do you?"

"No, I don't." Lala added pointedly: "Have you seen her lately?"

"No, but she's been pretty busy."

"Do you miss her?"

"I've been thinking about her a lot," Cab admitted.

"Wrong answer."

"Not in the way you mean," he replied.

Puzzlement crossed Lala's face, but she didn't press him for an explanation. She wandered toward one of the sofas and put down her wine glass on a walnut table. He came up behind her and stroked a bare shoulder.

"I tried calling Ramona," Lala said, "but I didn't reach her."

"She's busy, too."

"I don't believe what they're saying about her in the press."

"As a cop or as a cousin?" he asked.

"Both. I've known her for years. She's a good person."

"She admitted that Lyle consulted her about the hit and run," he said.

"Only in general terms. Not about Deacon specifically or about the accident."

"Ramona is smart," Cab said. "It's hard to believe she didn't make the connection."

"If she did, she would have taken it to the grave. She's a lawyer."

"I'm not sure I share your charitable opinion of lawyers," Cab said. He kissed her neck, but she tensed. "Sorry, I didn't say you were wrong about her. Sometimes I can't resist playing devil's advocate. It's a terrible flaw."

She relaxed and turned around. "I apologize. I'm the one who's being sensitive. You're right, I don't know the truth. I only know what I believe."

"That's good enough for me."

"You're buttering me up, but I still think you're more interested in getting my dress on the floor."

"Guilty."

Lala ran a finger along his chin. "Would you really come back home with me tomorrow?"

"Yes."

"That's an incentive, I'll admit."

"Good."

She picked up her wine glass again. "So are you serious about taking up special investigative projects? Or are you going to stay unemployed and watch soap operas and knit sweaters for your cat?"

"I don't have a cat," he said.

"Oh, that's right."

"I am serious," he said. "In fact, I'm thinking of taking on a partner for my agency."

Lala's eyebrows arched. "You and me? I'm flattered, but don't you think that's a terrible idea? We don't exactly thrive when we spend all of our time together. A night here and there is more than enough. Besides, I'm a cop. That's all I ever wanted to be, and that's still what I want to be."

"I know. I like you as a cop. I wasn't talking about you."

She looked somewhat crestfallen. "Then who?"

Cab nodded at the girl on the balcony, who continued to stare dreamily at the Gulf waters.

"Peach?" Lala asked.

"Peach," Cab said. "What do you think?"

"Actually, I think it's a great idea. Have you talked to her about it?"

"No, not yet. Will you put in a good word for me?"

"I will."

They kissed again. Lala turned for the balcony and left him alone. He knew she would stay the night, and he would leave with her in the morning, and life, which had been on hold for a while, would begin again.

Lala slid open the patio door and went outside and closed it behind her. He watched the two women together, Lala and Peach. There was something close there, an intimacy of friendship, an easy familiarity. Peach hugged her. Lala smiled, and he saw genuine affection in her smile. Lala had a big family, and Peach had no family at all, but the thing about big families was that there was always room for one more.

Then there was himself and his mother.

"Penny for your thoughts," Tarla said.

Cab jumped. He hadn't heard her arrive. His mother still had the ability to appear miraculously at his side out of nowhere. "A penny?" he said. "You can afford more."

"I'm retired on a fixed income, darling. I'm economizing. Anyway, you look happy. Is something wrong?"

"Oh, it just occurred to me," he said, pointing at Lala and Peach, "that those two women are likely to be in my life for a long time."

"Well, I hate to ruin the moment for you," Tarla replied, "but so will I."

"Despite my best efforts?"

"I'm afraid so."

"Just so you know, I'm going back to Naples with Lala tomorrow," he said.

"Finally! No offense, darling, but you were starting to get on my nerves."

She winked at him and patted his cheek. He looked momentarily dismayed, but then he smiled. Tarla was Tarla and would never change. She was dressed to kill, as she always was. She was beautiful, as she always was. The drive between Naples and Clearwater didn't take long in the Corvette. They still had things to talk about and things to work out.

"I have to go annoy the chef," she said. "Try to stay out of trouble until I get back."

She tossed her blond hair and strolled away in her three-inch heels, leaving him alone. With nothing else to do, Cab headed for the balcony to drink up the evening sun, put his long arms around Lala's waist, and offer Peach a job.

EPILOGUE

Caprice Dean sat on a bench in the gardens of the Bok sanctuary, under a sprawling ash tree that dripped with Spanish moss. Florida had never seen a more perfect December day. The air was dry. A noon sun was warm but not hot. The tower was at her back, its carillon playing a Shaker hymn that competed with the chatter of the birds. Her briefcase sat on the ground beside her. There was plenty to do, but she left it alone for now, so that she could enjoy the view across the green lawn and down the slopes into the orange groves.

She checked her watch. He was late.

She'd prepared carefully for the meeting with him. You had to approach every negotiation as a war, and all your weapons were on the table. Women were the hardest, because she'd always found them to be inherently untrustworthy around other women. You couldn't believe anything they said to your face. Men were easy, because they were creatures of desire. Senators or accountants, they were all the same. Undo a button, they were yours. He was no different.

The Shaker hymn ended. Another song began on the bells. It took a few notes, and then she recognized it. That song. That was the one. She stood up automatically. She didn't need to hear him to know he was behind her. She swung around, and he was watching her. Tall.

Handsome. Ironic smile. Knee bent, hands in his pockets. She erased the memory of the song, even though every clang of the bells pounded in her brain, and she gave him a casual smile.

"Hello, Cab."

"Caprice," he said. He cupped an ear and cocked his head. "Pretty, isn't it? I told them you had a special request."

"Interesting choice."

He came and sat down on the bench beside her. She sat down again, too. His arms draped around the back of the iron railing; she could sense his hand behind her shoulder. His legs jutted out, ridiculously long.

"I checked the concert program from the Labor Day event," he said. "This is the last song they played."

"You've been busy."

He listened to the music in silence. "You know, Tarla's right. This sounds a lot like Supertramp."

"It's not," Caprice said. "I picked it."

"Yes, I know." He smiled at her. "You look gorgeous, by the way. Not that that's a surprise, you always do. They say politics ages people, but you seem to get younger."

Normally, she would have flirted back. This time she didn't. He had her off her game, and she didn't like it. "I appreciate your meeting me," she said.

"Of course. This is a beautiful spot. Although it must hold difficult memories for you."

"It does, but you can't change the past. This is one of my favorite places."

"Even though your fiancé was murdered here?"

"Maybe I come here to think about him. Did you consider that?"

"Yes, but I don't think of you as the sentimental type."

Caprice frowned. She wasn't accustomed to people playing games with her now. "I've been keeping tabs on you," she said. "And on this new investigative agency of yours."

"I'm flattered," Cab replied. "You've had a lot on your plate these past few months."

"Well, you didn't give me much choice. I have sources who tell me that you've been scouring through my past. Talking to people who know me. Digging up college and law school friends. Finding staffers and volunteers who worked on Birch's campaign. Not just you but Peach, too. I'm used to reporters looking for stories and background, but when I saw your name, I couldn't help but wonder exactly what you were doing."

Cab shrugged. "You hired me."

"And then you quit, as I recall."

"Oh, I never really quit after I start something. I just change allegiances. I'm like a politician that way."

"Funny," Caprice said, but she didn't smile or laugh.

"I can't help but wonder why you hired me in the first place," Cab said.

"You already know that. I suspected there was a threat against Diane. As it turns out, I was right, even if I didn't realize the danger was inside our own organization."

"Yes, I saw your press conference," Cab said. "How you added security, hired a detective. Very noble."

"I believe I credited you with saving Diane's life," Caprice reminded him.

"You did. Thanks. That's good for business."

"So what's the problem, Cab? The job is done."

"It is, but I'm a little like a dog with a bone. I just keep going back to it when I should leave it alone."

"That doesn't explain why you've been doing all this research on me." She smiled, and she made love to him with her eyes. "Why, I would almost think that you've become obsessed with me, Cab."

"That would be easy for a man to do," he acknowledged.

"Do you want back in my life? The door is still open."

"Even now?"

"Even now," she said. "Nothing has changed for me as a woman. I'm still attracted to you."

"And you always get what you want," Cab said.

She grinned. "Most of the time."

"Look at Ramona Cortes. She was an enemy. She had the upper hand against Common Way in the election, but then she was neutralized. Destroyed. No charges, no crimes, just clouds of suspicion."

"Charges can be proved or disproved," Caprice said, "whereas suspicion lasts forever."

"Yes, how convenient. It cost her the campaign. It forced her to resign as attorney general. The investigation into Common Way wound up dead in its tracks. You got everything you wanted. Yet again."

"Apparently I did," Caprice agreed.

"Almost as if it were planned that way from the start," Cab said.

"Oh, now you're giving me more credit than I deserve."

"Am I? I don't think so. I think it would be a huge mistake for anyone to underestimate you. You're brilliant, beautiful, and absolutely ruthless."

"How nice of you to say."

"The information about Ramona, you were the one who planted it, weren't you? After Lyle died, you would have had a copy of the invoice that the law firm sent to him."

Caprice shrugged. "If I ever saw it, I'm sure I didn't give it a second thought. No, I imagine some Good Samaritan inside the law firm had an attack of conscience. It's a big firm. Besides, does it really matter? The truth is what it is. Ramona knew about Deacon ten years ago."

"But so did you," Cab said.

"Me? Don't be ridiculous."

"Lyle didn't tell you? His fiancée?"

"I'm sure he would have told me at some point, but Lyle was protecting Deacon. A tragic mistake, as it turns out, but Lyle always had integrity."

"Yes, he did," Cab agreed. "You know, Rufus Twill told me something about Lyle when I met him. I didn't really think about it at the time, but I should have. I got too caught up with Drew as a suspect in the murders. My mistake."

Caprice waited, a smile frozen on her face.

"Rufus said that Lyle called him shortly before Labor Day," Cab went on. "He said they needed to have a talk. Did you know anything about that?"

"No."

"Do you have any idea what Lyle wanted to talk to Rufus about?"

"None at all."

"Really? That surprises me, with the two of you being political partners. I mean, I can't see Lyle going to the press about his brother's hit and run. He was already in touch with a lawyer about that. On the other hand, I *can* see him deciding to blow the whistle on Birch Fairmont, can't you? He found out what Birch had done to Diane. He couldn't live with it. He knew his candidate was a monster, and he was going to slay him, regardless of the consequences to the Common Way Party. Regardless of the consequences to *you*. You said it yourself, didn't you? If Birch had been exposed, it would have been a disaster."

"Where are you going with this, Cab?"

"Well, I just keep going back to the amazing fact that events always seem to work out exactly the way you want them to. Birch didn't get exposed. He got killed. He became a martyr. Common Way became bigger than ever. Instead of losing everything, you wound up with even more power and money than you started with."

"Only by losing the love of my life," Caprice reminded him acidly.

"The love of your life? That's sweet, but I recall you saying your relationship was mostly political. And if Lyle talked, well, that would have been the end of his political usefulness, wouldn't it?"

"How dare you," she snapped.

"I'm afraid emotional outrage doesn't become you, Caprice. It's not convincing. Isn't it remarkable that Deacon chose to kill Lyle because he was afraid of going to prison for the hit and run—and yet he chose to do it in a way that also took care of a huge political problem for you? Birch dead, Lyle dead, it was like winning the lottery, wasn't it?"

Caprice slapped his face. Hard. Cab touched his cheek, which bore the crimson mark of her hand. He laughed. "Are those nails or claws? 'Tyger, tyger, burning bright, in the forest of the night. What immortal

hand or eye could frame thy fearful symmetry?' Peach reminded me
about that poem. I couldn't help but think of you."

"Shut up."

Cab smiled at her, completely unaffected. His calm drove her crazy.
He reached inside his pocket and slid out a photograph. "See this picture? I got it from an electrician in Ocala. He's a reformed member of
the Liberty Empire Alliance. A true believer who ran out of anger. It's
a picture he took outside an Alliance meeting in the spring ten years
ago. They don't like pictures, but he was actually shooting a photo of
where his car was parked because he was pissed that he got a ticket.
Turns out he got a few of the Alliance members in the background of
the photo. Anyone look familiar?"

She didn't look at the picture. "No."

"The kid with the red hair? Definitely Deacon Piper."

Caprice shrugged. "Good for you, Cab. You've discovered concrete
evidence that Deacon had Alliance sympathies. That explains a lot. He
killed Birch for the Alliance, and he killed Lyle for his own reasons.
Ham Brock got him to do the same thing to Diane. Probably with
Ramona's encouragement."

"And once again, things work out perfectly for you."

"I don't like your tone, Cab."

"No? The thing is, I went to see Ham Brock again last week. I
showed him the picture. He thinks Deacon was the mole inside the
Alliance back then. And that made me think about you telling me
how you always liked to have your own person on the inside, report-
ing to you. Did you use Deacon to spy on the Alliance? Were you
already thinking the Alliance might be useful to take the fall if things
went bad with Birch?"

Her first instinct was to give in to her agitation, but she held herself
back. She knew he was baiting her. She wasn't going to let him win.
Instead, she eased back on the bench without a care in the world.
"Ham Brock," she said. "You consider him a reliable witness, do you?"

"In this case, I do. Did Lyle know you were using his brother as a
spy?"

"Of course not, because it's not true."

"Just to satisfy my morbid curiosity, how far did the relationship with Deacon go? Did you sleep with him?"

Her head snapped around. "You're on dangerous ground, Cab."

"I just wondered if Deacon was in love with you. It seems like he was ready to do anything for you. He killed Birch. He almost killed Diane. He even made sure you wouldn't get blamed if he got caught. That's chivalry. Deacon meeting with Ham Brock a few months ago— that was a nice touch. Brock said Deacon spent half an hour bragging about everything that Diane was going to do against supremacist groups when she was elected. Were you hoping that Brock would put out the word? More rumors about the Alliance when Diane was killed? Of course, it didn't really matter what Deacon said to Brock. If Deacon got caught, the meeting alone would make people assume the Alliance was involved."

Caprice said nothing at all.

"Not that Deacon planned to get caught," Cab said. "He intended to frame Frank Macy. But what was your plan, Caprice? Did you plan to kill Deacon all along?"

"Ashes to ashes," Caprice said in the doorway of the garage.

Deacon had the gun in his hand and pointed it at her with a swift seamless whip of his arm. Instinct. She didn't flinch. Instead, she stood there, rain-soaked and wanton, her clothes like film on her body. The tiniest of smiles creased her face. Strange how she could smile knowing what was about to happen, but then, how could you not smile when you will soon have what you have always craved?

She came to him, dripping. "Are you scared?"

"No."

"It will all be over soon."

"I know."

Her fingers stroked the barrel of the gun, which was hard and long. She felt his excitement.

"I want to see the body," she said.

He took her hand and led her to the car. He popped the trunk, and when she saw the dead eyes of Frank Macy staring at her, she quivered.

It wasn't fear; it was arousal. She put a finger to the wound and let one of the corpse bugs climb onto her nail. She twisted her hand, making it run in circles around her finger, and when she was done playing with it, she crushed it under her thumb and dropped the carapace back among its brothers.

"Do you think this will work?" he asked.

"Trust me," she said.

"There's a chance—I mean, it's possible that I won't make it. I've protected you if that happens. You know that, don't you?"

"I do. Thank you."

That was the limit of her emotion. She'd always known his place in her universe. He was a useful tool to her, but if he died, if he was exposed, she would walk over him like litter in the street.

"There are days—" he began, but he couldn't finish his thought. He couldn't go there.

"We all make sacrifices," she said.

She heard him try and fail to keep the bitterness from his voice. "And what's yours?" he asked.

She put her hands on his face. He responded like that blind, dead insect, unable to stay away from her, despite the consequences of what lay ahead.

"Mine is living with who I am," she said.

"You said you never fired a gun before," Cab reminded her. "Isn't that what you told Deacon in the sunroom? All those shots went wild. Except for the last one, which killed him. Dead in the center of the back. Perfect aim."

"Luck," Caprice said.

"Yes, you are a very lucky woman. Except I found a shooting range not far from where you grew up. They still remember you. The pretty teenage girl who was as sharp as a sniper. They're proud of you, by the way."

"I hadn't fired a gun in years," Caprice said. "And I don't think I'm under any obligation to tell the truth to a murderer who's threatening to kill me."

"That's true," Cab said. "You know, I really have only one question for you. There's one thing I'm not sure about. The whole plot with Diane, that was you all along. That's why you hired me, isn't it? To point me down the path, to give the whole thing credibility. You used me from the start. I don't like being used, but I admit, you're good at it. As for the Labor Day murders, I wondered whether it was your idea or Deacon's, but come on. Deacon was a kid. You were the brains. Killing Birch and setting up the Alliance? Political brilliance. No, the only question I have is about Lyle. Did you know Deacon was going to kill him, too, or did he surprise you? I'd like to think you didn't know that was coming. I'd like to think you weren't acting your horror when he put the gun in Lyle's face and killed your fiancé. Sadly, though, I don't believe it. You told Deacon exactly what to do. Everything."

Caprice took a breath in and a breath out. "What a fascinating fairy tale."

"Isn't it?"

"These are extraordinarily serious allegations to level against a woman with my power," she said. "You do realize that."

"Yes, I do. And you do have power. That's what you always wanted, isn't it? I talked to your friends in college. They have exceptional admiration for you. They'd never met anyone so ambitious and so single-mindedly focused on achieving what she wanted. They all considered it to be one of your virtues."

"I hope you don't plan to go public with these crazy ideas, Cab," Caprice advised him. "As far as I can tell, you don't have a shred of real evidence of my doing anything wrong, least of all the terrible things you've talked about. Not that you could, because none of it is true."

"I'm not wearing a wire," Cab said.

"In my business, everything is on the record."

"Of course."

"You really don't want me as an enemy, Cab. Trust me on that."

"I think it's a little late for that," he said.

"Yes, I think you're right."

"Anyway, no, I have no plans to go public with any of this," he told her. "Not yet. I've been looking into it for months, but I can't find any useful evidence at all to prove anything. Even though I know you're guilty as hell."

"Why are you so sure?" she asked.

"Honestly? Because my girlfriend really, really doesn't like you. I trust her judgment, but I suppose a prosecutor and jury would want something more. Which I don't have. So you win, Caprice. For now."

"I usually do."

"However, I'll be keeping an eye on you."

"I bet you will." Caprice saw an aide gesturing at her from near the beautiful tower. The music of the bells had gone silent. It was time to go. She stood up, and so did Cab, and the two of them shook hands. The security personnel who had hovered at a distance drew closer.

"Don't be a stranger," she said to him. "Good-bye, Cab."

"Good-bye, governor," Cab replied.

AUTHOR'S NOTE

Cab Bolton first appeared as a character in my novel *The Bone House*. I planned the book as a stand-alone, but readers soon demanded to see more of that tall, rich detective. I hope you enjoyed his return. With this book, I now have two parallel series, one featuring Cab and one featuring Lieutenant Jonathan Stride of the Duluth police. You can also look for my stand-alone *Spilled Blood*, which won the award for Best Hardcover Novel in the 2013 Thriller Awards.

You can write to me at brian@bfreemanbooks.com. I welcome e-mails from readers around the world and always respond personally. Visit my website at www.bfreemanbooks.com to join my mailing list, get book club discussion questions, read bonus content, and find out more about me and my books.

You can "like" my official fan page on Facebook at www.facebook .com/bfreemanfans or follow me on Twitter, Instagram, or Tumblr using the handle **bfreemanbooks**. For a look at the fun side of the author's life, you can also "like" my wife Marcia's Facebook page at www.facebook.com/theauthorswife.

Finally, if you enjoy my books, please post your reviews online and tell your friends. Thanks!

ACKNOWLEDGMENTS

I lost a dear friend in the publishing industry as we were putting the finishing touches on *Season of Fear*. My agent, Ali Gunn, discovered me in 2004 with the manuscript of my first novel, *Immoral*. She was my agent, ally, friend, and supporter for all of the past decade. Ali passed away tragically and unexpectedly in 2014, leaving a terrible hole for everyone who knew her. This book, like my other books, is in your hands because of Ali. I will always be grateful to her for shaping my career.

I'm fortunate to work with an amazing team in the publishing industry, especially everyone at my worldwide publisher, Quercus. My thanks to David North, Rich Arcus, Nathaniel Marunas, and the entire Quercus team on both sides of the Atlantic.

This is my first book since *Stripped* to be set outside the Midwest. I'm very grateful to Mary and Roger Stumo, who allowed me and Marcia to use their condo in Indian Rocks Beach while we were doing research and scouting locations for the book. Most of the locales in this novel are real places, which you can find on Google Earth.

I have some wonderful readers who help me with feedback on early drafts of my manuscripts. They play an important role in shaping the final book. So big thanks to Marcia, Matt and Paula Davis, Terri Duecker, Mike O'Neill, and Alton Koren. Our three cats, Heathrow, Gatwick, and Baltic, also contribute to each book, but their "help" typically consists of sleeping on my keyboard and in my chair.

Speaking of Marcia . . . you will see her on the first page of every book, and after thirty years of marriage, she's the most important person in everything I do. So if you enjoy my books, the thanks go to her as much as me.